a novel

BONE

DOGS

Roger Alan Skipper

COUNTERPOINT

BERKELEY

All thanks to:
my tireless agent Farley Chase
my astute editor Roxanna Aliaga
and to Connie, who puts up with all this crap

Library of Congress Cataloging-in-Publication Data
Skipper, Roger Alan.
Bone dogs : a novel / Roger Alan Skipper.
p. cm.
ISBN-13: 978-1-58243-563-3
ISBN-10: 1-58243-563-4
1. Losers—Fiction. 2. Identity (Psychology)—Fiction.
3. Architecture—Conservation and restoration—Fiction.
4. West Virginia—Fiction. I. Title.
PS3619.K568B66 2010
813'.6—dc22   2009040509

Cover by Attebery Design
Interior by David Bullen

Printed in the United States of America

COUNTERPOINT
2117 Fourth Street
Suite D
Berkeley, CA 94710

www.counterpointpress.com

Distributed by Publishers Group West

10 9 8 7 6 5 4 3 2 1

In memory of my father, Sibre Breshloch Skipper
friend
philosopher
hero

But just let me tell you something, son,
a woman's love is like the morning dew,
it's just as apt to settle on a horse turd as it is on a rose.
Larry McMurtry, *Leaving Cheyenne*

*A*ll I have to do is think of that place and I can see the green inside his mouth. Smell his smell and feel his old cornhusk voice rustling in my ear. Hear bones rattle and swallow back the licorice of pure pants-pissing terror. So I'm careful not to go there, even in my mind. But now it's come up again and there aint a prayer of thinking on anything else.

I got a theory that the way to get shed of a bad memory is to lie about it. Rewire the bones of the truth into some shape you like better and stitch new hide over it and pump it full of air and patch any leaks and poke it with a stick to make it run and bark and chew up the bedroom slippers and poop in the flowerbed. Make it do it over and over and over till you forget that the original version was a cat. Make your own facts.

It's tempting to try that.

But then there comes a night when I wake up shivering and sweaty and something whispers in my ear that I've already done it. That this is the good version. The best I could make of it.

I dont even know anymore.

CHAPTER 1

I was cocky then, like you are when you're not yet forty, and so innocent I thought I was jaded. That's hard to get a handle on now. I'd had a bellyfull of the same old roads so one day I lit out for new territory. Jogging had just about put paid to my gut but there was a little donut of fat that wouldnt go away and it wouldnt get in time with the flop of my flat feet either. My knee joints had bar-floor sweepings in the liners. That's what they felt like. Busted glass and pulltops and cigarette butts. Evening was coming hard but the road was July hot and punishing me for going where I had no business.

Downhill on the lake side of the road were these big wood and stone houses lollygagging in the shade of red oaks and sugar maples older than the great-granddads that had made the money to pay for these vacation homes. Some of them you couldnt even see. Just a little carved cedar sign at the end of a curly paved driveway. Down on that side of the road is where you stayed if you drove down from Wheeling or over from Charleston or in from Cincinnati or come floating down out of the end of an eagle. Just so you were from somewhere besides here.

But if you were a local like me (but with sense) you would haul your butt back where it belonged before some cosmopolitan pit bull with an acquired taste for redneck tenderloin blew out of one of those peaceful, pretty driveways. The owners hollered at the dog when that happened but they never chained one up or laid the belt to it. Not unless it had made too much racket while it gnawed your hind leg loose. Then they might hold back a dog biscuit or call it a naughty boy but not so it would hear and develop a complex.

So I got to thinking on that and turned up the hill away from the lake onto a gash of a dirt road. As soon as the hard road fell out of sight I was in the real Green County. Clearcut slashings headhigh with bramble and devil's walkingstick and snapped-off saplings. House trailers with round corners and crooked creosoted telephone poles and dirt-and-rock sandboxes, made of blown-out truck tires, full of crosseyed kids.

The heat was searing in a cauterizing way. Healing by fire. My body had flushed itself of alcohol till on occasion I recollected my name and where I'd been the night before. And I'd held gainful employment for two months. Consecutive. Two months consecutive might not haul your ashes the way it resonates with me. To me those words felt like the Army ribbons that imbecile Johnnie Snider wears on his wifebeater shirt.

Linda'd even come back home. She was partial to that consecutive stuff too.

And I always did like a road with grass growing in the middle like that one had. Life was good. Then I came onto a house.

The picture of that place is burned into my head like the sun would be if you stared at it for a week or two. Consecutive. The cheap doublewide house—two trailers hanging on to each other like a couple of drunks walking the train tracks at night—at first seemed new. The dirtpiles that the bulldozer drivers push up to make sure all the trees are killed and to make a place for the delivery truck to back into were lumped around where the yard should've been. Like the house had been delivered today, and tomorrow or the day after they'd move it to where it was supposed to be. A scarlet tanager stared down from the roof's edge like it had come home to find this abortion of a dwelling where its nest had been. But weeds covered the dirtpiles and the roof shingles were humped and scabrous. The siding had faded to that calfshit-green patina I've never seen growing on anything but manufactured housing. This West Virginia chateau had been dumped off a while back.

A pickup truck so old I couldnt right off name the maker rusted at the edge of the road with its tires sunk into the mud and the bed spilling bottles and cans and plastic bags. The whole place as dead as Methuselah's digger.

Then there was a skinny washed-out woman glaring at me through the windowscreen and an old man sitting right there beside me in the pickup. All at once.

My feet jimmied out of sync and the road tilted up and whacked me in the face and I bounced up grinning like I wasnt goosy but had run my snoot into the dirt just to bring a modicum of levity to their day. How you all doing? I said.

The old man's eyes hoed around over my short, skinny legs and knobby knees and my little chub gut—everywhere but at my eyes—but he didnt utter a peep. I saw a face like his once in *National Geographic*. One that had way more to say than I wanted to hear. Black eyes like groundhog holes in a field of last year's stubble. Gray wilted hair scattered so scarce you might later remember him as bald. His head was not quite symmetrical, like some third-grader had fashioned it from clay.

You take care now, I said and ran on.

It's bad enough that God and fate and the devil and the county government are all fighting over which one gets to run you off the road next. Right there ole Ma Nature herself gave a jerk on the wheel. If the road hadnt deadheaded into an elephant's nest of bramble and greenbriar and pokeweed taller than I could spit, I'd have just trotted on to wherever the road come out and never set eyes on that place again.

But it did so I didnt.

I made a waterhole in the dirt and excavated a gravel from my knee and clopped back down the way I'd come and when I passed said, Well there you are again.

He stared down his crooked nose like a leaky barrel of slug guts had rolled past. There's plenty that looks at me in that same tone of voice but I didnt think some guy in a pickup full of garbage had that entitlement yet. I knew right off I was going to make him like me. Whatever it took. Or at least admit that I existed.

Or kill him.

Whatever worked.

Every day I ran out there and every day he was in the pickup. Never eating or reading or sleeping or listening to the radio but just sitting there like old men sit. Like if the pickup ever decided to hoove up out of the mud and depart he wasnt going to miss out cause he'd went to shake the dew off his lily right then.

The woman always glaze-eyed me through the screen until one day an airconditioner took her place. Then her snout showed in the middle of the peeling door's three diagonal panes. Whether she had radar that picked me up or whether she was mounted there permanent like a deer head I wasnt sure. What eyes. Like Mom's.

Every time I'd grin and say something nice and when that didnt work I'd rip off something asinine like, What a cool place. I'd just as well have conversed with a huckleberry. I was losing interest and about to just let them go ahead and despise me if they were so fixed on it but then the woman turned up missing.

Women are like that. They look out the window. Then they stand at the door. And then one day they're gone.

The whole climate changed when she vamoosed. The light had a finer consistency and the air was fresher and the old gray dude seemed tickled to see me lumber past. Once his lips even moved but no words came. His mouth had been a dry hole too long to start gushing right off.

Real late the very next Friday night I dozed off with the TV on and the volume jacked up the way it does when it thinks nobody's listening. After a while here come Linda like a bear that had sat in the campfire coals. Waking-by-yelling-woman sets my teeth on edge so to spite us both I stayed there in the chair and let the volume beller all night.

Come morning I was dilitary and snotty and I was the sociable one of us two. She'd revised the Ten Commandments to accommodate the hay crop in the yard and the broken washer and the stopped-up sink drain and then altered the Revelation's judgments to reflect the new rules. Just specially for me.

I likely should of cried holy holy holy and done a burnt offering and then doubletimed over to the neighbors and borrowed his mowing scythe and chopped down grass till I found the lawnmower. But what I did was go for a run. Once I'd discovered endorphins I liked them near as good as Keystone Light. So when the wheels came off at home I'd run down the road for a fix. That's the worst thing about living in a mobile home. The wheels come off too easy.

It was dead slam in the heat of the day and my shorts wadded up like a barbwire jockstrap and my shirt stuck fast everywhere there was to stick. A legion of demons disguised as deerflies lit down and herded me along toward hell. Linda's voice still nagged in my ears like a rat gnawing in the eaves.

When I went past the old man I said, Top of the morning to you sir. Like a rattlesnake would ask how you doing.

A rattlesnake would have offered more response. When I got to the end of the road I didnt even stop to blow and go to the brush like usual. The time called for the old gray fart to either make some noise on his own or I'd rattle him like a squeezetoy to see if he had a squeaker in him.

But when I came bulling down the road his bonepole arm slid out the window with a can of beer. Little tears of sweat on the can. So instead of ratcheting down on his neck I wrapped my fingers around that can instead. Laugh lines crinkled around his eyes when I turned it up. That sour-crisp icy sliver sliced into my belly like an orgasm. Only better. One that hung on for a bit.

Better set a spell. A voice like a bat lost in a field of dead cornstalks. He opened the door and sat sideways on the seat. He was a bag of sticks with hardly any sticks in it. Hands like kindling. Empty gray workpants, or barely inflated. Nearly deflated. I looked into his eyes and thought I saw a little boy inside who'd hauled that wrinkled skin over his head like a pillowcase.

I plopped down just behind the cab where the fender stepped into a running board. It gave under my weight but didnt let me clear down. Sitting beside him where I couldnt look head-on gave me the fantods at first but I cant stand up and drink very good for any appreciable length of time.

I flipped my empty can over my head and heard it roll off the other side and he handed me another one even better than the first. I was on the third before it occurred to me that I was the only one drinking and that I hadnt said word one. If I wasnt catching my breath from swallowing I had my mouth stoppered with the can. I was jacked up on endorphins and cooled with hard-earned sweat and my lungs were blown clean and the beer was good, man. I drained the third can and said, Now that there hit the spot. Aint you having any?

I dont drink.

Well I did. So I had another one.

What's your name? His voice even drier and woreout than the man.

Tu, I said. Tuesday, actually, but everybody calls me Tu anymore. Actually it's Andy. *Actually* it's Andrew. Grunts and monosyllables and scathing looks is how I communicate when I'm sober if I decide I want to communicate at all. But forcefeed a few beers into me and I yap like a spotted puppy. Tu. Tuesday Andy Andrew Price. What's yours? I let my lips touch together so he'd know that even after I started talking I *could* shut up if I wanted to.

Lilo, he said after a pause that left me ready to bust.

I laughed. How'd you ever acquire a handle like that?

They give it to me in Nam.

The booze gave me enough backbone to lean forward and give him a good tire kicking. He stared at the ground like an old dog at the pound pretending not to give a rat's ass—adoption or euthanasia was one and the same to him. Officer? I said.

Draftee. Grunt.

Liar. Nam had happened to folks not that much older than me, not old geezers like him. But then his eyes flickered my way and I wasnt so sure. Did you lie low, Lilo? Is that why they give you that name?

It dont mean nothing. It's just what they called me. How'd you get yours?

That old rip Miss Brodan at the unemployment office hung it on me. Said if she got me a job on Monday I'd be back to the office on Tuesday if I could get out of bed. So people got to calling me Tuesday. Then I ran into crazy Johnnie Snider in the beer aisle at the Food Fair and he said, Hey Tu, and Mr. Polk the English teacher overheard him from the next aisle and said, Et tu, Brute? and I hollered, If you're going to quote Shakespeare quote the whole damn passage, but he couldnt remember it any better than me. Then I got throwed out of the store for hollering in public—they make up rules special for me right on the spot—and that got norated around and everybody took to calling me Et tu and naturally that pizzled out to just Tu. People's too lazy to say more than they got to. The name wouldnt of stuck if I hadnt set out to whip anybody that used it. But if I was drunk enough to endeavor to whip on someone, I was too drunk to get it done so that just made them say it more. I dont care anymore. Kind of like it, in fact. You can call me that all you want to.

With about as much subtlety as a hog eatin ham I let slip how I concealed my superior intelligence so people'd not be intimidated and like me better and how brave I was to be out running considering my bad heart genes and all. Then I corrected his orientation toward religion and politics and women and recited Tennyson's "The Eagle—A Fragment." Wrapped my tongue around all those hard consonants—*He clasps the crag with crooked hands*—and floated them out like milkweed fuzz. And I thought that my rendition of "Yesterday" gave a real nice balance to the performance. He wouldnt clap along with me after the song but I could tell he wanted to. I blathered on proud as a whore pregnant with twins for getting him to open up.

But after a spell the hot breeze in my wet hair and the constant hoarse late-summer locust din lulled me into a stupor. I stared off into the woods without seeing it and all of a sudden everything snapped into such a sharp focus that I could make out a gypsy moth caterpillar feeling his way down the furrows on a white ash tree at the edge of the yard. The scene jittered sideways a few inches and then back. I clawed up and hung on to the door but it wouldnt stay put and I told Lilo it was nice to meet him and then things shifted a foot and another and then everything came loose from its foundation. I just made it around the turn till I was sick.

That's happened a thousand times but I'm still flabbergasted when everything in me comes up still cold. And that after I get shed the stuff that made me so drunk, I'm drunker than before.

I flogged home with my head and stomach battling over which one got to bring me down and the big hole in my gut filled up with mad.

Linda was gone and I was locked out. Like I'd knowed if I'd bothered to think.

Getting the key she didnt know about from under the brick was no big deal but once that chunk of dried clay nestled in my hand I got a new inspiration so I beat the glass out of the door instead. Hollering, I love you, dammit, with every whack. Not sure if I was talking to the brick or the door or me. Part of me stood off and watched like at a freak show at the fair.

After I worked the nasty all out I chucked the brick into the neighbor's yard.

How could she do that?

I hadnt had a drink for a year. Six months anyway. Or a good while at least. And then just one time I'm late coming back from a run and she *assumes* I'm on a tear and will come home with a mad on so she lights a rag out of here with no note nor nothing. It dont make any difference that she was right. That aint the point. If it had been her that didnt come back I'd at least worry awhile. Go check if a coaltruck had got her. Not Linda. She just leaves.

I never liked her that good anyhow.

I kept my stomach settled with fresh beer and relaxed in the trailer's quiet and enjoyed being by myself. But then a week later the Green County deputy served papers on me and I got to missing her. The next morning I smoothed the dew-soaked papers against my knee and just then a stinkbug landed astraddle of the legalese and followed a sentence like he was leaving words behind. Like poop. Or semen. His smell hung on my fingernail even after I scrubbed the guts off in the dirt. I had to laugh at what she was asking because ole Tuesday wasnt even doing Mondays anymore. You cant gin blood out of a crabapple. And you got to quit whatever you can. Even if it's work. After the sun fried the soggy out of the papers they wandered off with the wind.

It took a couple of days to get lonesome enough to do anything about it and then I loped up and sat with Lilo in that old pickup every day. I didnt know him from Adam's off ass but that meant he didnt know me either, and that made him right off one of my best friends in the whole world, and I couldn't see that he had a lot to pick through either.

I've set on rockpiles that were more comfortable than that truck. You had to heel to starboard because a broken seat-spring rewarded uprightness with a sharp prong in the ass. The cardboard pine tree most likely had an evergreen scent at one time but now it smelled like an old folks' home. The door clicked shut just like the one in Dad's old Dodge. The car I killed Matt Tamper with. So I was cautious to be talking whenever it closed so I wouldnt have to hear it. Or any other time just to be sure. But Lilo's big cooler sat between us always full of beer and *that* made it a pleasant little place.

To pass the time I posed provocative questions like where God came from or where Lilo came from or where the beer came from but if he ever answered I dont remember it.

We got to be one organism. I was the mouth and he was the ears and the pickup was our shell. Our exoskeleton. He'd close his eyes and lean his head back against the cab and grin like he was making sport of me but he wasnt. Just content that my chatter drove back whatever had him surrounded otherwise.

Then one day he wasnt in the pickup when I came up the road. I stopped as soon as I saw and had one of those rare moments of epiphany. Not that periodic stunned comprehension of what a USDA certified hindquarter I really am but a stark pen-and-ink drawing of our relationship. Lilo knew what time I went to the bathroom and the names of every dog I ever owned and its forebears and offspring and what my fat neighbor's double cousin ate for breakfast.

I didnt even know his name. Not the real one.

He'd sucked what he needed from me so slick that I didnt know what was missing or even that anything was gone. My toe scratched *Lilo* in the dirt and then scrubbed it out. If he'd hailed out of the house while I was weighing free beer against parasites I'd have trotted up and drank beer and wobbletongued all day like always. But he didnt.

I turned away and didnt go back.

Besides, I didnt need Lilo's beer anymore as soon as everyone saw that I'd earnestly swore off reform. As soon as you give up, the government piles in to battle over who gets to support your habits. I couldnt get drunk in peace without a representative from one agency or another hammering on the door.

Just down the road from my trailer at the Ace in the Hole Bar—I called it the Ass in the Hole just like anyone familiar with the owner would—I'd wear out my welcome in a few hours and then I'd stagger home to drink and converse at the dog. She wasnt as tough as Lilo, though, and she lit a shuck after a couple of days of that. Not because I forgot to feed her either. She just couldnt tolerate to hear any more. Neither could I but I had to stay there and endure.

Once in a while when I was dried up enough to run or too soused not to I'd pound the pavement again. One day I jogged up Lilo's way. A rabbit squibbled away in spurts when I got close but that was the only tracks life had left around. The pickup was empty and dust had drifted in through the open windows. A dead smell was accumulating in the cooler and the beer was gone. A sultry yellow moth floated on clear water like it had been white before it mopped up the impurities.

An upset backhouse wouldnt have felt any more deserted. My holler brought no answer. I'd never been inside and I sure didnt want to be now but my feet took for the door like they ran on rails. The airconditioner moaned and oozed water into a green puddle beside the stoop. My knock came up empty but the plastic State Farm Insurance calendar I had instead of a policy had slipped better bolts than that one. I yelled into the cold air that poured out the door. Hey. Lilo.

It was a tidy place. Lilo hadnt made any clutter a-tall because he'd been sitting in his chair for a while with his head laid back and eyes closed like he did in the pickup. His smile was mostly an insufficiency of lips because he'd started to shrivel up like an old mushroom.

I should of felt something but it wouldnt come. The air was parched and chill and he didnt stink all that much. Not like a man dead that long ought to. A trace of spiderweb picketed the top of his head to a plastic sign on the wall. GOD BLESS THIS HOME.

The stack of unopened mail on the bedroom dresser was all made out to Walter R. Fraley or Beverly Fraley. Walter R. Lilo Fraley. A name too late to do us much good. Some of the envelopes held checks and I contemplated kifing a couple but I wouldnt do that. The skinny woman's leftovers hung around here and there—old shoes in the closet and a hairbrush in the medicine cabinet and a felt-and-magnet spray of purple flowers on the avocado refrigerator door—but the big stuff was gone. She had moved out permanent. I pocketed a pretty hair barrette that I found on the living room floor just for a rememberer of my time with Lilo. Nothing else. And that's the truth.

I wasnt real gung ho to move Lilo but if there was another way to get at his wallet I didnt know it. He wasnt stiff like I expected but slack and soft so I only had to shift a pound or so of him. When I did his teeth parted and showed the soft green of old cheese behind. My stomach skun the cat and I looked away and havent cared much for cheese since.

Once I got two fingers on it the thin worn billfold slipped right out. Inside were three dollars. An old likeness of a couple posed unnatural and awkward on a rock. Holding hands. A waterfall in the background. Another snapshot of four muscley Marines with shirts open and caps akilter and cigarettes smoldering in the corners of their mouths. Lilo's black eyes looked like bullet holes in a stopsign. An American Legion membership card. An expired driver's license. I grunted at his birthdate: 1951. Only eleven years older than me.

Forty-six years old? Man. I thought *I'd* been rode hard and put up wet. He looked eighty. When I tossed the wallet on the dresser with the checks my face in the mirror wasnt a spring chicken's either. The only way to beat gravity is to wrinkle instead of sag and I hadnt even pulled that off very good. But that could have just been the light. Or maybe the shock of finding my old buddy expired had aged me some.

In the dining area—not a room, but a space just big enough for a little faux-Formica table—an aquarium stood on a rotteniron stand. Bubbles beat their way up through the thick water but all the fish were on the bottom. Some just bones. Others blobs on the gravel. Nothing left to eat them. They'd been dead for a long time and not just since I'd last visited Lilo. Like maybe since the woman left.

Lilo's green-cheese mouth was bad enough but those rotted up fish made everything take one of those sidesteps and I tore out the back door and fell down the steps with my face in the high grass. Everything that shot out was hot and that surprised me even more than when it's cold. When I could stagger up with my hands on my knees I spotted an old doghouse deeper in the weeds. I sat on it until I could walk better. Then I saw the chain pulled up semitight by something hidden in a clump of goldenrod. Dont. I said it again and again but I kept going anyway.

The collar had been bright red once but now just glowed soft in the green weeds like hot coals. He'd been a big dandy. Anything apast that was hard to tell. Wrinkled rags of skin and handfuls of bleached hair hung over dirty-white bones. He'd been dead a year or more.

Then there was no way to fight off that memory of *my* dog dead at the end of his own chain and the two pictures swirled together and around and around the toilet bowl I was in and then chugged down the hole and left me there in the right-now with no place to go.

I pictured Old Blue, if that had been his name, whining and barking for help and then breaking over to sit and watch down the road for someone else to come. Someone who would listen. He just sat there and laid hard against the chain till he wilted down over his bones. And Lilo just sat there and let him wilt.

That's when the dream commenced. I'm jogging with Old Blue, just his bones and a couple of patches of hair, and some of the bones have rattled loose and left a gap here and there. He clatters along with a big possum-grin on his face without ever stopping to poop or anything. His head cocked like he's listening and matching me stride for stride. I run faster and faster and my pulse ratchets up and my breath burns in my throat, run so fast that I come loose of the ground but I still cant pull away from him. Then my legs tangle and my face crashes into a road that somehow has gotten above me and I sit up in bed sweating like I really have been running.

I always reach for Linda. Always forget that she's not here anymore.

CHAPTER 2

The town of Ransom was nine miles from Lilo's and seven from mine but Lilo made more of a stink downtown than he did inside his doublewide. After a steady news feed of runned-over dogs and drunk-and-disorderlys and casual infidelities, unattended death under suspicious circumstances was fresh hot meat for the rumor grinders.

Libby at the grocery store nailed the date Lilo died. One morning she'd taken Lilo's phoned-in order but he didnt seem to be home when she delivered it. And her not even an hour later than she'd promised. She reckoned he'd got a burr under his saddle and ordered off someone else so she hauled it all back to town. But he hadnt, and the coroner said that date was consistent with his forensics. Which probably amounted to a sniff test.

Not that she'd take offense he started buying somewhere else, Libby claimed. Even with the delivery charge she couldnt show a profit trucking stuff to the unpaved end of hell's half acre and besides that it wasnt right to be buying all that beer and just a thimbleful of food. Bothered her conscience (now that it was staked out for public analysis).

The lake squawkheads opened up on the others' trail and said they'd all seen me headed up that way near every day until that aforementioned day and then I stopped.

And wouldnt you know that my bar tab at the Ace in the Hole started up again on that identical selfsame date offered forth in prior testimony.

While all this was going on I sat on the porch and practiced tying a hangman's knot so it'd be done right when the mob showed up instead of being strung up in a manner that would strangle me over a week or two.

Doc Crawford put in his nickel's worth and said that he was surprised Lilo'd hung on that long with everything that was wrong with him. He'd stepped in some unwholesome stuff over there in them rice paddies. Even when he'd kept his appointments and took his medicine Doc gave it a short time till he was underground inspiring the cabbages.

Sheriff Hawkins clinched the spikes though when he let slip that none of Lilo's disability checks were missing and that there was a fifty-dollar bill in his wallet. I wouldnt have took it but boy was I grouty that I'd looked over it. After that all folks could do was look sour at me and mutter because money left on the scene ruled me out in their thinking. I fastened the ends of the rope into a blood knot and hung it off the outside light as a reminder not to jump to conclusions.

For a while it looked that my life would come to a satisfactory resolution: I'd either drink myself under or someone at The Hole would throttle me to shut me up and either way I'd be out of this mess.

Then Linda came back and screwed it all up.

I was reading *Moby Dick* again between looks at my watch to see if the bar was open yet when tires crunched in the driveway. Anything old call-me-Ishmael had to say I'd worked out years before but I still got a tickle out of Ahab's hissies.

No engine roar along with the tires. So not Mike or Dave. That left bill collectors and government workers. I clicked off the lamp but a key rattled in the lock and my heart cut a little unplanned shine because Linda was coming home. Be still my perfidious heart.

Andy? she called into the gloom. Never Tu or Tuesday. Sometimes I called her Sweetpea but just when I wanted something. That didnt work as good as it used to but sometimes she was so fanatical for something nice that she'd still do what I wanted when I called her that.

Sweetpea, I said. Like she'd just stepped out for the mail.

Linda turned to someone behind her and this absolute rhinoceros of a woman plugged the door hole and I could see again. The porch groaned when she stepped up into the trailer. Low heels and a wide-belted dress that would make linguine look fat and a purple scarf that turned her red face maroon. Linda's suitcase dangling like a lunchbox from her hand. Half a pound of necklace slithering amidst her chins. The official seal of a green folder under her arm.

What's the protocol? Do you bow or kiss her ring? Shut the door when you leave, I said. I been working on this stink a long time and I dont want it to get loose.

This is Barb from Social Services, Linda said.

Aint this my lucky day.

The woman's voice as sweet and textured as she wasnt. We need to discuss a few things, Mr. Price, and then I'll be delighted to go.

Spit it out and git then. I got a sight of stuff to do.

You shut up and listen, Linda said. Please? Her brown eyes picked at my dirt and whiskers.

Well boy if this dont throw a kink into the day. I shuffled into the kitchen.

Linda piled trash over onto the kitchen counter and wiped the crusty table with a wet rag. Barb sat on the edge of the chair so she wouldnt have to touch the back. These, Mr. Price, are the conditions for Linda's return, Lard said without a preamble or table of contents. Right to the sex scene. Like I'd been on my knees begging. She balanced a cockroach-sized pair of glasses on her nose and read a half-hour's worth of musts and damn well better must nots during our cohabitation and the ramifications of failing to engage the mainstream of society.

Engage? I said. I come within a frog's hair of drownding in it.

She went on like I'd never interrupted and when she wound down I picked at a snot-colored scab on the tabletop that the rag hadnt bothered much and said, Go over that ram thing again. I'm bemuddled. We talking goats or we into Dodges here?

Her little pigeyes didnt waver.

You know I aint totally responsible for my actions. I been diagnosed as a omphaloskeptic.

She blinked a couple of times and smiled and said, Yes. I can imagine that you're fascinated with your own navel. Suffering from hypochondria as well, no doubt.

Son of a gun. And this fat government-inspected heifer had to be the one to know that word. Now it was ruined. Like when Dave run all over the country on his motorcycle and would stop at little pumpkin-roller gas stations and get a gallon of gas and go to pay for it with a hundred-dollar bill and they couldnt cash it and would tell him to just go on. Till some old woman smoking a cob pipe dug down between her bubbys and counted out change and had a handful left. I told him to just get another hundred-dollar bill but he said it wouldnt never be the same now. Like a hymen.

Linda shuffled her own stack of papers and offered to lay off lawing me if I'd go back to steppin and fetchin in a satisfactory manner. I never expected to be any more rid of lawyers than I was flies but the chance to get shed of one this easy didnt come along every day. Whatever, I said and signed the papers and waved away the consequences and Barb left with them.

She loosed one last glare from the doorway. Next time, Mr. Price, it wont be this easy.

What did I do? I said. Specifically. Other than just generally shooting short of the characteristics of acceptable husbands someone wrote in one of your books somewhere?

If you ever lay a hand on your wife again I'll personally commit to seeing you in jail.

I never done no such . . .

Shut it up, Linda said and pushed past me and hustled Lard out the door and they talked a few minutes and the car left and Linda was back where I could talk to her and even hug her if I wanted to. But I wasnt about to want to first.

You're reading that same book again, she said when I'd just about give in. What's it about?

I looked at what remained of the torn cover. A cartoonish picture of a white whale. It's a fishing book.

She stared at the ragged paperback. How are you? Like she was reading the words there.

I dont know how it could hardly get much finer. It aint as good as I thought but way better'n I expected.

I didnt ask how she was but she let on like I had. I'm all right, she said. She wiped hard at dry eyes and then turned in her chair and leaned over and pulled me to her. That made me squishy inside but hugging sygogling on a wooden chair aint good for your back so I turned her loose.

Why did you start drinking again?

I opened my mouth to tell about the old man and the skinny woman and the fish and the dead dog and said, I dont know. It just happened. Why is it snakes always wear Kmart shoes?

I got a good look at her then. At the yellow crescent almost gone from under her eye. Whoa now. What we got here? I pulled her cheek down where I could see it good.

She pulled away and turned her head. Dont change the subject.

How'd you get a black eye? Things were starting to cipher up: the official escort home and the warnings about abuse. You been at the *shelter*? And knew it to be true. You've been at the shelter. You didnt go home a-tall.

I'm back now, so dont worry about it. Where I've been doesnt matter.

The hell it dont! You think you can haul out for no cause and then one day out of the blue come waltzing in with some fat drill sergeant and a wheelbarry full of legal papers and tell me it *doesnt matter*? Come home with a black eye you laid onto me and it *doesnt matter*? It was a relief to have a good hard mad to teeter on the edge of. Desperate relief. Like when you find a place to piss after you've gotten resigned to making water in your pocket. Leave me here with a broke-down washer and nobody to cook and tell me it *dont matter*? I made my voice go low and hard: Now you tell me about this here eye.

I ran into the edge of a door. All right? Defiance in her eyes and dead things, too. Things I'd caught and killed hanging there like taxidermied fish.

You know what that sounds like? Run into a door?

I dont care how it sounds. She hugged herself and walked to the window with her breath brushhooking at the stale air. She stared out like Lilo's woman and I thought, man, she just got home and already she's scouting for a place to go.

When she turned back she'd gathered her face up. She dug in the tissue box but it had been empty since the first time I ran out of toilet paper. Yuck! she said from the bathroom and blew her nose. Her voice had a fish-scaler edge when she returned. I'm staying. You do what you want.

How could you tell people I blacked your eye?

I didnt tell anybody anything. They draw their own conclusions.

Only that one time did I ever lay a hand on you, and I didnt hurt you then, I said. I'd busted everything else, but not people. Sometimes I felt like the one that needed a shelter. I massaged the lump on the edge of my ear.

Your words are worse than fists could ever be. They hurt more.

Why didnt you just cuss me when I hit you that one time then instead of clipping me with the soup dipper?

I dont fight dirty like you do.

Seven stitches to zipper my ear back on? That aint dirty?

I dont want to talk about it.

Maybe if we'd talk about stuff we could get shut of it. But I could tell from the bulge of her jaw hinge that she'd clammed up. And then you laughed. Hit me with the dipper and then laughed. How can you do that?

I laughed because you were ridiculous. Carrying on like your ear was torn off. And when I get a chance to laugh I take it. Seldom as it is.

All right. Chase it apast me one more time and I'll see if I can count the points. You run into a door and blacked your eye and since you had a black eye anyhow you decided to haul off to the shelter.

Would you rather I went home with a black eye? How long do you think it would be till Sammy and Slick showed up to have a little chat with you?

I worried at my scar tissue to take my mind off of her brothers.

Where am I supposed to go? I cant come here because you're on a binge. I cant go home.

My arms crossed. Stone faced.

Have you paid any of the bills?

Interrogater to interrogatee in one smooth step.

Did you even pay the electric bill? Or the lawyer?

My determination to shut my flap went up like spit on a griddle. I'll pay McKevey when they lay me in the grave.

Who'll keep you out of jail next time?

I wasnt guilty and you know it. They just said I stole so they could fire me and not have to pay unemployment. She flinched when my fist crashed into the table. And dont you pay him, either. Not one penny.

What happened to the dog?

Maybe she run into a door. I dont know.

Did you feed her?

What do you think? Most of the time I had.

Did you kill her?

I blew up out of the seat and forced her eyes away with a glare. What kind of monster do you think I am? She just left. I kicked at the table leg but not hard enough to crumple up my toes. Maybe she run off to the shelter. Maybe my words *hurt* too bad. Too close to the truth.

She smiled. What happened to *your* eye?

I rubbed the scab from where I'd banked my head off a guardrail stumbling home from The Hole in the dark. Maybe I got the rickets. Does that give you scabs? I aint much of a cook.

She laughed from way down in her belly the way she does and I loved her to death.

While I scoured dishes Linda tossed iridescent food from the refrigerator. Some of the plates I had to do over because I was watching her instead of what I was doing. The refrigerator's cold light twinkled in her warm brown eyes and glistened in her hair and made my skin itch. The fine wrinkles on her face made it look like highdollar leather and the gray streaks in her hair looked like they'd been done apurpose. Her hair was longer than I'd remembered, not that I'd paid much attention while she was here, and she filled her black slacks and white blouse in a way that was full and mature but firm and uppity. Maybe her boobs had let down a tad but that just made them look comfortable where they were instead of like they were hanging onto a cliff for dear life. Somehow she didnt look as skinny as she used to be but I'd bet she still weighed 117 pounds like always. I had missed her, I realized, and I was anxious to get the place cleaned up so I could demonstrate that. The silverware was crusted even worse than the dishes.

She made a snoot into the produce drawer. She had more nerve than I did to even look in there. What about Ahab's big question? she said.

Excuse me? Startled into civility.

Moby Dick. Your fishing book that you read over and over. Who pulls the levers? Is God in charge, or are we? Or does fate have the determining whack at life?

If you've been fifteen years hitched to the same woman you'd think you'd know which way she pulled. Or not. You read it? I said. I didnt know you had the time.

When would I have time to read? Oh, any evening till midnight or so, or weekends or holidays . . . any time you're gone. But I have to subtract my time at work from that, so . . .

Time to get off of that course. Did something in the corner of the apple bin inspire this conversation or did you come up with it on your own?

Unexpected events. Are they fate? God's doings? Or just luck?

Just tell me what's got hung up in your berry patch and then you'll know what I think without having to beat all around the edges trying to flush it out.

Her back swelled with a deep breath. I'm pregnant.

Linda kept on working like nothing had happened and without any warning the knife I was washing got so hot I couldnt hang on to it and it jumped out of my hand and whooshed through the air and stuck handle-side-in through the paneling by the window. The point sticking back at me like I'd done something wrong. It stuck there for a moment and started to sag and clattered off the floor. Well look there what that thing done, I said just as Linda locked the bedroom door.

I slid down the wall outside her door and sat on the floor for a while. Pregnant. The word loose in my head like a pinball, caroming off the bumpers and lighting up thoughts like bonus points, faster than I could keep track: I'm a whole man after all . . . why now, after all these years . . . do we even want a kid . . . we're too old . . . will it be a boy or a girl?

No. No way. The baby is mine.

For once my feelings couldnt find any words and I felt like a touch-me-not ready to bust so I scrabbled up and lit back into the cleaning. The kitchen didnt take long to dung out and I moved to the living room and made a quick dent in the garbage there and was starting to feel adult and responsible like a father should and there was Linda's purse.

I shut it up again quick and turned the TV on loud but that twenty inside had seen the light and was bawling to be let out. Rather than let it wake up the neighbors I set it loose but left the five and two ones there. The twenty was a lot happier in my pocket.

It's not stealing when you're married. Just joint ownership.

When most people sneak they ease the door shut nice and soft then let the bolt hammer home like a fart in the choir loft. I always let the bolt ease into the latch like a whore into a tent meeting. I dont know why I sneak. She knows where I'm going. And when.

Just outside the trailer park the roadside gravel turned crisp under my running shoes. The evening sun burned clean on my skin and now that I didnt have to think, I could, and the air smelled like cut hay instead of dead grass.

I was going to be a dad.

That part of my life wouldnt mesh with the rest of it. Like a 1,000-piece jigsaw puzzle with 350 pieces missing from the middle. One side a close-up of the inside of a spittoon and the other a field of daylilies. It was going to take some imaginative pieces to fill in the middle.

I was going to be a dad.

Or not. Hows come after all these years the blanks I'd been firing hit the bullseye? I'd pickled my libido but Linda hadnt. My mouth tasted like I had a penny under my tongue and I saw Linda with a faceless shape looming over her in the dark. But where would she get a lover? She didnt have any friends of her own and I couldnt imagine her going to either one of mine's funeral. Much less to bed with them.

But I hadnt known that she read either.

Maybe she didnt even go to the shelter. And where did she get that black eye? Not in Sunday school for sure.

A horn blew and a big-tired pickup with darkened windows labored past and I realized I was standing out in the narrow road staring back toward the trailer park with my chewed-over nails biting into my palms. A crow swooped from behind the trees so close that I could hear the wind whistle in his wings and his caw sounded like barroom laughter.

There I'd done it again. Rolled some imagined insult around in the barn-yard that was my mind till it was as big and filthy as a cow. I closed my eyes and shivered away the dark.

I was going to be a pap.

On the last little downgrade to the bar I broke into a jog and sung one of my beer-drinking songs in time with the slap of my feet.

> *The pantry is scanty, the money jar's dry,*
> *Bread full of maggots and dirt in my eye.*
> *So set up another, a toast to my mother,*
> *I'll swallow my sorrow away.*
> *Too-doodle-dee-doo, de-oodle dee-ooo . . .*

The Ace in the Hole sat alone like an oasis. Or a monument to where some-one important had died or got wounded in the front side. The rattle of the old cooler compressor was a comfort and the dented doorknob was warm and familiar in my hand. The gloom and sounds inside were a balm to my eyes and ears and the odors would gag me the next morning but just then were the smells of home. Cigarettes smoldered in ashtrays. Pool balls clicked. Sawtoothed laughter from the bar. Stale beer cooked in the trash-can. Deodorant biscuits wasted in the urinal. Sweat and perfume tangled in a most seductive way. Northern lights danced across the jukebox and an old Gatlin Brothers song oozed into the artificial twilight.

Neither of my friends was there so I sat at the empty end of the bar. Ace and two regulars were peeling tickets and making side bets. They shuffled money back and forth after each tip and didnt seem overwhelmed with glad to see me. After what felt like an hour Ace hurried down and glanced back toward his gambling. What'll it be? Meaning let's see the cash, Buck-wheat.

I slid the twenty across the worn top.

You get ten dollars to drink on and ten comes off the top of your tab. He glowered and hung over the bar like a haired-over hippopotamus that had somehow hooved itself erect. *Hippo erectus.*

I had brains instead. I'd ruther you took it off the bottom. And give me a Bud this time.

He snatched away the twenty and gave me a Keystone Light that I had to open myself and he made change and tore back to his gaming and I waited until he gathered his tickets and said, How about a glass here? These here cans look like they been stored in the chickencoop.

The corner of the glass made another half-moon in the bartop when he sat it down. But for once I kept my trap shut even after two or three beers. When Ace brought the fourth one he said, What's amatter with you tonight?

Just mellow, I said. When I had nothing to say I wouldnt shut up till first frost. Now I wanted to keep my news to myself.

But I couldnt.

Ace, I hollered and motioned when he looked up. After a while he came. Guess what, I said.

I aint got time for it.

Listen, I said to his back and trailed him back down to where the action was.

Frank was an old wingnut-eared cowflop that didnt even let on not to despise me. When you gonna get a job, dirtbag?

I had a job for this neighbor ole Bunker Reddy back where I come from, I said. He got me to help load some cows in his truck one time. But every time we run em into the skinny end of the loading chute back they'd come all googleeyed and it was get out the way or be toe jam. Hoof jam.

That aint what I asked you.

Cows is like that, said this skinny coaltruck driver named Luther who drank fifteen or twenty Milwaukee's Best and chewed up half a jar of beef jerky every night without ever getting drunk or sick or putting on lard. Bullheaded. Cowheaded.

Old Bunk said, This aint a-working, I continued. He set down central of the pen like a idjit and beat two rocks together and hummed "Froggy Went A-courtin" like the cows had requested it. I climbed up on the fence where I could laugh better. The cows milled around like cows do and winked away flies and pooped on their hind feet. Bunk just kept pecking those rocks together. After a while they got to be all over fidgets and one let a fart through her nose and lowered her head and glared at Bunk through the bars of the pen. Then all the heads came up and they got to snuffling and shuffling and that alpha-male cow took one step in Bunk's direction and then they were all crowding to be first up in the pen. I reckon they'd never got to look close at a crazy man before.

A crazy man and a dirtbag all at one go, Frank said. Enough to make em go dry.

That dont sound crazy to me, Luther said. That's the way cows is. I bet they went right in, didnt they? I could tell you another . . .

I jumped back in before Luther could light out on a tale of his own. It took a bit for me to remember to close my mouth and shut the gap behind them. Old Bunk scratched the hairy knot on the top of their heads that cows got instead of a brain and reminded them what a honorable thing a hamburger is. Inspired them to feed the starving pygmies in Ethiopia and Kentucky and all godforsaken places. And after a spell they looked right proud and distinguished and content there in the hamburg pen.

The others laughed but Frank looked like he had his nuts in a vise. What the hell does that got to do with you getting a job?

Well, if someone sets on a jobsite and whangs two rocks together until I wander in to see what's going on and somehow I get hornswaggled into working while I'm there, a job and me might make a temporary acquaintance. But otherwise I aint going nowhere near one.

Red flushed up Frank's face and Ace and Luther laughed at him. His beer went down in one long pull like he was heading out so I blurted out my news. Hey, guess what. Linda's about to find pups. I'm gonna be a dad.

Frank froze and looked at Ace and Ace looked at Luther and Luther looked at me and then cut me out of the loop and looked back at Frank.

Oh, God, Frank said. Then there'll be two of you. He swiveled off the stool and went to the bathroom. Big ears making his head look like a haired-over butterfly.

You think it's yours? Ace didnt grin.

Aw, bite me.

I done swore off pork.

But I'd told them what I had to get shut of and I went back to my end of the bar and savored the glow that grew in my belly as the cold beer went down. I considered the fork this baby had thrown into my road.

———

I left my last forty cents for Ace and took the final beer with me and let it bump along the guardrail as I felt my way home in the warm dark. Bats flittered against the sky but a bobwhite's optimistic voice canceled them out. The trailer park was friendlier when you couldnt see it.

The cleaning had gone on without me and a shirt and pair of jeans had been washed in the sink and laid out beside the couch. I didnt have to try the bedroom door to know it was locked again.

My beer had gone flat and I couldnt finish it. Sleep finally came but that old bone dog came along with it. Twice I had that dream. When I reached for Linda the first time I spilled the beer into the carpet. The second time I got a handful of wet fabric and thought for a bit I'd wet the bed.

Linda was back but she wasnt there.

Before the sun split the trees I'd showered and tried to hack away a week's worth of scraggly whiskers without seeing the thin mouse-colored hair and the saggy shoulders. I'd lowered the mirror so I wouldnt have to stand tiptoed but I'd overdid it and now I had to squat. That didnt make me feel tall. Just stupid.

The spilled beer had sponged up into my clean shirt and pants. I smelled the clothes I'd taken off and selected the eau-de-beer ones and slipped out the door again.

The lawnmower had grown fast in the weeds but I muled it loose and changed the oil and cleaned the plug and excavated a mouse nest from the air intake and beat the dirt out of the filter against my shoe. I jerked the rope for half an hour or more but I just couldnt get it started.

CHAPTER 3

Till Linda stepped out to tell me breakfast was on my determination to change my ways was hair near yanked away. I reeked of spilled beer and of the sour-milk smell that oozes out of a drunk's hide come morning and slid in between was a rotten sweat smell. A stink sandwich.

Same old.

So I kicked the lawnmower over onto its side and tore a hole in my good running shoe and then when I flipped it back up the handle caught my funnybone. While I was jumping around like a chicken after a junebug and holding my elbow I tromped on the wrench and the ratchet went *ruk-k-k* like a frog and the handle cracked my ankle. I fell down and added grass stains to my knees and a brand-new word to my vocabulary—a word I'd never heard that sounded like *noktublerferdurum* jumped out to handle the stuff everyday cussing couldnt touch.

Linda stepped back off the stoop and slammed the door when I kicked the mower. By the time I cussed the mower till flies couldnt light on it and throwed the wrench into the street and stomped a couple square yards of grass into green mud I was feeling better. By then the door was locked. Not the bedroom door but the front door.

The neighbor stuck his greasy mug out and hollered, Hey. Do that again. My wife missed the first show.

Is that your wife? I said all pop-eyed. You better tell them guys that come around and needle her while you're at work. I bet they dont even suspect.

He laughed mean. Make sure you aint one of them or you'll be rat food.

Speaking of rats. You best tell your kids I've put poison out. They might ought stay away and not steal anything for a spell. At least until the D-Con's all ate up. It just aint safe right now.

He hawked spit my way and slammed the door.

That was before breakfast on the day I intended to clean up my act.

I considered lamming out the plywood that plugged the hole in the door where I'd bricked the glass out but that last fit ran me out of gas so I sat on the stoop again. I'd whittled away most of the floor mat with a butcher knife trying to trim the WELCOME off but what was left was dewsoaked and it felt like dipping my butt in icewater. Blood rivered in my ears and my heart hammered like a fifty-dollar pickup.

With my eyes closed I couldnt see the swaybacked trailers and broken toys and rundown cars and scattered trash that made life in a trailer park so colorful and picturesque. And the yelling and the crying baby and the rusted muffler on the car that had been idling for a half hour or more sounded slippery like a bad dream that would slide away if you tented up and concentrated hard enough.

But they didnt.

After a while the door creaked open and gouged me in the back and Linda said, Andy? Like maybe I'd metamorphosed into a cockroach. Andy? Like someone else had decided to sit on the wet mat where she couldnt see them.

Tis I, Andrew Price, a friend of your'n. We'd watched a Civil War special where some skinny redneck geek had answered that way to a sentry's challenge. Linda had found that funny but not this.

Are you back to earth enough to eat?

I come back oncet but couldnt find no intelligent lifeforms there so I've went off again. I'll be back to try again dreckly.

An apology from her was likely too much to expect. Come on, she said. A gust of wind slammed the doorknob into the pocket it had forged into the siding and daylight flickered where the plywood was falling out of the frame. Take your shoes off.

They're clean, I said on the way to the table. Stomped clean, I figured. I looked back at the dirt and grass I'd tracked in. She muttered something I elected not to hear and fetched a plate of French toast she'd kept warm in the oven while I cooled. The crusty bread swam with butter and syrup and the smell was almost enough to make me faint. Syrup dripped from my chin while I tried to wallow the first bite into a manageable chunk while I jibbled up the rest into bitesized pieces. Strong black coffee in a glass.

I dont know where the cups are, she said before I could complain. I guess you broke them.

You cant break a plastic cup (but you can tote them off and forget them somewhere). Where'd you get groceries at? I said.

They delivered from Pete's last night while you were at the bar. But you stole my money. I had to charge most of them.

I didnt steal no money, I said. I stole *some* money, I thought.

Her eyes probed mine for a long time but I wouldnt look away. So what did you eat while I was gone? Everything was spoiled or moldy.

I shrugged. Pickled eggs and sausages out of the big jugs at The Hole? I wasnt sure. She sat and watched while I cleaned the skillet and emptied the coffeepot. My belly felt like a cider jug that had been left in the car on a hot day. When I burped she took it as a signal to start with the news. Her mom had been sick again and her crazy youngest brother Slick had broken his arm and her crazy oldest brother Sammy was moving from her home place in up in Union County to Cincinnati for a better job.

What'd Slick do, hammer on the wrong person? Or did Sammy get bored and whup little brother just for practice?

He broke his arm playing volleyball. And you quit saying that. They're not that way.

Playing volleyball. When's he going to grow up? He is, what . . . thirty?

He's thirty-one. Two. So what's going on with your buddies?

Nothing breathtaking came to mind. Mike fell asleep in the pickup and dropped a cigarette ash onto his new shirt. Dave put his income tax refund into a new outboard motor just to spite Sharon for running off again. None of these were anything Linda needed to know.

I started to write a story once about this little redneck boy that grows up . . .

Linda finished my sentence . . . and your professor said that redneck and growing up created a contradiction in terms and wouldnt let you write it.

Oh, I do know something. Mike's piles has flared up again. He's going to get them reamed out. Get his butt relined.

Linda's laughter didnt sound belittling so I gave it a little shot along with her. I reckon if you squinted at it from the corner of your eye and ignored the pain in Mike's hind end it was a little funny.

How do they go about relining him? she said.

I think they intend to drive a ham up his butt and then pull the bone out.

We laughed hard then but there was an offtone of desperation to it.

Like if we could keep it up the real problems would have to go away. After a while we gave up on it. What's your plan? Linda said.

I'm going to start the mower and make a little hay while the sun shines.

Then what? Edge-free words that didnt give me the option of ignoring them by taking offense.

That depends when I finish. Maybe I'll put the insulation back up under the floor. Where I'd pursued a mouse that had gnawed while I was trying to sleep.

And then?

Days in this part of the woods aint got but thirty, forty hours. What she wanted to talk about I didnt.

What are you going to do long term? You need to think about it.

Yeah, yeah. I dont think that good while I'm working. Them two endeavors aint compatible. The door slammed behind me as I left the trailer . . . just a little warning: Dont push.

She pushed. From the stoop she said, Whether your problems go away is up to you. But I will if they dont.

The neighborhood kids must not have been out of bed yet because the wrench I'd thrown into the street was still there. It was a shame that the two families that mostly filled the trailer park didnt mix. The Henchports wouldnt work and the Salters even stole from each other. If they intermarried, their kids would be too lazy to steal. These kids were lazy enough but their thievery was top shelf.

I wrenched the mower up alongside the cylinder head to show it what would happen if it didnt start on the first pull. Yeah right. Most of the old gas drained into my good shoe when the fuel line came loose and I refilled it with some fresh and finally the engine gagged and hawked. I cleaned the spark plug again and it fired and settled into a ragged rumble in a cloud of blue smoke that dwindled to a haze after a few minutes and the exhaust got throaty and strong but not strong enough to cut grass without stalling. Not this grass anyhow.

But each time I swallowed down my bile and yanked her again.

I'd have give out on it if the neighbor hadnt stuck his head out the door and cussed me for the racket and after that I couldnt quit. The blades clattered and I found out what had happened to the brick I'd tossed into his yard awhile back. His grinning face popped up in the window and I almost

threw the brick at him but I wet my middle finger and chalked up one for
him instead and put the brick back with the others around the weedbed.

By early afternoon the place didnt look abandoned. It looked like white
trash had moved in.

A whiff of my shirttail when I wiped my face reminded me of another
chore. I dragged the washer out into the hallway as far as it would go and
squirreled over the top and hunkered in the corner and cussed and wiped
away spiderwebs and unscrewed the back panel. It didnt take two minutes
to find the problem. A screw on the rubber-boot-clutch-thing clamp had
rusted off so the motor spun but the drum didnt. In the shed I found a
woodscrew that would half fit in the hole and a screwdriver that still had
enough edge to drive it crossthreaded into the hole and directly the sound
of dirty clothes getting born again sloop-slooped through the trailer.

A three-cent part. And I'd been going to the Laundromat for months.
Or someone had.

That's what I was missing, I reckon. Some three-cent part. But I'd of
needed a two-hundred-dollar-an-hour mechanic to figure out which one.
And if I'd had two hundred dollars I sure wouldnt spend it on a head doctor because for ten dollars I could adjust my head till it didnt know it had
a problem.

The insulation was just as easy. The staple gun was rusted into one lump
so I nailed the paper edges with roof nails and felt righteous with honest
sweat even in the filth and gloom underneath the trailer.

I felt so good I went for a run. Linda watched out the window as I left
so I turned up the hill away from The Hole. My shins were knotted up for
half a mile or so but they eased up and I sweated out the drunk stink and
felt like a new man when I headed for the shower. Some old hillbilly song
was bubbling inside:

> Lookin' down from the mountain high,
> Thirteen polecats wander by.
> Flattop's got a busted string,
> But listen to me sing, Sol,
> Just listen to it ring.

That's all the words I knew but I let fly in a thin reedy tenor that sounds
like a peepfrog blowing a juiceharp. But in the shower I pretend I'm Bill

Monroe and that high lonesome sound is bounding off the walls of the Old Ryman.

While I was drying my hair Linda's lips touched my neck and her cool fingers slipped under my arms and hauled me back against her bare skin. I was red-combed right off but gave her no more attention than I would a wood tick till my teeth were brushed and my hair combed and then I sashayed her to the bed and did the only thing I know of that you can get two months behind on and catch up in way less than a minute. But she told me I was a stud anyway. Let me give you a back rub, she said. All of my sore muscles got grubbed out and some that were just lonely and before long I was anxious to rip again. The idea that I was shooting live ammo didnt hurt any.

Then I got to craving a smoke though I hadnt smoked for years and that made me think about when I was attached to the public tit and had to fill out questionnaires all the time and one asked if I smoked after sex and I said that our electric was shut off and I couldnt turn on the light to look. The memory made me laugh out loud and Sweetpea laughed too though she had no idea why.

We lay there clean and sated as if we'd been fileted and floating like bubbles on a bathtub and mine must of floated off by itself because when I woke I was alone. I could hear Linda in the kitchen but feel her right there beside me.

We had pork and beans for supper doctored with bacon and onions and peppers and barbecue sauce and I ate a dog's bait of it till something tore loose inside. Then we washed dishes together and teased at the subject of being parents without ever facing it square on. She'd had time to fool with the thought but it still left me juberous.

I thought I'd swallowed enough for a week but she made a bushel of popcorn and drenched it with enough butter to kill us and enough salt to make us euphoric while we died. Eating gave us an excuse not to get in trouble talking and we both pretended to watch TV.

Dave and Mike put end to that when they come herding in the door without knocking. Like they do when Linda is gone. Well. Sweetpea, Dave said.

Most times it took a minute or more for her to get homicidal toward him but her sparks glittered in his pale eyes before he'd even shouldered past the door. Wipe your feet! she snapped but he was halfway across the living room and the fat parts of the grass and dirt was off by then. Mike peeked at the bottom of one boot and had enough sense to hunker down into the nearest chair.

Aw, look at that. Git me a broom and I'll clean it up. Dave made more mess as he swaggered back toward the door.

Just sit down. I'll clean it up after you leave. Sounding like she'd like to start cleaning right then.

I took one shot at making peace. How about some coffee?

Nah. Mike was fifty but looked old enough to retire.

Come fishin with us, Dave said. The bass are schooled up till it aint never gonna get no better than it is right now.

I saw me holding a sag-bellied bass for the crowd at The Hole. *What'd you catch him on, Tu?* Linda wheeled off toward the kitchen but stopped short with her arms crossed.

Now's the time, Mike said. Them big old hogs are really laying on the lard.

That's just what we need. A bucket of fish lard. A coon couldnt snarl better than Linda when she put her back into it.

I reckon I'll stay home tonight, I said. And when I looked at Linda standing there that's what I wanted to do. Home life was good. She worked me like a rented mule today, I said, and I think I've broke allergic to it. *That's a real dandy, Tu.*

You dont never catch the big ones cause you dont never go when they're bitin. When Dave propped one foot on his knee a glob of crayon-yellow showed in his boot's knobby tread.

Linda didnt miss it. Dave, you've got dog poop on your shoe.

Aw, hell. Aint we a bunch of hogs. He was lithe and lean enough to spring up without uncrossing his legs.

Just sit. Dont track any more than you already have.

I cant take him nowhere. Mike laughed but kept his feet pulled back under the chair where Linda couldnt get a good gander at them.

I swear it's near a chore to visit when you're here, Linda. Tu dont worry about the floor like that. Dave cocked his head to his good eye. I suspected he was looking at her shiner but he didnt mention it.

Then dont visit if it's so hard.

He grinned and skinned a cigar and threw the wrapper onto the coffee table and then laughed and retrieved it before she could erupt again. What you get so worked up about a old woreout floor for? He groped in his pocket and withdrew a battered lighter.

Dont you dare light that stinking turd in my house. *Turd* was a cuss word when Linda said it. Mike mickeyed with the TV remote and I burrowed into the chair and pretended they were fighting over smoking instead of me.

Dave scratched in his tight blond curls and chewed the cigar like some things were beyond his comprehension. I see we done wore a hole in our welcome. He smacked Mike on the leg. Let's go catch some hawgs. He uncoiled and hopped on his cleanest foot toward the door and in passing hugged Linda and she responded with a fist to his ribs. One with some steam behind it. Broken glass in his eyes but he laughed. Come see my new motor, Tu, he yelled from the stoop's edge. He scraped his boot there where someone else would tramp in it.

I'm just gonna look at his motor, I whispered. So he'll leave. Linda's snort bit into my back like a rake as I closed the door behind me.

Dave twisted the tab from a fresh beer and tossed it into the yard. Foam dissolved on his knuckles and I imagined I could hear the tiny yellow bubbles pop. I'd offer a beer but Linda might desackulate you.

From the big cooler in the center of the boat ice clunked as the cans rearranged themselves. Linda's snort replayed in my memory even more irritating than the original. She's got half a freezer full of mountain oysters, I said. She aint going to dirty up her knife for just two. The icewater electrified my sweaty hand.

Aint that a dandy motor? Mike said. But it looks like a diamond ring on a bag lady. A curl of brown paint feathered down when he thumped the dented boat's side.

That thing will tear the transom clean off, I said. The motor was too big. Too clean for the boat.

It aint but a twenty-five. Hell, you could put a forty on it. Them rating tags is just to keep the manufacturers from gettin sued. Come on and take a ride. We'll drop you off at the point when you want to come home and you can walk back from there. Grab your pole and let's git.

Linda was watching out the window as we left. I didnt give her that black eye, I said.

Dave steered with his knee while he lit his cigar and then spit a bit of tobacco out the window and said, She looks good in black. All women does.

She's gonna have a baby, I said.

Well hell, it aint no wonder then. That'd give my woman a black eye for certain. Maybe two.

When's it due? Mike said.

I dont know. I never asked.

You want me to drop you grandmas off down at the preschool, or are we goin fishin? Dave said.

The clamor of frogs rose like a privacy fence as we rumbled toward the lake. The autumny smells of copper pennies and woodsmoke promised frost soon. Dave messed my hair and said, I like you, little buddy. Sitting down, my eyes were level with his.

You watch it now, I said and combed my hair with my fingers. I'm just liable to kick the shit out of you and then kick you for shittin. Feeling better all the time.

I'm glad you fell back off the wagon, he said. You aint cut out for that prissy-clean life.

I didnt *fall* nowhere. I *jumped* off. We laughed together like frogs.

The fishing went like night fishing goes. We got cussed at for fishing around private docks and then drifted into a shallow muddy cove and threw out our minnows and ate Slim Jims and drank beer and lied and laughed. Mike got hung up and turned on the flashlight and the beam tracked his minnow swinging like a pendulum from a tree twenty feet beyond the edge of the water. We caught fish in spite of ourselves but the big old sow that would bring me respect never came my way.

I remembered Dave's bragging as we tore through the utter dark—*listen to that motor whine; sounds like a cat with its tail in the fan belt, dont it?*—and the bursts of red from his wind-fueled cigar ash and the sphincter-clutching obstacles in the black water. I recalled the rocks biting into my knees when I fell down as we loaded the boat back onto the trailer and the cold water in the good shoe that I hadnt torn on the mower but spilled gas on and the rainbow that flared around it on the water's surface. And there was Dave's and Mike's laughter as they dumped me on the stoop and staggered back to the truck.

A road-killed skunk hung heavy across the trailer park and that looking-down-on-the-polecats song was on my mind again and I sent that high lonesome cry out through the trailer park over the cursing and slamming doors. A yellow wedge of light when Linda peeked out the door. The snick of the lock.

Later, much later, the discovery of the bluegill Dave had slipped into my pocket instead of the handkerchief I needed to wipe away the sick and damp and age and fatigue from my face.

I found the key under the brick and let myself in and slept on the couch without testing the bedroom lock. The old dream came but a new one, too, of a slick fast passive boat driven helter-skelter into docks and stumps and moored boats over the water and under the water and soundless but for the screams that echoed back from the hard black line of forest.

CHAPTER 4

I slipped into morning like an old cripple trying to ease down into a too-hot tub. My head throbbed and a sour paste glued my tongue to my teeth. Some kind of hair paste. The noise that had dragged me from sleep came again. The intimate liquid tearing of someone turning guts inside out. The night was scattered through my mind like a busted flowerpot. My fingers smelled of fish and bits of scenes and of what I'd said or tried to say and feared I'd said but hoped I hadnt chased each other through my mind down a random path and with no common denominator. But I couldnt remember anybody coming home with me. And there was a dim recollection of Dave's and Mike's drunken laughter as they roared from the driveway.

That burlap sound again. What had I dragged home this time? When the spinning in my head whirled down to where I could jump the rest of the way I lurched toward the bathroom and whatever part of the night had slipped past me. Linda's body hung from the toilet in the near-dark of daybreak. Her back arched and the sound ripped at my own insides. Her mouth when she turned my way was a waxy embarrassed scar hacked in the shine of her pale face. I flinched away.

Not Sweetpea. Please no. Aw. What's got into you? I said.

I'm not drunk. It's morning sickness. She laughed or sobbed into a folded towel.

But the idea of Linda's hollering for Huey like a common bum had jumped the fence and my stomach surged and I stumbled outside and held on to the trailer's corner and had a go at it myself. My legs spraddled far out so I wouldnt splash on my bare feet. Far out, man. Two fascinated kids that in other neighborhoods might have been paperboys but here most likely werent in yet from a night of thieving stopped their bikes to watch and then spat in the dirt and laughed as they pedaled away laughing like they'd never turn out like this.

Then Linda and I laid up sick in the bed. One was from the life growing inside and the other wasnt. The bed trembled as she cried. Sometime later she went still and cleared her throat. I rolled toward her before she could say anything and rested my hand on her belly and felt for the little squid that wiggled there. So eager to leave that warm safe place for a world a dog wouldnt tolerate. Her words didnt come. Just silence framed by the sound of a leaking toilet. When she rolled away my hand trailed across her back and fell into the warm pocket where she'd been. She squeezed my dirty hand and said, Come on. I'll fix breakfast.

If you get a bag of horsemanure for Christmas you only got but two options. You can cut a rusty about the unfairness of life or you can noodle around in the bag to make sure there aint still a pony in there. I guess it had sunk in that I was all she'd got, so she dug down like she'd already *seen* the pony and just had to hold her nose till she caught ahold of it.

Dave showed up just before nine that morning. At least he knocked this time but Linda flew between us like a she-bear. Go away, Dave. Leave him alone. Leave *us* alone.

Easy, hon . . .

You shut up, Andy.

Aw, Linda, give us a break. Dave tried to crowd past her objections.

Go away! Now! Her arm barred the doorway and her knuckles flashed white where she clutched the jamb.

He went cabbage-faced and backed onto the stoop and tucked his beer under his arm and in one slick movement touched her discolored eye and then made a crucifix of his index fingers and extended it toward her face. Easy, babe. His voice as emotionless as his face. See you at The Hole little buddy, he said over her shoulder. Gravel ricocheted from the lawnmower as he spun from the driveway.

Daggone you, I said to Linda. You cant treat my friends like that. We'll talk, I yelled to Dave but he was gone and I was glad and ashamed that he was.

You and your talk. Sometimes I think that's your addiction more than the alcohol.

Maybe you should have a go at it once. Get stuff off your plate so you dont have to eat it again. Like how you got that black eye.

You want talk? Try this. She grabbed my cheeks in both hands and spit the words out with spaces between them like she was trying to get through to a cucumber. I've waited a lifetime for this baby and I wont bring it up under the influence of a drunk. Straighten up or I'll leave. But decide now. Right now.

You dont want him under the influence, huh? If I could make her laugh we could stagger past it.

Right this minute. Her fingernails bit into my cheeks and I pushed her away.

This was a definitive this-is-your-brain/this-is-your-brain-on-splo moment. I whistled while I tried to scout a path around and then tried my best hounddog look but she just got meaner. Well why didnt you say so instead of beatin around the bush, I said when I had to say something. Sure. Let's give er a try. I imagined that my spine crackled as it straightened and stiffened.

Monday morning Linda went to work on me instead of to her usual job. Get up, she said. The sun wasnt but she thought I should be.

I pulled the covers over my head. What for?

She whacked me with something that didnt hurt but when she did it the second time I threw back the covers. With her snarled hair and ragged old nightgown and waving a broom, she was a witch pure and simple. She swung again and I caught the broom and jerked it away. I went after her as far as the door and she laughed and stuck out her tongue from the far end of the hallway.

What I wanted to do was to bust her childish head, but damned if I didnt love her right then. I groused and banged the cabinet doors but I showered and shaved and then got another great breakfast and a haircut. She was diligent to let hair fall in my face and to pinch and pull with the dull scissors and to harrow the back of my neck with the razor. She expected thanks for all that, of course, and then we lit off to find me a job.

Car-less, we walked like common vagrants along the shoulder of the road the half-mile to the intersection at The Hole, Linda in front, then caught the little ragtailed public transit van into Ransom. The first place we applied was at a lumberyard. It aint no use to stop here, I said. I already worked here once. I might just as well have argued with a stump.

There's an old geezer named Walt Bonnar lives in a tarpaper shack along Spring Road just past the bridge. Up in his nineties. A while back Dave's dad Bud took Walt on a day-trip to Bluefield. They just drove down and walked through the mall and ate at Long Dong's and then came back. Walt didnt seem too bedazzled by his first trip out of the county. Bud was fractious cause he'd only took the old goat there to see what he'd missed louseing around his shack while the world went round and round without him even knowing it turned. Well, whaddya think? Bud finally said.

Old Walt looked him over careful and then said, I knowed the world was big and fiercesome but I didnt have no idee she was anything like that. He spat snuff juice out the power window and slid down in the seat and pulled his cap down and took a nap till they got back home where he could do something.

That's the way I felt when I got that job. I knowed workers were hard to come by but I didnt have no idee the labor market was anything like that.

I wasnt immigrant enough to waste time filling out a application where I'd already worked once so I just went straight to the bull goose's office and stuck my head in the door. How's about another job, Ken? I said before I noticed that he was on the phone. He held the receiver against his chest so I plowed the rest of the row: My woman says I got to get a job. That was self-inspired and not anything I learned in the job-search classes that Miss Brodan made me pretend to sleep through before she'd process my unemployment claims.

He laughed like the joke was on him. Your timing is impeccable, Tu.

My haircut aint bad either, is it? That kind of stuff runs out my mouth whenever I'm in shock. Pieces of new-cut hair twinkled down onto his desk when I stroked my head.

He held up one finger and stuck the receiver back to his ear. Wednesday afternoon's the absolute soonest I can get it there, he said. I'm sorry, but we're just overwhelmed and that's how it's got to be. While he listened his lips tried to shape words that never came and then he set the receiver back into the cradle. Can you start right now?

You mean like the instant before next? The idea was like spit in the face till I considered the tramping and groveling that was on the other side of the flapjack. I shrugged. Let me clear it with the boss.

Linda was sitting on a highdollar rotteniron garden bench sipping Dr Pepper and making the bench look worth the price. See! she said. Like she'd never hoed the tiniest little seedling of doubt. The pop made her kiss cool and sweet. None of the people coming in and out of the store looked our way. I had half a notion to start a stir to draw their attention and then kiss her again. Even if she did have a black eye.

———

The lumber to build the *Mayflower* probably came from Workman's Contractor Supply, and there was most likely some roundhead like me to load it into the customer's wagon. The task would have been easier then. You wouldnt have had to insert a ten-foot board into a five-foot car without touching the upholstery or construct a hangglider out of a Hyundai and a sheet of plywood and two pieces of balers' twine. And there wouldnt have been fifteen bit-chomping customers helping you out by blowing the mouse nests out of the horn and expanding their vocabularies with new cusswords. Patience was still a virtue back in colonial days and people would have seen that you were doing your dead-level best and sat and spit on the mule's tail while they waited their turn. Workman's full inventory drew folks from all over Green County and every one of them knew enough about me to despise me without reservation. People that had no more use for a two-by-four than they did for Socialism stopped in for one just so they could lower their blood pressure by getting off on me. The physical side of the job was just as hard as the emotional. For a while there I had to drag my butt home in my lunch bucket cause I'd worked it clean off and was too tired to pack it under my arm. I reckon I was still five-eight but I felt wore down to four feet tall.

Not once did I catch a ride that turned out onto Hungry Holler Road and past the trailer park. Every evening I got expelled into the parking lot at The Hole all hot and dry and out of gas and self-esteem. The bass notes from the jukebox and the faint smell of cigarette smoke leaked through the cracks like vines that caught at my pantslegs and tugged at my sleeves. My calf muscles (on the way to becoming cow muscles) would tremble as they scooted my shoes up the hill toward home and Linda.

Years ago when I quit smoking I carried a coffin nail behind my ear until I got it licked. The smoke was there anytime I wanted it and it was like a billboard ad that I was quitting. Once in a while I'd slope off and smoke it and then put up another one and nobody knew the difference. After a time not smoking was what I did just like smoking was what I did before and I threw it away and didnt fool with it again.

Drinking aint that way. The Hole was there every night where I could see it and hear it and smell it but I couldnt take it down for a couple of tokes and put up another one. Many a night I stopped and looked back down the hill on my way home to Sweetpea. But if I went back down there there'd be no Sweetpea to come home to.

I've heard of folks got saved by angels from that first drink back. One feller told me his dead mama stood in the doorway of the bar and wouldnt let him past. She must of croaked again cause he was drunk when he told me about it. But dried limabeans saved me this time. There's nothing better except maybe a ramp sandwich with a can of sardines on the side.

I'd seen the beans soaking that morning and my stomach growled so that as I hitchhiked home the kid who gave me a ride laughed out loud. I grinned and said, We're having limabeans for supper. That was the G-rated preview. He laughed and let me out just as Mike rolled into the parking lot at The Hole. He asked me in and I looked up the hill and tallied losing Linda and a pot of beans both. Nope. I cant. Not even for one.

He didnt goad on me the way Dave would have.

Where's Dave at today? Feeling like I was talking to half a person.

Playing softball. Thinks he's still a kidlet. Tomorrow his hamstrings will be drawed up tighter'n a black bull's butt and he wont be able to scratch his ass. Mike looked younger himself away from his junior of twenty years. I'd forgot how he could go on. The time got away and in the middle of a windy he said, Uh-oh.

Linda's lips were like baling wire as she first came down the hill but her whole face pinched up till she got to us. Your supper's getting cold.

Aint you even gonna be nice and say hi to Mike?

Mike eased back a half step like he wasnt feeling left out.

Has he said anything nice to me?

I could probly do it, he said.

Well let's hear it then.

All right. He lifted his hat and scratched his head. You dont sweat too fierce for being knocked up.

I felt the tension go out of her and her claws eased about halfway out of my arm and her lips quivered on the end. Dern you Mike. Dont make me laugh when I'm mad.

A few minutes later we were strolling up the hill. You two behave yourself, now, Mike called. I waved as he disappeared inside. The talk had given me a slight buzz. The limabeans were something special.

Workman's closed at two o'clock Saturdays, and that afternoon I'd brought home a roll of windowscreen to try to do something about the flies that wandered in and out of the trailer like tourons at a yardsale. The afternoon sun was a torch, the way it is when you're not free to fan yourself or shift your britches. Drops of sweat freckled the screen and the garbage cans I was using for a worktable.

If I pulled the screen up snug I didnt have hands enough to worry the rubber cord into the groove. But if I concentrated on the groove the screen bagged like an old woman's sweatpants. I was fixed too hard on the job to notice a car ease into the drive. The cord was started but when I shifted my hold on the screen it started to ooze back out. Dammit to hell! I hollered and kicked the garbage can.

You got to be patient with it. Homer Lawton's unmistakable axlegrease voice. My heart turned into a thundermug and my bowels felt like I needed one. The air all of a sudden stunk of septic systems and Dumpsters. Freda Lawton smiled like my language hadnt bothered her at all.

The trailer door flapped against the wall and Linda thundered down the steps like a runaway buffalo squealing Mom! Daddy! She looked old and fat and I looked down embarrassed when the neighbor's head peeked out the door. When they'd settled down Freda gave me a hug around the belly. It's good to see you, Andy. She looked like Linda freeze-dried.

I patted her on the back easy so I wouldnt break anything. Hey, it's good to see you all too. There ought to be a trophy for telling one like that.

You girls go get the girltalk out of your system, Homer said. Me and Andy'll finish these screens.

There aint no call to get your clothes dirty. (Please go away.)

Take more'n this little job to filth up my duds. Hog hair bristled where he rolled up his sleeves. He looked soft but I knew better. Where's your screen tool at?

I guess I dont know too much about this.

Aint you got a jar lid? Anything round with a grooved edge. He poked through my shed without asking and returned with the lawnmower's gas cap. He rolled the cap along the cord and stretched the screen tight at the same time. Made it jump together like the groove was pussy and the cord was a teenager's hoe handle. If you haul it thin it'll go in but it wont hold. Let it big and mash it in like you was helping a fat woman into the backseat. Now you do one.

Coordinating the gas cap and the rubber cord and screen wasnt as easy as Homer made it look but that little bit of knowhow was all I needed to get the next one fixed to his satisfaction. We didnt talk about anything but what we were doing so I neglected to be fearful. The last screen thrummed like a banjo head. He held the stepladder while I fastened it in place and we even joked a little bit.

My trepidation came home with kittens when we went inside. Those other sit-downs we'd had were full of threat and ultimatum and hard to digest but this time the air stayed static-free and nobody mentioned Linda's eye and I elected not to bring it up. Linda said to tell about my job and I was hard put to keep the swagger out of my voice.

Then I realized it wasnt news to them or they wouldnt of been there.

The talk started to miss on a couple of cylinders. Freda eased back from the edge of the couch and Homer fiddled with his pantslegs. Let's go for a little spin, he said.

Not if I got any sense left a-tall, I thought so I said, Sure, why not.

Jump up front, Freda said as we climbed up into the big Buick. The car was everything I didnt have in one package. My neighbor stared out the door as clueless as me and we traded telepathic middle fingers.

The women gabbled in the back while Homer and I hunkered under the air vents like hunters in a duck blind. My mind ran out in front but I couldnt see where we were headed. We cruised past the downtown loop and its lawyers and social workers and deputy sheriffs and then the blinker came on at D&R&AP Junior's Used Car Lot. The crooked marquee beside the entrance said PEACH SALE TODAY. NO CHERRIES. NO LEMONS. Or would have if all the letters were still there. Two of the o's were red among the black.

The salesman came lunging out of his little shack wiping his mouth on his snotrag and said, You're back already. His mouth still full of sandwich.

Homer pushed past him and led us to a ten-year-old Subaru station wagon. What do you think of that vehicle right there?

As many pairs of shoes I'd wore out it looked like a Porsche. I looked at Linda but she wouldnt meet my eye. We need a car bad with the baby coming and all, I said, but we cant swing one just yet. I could hear something rattling down through the branches but I didnt jump right out to catch it. Sometimes those walnuts turn into bird droppings.

I'm gonna loan you the money.

And you dont have to pay us back, Freda said.

You keep out of this, Homer said. This is between me and him.

I cant pay you for a while.

I reckon if you could pay it back right now you wouldnt need a loan. Aint that right?

A knot or a hairball or something had caught in my throat so I looked the car over instead of saying anything. When I looked at Linda she shrugged like I was the boss. Putting on a show for her folks. I *will* pay you back, I said. You can go ahead and put the paper in the piggybank and count it in.

Homer shrugged. I got more important things to do than count money.

The screwdriver slipped and nicked my finger while I was fastening the temporary plate and I bumped my head when I put the insurance binder in the glove box and Linda raked the gears when she downshifted to follow her parents into Denny's parking lot. Freda flipped the page of my menu from the cheap stuff to the dinners. The tea was sour. There were no bone dogs or motorboats around. This was no dream.

Our eyes hung solid when I shook Homer's hand beside the car. Freda hugged hard and I gave her one back but she didnt break. Linda waved until they were out of sight and then drove us all around in luxuries long forgotten. Linda a madame inspecting the whorehouse and me in a daze that hadnt come from a bottle.

CHAPTER 5

The sunrise the next morning either had new colors or I hadnt noticed it for a while. I'd been dry for a month. My eyes didnt slip off the mirror when I shaved.

Linda bushwhacked me. Let's go to church this morning.

I was caught up in admiring myself and I said, Okie dokie instead of hmmm? I wanted to cram the words back in but they were out and I never let on. But I hated those words. She never said, Are you serious? or anything that would let me make a joke out of it. So she put on her best clothes and I put on my worst mood and off to church we went.

A new white straw hat haloed Linda's head and shiny black heels made her ankles young again. Two longs sweeps of hair fastened at the back framed her innocent face. The rest fell like lace over her shoulders. I'd banned Bibles from the premises but one snuggled against her breast as natural as if a ginseng had sprouted there.

You blindsided me, I said. This was figured out ahead.

She smiled with her mouth but not with her eyes. When she locked the door behind us the pretty barrette I'd found at Lilo's flashed on the back of her head like an imbedded jewel.

My call was to go across town or out into the country where nobody knew us but she firmed down on the little Ransom United Methodist church just apast The Hole. Dont worry, she said. Anybody that goes to church wont know you.

It's interesting to note the things that embarrass the shameless.

I was about as anonymous as Abe Lincoln. Larry from work was there and Pete's Grocery Joni and that old rip Miss Brodan . . . I knew more than not. Linda's clear alto during the song service drew looks from the offkey gum-rattlers around us but my glare put their eyes back under the porch.

Voices bounced from the old stamped-steel ceiling and fell down like a grapevine snarl till I got tangled up and was singing inside. Lyrics that wouldnt stay down. Tunes that rose up to wrassle with the organ.

> *My faith rests not in mortal plan,*
> *But in God's palm, rock laid for man . . .*

My faith was under the rock, not on it. Dead and cold as the dank basement air that clanked through the ductwork.

Then the preacher squirreled up to the pulpit to shine his big gospel spotlight on our pitiful souls. That's the part I hate the most. If you have a soul like Linda's you luster up like an angel. But when you illuminate a pile of dog vomit like me you get dog vomit all lit up to where you can name the individual chunks.

Fifteen words into his sermon I had remembered how to slope off into a daydream where words couldnt hound me. This preacher's quiet voice grew louder, more strident: Dad's voice. I was a gradeschool kid again and back in my regular seat at the outside corner of the next-to-the-front pew. Dad stood just in front of the pews with his face hotted and gasping for breath between long rips of hellfire and damnation. The congregation egged him on. Amen. Hallelujah. Bring it, brother. His damning finger pitchforked through the crust of iniquity that was growing over the souls of the bigger kids just behind me, then held them like hot dogs over the flames of hell. His skewer never quite gouged me but the sludge inside still swelled and leaked into the flames just below. What crowded out I never knew but it sure made the fire snarl.

The adults' vinegar petered out when Dad turned their way. He stalked them now, paced back and forth while his voice soothed their fears, then struck with shout and finger. When he fired Myrtle Yunker's way she jumped and jarred the red head in her lap from its beauty sleep. Eight-year-old Jenny glared at me like it was my fault and ground her eyes with freckled hands.

Dad's voice went loud and soft and loud and soft until it gathered a rhythm that turned meaningless and hypnotic. With my head propped against a hard pew rather than nestled in my mother's soft lap I drifted away to dreams filled with jealousy and envy and covetousness—grownup terms I knew all too well.

Linda elbowed me in the ribs and I grunted loud enough to wake myself up. The lady beside me covered her mouth and coughed to let off steam so she wouldnt blow snot on herself trying not to laugh. This preacher still oozed soft words and I actually listened for a while even though it wasnt any of my business. Near as I could tell the heathens were getting a day off while the good folks pulled the plow. I looked at the open empty faces around me and realized he probably hadnt been prepared for sinners.

His topic was guarding the gates of the mouth. *I will keep my mouth with a bridle, while the wicked is before me.* He held the Bible up close to his face while he read and then blinked our way like he wasnt sure we hadnt went home while he was occupied with his scriptures. He leafed through the pages longer than Dad could ever have kept his mouth shut and then read again: *Set a watch, O Lord, before my mouth; keep the door of my lips.*

Tell me about it. Get caught up admiring yourself in the mirror and let fly a okie-dokie and you'll find yourself hunkered on a oak pew that bites into your back like a hickory switch. The preacher was smiling and forgiving and encouraging us as he stepped down from the platform and I was dumbfounded that the sermon was over. I looked at my watch. Dad wouldnt have even have eased off the choke yet. This biblethumper just gave a lick or two of admonition and then a big attaboy so we would know he didnt mean to offend us and then we all go home. Imagine that.

I should have known better. What I'd thought was the benediction was a hymn to segue us into a baptismal service. Like the national anthem before a ballgame.

How they were going to pull this off without a pond or a river kept me awake for a minute or two but I saw right off they werent forty-gallon dunkers but head daubers. His voice droned on like rain on the roof and I drifted off again to the past . . .

. . . the accordion groaned and wheezed and battled the faint out-of-tune singing sucked dry by the wind. Hands clapped along but stragglers and time-jumpers made the rhythm ragged.

> *Come through the water, the water of love*
> *That flows from the throne above;*
> *Leave the past 'neath the surface, emerge with a shout,*
> *Wash away every remnant of doubt.*

I closed my eyes and latched onto the whine of late-summer locusts. My only touchstone to anything normal. We werent at a river but mired in a stagnant farm pond that wasnt flowing from the throne. Wasnt flowing nowhere. Mud extruded between my toes and I sunk deeper with every word as I waited my turn in the shallow water. Deerflies buzzed my hair like baby demons and I swatted and missed again and rubbed the stinging welt on the back of my neck. A cow bellowed a warning from the old world but I was already herded through the door to the eternal.

The water had been warm as cowpiss in the shallows but as the line squished forward the chill made me want to either get in or get out. Swamp air bogged down in my throat as the water lapped against my ribs.

Hands that werent clapping were raised and waving with the cattails in the hot breeze. None of the drownded-rat candidates that had their dunking over with looked near as miserable as I felt waiting in line. Jenny Yunker was lit up like a lantern as she dried in the sun.

Dad grappled my arm when I reached the front of the line and then a deacon snared the other one and they turned me to the crowd to pass muster. The familiar wrinkles and moles and chapped lips that always grinned and soft eyes that labored behind out-of-kilter glasses were hostile and strange from this new vantage point. Like a frog would contemplate a gigger.

Andrew, do you profess Jesus Christ to be your personal Savior? Mom could have heard him at home. I nodded or thought I did. The stink of tadpoles and barnyards was liquid and warm when he clamped a handkerchief dark with muddy water across my mouth and nose. I baptize you in the name of the Father and of the Son and of the Holy Spirit. They swept me back and under and water crashed in my ears and while I was under the praying voices sounded like crows on an owl.

Before I could even open my eyes I stumbled toward the bank and wiped water away with wet fists. An old woman that smelled like coffee grounds and with a tag sticking up from the back of her black dress draped a towel over my shoulders when I joined the finished ones on the bank. I tried to pray but my mind was used up with the flies and the mud and the cold clothes and the hot hot sun and that one bull voice that spoke in tongues, the same line over and over: *lalla korabbo mobonni shay hundi osaka.*

Finally the dunking and the singing and the praying and the testimonies were over and we gathered around a haywagon layered with chicken and sliced cheese and salmoncakes and potato salad and pickles. Flies from the barn over the hill wiped their feet on the food and people cleaned their hands on my back while they patted and rubbed and rattled on about how proud I'd made them.

Jenny Yunker hugged me like she'd been baptized for years and was welcoming me into the club but while she did she whispered, You're supposed to be *saved* first.

Before we left I liberated a katydid down her back. The coffee-ground woman thought Jenny had a dose of the Holy Spirit and hollered Hallelujah over and over till the bug crawled loose and Jenny tamed down.

That was my first amen of the day.

As Dad drove the old Dodge home his white waterwrinkled hands clashed with his puffed red face like two different people were knotted together under his coat. He bumped the wornout steeringwheel back and forth to keep the car on the road. He was right there where I could touch him but off somewhere I couldnt go. From the way he hummed it must of been a right nice place.

I dropped my stinking clothes on the porch and scurried naked to the bathtub and felt the unfamiliar feathers of embarrassment as I ran through the house.

Dad was studying at his old rolltop desk when I came downstairs so I left him be. The lazy no-quit strokes of Mom's hoe rattled in the garden's rocky soil. The peas I plucked from the vines and stripped from the gnarled pods were cool and sweet inside.

Mom, have you been baptized? The hoe kept on clicking.

Probably.

What's that mean? Dont you remember?

The hoe became a prop. I remember, all right. I wasnt lucky enough to be dipped in the middle of the summer. It was wintertime, just before the river iced over, when I got mine. She made a face. I'd like to forget it but I cant. They figured it would be preferable to kill us in the icewater than to risk letting us run heathen till spring.

Then hows come you say you were probly baptized?

She returned to her hoeing. I was baptized but I dont think it took on me.

What's that mean?

She rumpled my wet hair. You're just like Fiddler on a coon. You wont let go. Our dog Fiddler nosed the air and collapsed back into the grass. His long sigh shuffled his feet into a new arrangement. It didnt change me any, she said.

Will mine take?

Your daddy did it, so I reckon it will. He wont have it any other way.

Oh. I didnt know whether to be happy or not so I turned my attention to Fiddler. He opened one eye to watch me run toward him. I jumped high like I was going to land in his belly but spread my legs just before I landed. His big tail thumped in the grass. You smell like dog, I said. He must not have cared because his tail thumped even faster.

Dont be ridiculous, Dad said. Of course your mother's baptism took.

She said it didnt change her none.

It's not *supposed* to change you. It's a sign to others that you are stepping forward, that old things have passed away and all things have become new. That you're already changed.

I didnt step nowhere. I was pushed.

He looked at his paper. Perhaps you were pulled.

It *felt* like I was pushed.

The pencil started up again and I figured we were done. I turned to leave and he said, Each one of us is pushed by something, Andy. But we're pulled, too.

When I told Mom the good news about her baptism she wheeled from the sink with broke-up jars in her eyes. Your daddy knows a heap about the Bible but not one goddamn thing about me.

I covered my mouth and ran from the kitchen praying as I went that God wouldnt strike Mom down dead, though I was the one needed to be cut down but I wasnt sure why.

. . . everybody was singing again and I was confused by this preacher's voice and the benediction was given and Linda and I were moving and everybody was shaking our hands and making over us like we were real people and inviting us to come again.

I dont think so. Not if I can keep the mouth guard awake. But it was a nice change for people to shake my hand even if that would change when they knew me better.

How did you like the service? Linda said on the way home.

Same old crap, I said. I felt chilled, like a door was standing open.

Good, she said.

CHAPTER 6

Earwigs and hard work and leprosy have a common denominator: They get into everything. Permeate it. The Bible tells how leprosy would infect even the plaster in a house so that the priest would come declare the house contagious and then they'd burn it and post a guard on the ashpile to holler Unclean, Unclean every time someone wandered close.

Hard work had infected my house like leprosy. The mirror was out of whack because it showed a taller, thinner man with no love handles but just a smidgen of a potgut that would be gone in another month. The scales were haywire by twelve pounds, too. Hard work is one insidious and pervasive animal.

Workman's customers showed signs of infection, too. One day Ellie Groves said, How long you been here now, Tu? The day was cool but his T-shirt was wet down the back. Damp half-moons on the sheets of drywall we slid four at a go into the back of his truck showed off the size of his grip.

This is the selfsame Ellie who one time asked my height and then said, Must of been one hellish dog to make a pile that high. So maybe I was a bit more oysterish than I needed to be. I shrugged and mumbled, Month, maybe, and stiffed up for the rest of it.

Thanks, he said and left and after a while it sunk in that there wasnt a punchline.

Other customers started showing the signs of a high fever by talking out-of-their-head stuff like, No problem, or, I aint in a hurry, when I'd get behind. Then Doug, one of Workman's truckdrivers, came down with it. I go past your road every day, he said. You just as well ride with me. So Linda got an extra hour of sleep in the mornings and I got home on time every evening. Doug's infection spread to the guys in the lunchroom and they started to shuffle together to make an extra seat instead of sprawling wider so I'd have to stand. Even Ken, the owner, caught a touch of it. He didnt catch a big enough dose to compliment me but he gave himself an extra pat on the back when he said, I'm never too old to be amazed.

Me either.

With my old friends, though, the milk had went blinky. A few days after I jawed with Mike in The Hole's parking lot him and Dave showed up at the trailer with their hands empty of beer cans but both half crocked.

I'm taking off my boots, Dave said. See, Sweetpea? I dont even do that at home. Dirty folds zigzagged through his socks toward holes in the heels. No beer neither, he said. You want to frisk me? He turned out his pockets and loose change and some blue fuzz scattered across the floor.

I wouldnt touch you with a cattle prod, Linda said.

By hell she does like me. A hard edge of sarcasm in everything they said to each other. Mike was nice and cracked jokes about Linda's belly that made her giggle but Dave soured even that. If that baby looks like me, he said, give me a buzz so I can hightail it out of town.

Not until everyone stared at me did I realize how loud my laughter was.

And how would you know if you got another buzz? The disdain in Linda's voice finally brought down the mask that Dave wears when he's hurt or confused.

You been fishing? I asked Mike. Feeling like it was my duty to head off a flood but keep the crick from going dry.

Not for a week or so. He told a story about Dave hooking himself in the butt and turning in a circle all the time he unhooked himself that had been funny the first half-dozen times we'd heard it. When he finished we were done for. The kitchen clock ticked like it was dealing out piles of blame.

Mike coughed and said, Well, you look as happy as two pigs in a pod. We laughed good and hard because we knew it was all coming to tassle and we wouldnt have to let on anymore. We all promised to get together while they laced their boots and then they sidled out the door with their hands buried in their pockets. Looking naked without beer cans.

See you, buddy. Dave had always called me Little Buddy and his goodbye felt cold and final. Linda still worried I'd sneak off with them but I never again got invited. The stink that repelled others attracted them like fruit flies. When I cleaned up they flew away.

———

So it was just Linda and me.

And the dog.

When I tried to open the door one morning, our long-lost mutt was curled on the mat. Her tits bloated like exclamation points on her fat belly: Free! Puppies! Coming! Soon! She was so pregnant and ugly that I loved her instantly. Aw, Funky! Where you been, girl? We missed you. She snorted and shuffled deeper into the mat. I squatted and tried to reach around the door to pet her. Come on, sweetie, let your old man out. Her bared teeth were yellowed and dull but her growl wasnt.

So much for making nice. Move, slut. I've got to git to work. I rammed the door into her and she crowded in as I crowded out. Glaring at me like I was the one who'd been out whoring around.

I drew back to give her a little welcome kick but just then Linda loped out of the bedroom and gathered the dog fleas and tits and all into her arms. Then the whimpering and slobbering started and the dog's behavior wasnt one bit better. I shook my head and went to work.

A family of three again, we did family things. Hi-ho, off to work we'd go. Talk about work over supper. Scratch fleas. Fight over the one good chair. Piss on the neighbor's flowers and crap in the middle of the street. Watch TV. Read magazine articles about how to bring up a baby not to be like me. Get a back rub. Give a back rub. Shed hair. Listen to the baby gurgle in Linda's belly. Go to bed. Get up and do it all over. Pretend it was good.

Except I didnt have to pretend. Life dont get any better.

If you've never cashed a welfare check or ducked behind your jacket's collar while the cashier makes a big fooforaw out of cashing your food stamps then you dont know how to appreciate a real paycheck in the hip pocket of your jeans. One you got with sweat and splinters. I know people talks about welfare check day like it's a special occasion. First of the Month. Like Fourth of July. Not me. I took the money, naturally (*naturally*: by nature; without special teaching or training) but I tried not even to think about it much less fixate on it. But earned money is a whole different animal. It floats in your pocket and threatens to lift your feet clear of the dirt.

I had everything I could want when Doug dropped me in The Hole's parking lot that Friday evening: a check in my pocket and bull in my stride and new cable in my muscles and a chunk of time I wouldnt have to account for.

And a raging hunger for someone to recognize all these things.

The evening lay ahead like an oats field ready for the combine. Just like I planned I fooled with my shoestrings till Doug was gone and then followed the sounds and smells into the bar. I parked my lunchbox in the corner while my eyes adjusted to the dark. The little bar was jammed with the Friday-night crowd: the terminally unemployed and the after-work regulars and a few late-season lake people. The stools were all filled so I grabbed Dave and Mike by the underarms and nosed in between them. Dave's expression brightened for a second and then went flat. He turned back to his beer.

Well looky here, Mike said. You dig out under the fence?

Nah, I said. Linda started working late Fridays. Folks likes to rent their tools on Fridays so they can get a early shot at it on Saturday morning but ole Heller cant cut all them hours anymore so she's picking up the extry.

Mike's whistle got everybody's attention but Ace's. I'd expected to feel good as I met eyes up and down the bar but that other emotion blindsided me: I felt sorry for them.

Ace's big face loomed in the gap. Where you been, man? Not like I missed you but where you been hiding, dirtball? He took my outstretched hand before he could process it and I liked the way my palm stood firm and hard inside his grip till he ejected it back onto the bar. He wiped his hands on a bar rag. What you drinkin? (You got any money fore I go to the effort of gettin a beer?)

Nothing. I just stepped in to put this on my tab.

Ace held the crisp new fifty up to the light and made me want to take it back and give him a dollar instead.

Get ole Tuesday a drink on me. One wont hurt him none. Mike's cracked nails nudged forward his little pile of bills and loose change.

No no. I dont want nothing.

Dave's fingers dug deep into my arm. You aint goin fore you have a drink with your buddies. You got to drink one. And tell a story. Tell us about Tuesday Price going to work every day. I cant hardly picture that.

Give me a Diet Coke then.

Ace had already pulled a Keystone Light and he slammed it hard back in the cooler and went to the other end and extracted a Pepsi. That's as close as I can come. He ignored Mike's money like he wasnt going to stoop to dealing pop.

Then my ears were ringing like they do in those moments when you ask yourself am I really here? Is this really happening? And you aint so sure.

Dave had turned back to his beer so I guess he didnt want to hear a story after all. Just tell one of his own. Ace and Mike leaned close together over the bar and not enough scraps of their conversation leaked out for me to make sense of it. The Pepsi was old and flat and metallic as a frozen sled runner.

A couple of tourists on the other side of the horseshoe bar caught my eye and waved. Straight white teeth. Baseball caps that laid down against the head with no billboard for advertising. People I'd forgotten that obviously remembered me. I nodded. How you doing.

Come on over. They shuffled their stools apart to make room for me and started a resentful chain reaction when they bumped their neighbors.

I glanced up and down at the sweaty backs of the locals on my side of the bar and allowed myself to be reeled around and into the open space they'd made. Winston, right? I said. Thirties maybe, trim and compact with a firm grip. Good clothes. Rich folks out slumming. Looked like a Winston to me.

No, it's Jake. And this is Art.

I mix you up with Winston every daggone time. (Must be nouveau mo-nee to have two-dollar names like that.)

You do remember us, dont you?

Not a clue. Heck yeah, I said. That was a hellish drunk front rolled through here that night we was talking but I aint forgot it. If I stored up the names of everybody I'd ever bullshitted there wouldnt be room for the bull.

Tell Art about your father's goat and the Jehovah's Witnesses. You have to hear this, Art.

Sounded like a great story to me but it's hair near impossible to make up the same lie twice. Ah, I'm not in the mood for stories tonight, I said. I showed them my Pepsi for explanation.

Who's the turkey you were talking to? Art nodded across the bar and the floor trembled as his leg bounced on the tip of his toe. The one with the smart mouth.

That there's Dave Sinko. I leaned against the bar rail with my back toward the other side of the horseshoe and lowered my voice so Jake and Art pulled close. Let me give you a free tip before you get into a fracas with him. If you start you best be prepared to kill him. Cause that's what he'll do to you if you dont. He's tough and he's dirty and he dont never quit. He cant even hear the fat lady sing.

They looked at Dave and back at me like maybe I had the wrong guy.

I shrugged. You do what you want. It dont matter to me. If they wanted to go to the hospital or to the great white beer garden in the sky it was okay by me.

Art's leg quit bouncing. Aw no. I just wondered who he was. Is that his father?

I laughed because I knew they were talking about Mike. You keep that up you'll have to whip Mike too. They're just friends. Not even related.

I thought everyone up here was related. Jake grinned and bumped me with his shoulder the way people do when they want to make an ass of you but want it to sound like a joke. One big happy family.

I drank from my Pepsi so I wouldnt have to fool with my expression and while I did a story or the beginnings of one got to cooking. Either of *you* guys from a big family?

Seven, Jake said. Five plus my parents. Art shook his head, still looking over my shoulder like he was watching an accident with lots of blood and body parts still coming loose.

I laid it out slow so it wouldnt get ahead of my imagination. They was thirteen of us. Fifteen with Mom and Dad cept she got gored by a Holstein bull when I wasnt but four.

You mean like fatally? Art said. If you put on a good haunted inbred face and got enough pone in the accent tourists would park their big-city cynicism at the door like I had my lunchbox. Carry in their gullibility the way you pack popcorn into a movie theater.

I see you aint been around a Holstein bull or you wouldnt ask that.

Are they the black ones?

No, them's Anguses. Pacifists next to Holsteins. There wasnt hardly enough left of Mom to have a funeral but we done up a short one anyhow. Just one banjo and a couple of fiddles and no figure callin or nothing. (I could smell the dirt and the cut roots stobbing into the hole.)

And then the only one of my brothers that was a girl, Lucinda, she got run over by the church bus trying to save her doll baby. Deliberately ambiguous syntax but they werent attuned to the subtleties of good storytellin.

Jake looked at Art and Art shrugged like there wasnt any call to *disbelieve* it. Damn, he said.

That was just one of them things. It dont even concern what happened. The Pepsi tasted better now and the past was coming clear and heavy. That left thirteen of us, every one a man in one house. Jake, you come from a fair-to-middlin family so you know you probly didnt get as much attention as maybe Art here.

Jake shrugged. Yeah, sometimes I felt that way.

Well right here's the way it was in mine. An edge of indignation dressed off with resolve in my voice. Even without no one to check my homework or go to the P and TA meetings I made it through school. Even high school. Got me a diploma to prove it too even though it's got a grocery list on the back side. The teachers never even noticed me that I could tell. And then the day after graduation I enlisted in the Army but that was worse than home cause then I had a hunderd and fifty brothers and if someone paid attention to you it werent nothing you was looking forward to.

Art was looking over my shoulder again so I skipped past two or three wars.

Anyhow, I was gone four years. All through that fourteen-hour bus ride home I thought on the parade they'd throw when I lit down there. Not ticker tape and convertibles but Allis Chalmers tractors and mixed-breed pickup trucks with shotguns in the gunracks and foxtails on the antennas. The same kind of shindig they throwed for crazy Johnnie Snider when he come home from Korea. That's what I had laid out in my head. I paused to drink from my empty can.

Who's Johnnie Snider? Art was determined to sidetrack my story.

He's the town idiot but he's the only war hero we got. Too dumb to know that anybody was shooting at him. Thought them bullets was junebugs. But anyhow, after that long ride the bus dumped me on the long end of town. There wasnt a solitary soul around and the pay phone at the bus stop ate up all my money and never even give a dial tone. There wasnt a thing to do but light out walking. I allowed a little space for them to grin at each other and then finished my story.

So I had to hoof it all the way in dress slippers and I got a blister between my big toe and the little one on my off foot and the suitcase handle stretched out in the heat till I couldnt hardly keep it off the ground anymore. I come in the back door into the kitchen and it hadnt changed one little bit. The dirty dishes in the sink looked like the same ones that was in there when I left. Same ratty tablecloth. Same faded picture on the wall. Still a big X of duct tape where the ruffled grouse flew through the windowscreen and the selfsame identical hoe marks on the ceiling where Waldo tried to kill it and a piece of paneling in the screen door to cover where it went out. The whole place was just like I left it. Someone cleared their throat behind me and I turned around and there was Dad. He hadnt changed much either. He'd grayed up on the corners and dried out a little more but not much. We stood there for a long time checking each other out and his eyes went over my haircut and my shoes and settled down on the suitcase.

And after a spell he said, Where in hell you think you're going?

After they laughed out I promised to tell the billygoat story next time we shook hands and I went around and slapped Mike and Dave on the back. Ace snatched away the empty Pepsi can like he was ashamed for it to be on his bar. I'll bring you more money next week, I said.

He snorted.

I felt like a bull with the keys to the cow barn as I started up the hill toward home. At the edge of the parking lot I remembered my lunchbox and went back after it. The gap where I'd stood had healed like I'd never been there. Nobody looked my way.

I was a bouquet of feelings as I walked home through clabbering darkness: shaky unease from a close brush with alcohol and the sting of rejection and the amphetamine of acceptance and the heady shame of a good lie. But I'd tiptoed along the pit without falling in. Pulled it off without alcohol.

A shadow darted between my feet from the roadside grass and I dropped my lunchbox and jumped out onto the pavement and drew back my foot to kick it and saw it was just a toad. It was so ugly and bloated and hideous that I felt sorry for it. The toad shifted in the gravel to face me head-on for a moment and then jumped toward the road again. I know you like it out there where it's warm and comfortable but that aint a good place for you to be, I said. I plucked a big burdock leaf to keep it from pissing on my hand while I folded it inside and tossed it back into the weeds.

My softness shamed me and I glanced up and down the road and picked up my lunchbox and started home again. I stopped and yelled out into the darkness: I aint ashamed. Something I cant imagine ever saying before. The old cockroach was metamorphosing into a man. Some other Tuesday. Super Tuesday.

I must of been too deep in my head doctoring to hear the car slow as it came up from behind. The food trash missed but ice and soft drink sprayed over me like the devil's piss as the drink cartwheeled by. Teenage laughter and Saab taillights fell away over the hill's crest toward the lake. My cussing made the dark feel heavier.

By the time I'd reached the trailer park a black longing for my bull-gored mama and bus-mashed sister was as real and cold as my wet shirt. You never had a sister, I said as I shuffled into the driveway, or a bull. Just bullshit.

I didnt see my fat neighbor till he laughed. Talking to yourself again, poophead?

What you doing? Waiting a turn with your woman?

Listen, dirtball. But he couldnt think of anything to follow it up.

I started to go inside and turned and said, I'm sorry. That was uncalled for. I just had a bad hair day.

I surprised myself but must of shocked him speechless.

The dog didnt race out the door for the flowerbeds like she usually did so I figured she'd took off again. Good riddance. Cold tuna and bread was all I had energy for but there were only a few dishes so I washed them along with my thermos. That was fortunate because when I opened my lunchbox I found that while I was telling lies I couldnt get shed of, someone had donated a pack of red knobby-tread rubbers for Linda to find.

Then I found out why Funky hadnt greeted me. She was under the coffee table curled around a squirming mess of white and red and black and brown puppies. Not all the colors on any one dog. In front of my chair was a dark stain that I knew I'd Rorshach till Jesus came. Like I do. Every time I came near she growled. Easy, girl, I said. I dont want your puppies. I dont even want you, you stinking bitch.

She snarled again.

Guess what! I said when Linda opened the door. Funky had her pups.

The trace of barsmoke that clung to my clothes put a charge slam up her bunghole. Her hand froze for a second and then the door flew shut so hard that the plywood hopped out of the glass frame. You've been to the *bar*, you *jerk*! Did you think I was *kidding*?

I was as quick as a fairydiddle but barely caught her before the bedroom door slammed shut. Linda, listen . . . I didnt . . .

Freckles of her spit splashed my face and she thrashed her head back and forth and tried to tear away. Leave me *alone*. Get away from me! I'm leaving.

Listen to me. Elbows and heels hammered the paneling as she fought to get loose from my grip. Her fighting finally petered off but her breath shot me in hard angry whistles. I stopped there to make a payment on my bill, I said. Smell my breath.

Yuck. You smell like fish.

Would you rather I smelled like beer? I tried to keep my voice from rising but I'd had just about enough. I drank a stinking Pepsi and paid fifty dollars on my bill. Call Ace if you dont believe me.

Her eyes changed, but not enough. I dont want to talk to him or anybody else in that filthy place. Angry eyes again. Why didnt you let me make the payment so you wouldnt have to go in?

You just said you didnt want anything to do with that place!

Why didnt you mail it, then?

Talking was useless until I could get a bridle on my voice. Look, I said when I could. I drank a Pepsi and talked for a few minutes and paid some money on my bill and I came home. Mad was sneaking in again. Next Friday when I get paid I'm gonna stop again. Drink a Pepsi and talk for a while and come home. Unless I figure you're going to throw another hissy. Cause then I aint coming home a-tall.

I dont want you there.

Well you dont get everything you want, do you?

Everything? *Everything?* She pushed past me and went to Funky's squirming brood. You poor baby. The mutt whimpered and wagged her tail and Linda kissed her on the lips. Some things would utterly gag a man's ass.

Even back before everything went to pieces she used to dream that I'd done something atrocious and the next day she would treat me like it had really happened. I always knew it was coming, but it always took me by surprise.

That night I had the dream again. The first time in a while. Old Blue's skeleton come rattling out from the heavy grass alongside the road and we tore along faster and faster, running away from one thing but toward something else and both of us looking scared in both directions. One side of his head was busted in and he snapped at me every time that caved-in skull swung my way.

But this time when I reached for the old woman she was there. We hadnt been on speaking terms when we went to bed but she rubbed my back and whispered something over and over. What the words were I couldnt remember in the morning but they sure worked that night.

Next morning when I walked down the hill to catch a ride the toad was a map of Georgia in the center of a stain splashed oblong by passing tires. I added my spit to the fluids already drying in the morning sun. Toads is so damn stupid. Do what they want even if it gets them killed. A pair of crows in a blighted chestnut hurried me on so they could get their turn in before it dried clear up.

CHAPTER 7

That afternoon I figured out why Linda'd blown up all out of scale to what I'd done. I doubt she'd admit the hookup but it sure cleared it up in my mind.

The place where she worked was grinding down to nothing and she was afraid she was going to lose her job. I guess that could work on you, but still. She worked at this tool-rental place where the only things older than the owner were the tools and the books. Ole Heller had a bookkeeping system so old the first half was in Roman numerals. On animal hides. But he'd vote straight Democrat before he'd change one thing. He drank Maalox by the quart but the fear of labor unions and computers used it up quicker than he could swallow.

Any of those things, a computer or a Democrat vote or a union, was about as likely as a copperhead learning to tapdance. Heller's only had two employees. Ermie could lift a ten-horsepower log-splitter over his head but he couldnt even spell *union* and thought one was a pipefitting anyway. And Linda would have loved a computer but she knew the business was down the toilet and needed more work not less. So she kept the abacus greased up and the safe full of Maalox and kept her mouth shut.

Then Heller got to thinking maybe they werent open enough hours so he decided to stay open Friday evenings but since his second hernia from carrying crates of antacid he didnt have the starch to stick it out on regular days. Linda jumped at the chance for a few extra dollars.

But it wasnt going to last. I wrote three rentals last night, she said. A drain snake and a pruning shear and a hammer drill. That didnt pay the light bill.

There, thought I, lies the *real* source of her angst. Not my stopping at the bar. So I immediately felt cocky again. Big deal, I said. What if Heller's does go broke? It'll give you time off to have pups and then you can find a real job. I reckon I can take care of one woman. At *least* one.

Funky butted in and nosed my leg and sat and stared at me. What do you want, mutt? Ka-bump went her tail against the floor.

She wants you to look at her puppies, Linda said.

Yeah right. And then she'll bite my gizzard out.

She wont. Look at her. Aw.

Surprise, surprise. Her tail thumped away while I examined the pups. Four splittails and two bulls. Ugly to the bone. In the marrow. How's come you're so friendly all of a sudden? I said.

She cold-nosed me in the face. A female. Thus under no obligation to make sense.

With energy leaking out my earholes, I patched and painted on the trailer and changed oil and rotated tires on the Subaru and raked what few leaves that had blown in from some exotic place that had trees. My brain must of been befuddled on adrenaline or testosterone, because sometime during supper I realized that I had just contracted for church again the next morning. I despised the words before they were out of my mouth, but I never let on. I went for a run instead.

The day sat down cool and clean, but till I'd finished stretching a fine sweat had popped out. Within a mile it ran like a spring flood. The pounding of the road and the whistle of my breath faded into an easy monotonous rhythm that turned my mind out to roam.

We'd been thirteen when Matt Tamper taught me how to run. There aint nothing to know, I'd said. You move your legs faster than when you walk.

The way you naturally want to do something is almost always the wrong way, he said. You cant just rip off running. Not with tight muscles and thick synovial fluid. While I tried to stretch everything he did, he explained about the joints and muscle fibers he'd studied in the books he'd checked out of the library. If you're going to be a high-performance machine, you have to fine-tune every part.

I was kind of set on bein a stallion stead of a machine, I said. Less it was to be one of them tables with the stirrups naked women put their feet in. I could be one of those.

I'm not. He pushed against the front-yard apple tree and mashed his ankle into an angle I'd never seen one make. Not one you wanted to use again. Running's going to pay my way to college.

You got to make a pick. Yesterday you was a brain and now you've swung over to jock.

Only an idiot would suggest that you cant be both.

I smarted under that and kept my mouth shut.

Go against the grain, he said as we jogged out the driveway. Your body wants to go fast at first. Hold it back till your capillaries get distended and your muscles warm. Later, when it wants to loaf, stick a prod up its butt. You're the boss. Make your body listen.

We ran down the road against the grain like we had some clue as to where we were headed.

How'd you get so many girlfriends, Matt? We were still in an easy lope, but I was already struggling to get the words out.

They're not girlfriends. Just regular friends. If he was using any air it didnt show in his voice.

If you was going to pick out a special one, which one would it be?

It wouldnt be any one of these hillbilly goat ropers. I can tell you that much.

Good. I was afraid he'd latch on to Jackie Collins. I'd asked her to be my girlfriend and she'd stuck her finger down her throat but I knew she liked me. *I'd* take one of them, I said. Two, if I could get them.

He snorted. I'm going to college and run a four-minute mile before I get tangled up with girls. And then it will be one with big hooters that knows English and doesnt smell like silage.

For the next mile I struggled to keep up but finally stopped and leaned over with my hands on my knees. Matt jogged in place and studied his watch. Look, he said. We're a mile and a half from the house. I'll go out to where the big culvert goes under the road—that's another half mile—before I start back. You'll have a mile and a half, and I'll have two and a half miles. Let's race.

I ran the numbers through my head and knew there was no way he could beat me if I kept moving at all. But I still bolted off running before I yelled back over my shoulder. You're on.

When I glanced back he was almost out of sight, moving like spilled hot oil. My diaphragm was tearing loose around the edges and my thighs were afire but I remembered what he'd said: Make your body listen. It paid attention for a while but then my rhythm started to fall apart and the air turned to clods in my throat and when I looked he was far back but coming hard, sunlight flashing off arms and legs that looked like working pistons.

Somehow then my mind found a cold corner away from the fire and took charge and lashed my limbs into cadence and dragged air into my lungs and even when my body died in the last hundred yards, my mind punished the corpse till the only option was to fall forward, away from the whip.

The pounding of his feet carried me the last few feet and we crashed together through the lawn gap and glanced off each other and plowed into the grass on separate sides of the walk. I lay facedown and drew great draughts of air that held no oxygen and each pore in my body itched with sweat that couldnt get out fast enough.

I won, I said when I could.

Like hell you did. He was already sitting up and wiping his face on his T-shirt.

Dont talk like that. My mom'll hear you.

Whoop de doo.

I reckon I never did beat him at anything. But he was my friend—my only friend—and I loved him to death.

More than twenty years later, it was good to run again. Satisfying to feel my stride and breathing and heartbeat fall into sync as my second wind came up. For once it felt like I wasnt spoiling the air but just using it. The falling darkness wasnt to hide in but merely the end of a long, hard—and wholesome—day.

And church the next morning wasnt as bad as it could have been. Nobody went to hell or nothing. At least not right during the service.

Life fell into time just like my running had: a *good* routine of working and running and talking. Finally I could foretell what I'd be doing at 10:22 A.M. the following Wednesday and not get the thimbleshits from it. And at 5:30 on Friday I'd stop at The Hole to drink a Pepsi and shoot the breeze and make a payment on my tab. The Friday after that I'd do the same.

For one more week I'd drink a Pepsi, at least.

It wasnt alcohol I was craving that third Friday evening, but the *taste* of a beer. Lemme try one of them non-alcoholic brewskis, I told Ace when I handed him the weekly payment.

Two of them and you'll be right back in the bottle and your tab will be up where it was.

And you'll act like I'm the stupid one. You let me worry about it. But there was nothing to worry about. The taste was flat and bitter and after one swallow I was anxious to leave. The customers werent having as much fun as they thought. Their faces were haggard and their laughter had ragged desperate edges. Like it was laugh or cry. No other option. Smoke stung my nose and eyes and hung on me like graveclothes after I left the bar. I hated it.

Till Linda got home just after 7:00 I'd carved slices of deli rye too thick for the toaster so I browned them in the oven. I stacked on sauerkraut and jack cheese and corned beef and nuked the sandwiches till they globbed up and then doused them with Ranch dressing and opened a jar of pickles and made a jug of frozen orange juice. Eating dont get any better than that except in the spring when the ramps are first out of the ground.

I kissed her at the door so she'd smell the beer and hugged her tight so she couldnt bust anything when she threw her fit. It's just near beer, I said. Non-alcoholic. Call Ace if you dont believe me.

Whatever. Can I go now?

Aint you going to have a cow?

Come on. Let me go. It's been a long day.

I turned her loose the same way you'd leave a panther go from a legtrap but she didnt do a thing but be surprised I'd fixed supper. She slid down and rested her head on the chair and closed her eyes and went m-m-m-m even though she dont care that much for Reubens even when you have the right dressing.

Doing something nice for her felt even better than the other way around and I figured right there to attempt it again sometime.

I want you to do something for me. Like she could read my mind.

Okie doke. Oh, mouth guard. You slovenly delinquent sonofabitch.

You have to promise.

I *said* okay.

Say it.

It.

She sat up straight and I could see the evening sliding toward the guard-rails and I thought oh hell with it. I promise.

Good. She got up and ran dishwater in the sink and said, Tomorrow morning we're going to get your driver's license.

My heart soared over the fence but caught on the barbwire. No way. Doug takes me to work every day. I dont need a license. We aint got but the one car anyway.

Her hand was warm with dishwater that felt like blood. What about when I go to the hospital? We going to call Doug then?

There's a wealth of people would take you for that.

She squeezed my arm and dismissed it and gathered the rest of the dishes from the table. You're the one that's taking me. That's part of our arrangement. For me to stay.

My fist crashing into the table startled me but she didnt even blink. The orange juice went over but she moved just enough to let it wash over the side without splattering her. I wanted to drive my fist into the smug line of her mouth but I kicked my chair over instead and felt my toenail peel away like an orange rind. There aint no arrangement. You're making the rules up as we go. My voice shook as I sat the chair back in place.

She smiled like I'd said I liked her hair. There's plenty of arrangement. I just havent told you all of it yet.

A red spot was growing on my sock and I fled to the bedroom before she saw that and made sport of it. I changed into my running clothes and ran off into the near-dark chill without stretching. My toe throbbed but I ran right over the pain. Nursed it, in fact, in hopes that it would get bad enough to dim that years-old picture of Matt's broken body.

When I couldnt run any farther I stood head down, trembling and winded, and gathered my bearings. The smell of a charcoal grill was rank as a crematorium and close by a dog barked low and hoarse. I was out by the lake houses, out toward Lilo's, the last place in the world I wanted to be. As I stumbled back toward home I heard the unmistakable rattle of the old Subaru and headlights pinned me like an insect in a collection. Linda turned around in the next driveway and then idled alongside until I reached for the door handle.

Neither of us spoke. Linda hummed like nothing had happened.

The Motor Vehicle Administration didnt open until nine o'clock. By then I'd coffeed my way to a caffeine high that made my nerve endings feel like they were waving on stalks and I fidgeted like an addict. Linda went along in to make sure I didnt take a powder out the back door.

The application questions all started *Have you ever?* but they werent the right questions. Not the ones that would keep a killer like me off the highway.

The written test was simple enough for a groundhog to pass, and I knew that Linda would bring me again next week if I marked the wrong answers apurpose. The seatbelt chattered in my hands when I started the driving test but the little car chugged to a smooth stop between the parking poles. The pedals cycled under my feet like they'd never left. A shell-shocked face stared back from the laminated license. Linda laughed at the picture but it was me to a tee.

It's been *so* long since I had a chauffeur, Linda said as we started home.

I felt my way onto the highway expecting a TV-attracting pileup every second.

Was that so terrible?

I grinned, but the tires' vibrations went straight to my intestines. I'd never driven anything but the old loose-jointed Dodge so I zigzagged for a mile or so and braked way too hard at the first intersection.

You stop good, Linda said while she fumbled for the papers that had slid onto the floor. I'd forgotten that things were backwards in the rearview mirror; the driver of the bread truck on my tail was sitting on the wrong side of the cab. My whited knuckles showed the load of dread I tried to conceal.

When I finally switched off the ignition in the driveway I felt like it had been a close call for me but everyone else had died in the wreck. But I told Linda it was like riding a bicycle.

My dreams that night were such a mess—broken bodies that I couldnt identify and cars that wouldnt steer or stop and a preacher that flickered with soft pink flames while he served communion from a shoe and bloated ticks that popped out on my hide faster than I could peel them off—that when Old Blue clattered up alongside it was like meeting an old friend. He whined and rattled something against my leg. What you got there, Blue? I said. When I tried to prize the baby rattle from his teeth he bit me.

It's okay, Andy, he growled around the teeth that ground into my arm.

I screamed and tried to tear away.

It's okay. It's okay, Andy. When Linda was sure that I was awake her hand moved from its grip on my arm to stroke my chest. After my pulse slowed down to about two hundred she took my hand and placed it on her belly. Feel, she whispered.

The baby was kicking and twisting inside. Oh dear God, I thought, still mired down in the dream. Run, baby, run.

Linda stroked my chest and rested her head on my shoulder. Rain stitched the roof and mended the rent in my night.

CHAPTER 8

Time lit off at a dead run toward winter and I ran along with it. At first I ran just far enough to pop off work steam but as I toughened up I ran farther just because I could. While I remodeled my body I hit a lick or two on the trailer: patched holes and nailed loose trim and daubed some paint here and there. Little bits of nothing that made a noticeable difference.

Christmas snuck up on me like always, and there was an extra surprise in my pay envelope. Santa Claus gave the other new-hire a layoff slip but I got a 25¢ raise. My first raise ever. That's how they do employee evaluations at Workman's. You get the boot or you get the raise.

I was on cloud thirteen when I stopped at The Hole that Friday evening. Ace marked my payment in his little notebook and measured me over his dime-store reading glasses. When I'd kept up on the payments and stuck to the near beer, his attitude had lightened to where he could tolerate me, but all that did was make the place harder to leave.

Next payday I'll be clean out from under your old black thumb, I said. I dont know why. It just came out that way.

Ace's eyes jerked open like he'd come astraddle of an electric fence. You see any black thumbs in this here bar?

I scanned the crowd and by gum there were a few darker folks but their tint came from passing out in the sun and from rotten livers and constant basting in cigarette smoke. Inside we were all angry white males except for the one redfaced female that was beating on the jukebox because it did what buttons she pushed instead of what she said. Nope, I said. Looks like unanimous white trash to me.

Dave was sober enough to wink and rattle his empty can against the bar. This here'd be a dandy place to start a bar if you could find a bartender. If I cant get a drink pretty damn quick I'm goin to Alejandro's. Alejandro was from Ecuador or one of those places where the kids all got pipecleaner legs and hogbladder bellies. He served real food cheap and his coolers werent always out of whack and the place was clean and bright and he was Ace's competition and siphoned off the customers that had money or sense or upbringing.

But Ace hated him not for that but because his skin wasnt white and his neck wasnt red and he made a good living from smoking and drinking and gambling but he wasnt caught in those traps himself. Like Ace was.

Ace ripped off onto the pissing-away-everything-my-great-great-grand-daddy-fought-and-died-for mad-dog-frothing-at-the-mouth fit he threw every time people of color were the topic du jour.

Mike egged him on. If that old man was any relation of your'n he didnt die of no war wound. Less he got shot in the ass.

Ace was so mad he sputtered. He by god died at Gettysburg marchin up the hill right into the mouth of the cannons.

They likely tole him there was free likker up there could he but get to it, Dave said.

Or a bus to take him home. Mike drew on his smoke and grinned like a possum eatin peanut butter.

Ace whipped his wet rag down across the bar and said, Now that there's just plain ignorant cause they didnt have no buses way back then and if you had a gut in your head you'd know that much.

Sometime in the midst of his tirade Ace set me up a Keystone Light and right there in the middle of all the fun and ragging didnt seem just the absolute proper time to clear my throat and say, Scuze me mister bartender, but could I have a sarsaparilla instead? Especially since I started the whole thing. So I drank it and another one just like it and it was a nonevent. The alcohol didnt make me feel drunk or crazy or dumb. If anything I felt purged and manlike and anxious to show Linda my check stub.

I thought I had a straight face when I went in the trailer but Linda said, What?

What you talking about woman?

You tell me what you're so tickled about. She pinched my cheek. Right now, Andrew Price.

I handed her my pay envelope and she took out the check stub and shook it and looked back into the envelope and blew in it and then she studied the stub and after a while she closed one eye and looked at the ceiling with the other the way you do when you're ciphering in your head and finally she grinned but not as big as I thought she should have and said, Well, it's about time they realize what a man they got.

Just about then it sunk in how insignificant a quarter is and I could feel that my grin wasnt any bigger than hers. And that maybe she thought that now I was getting paid about what I was worth.

What do you want to do to celebrate? she said.

I told her what I wanted and her belly pushed hard against me when she hugged me. It wont be long till we can do that again, she said. So we went to dinner and a movie instead. As we left the theater Linda's hand rode on the crook of my arm. She was an inch taller and I imagined I was carrying her with her feet never touching the ground.

The other Christmas heart-stopper was a trip to Linda's home. My mouth guard was laying drunk somewheres when Linda proposed the trip to the northern part of the state and right off I had put out extra food and water for Funky and the pups and was driving north. My dander was still up about being manipulated again but heading for the hills still threw my ticker up in a higher gear.

The falling snow showed the difference between this and the black holidays I was used to. For years now Christmas had been strange liquor labels and fuzzy sick unfocused weeks that didnt seem to have lines between days and nights.

Around Shoehorn Lake the mountains got for real but the little Subaru pepped up to the challenge. Directly we nosed into a spot between a mini-van and a pickup amid a gob of vehicles that meant Linda's whole family was home. Freda hugged us before we could even stomp the snow from our feet.

I felt like a bug in a frog farm for a spell but after a while the smells of cooking clouded the windows and the noise chased the leftover filth for my mind. I'd forgotten what Christmas was.

I forgot the blessing too and my face burned around my mouthful of turkey while Freda prayed: Thank you, most gracious heavenly Father, for this food, for we have tasted it and it is good—Linda giggled—and for bringing this family together once again . . . I never knew her to joke, and that more than anything set me at ease. Even Sammy and Slick, right there within smacking distance, just acted like I wasnt there. And that's as hospitable as they get. Slick had a scab on his knuckles and his nose tilted a little extra to the left and Sammy was still unmarked but you cant fool me. I didnt know the kids. Nieces and nephews in faces and clothes that matched the wrapping paper under the tree. They made me feel old and dirty when they got too close.

As soon as dinner was cleared off, the tabletop was re-covered with games. I'd played pool and cards and craps a couple times when I could afford to fry brain cells and recreate both. But games like Payday and Clue might just as well have the rules written in Ethiopian for all I knew. I played for a spell but there wasnt any money bet and I couldnt see the point. Slick's woman Gina taught me to play solitaire on Homer's computer and to nose around on the Internet and that was fun enough to make me feel guilty.

All of it in one lump had my senses down on the overloads and sometime during the afternoon I slipped outside. The snow crackled under my feet. I hadnt leaned against the garage for long till Linda squeaked my way and gave me a cinnamon kiss. How you holding up?

All right for the shape I'm in. I pinched the gooseflesh on her arms. Looky there. You swallered so much turkey you turned into one. You ought not be out here without your coat.

I figured I'd better check on you.

You mind if I go for a ride?

She pulled back and pried at me with her eyes. You going home?

I shrugged and nodded. More reliable than talking.

Without giving me a chance to change my mind she hugged me and said, Be careful. Dont drive like a flatlander.

Get back in there fore you freeze my baby. Her tongue shot out like my little smack on the butt had dislodged it and she ran fat and flatfooted up the walk toward the racket inside.

CHAPTER 9

Home wasnt even an hour away. The snow stopped as I chugged toward where Union County snuggled up under western Maryland's armpit. Sun glittered from bareblown patches on farm ponds and feathers of vapor sprouted from livestock. As I got closer to the lake the vehicles stirring were Volvos and Toyotas with ski racks and every one running too fast or too slow. The locals had turned the world over to the tourists.

I swung into the parking lot of my old community college. The squat yellow-brick buildings stood like crawdad holes in the oatfields that surrounded them. Two new buildings were as ugly as the first but there was no sign of the stores and houses that sprout around most schools. Two students threw snowballs outside the squat little dorm. Stuck here for Christmas. Santa must of really kept a list on them. Their hair was shorter and they had poked holes in more places than their ears, but otherwise they could have been here when I left. I circled the school once and then parked and turned off the engine. The windshield fogged right off but I was looking into another time.

Our first day of classes hadnt felt like college but like a high school with ashtrays. I'd felt sorry for all of us but mostly for the girl in front of me. Other girls had worn dresses but not like hers. Hers was the kind on the rack just inside the Kmart door. Worn over a white short-sleeved top. Blue $9.99 canvas sneakers and no socks. I was self-conscious in my baggy jeans but I could put up with them better than Dad's sermons about tight ones.

I sat behind and to the left where I couldnt look at the professor without seeing her. She'd spent two minutes on her hair but not that particular day. Brown hair in a rubberband ponytail. Kind of. If she'd put makeup on the cat licked it off while she milked the goat.

The psych professor was bummed out about wasting his intelligence on such an inbred mob of delinquents in this educational backwater. He was even more pissed at the lawnmower that roared past the window every four minutes and fifty-seven seconds. Maybe he'd got a gig in human motivation, or at least his own, and now he didnt know how to turn it loose.

The morning was frosty but the afternoon was a blueskied oven. He slammed the windows to stifle the lawnmower but then the classroom smelled like fresh pork rinds. Other professors passed out the syllabus and sang the this-is-not-your-high-school song and dismissed. Hanratty was in a shooting feud with the lawnmower and with us and he started right in lecturing. We picked at our underwear and doodled pictures of morons and watched the clock.

Except for that girl. She looked as eager and alert as a hoot owl in a mouse migration. She asked questions and kept him fired up and made the rest of us look stupid. I didnt hate her yet but I had a running start at it.

After school I sat on a picnic table beside the parking lot with my feet on the bench. I wasnt in the mood for a smoke but when Jenny Yunker came out I lit one anyway. The revolted look she shot my way made lung cancer a reasonable tradeoff. Halfway down the walk she doubled back with her boobless chest heaving and her eyes wet and her freckles hot coals in her pale skin. Why do you hate me so? What have I ever done to you?

I pictured the way Deacon Daddy Yunker's hog jowls would tremble when she squealed to him. He'd pass my sin on to Dad but I'd skin that one when I caught it. *Cry "Havoc," and let slip the dogs of war*, I said, Shakespeare achurn in my head. Her trembling lips hunted for a Bible verse but there was nothing there would trump the Bard. Just soft answers and turned cheeks. She wiped hers and turned it and almost ran to her daddy's car.

I was still sneering in that direction when a pile of books spilled onto the table. Hi, said that girl. Do you mind if I sit with you? Scootch over. Five empty tables and I have to scootch over. You waiting for a ride?

I got a ride. I'm waiting for Matt Tamper. He's on the track team.

I've heard of him. She looked like she was trying to affix a dollar value to me.

He's my best friend.

I'm Linda Lawton. She held her hand where I had to shake it. You're Andrew Price. I heard your name in class. What are you reading?

Everything. I tapped the big Norton Anthology that already looked worn. Shakespeare. Tennyson. Keats. Even saying the names made me feel powerful.

Yuck.

I didnt care for that but I was partial to the way her nose wrinkled.

Is that what you're thinking about, sitting here alone staring at the hill?

I was writing a story. In my head.

What about?

It's a horror story about a guy that has nightmares so bad that after a spell he cant tell the real world from his dreams. He's afraid that if he wakes up he'll go from the real world into the nightmare one.

You do that all the time?

It's fiction.

I mean write.

Yeah. A good bit.

Could I read some of your stories?

I write some down in this journal that I keep. But I keep the most of them right here. I tapped my chest.

You ought to write them out. They sound good. Her hair had got loose from her rubberband and against the sun the brown strands turned white and fine as spiderweb. Her legs were tan and she sat spraddlelegged not like a woodhick but in a comfortable-on-a-hot-day way.

I dont want people to know everything that goes on in my head.

Why not? There wasnt anything she wouldnt ask or I could keep from answering.

I drew hard on my smoke and looked world-tough and mysterious. Knowing me probly aint the most wholesome thing to do.

Behind her eyes the lever chunked on an old mechanical adding machine. I doubt that.

I flipped my cigarette toward the parking lot.

Matt had slipped up behind us. He's a fake. He tries to be tough but he's a marshmallow.

I'm going home, I said. Saddle up if you're riding with me. I turned to Linda. You need a ride somewheres?

In that?

The old '48 Dodge sat all alone. The pig farmers had already roared off in multi-colored pickups the sewer rats in four-door Oldsmobiles and Pontiacs and Fords. A few in the sharp new compacts their big-shot parents had given them for a high-school graduation present.

Dad's old Dodge had gotten so decrepit that he was embarrassed to drive it. But I wasnt. It was so old it was classy. Hubcaps bigger than the wheels of the rich kids' little crackerboxes. Their cars would fit in my backseat. People couldnt pass without gawking at the half-acre of dashboard and the truck-sized steering wheel.

Linda wasnt impressed. No thank you.

I walked with my arms cocked like muscle kept them from hanging straight and I rolled my hips like Bunker Reddy's bull. She giggled and Matt laughed.

It was near impossible to stall the Dodge since it had fluid drive but I did it. The starter ground forever before the car started again in a thunderhead of blue smoke. We took off in a fit of leaps and jerks like I was spurring it and by then Matt was holding his sides with laughter. I pushed in the lighter and picked a smoke from the pack and tapped it against the wheel. While I did the wheels wandered off the road and gravel peppered the floorboards. I whipped it wide across the center and then back kind of into my lane and kept my foot down on the gas all the while. Matt's laughing dried up and he fiddled with the radio but got nothing but sparkplug wires. He flicked it off and whistled the most irritating tuneless song till we got to his grandmother's. *Mañana*, he said when he got out. He opened the door again. She bit you right in the jugular, didnt she? He hooted and walked up the path exactly the way I'd tried to.

But somehow we became a trio. She was our girl. Goodnatured as a spring heifer and as athletic as Matt and as wholesome as Dad, but she kept back the mystery I'd glimpsed in Mom a time or two. And they were my best friends.

I asked her what she wanted to be. Just me, she said.

A nurse? A lawyer? An accountant?

Just whatever comes down the pike.

You dont have plans?

No. I want to be whatever I'm natural at.

Then what you doing in college? That sounds like a plan to me.

I guess I just naturally ended up here. She'd given me that little smile that made me feel like my nose was being rubbed in something.

It sunk in that I was cold and I wasnt in college anymore. I stared at my watch and marveled how little time had passed. My mind said it was time to skedaddle but the numbers disagreed. When the windshield cleared I headed left toward more past that lay brooding and malignant just six miles away.

The town of Hardly had grown up. A mini-mall and a Big T-Burger and a Citgo station freckled the cornfields a mile before I expected anything. Even without the yellow buses I'd have recognized the long brick building in Kraymer's pasture as a new school.

But the downtown part was past due for burial. Ruby's and Delard's and the Western Auto were either closed or moved to the mini-mall that would die itself when Wal-Mart came. Some of the buildings had burned or fallen and were marked now by a handful of grass and a bench or two. Empty benches. The merchants had bricked the walks and bought fancy light poles but dandelions sprouted in the bricks and dogs had pissed the paint off the poles. The old school had a new sign that said Department of Human Development and I wondered what they thought it had been before. I didnt slow there but the memories struck out as I passed.

I forget my first day at that school but not Matt's. A new mid-year arrival trumped a two-headed turtle any day. Matt lit down in our cafeteria just after Easter in our sixth grade. The secretary who hoarded the locker combinations was off with the chocolate rabbit syndrome so all his books were in a crooked stack under his arm.

The new guy scanned the room and spotted my empty table and came my way. Hog-subtle Bennie Harper slid his chair back just as the new guy passed behind him. Bennie jumped up with a sneering apology but the new guy pirouetted around the scattering books and when he'd come full-circle they were back under his arm. Sorry for what? he said.

Bennie stood there with his teeth in his mouth but no words.

Mind if I sit here? he said at my table.

With my foot I pushed out a chair.

Watch my books while I grab some grub.

Sure, I said but he'd already gone.

What is it with you? he said when he returned. You pick your nose or fart or are you just a jackoff?

My face felt the color and texture of his meatloaf. I dont know what you mean.

He looked around at all the other packed tables. Hell you dont. He didnt even seem to care that a teacher stood not fifty feet away. Gray eyes walked over me as cold and impersonal as a stethoscope.

I got lots of friends at the Christian school but Mom makes me come here.

He pulled a bean string from between his teeth and flicked it on the floor.

My dad's a Assembly of God preacher and he shows up and rares on the PTA and the school board about the heathen teachers they got here and everybody thinks I'm like him so they dont want nothing to do with me. But I think he's right.

His face said something I couldnt interpret but I didnt care for it anyway.

I aint got any friends at the Christian school either. I just said that. Cause Dad throws fits there about their dumbed-down classes. That's what he calls them.

You're a holyroller.

You probly dont know what one is.

They talk in tongues and handle snakes and stuff.

That sounded like a good thing the way he said it so I said, Yeah. Then felt stupid. Not the snakes, I added. That's that other bunch.

His eyes dropped to his food and I studied his buttonup shirt and glasses with an elastic strap behind his head. Short wiry hair. Strong looking without big muscles. No bigger than me. But he was different.

What's your name? he said.

Andy Price.

You even sound like a Bible thumper.

Well I aint one.

What section you in?

I'm in 6-C. How about you?

He took a final bite of meatloaf and made a face and pushed the plate away and said, I'm Matt Tamper. He stuck his hand over like an adult and I shook it. Come on, he said and pushed his chair back.

We got to take our trays up.

But he left his on the table. He was halfway down the hall till I'd gone back and taken it up and caught up with him. Where's your folks live?

I stay with Margaret Stollings out on Fingermill Road. She's my aunt or greataunt or something.

I'd never known any kids who didnt live with their parents. Hows come you live with her? Where's your mom and dad at?

My mother's dead and I have no clue where my father is.

My face burned and I looked quick but he didnt seem aggravated.

You going to be my friend? he said.

Well sure. I looked around hoping someone had heard. I'll be your friend all you want.

Let's put these books in your locker then till I get one of my own.

By the end of the day I knew that we were in the same section and that we both liked to read. And that we shared a dont-give-a-damn attitude though I'd never heard it called that before. And that I wouldnt sit by myself in the cafeteria anymore.

I checked the rearview mirror and I was old again. The memories had been so clean that a kid's face wouldnt have surprised me. I'd intended to turn around at the college where the memories were good but instead I went on like a vacuum cleaner salesman into a biker bar. Knowing I was going to get my gizzard kicked loose but unable to come rid of the notion that I could make a sale in there. Knowing that vacuums and Harleys both carried dirt bags.

CHAPTER 10

Union Highway was salted and cindered but if I went that way I'd have to pass Beck's Hill and I wasnt ready to drive past where I'd killed Matt Tamper so I turned onto back roads. The snowplow had wandered like a polecat and left a path twice as crooked as the road. Snakes of blowing snow lashed the potholed blacktop. The Subaru spun on the steepest grades and stalled when I rammed it into a snowdrift at the end of our old driveway. Our rusted mailbox hung from the post with mouth agape and faded red flag raised. A yellow NO TRESPASSING sign was like a touch of freezer burn in a frozen world. The lane was cluttered with fallen limbs and deep snow hid more that skun my shinbones as I fought my way toward the house.

Paint peeled from the windows Dad had installed on the second floor. The porch ceiling had collapsed in one corner and the chimney had fallen away into the yard and left a dark stripe down the scaling siding. Corners of blackened bricks fanned though the snow toward the little barn. But the barn was either collapsed or scavenged for its wormholed chestnut boards. Only the cancerous top of the old Dodge showed above a snarl of dead goldenrod and vicious white thorn that choked the meadow beyond.

Here Mom had hoed in a rocky garden and Dad had sawed sweet pine boards—*Jesus was a carpenter, Andy*—and I'd yelled as my sled greased down the steep slope to the creek. But the cold blanket of despair that settled on me as I drew closer deadened the sounds and corrupted the smells.

The front porch steps were down and the door was gone and the windows were ragged dark holes. I stood numb just inside. Even in the frigid air mildew burned my nose. Graffiti blasphemed the walls and a longneck beerbottle stuck from the broken plaster. Old magazines sprawled in moldy abandon among broken glass and food wrappers and rotting clothing and collapsed furniture. The basement was a dank void that stunk of coal and mice. A chromed control on the furnace shone in the dark like a pinhole. I turned halfway down the stairs and retreated.

The second floor was in better shape. Dad had remodeled there, and it was safer from vandals too drunk or horny or lazy to labor up the stairs. Fix something downstairs, Mom would complain. I'm embarrassed to entertain company in our living room. But he wanted to practice where it wasnt so noticeable. They're church people, dear, he said. They know if they keep us poor God will keep us humble.

Snow filtered through the unlatched window in my bedroom just like it used to sift through the baseboard during winter storms. I'd curl under the hand-knotted blankets that covered my little bed and watch the white streaks nose onto the floor and wait for the clank of the furnace when Dad shook down the night's clinkers and stoked the morning fire. Then a rush of sulfur as the coal poofed into life. The door would bang and the treads would complain as he tried to sneak up the stairs. Always surprised when he woke Mom.

He'd snatch me up, blankets and all, and carry me downstairs and hold me over the cast-iron register that boiled dry heat into my little blanket teepee while our breath fogged into the kitchen's chill air. Just before the heat inside my blankets turned uncomfortable he'd fold the bottom closed and plunk me into the big wooden rocker that sat by the stove. In minutes the roaring furnace turned the room toasty and the heat and the smell of coffee would drag Mom and her cloud of gloom down to join us.

Now the swampy stink of the damp ceiling was so like the smell of joint compound that I could almost hear the whisper of Dad's trowel as he feathered the edges of the new drywall we'd hung together. Dad doing the work but giving me the credit. You're quite a man, Andy. He'd sat right there on an upside-down bucket and kicked with old white-spattered dress shoes at the tracks Mom scrubbed away later. His red face leaked sweat and the air whistled through his nose as he rested from lifting for both of us.

Papers in the dresser drawers had my name in the corner and were written in my hand but the ideas recorded there werent mine. An old spiral notebook bulged with sketches and stories and poems from another who'd shared my name. As I felt my way down the stairs I smelled buckwheat cakes and heard the rattle of pans and the murmur of voices and sweet laughter that turned hard and crazy and mocking. Cold mirth at the wasted remnants of all I'd ruined.

I ran. The place's smell snatched at me with dirty fingers and grabbed at my clothes and wormed into my lungs as I slipped and slid out the lane. My fingers and toes and ears and nose burned with cold. I shivered in the car and paddled my feet and blew on my fingers till the hard sparks of ice faded away. But the ice in my belly wouldnt melt. The folks that wrote the Bible lived in a hot place where fingers and toes never crackled in winter's fire. They thought hell was hot. I think it's the everlasting inferno of ice.

The Subaru spun but dug free of the snowdrift and I drove farther down the road looking for a place to turn around. I wiped the fogging windshield and cussed the idea of coming back here but finally the snowbanks widened at the parking lot of Dad's old church. Snowplow drivers took a break here to drink coffee and make yellow holes in the snow. The church was as peeling and sagging and abandoned as the house but it didnt look vandalized. I reckon it's hard to raise hell in a church. Only the hardest case could sprawl in a pew and drink and throw beerbottles toward the corner and write filth on the walls. Even if you believed in nothing some finger of fear would have to touch your spine and give you pause.

Before I could leave, an old red Chevy pickup with a bright-yellow snowblade pulled in behind me. A tall man in coveralls and floppy rubber boots jumped out and gallumped to my window. Everything okay? A voice with no mountain drawl but somehow familiar. He dug a snotrag from his hip pocket and cleared his cold-fogged glasses.

I'm just turning around.

He replaced his glasses and looked hard at me. Have you been inside?

I glanced at the church like I'd just noticed it there. I'm just turning around.

Sure you dont need help?

I got no problem at all.

Well I'll help you when you do, Andy.

I nodded and wheeled out of the parking lot and was almost out of sight before it sunk in that he'd called me by name. I looked in the mirror but the parking lot was empty. I dug through faces and voices and eyes and found nothing. I sped up till I was going way too fast for the slick roads but I couldnt outrun the chorus of old demons that commenced like faraway dogs but built to a panbeating din. I turned on the radio and filled my space with Christmas carols that came soft in spite of the volume.

I wanted to cut it south but Linda begged to stay till morning. Food and laughter eased my tension but I was still shaken and moody. While the others played games I played on the Internet but everything that popped up was dark and damned and long before the others were ready for bed I switched the computer off and retreated to the bedroom.

Linda followed me in and kissed me and said, I love you, Andy Price.

I love you too, Sweetpea Price. She was warm and soft in my arms. Hey. I just remembered something. I'd held one gift back from the big fooforaw. Christmas gathered a little magic as I watched her peel away the wrapping.

Ooh! Chanel No. 5. She smelled it and gave me another hug and kiss.

Shu-nell? I thought that was channel. That aint catfish bait? I better take it back.

She laughed and hugged me and stood up to return to the festivities.

I clutched at her blouse. Can we talk for a few minutes?

She nodded, but glanced out toward her family with such longing that it put a twist in my shorts. Go on then, if your damned old games mean more to you than I do, I said.

No, honey. What do you want to talk about?

Go on, I said. Sulled down and already determined to stay there. Anything magic left with her.

CHAPTER 11

Sleep would have been a good place to hide but I couldnt find it. Just that restless state where dreams and memories meld and clabber. You roll over and check the time and go to the bathroom and sometime during the night you realize the bad dreams aint leaving in the morning. I slid into a conscious stupor that floated on the spurts of laughter from the kitchen and once I thought I heard Mom's voice among the others and my thoughts wandered back up the mountain toward home.

Andy! Mom had called from the kitchen. Get in here and help set the table.

As the screen door slapped shut behind me Fiddler's wet hound nose snickered against the mesh. Voices in the living room like evening thunder. I stood on my toes to turn the faucet. The sharp smell of iron as the water came.

Clean up good. The bigwigs are here. She had rocks in her voice again.

Hows come the only time we have chicken is when they come? With all the bowls of mash potatoes and gravy and green beans and hot bread and Alison Reddy's hand-churned butter there was hardly any room for me to put down plates and cups.

You got your preachers, you got your deacons, you better have your chicken. Mom sounded tired and angry both. They're all cast in the same mold. Her raised voice chopped off the living-room conversation. Dinner's on the table, Darrell.

Praise God, one of the voices rumbled.

How could they be made in the same mold? Dad was medium-tall and stout as an ox, Mom said. Brother Yunker was big as an ox. Brother Bowles wasnt as tall as Mom and way skinnier. And Brother Thornton was like two of him one atop the other.

There's dessert, too, Dad said. So save room.

Yunker raised his eyes at Mom in her stoveside chair.

Blueberry pie, she said.

Oh, gracious Lord, Mrs. Price, he said. My stomach hurts already. Like she'd took the kraut stomper and pounded the food down his throat. One time I took a wee little sliver so Mom would get a piece too but the whole rest of the pie disappeared down his gullet anyway. After that I always took the biggest piece in the pan.

When Mom cleared away plates the white scars on her wrists showed beyond her sleeves. Talk stopped till she sat down again by the stove.

Mom? I said after the men carried coffee cups to the living room and their voices turned somber and serious again. Hows come you're a Mrs.? The other women's all sisters but you aint.

Dont say aint, Andy. After that I'd just as well questioned the dog.

But I tried again later while I scrubbed a pan in dishwater that had turned cold and slick. I like chicken too. Was I made in the mold?

She set down the bowl she was drying and hugged me so hard that she mashed the wind out. Warm and damp and smelling of flour and cigarettes and sweat. I ever catch you trying to fit a mold I'll warp your ass till you dont. She'd dripped dishwater on my ear and I'd pushed her away.

I'd always pushed her away. The more Mom had pulled me to her the harder I'd pushed her away till after a while she gave up on the physical clutching. But her need was always there like snapping turtles in muddy water. Especially when Dad was away. I could hardly wait for him to get back from seminary. I'd wait on the porch for two days just in case he was early. Finally he'd be there again.

Fiddler raised his head from my lap and just before I was sure I'd heard something the Dodge's faded top hove above the goldenrod where the road crossed the powerline and I launched myself from the edge of the porch to try and beat Dad to the mailbox. Locusts flushed from the dust in a rolling wave ahead of my flying feet and Fiddler loped alongside with his tongue trailing in the wind.

Dad leaned over the wheel like it was a pulpit and when he saw me he blew the horn and stuck his hand out the window to grip mine while I ran up the driveway alongside the car. Slow down, boy. This old car cant go too fast anymore. Mom watched through the screen door and wiped her hands on her apron.

Can I carry your books? I asked before he could get the door open. The leather bag bounced against my knees because it was too heavy to hold away to the side.

Mom took the suitcase at the door and held it while Dad hugged her. Darrell, she said. It always made me mad that she didnt act more excited to see him after all her pining around while he was gone.

Classes were good this week, Dad said like Mom had quizzed him about it. But those young kids make me feel awfully old and slow.

I bet you're the smartest one there, I said. At least you wont be no shittin redneck tambourine thumper when you get out of preacher school.

Mom gave a bark of laughter that jumped out like a touch-me-not and color ran up the sides of Dad's neck. Now just where did you learn *that*? His preaching voice hurt my ears there in the confines of the hallway. Mom laughed from the kitchen, this time a long string of clear notes. Dad looked her way like he'd go holler at her but then he squatted and his fingers bit into my arms. I guess that's what you're learning in school.

I'd practiced the words over and over but somehow I'd got them wrong. I tried to pry his fingers loose from my arm.

You hear how your son has learned to talk, Jasmine? His spit freckled my face.

Mom came from the kitchen and stood right behind him. You're hurting him, Darrell.

Dad turned me loose and pointed his finger at Mom but she folded it down like she was redirecting a pistol aimed at her face and said, That came from Bunker Reddy. Not from school. Bunk had stopped in to check on us and I'd listened outside the screen door.

Dad wheeled back to me. Dont *ever* say that word again.

Which one? But he was gone to wash up for supper before I could ask.

Their argument started again after supper and I didnt have to hear all the words to know it was about where I should go to school. Again. I heard hothouse tomato and heathen upbringing and well adjusted and sanctified. That was enough.

I sat on the porch swing and kicked Fiddler in the ribs with every swing and with every kick he'd wag his tail. Shittin, I whispered. Redneck. Tambourine. Thumper. Shittin redneck tambourine thumper. I said it louder and Fiddler jumped up and put his paws over my shoulders like I was saying hamburger and pork chops. He stood on one foot and stomped the other when I scratched his belly anywhere close to his tallywhacker.

When Linda fumbled her way into the dark bedroom, I was sitting on the bed with my head in my hands, wiping the sweat from my face with a shirt that smelled of Christmas gone sour. I'm awake. You aint got to tiptoe and cobble everything off the dresser trying to find the bed.

Her clothes rustled and thumped onto the floor and the bed sagged as she stretched out. I had such a good time, she said.

I hope you sleep better than I been. It's hotter than the hubs of hell in here.

Open a window.

Yeah right. Your old man would foul his britches if he caught his gas heat flying out an open window.

Aw. He's not like that. But she didnt get up to open a window.

Just before her breathing got too regular, I said, It was the winters that done him in.

What? She flounced and fluffed her pillow and hauled at the covers.

Dad. He could chop down the weeds and they'd stay chopped. At least for a while. And when he fixed the house it stayed fixed. But the snow would fill in the walk before he could even get back into the house. And he couldnt stand not to shovel it. Somebody might come. He couldnt leave it be.

Like you can?

I dont even own a snow shovel.

The bed shifted as she sat up. He's dead. Your mom's dead. Matt's dead. I cant change that.

Now that's just about cold.

You cant change it either. But we've paid enough. More than enough. So let's put it behind us. Let them rest in peace.

The temperature must of dropped below a hundred because the furnace kicked on with a blast of air straight from hell. You best get some sleep, I said. We got a long drive tomorrow.

That there's a bobcat track, I said. I was ready to bust with that knowledge, and with amazement that Dad would leave his books long enough to come see it.

Dad glanced at the print along the creek bank. No, it's a dog. It's too big for a cat.

It *aint* a cat. It's a *bobcat*. You cant see no toenails like you could on a dog track. Bunk said so and he's even saw them before.

Maybe so, he said like it didnt matter one way or the other. He took me by the hand and towed me far enough away that I couldnt look at the track while he talked. He sat on a stump and pulled me onto his knee like I was a little kid. The next time it rains that track will disappear, Andy. Gone as though it were never there.

But I still seen it. I'll know.

I'm *glad* you enjoy the forest, Son. God made it just for you. The bobcat, too, for that matter. But the whole world is just as temporary as that track. Do you know that word? Temporary?

I thought I did but then he explained.

It means unimportant. This life—Dad swung his arm like we could contemplate the whole of it from this old sawed-off stump—is just a test. This sin-dark world will pass away and God will fashion a new one for the faithful. A perfect world where all will be at peace. Where the lion will lie down with the lamb and we'll study war no more. He shifted and repositioned me on his knee. Andy, I need to explain salvation to you.

I've already done it.

But he wasnt listening to me. He told me God's plan that I confess my sin and invite Jesus into my heart. You can do that right here in the forest.

I done did it.

One more time wont hurt anything, will it?

I allowed that it wouldnt so we knelt with our elbows on the stump and our knees in the leaves only one of mine was on an acorn that augered a hole in my kneecap while I got saved for the six-hundredth time. We shook hands then like I was a deacon and Dad had tears in his eyes. On the way back he gave me a new silver dollar. You keep this to remind you of this day when salvation came into your house.

That dollar rode in my pocket for nigh onto twenty years before it leaked away through a hole. The edges wore smooth and you couldnt tell heads from tails. I looked for it for a long time but it was gone. I didnt spend it on drink, either, like Linda claimed. She always thought it was just a dollar.

Bunk Reddy's laughter was like coffee perking. Somebody best explain to them sheep the new order a things fore they wake up in bed with the lions, he said. They're liable not to stick around for breakfast. Long muscles crawled under his wet shirt as he pitched hay from the loft to his white-faced cattle.

Huh-uhhh. The lions will eat grass in the new world.

Bunk straightened and wiped sweat from his face with a hand too big for his skinny arms. God amighty. That means someone'll have to feed em. How many bales a hay you reckon a bull lion eats a day?

Dad says this world is temporary and that means it aint important. We're just here to see which ones is saved.

Commere. Bunk led me across the barnyard to his sagging garage. He walked sideways like a hounddog because one leg was twisted in the knee. I came up almost to his shoulder but he grabbed me by the hips and hoisted me up to where my head was in the eaves. Inches from my face a nest of baby robins gaped wide. What's them birds look like they're wantin?

They could stand some food, I said.

If you was to cram them full enough of worm sandwiches they wouldnt be hungry no more. That's *temporary*.

My head bumped the roof boards when I nodded.

I want to listen while you explain to them it aint *important*.

Boy, arent you chipper this morning, Mom had said a few years later as she flipped another corncake onto my plate.

My mouth was full so I pointed out the window to where the Easter lilies were blooming and the first swallows were swooping for bugs.

It's not spring so dont get your heart set on it. We'll have the sarvis snow yet.

Mr. Martz says they're serviceberries. Says people who call them sarvis are showing their ignorance. Before they had backhoes they couldnt dig a hole in the froze ground to bury people who died in the winter. They stacked them in the smokehouse and when the preacher came around in the spring they buried them all in one shot. Just about now—when the *service*berry blossoms.

She shrugged. Service or sarvis, those white blossoms mean another snow.

Aw, I dont believe them old tales. March came in like a lion and went out like two of em.

Yeah. It's the good things that never come around twice. She messed my hair like she was in a good mood but she wasnt. Will another snow put your sap down, you think? Or will you still be in love?

I just about choked on my cake. You're nuts.

Boys dont act the way you been just because the sun shines.

I hadnt intended to tell them about Matt because I knew they'd ruin it somehow but I was scared if she thought I was messing with *girls* and it got back to Dad . . . my mind shied off from what might happen then. So I started with Bennie Harper and the books and told her about Matt.

The flicker of interest she'd shown burned out when she found out I didnt have a girlfriend.

Can I bring him home some weekend?

You'd have to ask your dad.

That shot *that there* slam in the ass, as Bunk always said. But I asked him anyway when he was deep in his books and he said, I dont care, without even hearing what I said so I brought Matt home without asking again.

Matt leaned close and looked at the carving that had forever stood on the corner of Dad's desk. It was a complicated thing someone had whittled from a single piece of wood: Two round balls rolled loose inside four slender spiral posts that trapped them inside. Can I touch it? he said.

Be careful with it, Dad said. I made the corners too thin.

Matt stroked the wood the way I always thought I'd touch a girl if I ever did.

Dad made that?

Wow, Matt said. Have you made anything else?

Dad shook his head. No. I had to repent for the time I wasted carving that.

Matt set the carving down and read Dad's diploma. I'm going to college someday.

That's wonderful. Maybe you and Andy can go together.

Who said I was going? I thought. The idea was like a stinkbug in a raspberry and I spit it out before it could get me.

Then Matt made a fuss over Dad's old books and Mom's needlework—everyday trash that wasnt worth wasting playtime on—and even though it was Saturday when Dad was busy studying and Mom said we had to keep out of the way, they strutted and grinned till I wanted to kick all three of them. And when Fiddler sniffed him he scratched that special place behind the dog's left ear that only I knew about.

Raise your hands, Dad roared at church the next morning, and give the Lord a praise offering. It didnt matter whether I raised and praised like

Brother Yunker or sulked like one of the teenage boys that came to sit with the church girls. I felt self-conscious and awkward either way. Matt just looked around to see what he was supposed to do and then did it. He even started talking in tongues with the others till my elbow in his ribs shut that down.

You dont do that unless you cant help it. Sorry I'd brought him home with me.

Matt shrugged and didnt blaspheme the Spirit anymore but he clapped with the music and made a joyful noise unto the Lord till I wanted to punch him. I swallowed my sour spit and clapped too. Like it had been my idea.

Matt was even more obnoxious on the way home. You always that loud when you preach? he asked Dad.

He should of heard him before he went to seminary.

Dad smiled like he had when Matt bragged on his carving. It's just what folks expect. He laughed and told about finding a handwritten note in the margin of his roommate's sermon outline: Weak point. Volume here.

Then at dinner Matt turned his inquisition Mom's way: Why dont you go to church?

I stopped chewing my food but Dad just buttered another biscuit.

Mom placed her fork on her plate with great care. Matthew, that's none of your damn business.

He laughed like she'd told some stupid little joke but nobody else did. What talk there was for the rest of the meal was about ham or rain and not one word of it was mine.

When Homer Lawton's bedside clock read 2:41 I figured maybe I ought to let Linda get some sleep even if I couldnt. In the semi-dark kitchen I drank a glass of milk that seemed to go blinky before I could swallow. It was no wonder Linda's brothers had grown up so mean, if every night in this house was this long and hot. The couch swallowed me with a crackle of wrapping paper into the crack behind the cushions. Alone there where I couldnt hear Linda's soft breathing and smell her hair, my memories turned acrid and hard.

A pellet of coal seared the back of my neck where I cowered in the ditch along Fingermill Road and the sledgehammer of air from the coaltruck seemed to drive me into the mud. Wait up, I yelled at Matt, but he was so far ahead he couldnt hear me over the racket of the truck's Jakebrake. He widened the gap all the way up Beck's Hill and then waited at the top. Till I got there he wasnt even breathing hard.

I hate this road, I said when I gathered up enough air to talk. There's no shoulder. That D & G truck didnt miss you more than six inches.

Matt grinned. This is a great hill. You want to be a flatlander runner?

You're going to be a flat runner if one of those trucks hits you.

Dont be a wuss. Come on, I'm cooling off. He rolled his shoulders, then started down the other side.

I could hear another truck grinding up the backside of the hill. Let's at least run in the evenings when the coaltrucks are off the road, I yelled.

The weighcrews dont work at night, he tossed back over his shoulder. There's twice as many trucks then running twice as heavy and twice as fast.

I crouched as another handful of coal peppered my skin and didnt even hear the second truck running right on the tail of the first. How it missed me I'll never know.

I never caught up with Matt again, but it wouldnt have made any difference. He never took my advice or did what I wanted. It was always the other way around.

CHAPTER 1 2

Get us some cigarettes, Matt said.

No way, I said. I'm not gonna start stealing too.

It's not stealing. Not from your mom.

Later, far up the hillside by the creek, Matt's eyes glittered with the flare of the match. Smoke disappeared behind his long red ash like he'd been pulling on cigarettes for years. He blew a long plume and dragged again.

I held most of the smoke in my mouth but my head spun anyway. Dont it make you drunk?

He nodded and coughed and threw his short butt into the creek. Mine was only half gone but it hissed into the water beside his. I wondered if they'd float past the house. If Dad would see them.

I'll get us some more tomorrow, I said. My tongue explored the film the smoke left behind.

Not for me.

Dont you want more? (Arent we smokers now? Addicted?)

No way. I'm a runner. He seemed dumbfounded that I suggested more. I just wanted to know what it was like.

What's go walkabout mean? I asked him once when he'd threatened to do it again.

You walk about, like it says. In Australia, they do it all the time.

Where do you go?

Wherever you want to. There's no rules and you stay as long as you want.

Well bag that then, if there aint any rules. Dad wont allow it.

We'll just go regular camping, then. El Mucho ought to allow that much.

He'd never called Dad that to his face but I knew it was only a matter of time.

Maybe, if I dont miss church.

My old man would fill his pants if he could see us. I examined the campfire through the bottle of cheap whiskey and then passed it to Matt.

Muscles snaked in his arm as he shook the amber liquid and drank. We'll probably fill our own. This stuff is awful.

I caught the bottle, almost dropped it. Dont *throw* it, man. The liquor burned inside me like a single hot coal. Say me a poem, Buckwheat, I said.

You want one I learnt or one that I writ myself?

Say one you whupped up on your own, I said.

His words seemed to flicker and flare like the firelight as he locked his fingers behind his head and closed his eyes and quoted from memory:

> The Stalker
> *Without a trace our mind explores,*
> *Treads sacred ground, defies closed doors,*
> *Intruding, snooping, peeping Tom,*
> *Who's never brought to justice.*

But for fire's crackle, a vast silence eddied in the poem's wake. That's neat, I said. A log collapsed in a spray of sparks.

Why did your mom try to kill herself? The question an open palm across my face.

I dont know what you're talking about.

She didnt get those scars on her wrists from a crochet hook.

I took a longer drink that tested my gag reflex. I dont know. She's not crazy, though. Just depressed. Alcohol ricocheted through my veins and roared in my ears. A soft smoky fire had kindled in my gut. Dad says it's hereditary.

Matt went quiet but the talk had gathered momentum in me. More? I waved the bottle at him. He shook his head. Twin fires reflected in his glasses. The silence bore down hard till I said, Do you know anyone that ever went walkabout? When he didnt answer I bounced a stick in his lap. Dufus. Wake up!

I'm awake.

Do you? No answer. Something rustled leaves outside the fire's nervous ring of light. Far off a dog barked. Another farther to the north passed it on to a shrill voice on the edge of my hearing. Matt stirred and pulled the bill of his cap down over his face. My father did, he said. When my mom died. His sigh strengthened the atmosphere the faraway dogs had created.

How long was he gone?

He's not back yet.

Later, as I rambled about other things, his still form gradually faded with the fire until he joined the other lifeless shadows around the coals. The liquor's race through my veins turned hard and caustic and my throat swelled with bile and my vision swam till the embers traced circles and streaks. I'm going walkabout, I croaked, but I couldnt stand. I crawled a few feet and emptied my body of everything but the alcohol that speared me to dirt and decaying leaves as surely as a straight pin through a butterfly.

The next morning Matt was upbeat and talkative while I fluttered mute and nauseous on a flagstaff of leftover whiskey. My head pounded and I stank of sweat and puke and stale alcohol. Embarrassment about what I'd said the night before—though I wasnt sure what I'd said—sealed my fuzzy tongue behind trembling lips.

Matt wouldnt let me suffer in peace, but forced me onto my feet and into the woods, exploring. We went to the Cat Rocks, a new place to him, and he climbed and jumped as happy as if he had his right mind.

By noon, when we built a small fire and ate Spam roasted on a stick with grease dripping from our fingers, I was bragging about the bender we'd been on. As we packed for home in the late afternoon Matt made a face at the inch of liquid left in the bottle.

Gimme that, I said, and drank it in one swallow and gagged as it burned to the pit of my stomach. The fire continued to spread till it wiped away the last traces of the morning's sickness. Matt shook his head, repulsed and fascinated. I felt for once his equal.

Dont be depressed, young lady, Matt said. Get your head out of the slop bucket. A fast bluegrass tune was playing on the radio as he hauled Mom out of her chair and into a crazy reel around the kitchen. The rug slipped from under their feet and ended up a wrinkled pile against the baseboard.

Stop it, Mom shrieked, but her eyes sparkled and her cheeks flushed red and she didnt fight to get away. Another woman slipped into her dress—one that could dance, that knew the steps and the motions. A woman that loved dancing without shame or inhibition. She looped and twirled and shot away from Matt, then clutched him tight when their spinning brought them together.

Mom, I said.

Something snapped. Mom's face and voice hardened. Stop it. They whirled to a halt. Dont ever do anything like that again. Do you understand, Matthew?

For once Matt looked embarrassed. I was just trying to make you laugh.

That's *not* the way. Her feet cobbled up the stairs and left us in a silence as comfortable as a slug on a salt flat.

Whew. What got into her? Matt released air from puffed cheeks.

Who do you think she is? One of your girlfriends?

Aw, man, he said. I was just trying to add a little life to the party.

I snorted. This aint a party. This is my home.

You're worse than your old man. Matt fetched his hat from the living room and let the screen door slam behind him when he left. At least he only flops one way.

I found Mom staring out the window from the corner of her bed. Her back full of starch.

What's amatter with you? Matt was just being nice.

I shouldnt have yelled at him.

What did he do that was so wrong?

Come sit beside me. She patted a spot on the bed. I did, and she leaned her head on my shoulder. She'd never seemed this small before.

What's *wrong* with you, Mom?

A hot tear blazed down my arm and her body trembled. I dont know. I feel like I've fallen down a crack.

What the hell is that supposed to mean? The word gave me a little twist of pleasure. Her hand was a steel talon on my arm as she pushed away.

Andrew Price, you will never use foul language in this house again.

I said *hell*. It's in the Bible. Who says I cant say it? My anger was loose and I didnt care to catch it.

Your father says so, and I do too. And the church, if you need a third opinion.

I hate that church.

The whites of her eyes, wide around the brown centers, began to leak again. The church isnt the problem. I am. White hands hid her face while sobs gushed out between her fingers.

I felt like a pile of Fiddler's crap that had been tracked into the kitchen. I hugged her and patted her back. Spots and blemishes showed through the part in her thin hair. After a while she pushed me away and returned to her corner of the bed. She blew her nose on tissues from a box on the nightstand and cleared her throat. I wish you had a better mother.

I slid over beside her. You're a good mother.

Look what I've done to you. One solitary sob.

I was clueless. Speechless.

You cuss and smoke and drink and you dont go to church anymore.

Those things arent so bad. You do some of them too.

I know, she said. I *know*. Her shame settled over us like a shroud.

Mom shook the last pack of cigarettes from a carton. This is my last one.

Put em on the list, I said. Grocery shopping had gotten to be my job along with cleaning and cooking and every other thing that she was too depressed to tackle.

No. I mean this is the last pack of cigarettes I'll ever smoke. I'm quitting.

My laugh was meant to be nasty. You'll change your mind when the smokes get closer gone. Put it on the list now or you'll forget. I'm not going to make a special trip just for cigarettes.

The lighter was already in her hand and her eyes were squinted ready for the smoke. She froze for a second, then slipped the cigarette back into the pack. She walked toward the refrigerator where the grocery list hung but threw the pack in the trashcan instead. Please burn the trash this morning, Andy. She rattled up the stairs to her bedroom and didnt come out until dinnertime.

I burned the trash but I kifed the smokes first. Like Dad always said: waste in haste, you'll want in leisure. The first half of the pack lasted almost a week, the second less than a day.

I know what you're doing, Dad said. Not everything, I'm sure, but enough to be concerned.

Big deal. I didnt know everything I'd done either. Some of my drunks had ended in a brain-dead stupor that I couldnt remember.

The wooden balls in his carving clicked back and forth in his trembling hands. His office was cool but he wiped his mottled face with a rumpled white handkerchief.

Aw, Dad, I'm just planting a little wild oats. I'd been expecting this confrontation but wasnt prepared for it. I'm not a bad guy.

I pray that's true. But every day it's something new. Some new sin that's cropped up inside this house God holds me responsible for.

Well what is it now? What did I do today? Since I'd been so hungover two days before I'd sworn off all manner of sin for good.

I wont call it sin. But this almost scares me more. Because it's an indication of the direction your mind is heading. From his desk drawer he pulled my paperback copy of *Moby Dick*, only a month old, but already marked and dog-eared.

What's wrong with that? It's a classic, for God's sake.

Dad licked his fingers and paged through the book to a text I'd highlighted. You found this passage important: *I'll try a pagan friend, thought I, since Christian kindness has proved but hollow courtesy.* And this one: *But, alas! the practices of whalemen soon convinced him that even Christians could be both miserable and wicked; infinitely more so, than all his father's heathens.*

Are you going to censor what I highlight in a book now? How can I work out my own salvation with fear and trembling—like you preach—if I cant even ask questions of myself?

Are you working out your salvation? Or are you discarding it? Accepting others' easy answers that excuse the path you're taking?

Give me that. I ripped the book away but he grabbed at it and tore half the jacket off.

If he'd have shouted and banged his fist on the desk like he did when he preached, I'd have fought it out with him. But he said, Oh, no. Let me tape that up for you.

I cant deal with hurt when I'm mad. With polite.

I paused in the doorway. Get off my back. Let me grow up.

Framed by white curtains, Mom was a watching witch as I spun from the driveway.

I'd taken the first drink of the day before I was out of sight of the house and then lots more between classes. I'd peaked in Hanratty's class where I'd offered brilliant counterpoints to his ignorant philosophy, but by the time Matt and I waited in the car for Linda I was gritty with the leading edge of a hangover.

She'd better get her fanny in gear if she wants to be my girl. Matt looked at his watch.

I thought a college degree and a four-minute mile came before girls.

Yeah, well, I'm only three years from one and twenty seconds from the other. And that was before I met Linda. Those gray eyes were as cold and hard as train tracks.

What about the hooters? You said your girl was going to have big ones.

He grinned. Anything more than a mouthful's wasted.

I smashed my fist into the dash and knocked the rearview mirror crooked in the process and stared into my own crazy red-rimmed eyes. I think she ought to get to decide whose girl she is.

Here she comes. Ask her.

We both knew what her answer would be.

Oh good, Linda said. We're into the bottle again. Her clean spicy smell drove back the smoke and alcohol fumes as she slid in between us. She looked at my eyes and said, I think I'd better drive. She held out her hand for the keys.

I'm good. The day wasnt but I was. The liquor was hot in my blood and my senses were sharp. The Dodge yawed hard to the left as we roared from the college parking lot and turned onto the county road. Linda slid against me like we were on the Tilt-a-Whirl and her fingernails scrabbled on the dash as she hauled herself back to the center. Dust and smoke rose in a plume behind us and gravel rattled against the floor pan.

Andy, you bonehead! You trying to kill us?

Leave him alone, Matt said. If he thinks he's getting under your skin he'll go faster. Just like my old man, so grownup and reasonable. Pass the hooch, he said.

Aint you scared drinking'll hurt your running? As smartaleck as I could make it. He wiggled his fingers: Give it. Before I passed the bottle I took another long pull while I whipped the old Dodge onehanded around a curve. The turn took the play out of the steering but when the road straightened I needed both hands to stay on the hardtop.

Matt took the bottle and drank and offered it to Linda. Have a sip.

No way. Her nose crinkled.

I said have a little sip. He grinned though his tone was serious and pushed his index finger against Linda's temple. An imaginary pistol of finger and thumb. Or I'll pop you.

Dont shoot. I'll do anything you say.

I nearly ran off the road when she turned the bottle up. She coughed and choked and drank again.

Linda, what the hell . . . what are you doing?

Oh, lighten up. Maybe it's time I had some fun too.

Now we're talking, Matt said, and took another turn on the bottle. God, this stuff's awful. You hold the gun on me and make me drink some. Linda laughed and held her finger against his head. Here, he said. I'll take the sting out of it for you. He filled his mouth with whiskey then pointed at his lips and leaned toward her. When they kissed he passed the liquor to her. She coughed and laughed and kissed him again.

I threw the column shifter into second gear as I accelerated around the next turn. The back wheels drifted sideways on the pavement.

Hey! Linda said.

Why dont we drop you off at the go-kart track? You can work out your frustrations without hurting yourself, Matt said. Little dad.

The car leaned so far into the next turn that I didnt think it would roll back in time for the next turn but it did, and I didnt slow down. I'd shut their filthy mouths. I held the gas pedal flat against the floor until the rear end finally broke loose at the bottom of a hill and took us across the other lane and into the ditch in a geyser of gravel and roadside weeds. I twisted the wheel and we went fishtailing back across the pavement and plowed to a stop on the road's shoulder.

I took a very deep breath.

Matt's laugh was a nervous little whicker and all of a sudden he didnt look so cool, so tough. Maybe the sun was in my eyes. Or I'd gone blind with anger and frustration. But all I could see were the people who had everything figured out: Matt and Linda and Dad, each of them all settled and comfortable while I was still scrabbling around trying to find a place for me.

I could see that, and my fist in Matt's face. Come on, I said. Right now. Let's do it. I bailed out and started around the car but my feet slipped on the gravel and I almost went down and that gave Matt time to get out and square himself.

Linda was yelling something at first but later she just cried.

I couldnt hit him.

My fist would seem to pass right through him and then his knuckles would crash into my face. Stop when you're ready, he said. He wasnt even breathing hard. I've got all night.

Then he started preaching. I'm the best friend you'll ever have. Crash.

I hate to do this to you. Crash.

Why dont you give it up, man. Crash.

Then the words and the fists lost their distinction with one as harsh and meaningless as the other and somewhere in the background I could hear Linda crying. I was falling falling falling and then everything stopped with one last thump.

I'm still your friend, man, he said. Then his footsteps faded away down the road.

At some point I was aware of a concerned voice from a car that happened by and of Linda's reassurance that everything was fine.

Then she was helping me up and wiping my face with my handkerchief and wiping her eyes on the back of her hand. Oh, Andy. Andy Andy Andy.

My face felt shapeless and rotten when I felt of it. Air wouldnt pass through my smashed nose and my left eye was swollen nearly shut. Where's Matt? I said.

He took off jogging. It's not that far to his house.

I'm going to kill him.

Hush. She touched my broken lip. You've killed him enough.

If only that had been the end of it, I thought as the first wisps of daylight leaked into Homer Lawton's living room. The room was filled with scattered toys and crumpled Christmas wrappings and in the black-and-white shadows of dawn looked like an aerial photo of a disaster scene.

CHAPTER 13

The fart-and-mildew stench of the Dodge's backseat turned my stomach but if I turned my head from the stink the morning sunshine hammered at my eyes. The one that wasnt swollen shut. My pulse clattered like a tambourine and a dirty sock was stretched over my tongue. Tree leaves rustled outside the open door. My clammy bare feet stuck straight out into the dew-heavy air.

My pregnant bladder was being perforated by what my shaking fingers identified as a square bottle. I tried to make sense of the unfamiliar label. An ocean wave surged in my stomach and I clawed my way up and out the door. Dry heaves tore at my raw throat. I remembered none of it.

My churning stomach demanded attention but my bladder couldnt wait any longer. My jeans and shirt were gone and my shorts were on backwards.

You could turn your back, Linda said. She sat on a rock fifteen feet away but there was no stopping now. When I spun away I pissed all over my leg.

What are you doing here? The words felt like barbwire unspooling from my guts.

Praying.

Sarcastic? Dont waste your prayers on me, I said. I aint worth it. Now that I was moving around the shakes were really taking over.

I wasnt praying for you.

Where's my pants at?

They're in the trunk where you put them.

No trace of that in my memory. Oh, yeah. Right.

I slipped behind the car to get my hind leg in the hind leg hole of my shorts. Mud was caked over the car's side and splashed onto the top and windows. If you want to feel real good about yourself try waking up sick and near-naked in a trashed-up car and not knowing where you are. Or how you got there. Or what you did on the way there. Where are we, anyhow?

Oh Lord, Andy.

The surrounding woods held some vague familiarity but my face stuck out where I wasnt used to seeing it and made everything look different. Like my brain had been put down inside a anteater. I felt of a nose that had gone fat and purple and asymmetrical and of an eye lost behind a fold in a smooth hot mound of flesh and of a lip that lit afire when I touched it. Matt. Aha. A glimmer. That sonofabitch.

And I still had Linda.

And I was still drunk. I climbed on top of the car and tried to stand straddle-legged and beat my chest in victory but my left heel had mud on it and flew away without me and my knee made a dent in the top and I slid down the corner of the cab and hung by the nuts on the side mirror for a second and then slithered down in a pile like a road-killed possum with my head jammed under the front wheel. Where it belonged. Feeling extra special. Did you catch all that? I said. I hope I aint got to do it over again.

Linda made a sound my mind wouldnt let me interpret and she hugged herself.

I crawled from under the car and leaned back against the tire and tried to die. After a while I realized I recognized a lightning-struck chestnut snag that stood just off the edge of Bunk Reddy's back hayfield. I reckon there's a story of how we got way back here, I said.

Linda leaned forward and vomited between her feet.

When I was able to I felt along the car and opened the trunk and found that my shirt and pants were stiff stovepipes of mud. The pants closed like clams over my pale legs. I didnt try the shirt. All right, I said. Tell me all about it.

Linda hawked and spat and I thought she'd barf again but she looked at me and seemed to steel up with the comparison. You have to be kidding me.

I aint sure what happened. I got pretty drunk.

She put her head on her knees and didnt say anything.

It aint over between me and Matt. If he thinks giving me a slicking will keep me away from you, he's gonna have it to do.

Linda got to her feet and hugged herself and walked away down the logging road we'd come in on and I thought she was leaving me but she sat on an old stump before she got out of sight. Hunkered up like she was bawling but she could have just been sick again.

My shirt was a mess but it was in better shape than my pants so I folded it across the driver's seat and sat on it. The engine started with a roar that sent me into the shakes again. The exhaust system gone. The wipers just made the windshield evenly opaque so I got out and scoured a hazy oval through the mud with a handful of leaves.

I didnt kill more than fifty saplings while I backed and filled to turn around. When I stopped beside Linda, her eyes were dry but red.

I turned off the ignition. I meant what I said about Matt.

Dont play stupid with me, you jerk. You know Matt's dead as well as I do.

The info wouldnt process. Oh, he is not. I'm the one got the worst of it.

Dont tell me you dont remember. Dont you dare lie to me.

Dont *you* lie to *me*. Being dead aint something to fun around about.

Her eyes danced back and forth between mine. I guess you dont remember this either. She motioned me to the front of the car. The right front fender was buckled so the headlight cast down and away like Dewey Newcomb's off eye.

I dont know nothing about that. My guts turning to cold gravy.

If you ever told the truth you'd better tell it right now.

Linda . . . Lately when I get too drunk I dont remember stuff for a while.

She turned her back to me and stood cross-armed till I couldnt stand it.

What happened? You got to tell me.

I cant stand it if you go to prison. Her shoulders heaved when she sobbed.

I could feel my mouth moving but it wasnt making any noise.

I know it was an accident and you know it was. She turned and touched my swollen face. But nobody's going to believe that. Nobody.

Believe what? I didnt do anything. But doubt gnawed like a rat under the floorboards.

She stared at me for a long time and then stooped and stared at the fender the same way. Okay. Okay. Here's what we're going to do.

As she worked out the lie that would keep me out of jail, I sat with my head buried between my knees. Dumbstruck.

Tell it back to me, she said.

I shook my head. I aint going to do it.

Then enjoy your time in prison. She wheeled and stalked off with enough energy that I knew she wouldnt be stopping again.

Tell me again where we were when I hit that deer, I said when I caught up with her.

We glugg-glugged out of the woods and along the edge of Bunk's field. At the creek where we'd missed the rubble-rock crossing and gotten hung up and torn off the muffler, I stopped and switched off the engine and she waded out on her side of the car. I tore my shirt half in two and tossed one piece to Linda.

She bent and dipped her cloth into the water. I'll get the fender. It has to be done right. You get the high spots.

When my feet found the icy water I remembered mud and water slashing at me from a spinning tire. You were driving, I said. I pushed you out of the ditch.

After you missed the road, I was. She winced and made a face when water dripped from her rag onto her legs. Get busy.

I cant believe I got so muddleheaded I run in the crick. Staying on the road wasnt a problem as far as I knew. Remembering where the road went was.

More pieces of the night tore loose as I rinsed the shirt. My head stuck under the armrest. Linda yelling slow down slow down. Long fluid shelves of bottles. Matt saying give it up. But I recalled a stuffed red alligator, too. How do you tell what's memory and what's whiskey? You got to tell me what really happened, I said. I cant stand not knowing.

It's better that you dont get confused just now. I'll tell you later.

It wasnt something I *wanted* to know. Not ever.

My pants smelled like a swamp so I sat on the rocky streambed and scrubbed away what I could without taking them off. The icy water sobered me but the climbing sun beat at my head worse than Matt had. Cleaning the car seemed to take forever. Just a few swipes and the shirt was mud-heavy and ready for rinsing.

I stopped and looked around and realized that nothing would ever look the same again.

When we finished scrubbing, I loaded the muffler into the trunk. The pain from where the rusted edge sliced my hand was almost a welcome distraction.

You coming home with me? I said at the highway, after I twisted barbwire together to close the gap we'd torn through the fence. You're welcome to use our shower.

No. Take me to the dorm. I need to be alone for a while.

How many times have you had blackouts? she said just before we got to the college.

I shrugged. A couple of times.

How long does it take you to remember?

I shook my head and shrugged again. It varies.

Promise me something. Her hair was tangled and her clothes rumpled and muddy but my pulse juddered anyway when she slid close and stroked my chin and kissed me. Promise you'll get some help for your drinking. Whatever happens.

I shrugged. I'll try.

No. That's not good enough. You have to promise.

I said I'd try, dammit.

Dont forget what I know. Anything soft or warm gone. The door clicked shut a little harder than necessary. I pivoted the rearview mirror so that I could see my battered face and then turned it away.

I tried to practice the lie while I drove home but my thoughts kept going back to my near-nakedness that morning and I kept fantasizing that I'd gotten laid. There's a cure for a mind that slimy but there aint nobody yet survived the treatment.

Lord have mercy, Dad said when he saw my face. What happened?

I fell down the steps, okay? I brushed past him and started up the stairs. He followed and stood in the bathroom doorway while I washed the worst of the blood from my face and brushed my teeth.

I hope you took Matt home. Margaret Stollings has been calling all night.

I dont know where he is and I dont really give a rat's kazoodie. The bedroom door didnt have a lock but Dad didnt follow me in.

The man who shook me awake was too old and tired and red to be Dad. A deputy dog stood right behind him or I'd have crawled back under the covers. What? Amazed more that I'd fallen asleep than that they'd showed up so soon.

Deputy Murray wants to ask you some questions.

The deputy was beefy and dark but his voice wasnt. I got to take you down to the station.

Like hell, I said. I fastened Bunk's fence back up till the cows wont get out. I'll go back and fix it good when I get a chance.

Dont say anything more, Dad said. I'll get Chester Griffin and we'll meet you there.

Our lie felt transparent and fatuous and silly. You got to be kidding, I said. I need a lawyer for a fence? I didnt even have to fake shock when Dad said they'd found Matt dead on Fingermill Road, on Beck's Hill. Where he'd been jogging way into the night, up and down and up and down in the dark on the narrow road.

Found this morning by the same man who'd driven by just after our fight.

He did lay a serious hurtin on you. I'll 'low you that much, Deputy Murray said as he mashed me down into the backseat of the cruiser.

We buried Matt at ten o'clock on a cold day that brought the first taste of autumn. High cirrus clouds swept away any warmth from the pale sun. Mom and Linda and I huddled separate from the rest of the little graveside group. I dont remember much of Dad's eulogy. Gone home. God's child. Older than his years.

Tendrils of Linda's hair crept across my face like they were trying to find Mom. The same fat deputy and Ches Griffin stood just behind me but they didnt block much wind. The handcuffs were bands of ice.

Each mourner stooped to toss a handful of dirt into the hole, but Jenny Yunker threw hers at me and stooped for another. Her buckteeth fangs. Mom wheeled in front so none of it hit me.

Jenny, Jenny, Jenny. Brother Yunker hustled her away under his big arm.

All I could do was nudge a clod into the hole with the toe of my shoe. Give the boy a break, Don. He's not going anywhere, Ches said. Deputy Murray might have been deaf. Mom's black dress was dirt-spotted in the back.

I wont bump my head, I said as I climbed into the cruiser's backseat.

Caint be too careful. The deputy mashed my head down so far I couldnt even *see* the roof.

They grilled us like week-old pork but Linda'd figured it right. Every detail got checked every way there was to turn it and then they'd turn me on the spit some more but I didnt offer one word that we hadnt gone over. I found out later that she'd even had the pokerfaced nerve to take them out and show them the deer we'd supposedly hit on I-64 and there happened to be one there or close enough to where she said. And then to confront the 7-11 clerk in Barnesville. He sneered at the deputy and said, Well sure I remember her. She bought a bag of chips and a bottle of pop.

Everything they tried to trip up kept its feet and they couldnt do anything about the rest.

They sprung me loose the day after the funeral and I read all about it in the paper and they'd got it right for once or at least right the way we told it. How I'd decided to leave here and go south and get a job. How Linda had gone along with it till I got too drunk to drive and then she'd doodled around in that direction till I'd passed out and then brought us home. But just before she got me home I'd roused up and made her drive through Bunk's fence into his back field and she was afraid if she didnt I'd start a ruckus and somebody would call the cops and we'd be in big trouble. So she'd done it but in the fog she'd run off the rubble-rock bridge into the creek.

Nobody knew she'd gotten drunk after that.

We was lucky there was a deer where you said, I lectured her when we were finally alone. And that the 7-11 clerk didnt care for cops.

Aw, there's a dead deer every half-mile on the interstate. And I stop at that Barnesville 7-11 every time I go to visit Sammy. I always get the key to the john and buy a bag of chips and a Coke. The same clerk's always there and he always flirts with me. She gave me that old soft smile I hadnt seen for a while. But you're going to have to keep your nose clean now, she said. The cops will watch every move you make from now on. Her lips turning hard and thin in such a pretty face.

The cops picked over every bumper on every coaltruck that hauled on Fingermill Road but they never found the truck that ran over Matt. Go figure. But you could ass-end a hippopotamus with a coaltruck's bumper and never even dull the chrome. We'd repeated the lie so many times I started to hate the stupid, greedy truckdriver running overweight and too fast just to make more money.

Then I remembered that I was the one they were looking for and I'd have to wonder just how hydrophobied a person could get and still walk around and pretend he had his right mind.

Jenny Yunker was waiting just outside the station's door when I was released but she didnt ask questions or write anything down on her little stenographer's pad. I know you killed Matt Tamper, she said in a pussy little voice that nobody else could hear. Her freckles like blood spatters on her pasty white skin.

Whatever drugs you're on, I could use some of them, I said. Her smile was anything but.

Just after breakfast on the day after Christmas, in a flurry of goodbye hugs and coffee kisses, we packed the car to leave Linda's home. The weather forecast sounded more like The Revelation and my patience was showing daylight in places while I sat in the Subaru revved the engine and adjusted mirrors.

Homer tapped on the window and I cranked it down. Thanks for bringing our little gal home for Christmas, he said. And for coming along with her.

I nodded and he squeezed my shoulder.

CHAPTER 14

The cold front rolled down off the Great Lakes like a steamroller made of snow and freezing rain that chased us south. The sky ahead was clear at first but the overhanging clouds boiled past us from behind and crushed us between worlds of white and gray. When I stopped to pump gas into the Subaru my thin jacket snapped and rattled like the faded Confederate flag over The Hole's door.

Linda was like a turkey stuffed with cheer but I was mean and as full of bad stuff as a spring bear that hadnt blown its plug yet. All I could find on the radio was noise without rhythm and rhythm without music and commentary that wouldnt pose an intellectual hurdle to a crawdad. I turned it off.

I'm so glad you went to your home.

Good for you. I brushed her hand away and twisted the radio's dial and punched a tape into the player and ejected it after three notes.

The snow came without prelude and the lines on the road disappeared and brake lights flickered as traffic slowed and fell into single file. A few drivers skittered past in a wash of left-lane slush, but not many. My nerve was good enough to join them but my tires werent.

Far ahead red lights flared and the guy in front of me braked hard and I had to throw us forward into the seatbelts and when I did the driver behind blew his horn at me. Then when I backed off from the vehicle ahead to make braking room the rectumhead back there hammered his lights onto high beam. God rest ye merry, gentlemen.

Up here's a rest area. I have to stop, Linda said.

You got to be kidding. We aint hardly got started.

She patted her stomach. There's a baby where my bladder was.

You'd best get a dadblamed move on. When I eased onto the off ramp, the car behind surged ahead to close the gap. I shot the driver the finger before I saw she was a little old blue-headed woman. Singing. Probably "Silent Night." She waved. One of those wiggly fingered ones. With a smile. Women intuit from birth how to make men feel like a rat turd in the tater salad.

Dont bust your yingyang on the sidewalk, either, I said. I dont got time to be going to the hospital.

You just simmer, she said, and tiptoed off to the bathroom at about a tenth of a mile an hour. I scraped the windows again and then sat in the car and brooded.

I had killed Matt on Monday, September 10, buried him on Thursday, and was home free before the weekend. That Saturday afternoon I stared out the bedroom window at the halo of mist the falling rain made around the roof of the old Dodge. The tire tracks that led to where I'd parked it behind the barn were already disappearing as the surrounding weeds laid down for their winter nap. The following summer new growth of goldenrod and poke would hide the car completely. I looked away, toward the driveway.

It felt like Matt should come jogging up the lane, leaping over the puddles and shaking water from his hair. Instead a long gray shadow nosed into the drive and wallowed my way. Brother Yunker parked his Lincoln sygogling in the turnaround place so it would be impossible to turn without a lot of backing and filling. Deacons poured from every door: Yunker, Ellersly, Thornton, Armbridge, Blake, Malon, and Bowles—all seven of them. Black umbrellas opened like poisonous mushrooms.

I met them at the door. Dad's in his study.

Yunker shook water from his bumbershoot onto the floor. We dont want to intrude.

Come in, Dad said as they crowded into his study. My goodness. Dan, hello. Henry. Woody. Gracious, you're all here. Let's go where there's more room.

We'll just be a minute, Yunker said. Get Mrs. Price here, too.

Dad's hand picked at a shirt button. She's not feeling well. His study was big enough for about half of them. At least let me move these books. But he looked back and forth at their faces and didnt move anything. Nobody sat down. Andy, tell your mother to come down.

Mom met me at the top of the stairs dressed in a shapeless rumpled robe. Her eyes like a dog's that's chewed up a billfold. I stood in the office door but Yunker said, Excuse us. They got the door closed somehow but part of what they were saying carried: Darrell, we had a special meeting last evening . . .

After just a couple of sentences I ran from the house. I was soaked through to the bone before I got to the mailbox but I turned right toward the church and almost immediately reversed past the driveway again. My shoes turned to lead and my skin was numb with sleet but I pounded into it for an hour or more before I returned.

A deep rut in the yard where Yunker had backed the Lincoln off the driveway was already full of water. All around were clods of mud where they'd stomped their feet clean after they'd pushed him out. One of them had thrown their mudcaked handkerchief toward the house. Serves you right, you bastards, I yelled into the rain. You *dirty* bastards.

Dad pored over his papers like nothing had happened but his bald spot was a waxy red blister in the middle of his head. A puddle grew around me on the floor but he didnt look up.

They fired you, I said.

He jumped at my voice. You're soaked. Grab a towel before you catch your death of cold.

Didnt they.

The wooden chair creaked as he leaned back. They've been unhappy with me for a long time.

Dammit, Dad, you didnt do anything wrong. None of us did, but least of all you.

I serve at their discretion.

Just once—just one time—cant you stand up for yourself? God aint going to send you to hell for looking out for yourself for a change.

Dad started to say something but then he sat up straight and chewed his lip and picked up a paper like he always did when he dismissed me. He put it back down. That's kind of hard to swallow right now. Just after I've squandered my integrity defending your lies.

My bruised face throbbed as the blood rushed in. I dont know what you're talking about.

Why'd you park the Dodge out behind the barn? If you're innocent, why did you quit driving?

I dont want to drive till I get a handle on my drinking. I didnt kill Matt but I could have. The truth was clamoring to get out but it didnt have any better chance of getting out on its own than a bad tooth did.

He slid open the top drawer of his desk and sat looking into it. The day they found Matt I stopped out at the scene to say a prayer. He shut the drawer and fingered his papers. I really liked that young man. He had so much potential.

Big deal. I loved him like . . .

Dont tell me about love. A voice I'd never heard. He hauled open the drawer again and clasped something in his hand and hit the desk lightly with his closed fist. I sat down on the bank to pray, he said, and when I opened my eyes this was in the grass between my feet. He opened his fingers and showed me a hair barrette and when he did another hand tightened around my chest.

The memory lanced clear and crisp and colorless: Linda crouches in the headlights with her head down and fingers tangling through her hair. Matt a rumpled shadow in the ditch beyond. She raises her head and tears glitter like ice flakes.

It's a hairpiece. A barrette. So what?

Not just any barrette. It's one I carved from a turtle shell. The one I gave Linda the first time you brought her home.

I didnt have any words to contest that so my hand struck out at the pile of worthless trash on his desk and the papers looped and settled but the thin wood corners of Dad's carving collapsed against my hand and the freed carved balls ricocheted from the wall and rolled across the hardwood flooring making sounds like faraway thunder.

Dad was quick for a big man. He was around the desk before I could think and as he closed on me I swung a weak blow that glanced off his forehead but he was all over me in a smother of hot nursing-home smell. He crushed me against the wall till I could barely yell: What kind of a father doesnt believe his own son?

I love you, he whispered.

I struggled and my head smashed his face and he recoiled and fingered the red worm that crawled from his nose and looked at his fingers like the blood was coming from them. Like he couldnt figure it out.

Mom burst into the room but I pushed past her and fled from the house.

———

I saw Dad again the next morning as I passed through the living room on my way to run. Church had started without him an hour ago, but he wore his best pinstriped suit. His hands were empty and still and it looked like his mind was too. Flesh sagged on his face and his jacket looked like a leaky air mattress. Good morning, Andy.

Hey. That's all I said.

When I returned, Dad was gone. I read the note he'd written for Mom (still in bed): *Gone to get things from church. Dinner date three of us p.m.?*

I'd run the other way, not toward the church and Matt's muddy grave, or I'd have been the one to find him. Not Bunker Reddy.

If I'd been the one to discover his body, if I'd had just a few minutes alone to say the words I should have said earlier . . . maybe I could have found some peace with it.

But till someone bothered to tell us that Dad was dead, a crowd of the same people who had killed him were gathered around the ambulance like flies on a cow's butt. Their insincere hugs and half-assed condolences turned me as hard and cold as I've ever felt. Dad had gone about halfway to the church before his car skidded to a stop in the ditch. He'd even stepped over the electric fence. Maybe heading for the big cowshade poplar across the pasture. Hoping to cool the fire that had erupted in his chest. Or maybe going there to pray.

Even if the cows hadnt been gathered round to point him out, Bunk had said, I'd a seen him. Layin there like a roadkilt buffalo. He didnt go far nor suffer much.

It's *nasty*, Linda said as she clambered back into the car. Water freckled the back of my hand when she brushed wet snow from her hair.

The next rest stop's twenty-seven miles. You make it that far or do you want to go again while we're here?

She pointed toward home.

A wedge of three snowplows with a long string of headlights behind beat me to the merge area. I worked into the traffic and within a mile gave up advancing through the pack. The slashing of snowflakes was mind numbing and somehow soothing.

So what happened at your home place?

Nothing. Why?

All of a sudden you're wanting to talk about it, when all this time you had it locked away.

When? I never said word one.

Last night. When I wanted to play games with my family.

You dont have the foggiest idea what I wanted to talk about. It was the recipe for that clovey cake I was wanting. And it dont matter anyway, since you didnt have the time to give it up.

You're the one that got pouty. Not me.

You're the one didnt have time to listen.

I'm listening now. Tell me what happened with your dad.

Here's what I got to say on the matter. I eased a cheek from the seat and cut loose a little bit of yesterday's turkey.

She rolled her window down a few inches and watched the snow go by till I was ready to bust. Well? she finally said.

She could well all she wanted to, but I wasnt about to spill my guts. Just because she told me to.

You got to stop again? I said when the next rest-stop sign hove up through the snow.

How far to the next one?

Thirty miles or so. An hour, probly.

I can make it.

I fiddled with the radio and the wipers and the defrosters and the rearview mirror but after a while it all came busting out. In the Old Testament they cut off your hand if you hit your parent, I said.

She touched the back of my wrist like she was considering what a one-handed husband would be worth. Is that what happened?

I smashed his nose with my head.

Tell me, she said. So I told her what had happened that day with Dad.

She interrupted at the deacon's visit. But why'd they fire him? Did they think he was somehow to blame for Matt? I dont understand.

I'd wooled it around long enough that it was straight in my head. They *said* it was because of some kind of dirt Jenny Yunker dug up about before he came here. I wouldnt even listen to it. Because if there was one person on the earth that didnt have any dirt in his life it was my dad. He was hard and strict—I'll give you that much—and that's what frosted their punkins. But to get rid of him they had to blame him for my faults. And Mom's.

Jenny Yunker was that skinny blonde girl in our algebra class?

She was bony but she had red hair and freckles. Beaver teeth.

Why would she even care?

I dont know. She never did like me. But along about high school she got real nasty about it.

Linda didnt interrupt again until I came to the part about Dad finding her barrette.

Oh dear God. She turned her head to the window.

Dad lied, but he wouldnt have lived with it if he'd had the chance. He'd have come clean.

Just from what little I knew of him I can believe that.

And I'd already decided to tell the truth but I never got the chance to either. Cause he died before I could and then it was too late.

Her next words were long in coming and harsh when they arrived: So do you want your hand taken off by a surgeon or do you want me to whack it off with the axe?

It aint nothing to joke about.

I'm not joking. She turned away but not before I saw the tears behind her anger. It wasnt your fault. His heart gave out. He was going to die anyway.

But he wouldnt have died a liar.

What was his sin? Loving his son? Dont you think God forgave him that one little slip after all the good work he did?

Right there was the mouse in the cornmeal. Sin is sin, I said. There aint one lick of difference between a little white liar and a fornicator and a murderer. They all burn in the same hellfire.

Oh, what a crock. That same hellfire flashing in her eyes.

I backed off the car ahead before I pushed him off the road. If that's not the truth, then Dad was stupid. Cause that's what he preached. And he wasnt stupid.

What about God's grace? I *know* he believed that.

Oh, yeah, you got your God's grace, but that's conditional to God's laws. And there aint loophole one in the law. Dont think I aint looked.

If that's the way it is there wont be anybody in heaven. Nobody could ever be good enough.

One was till I sent him to hell. He lived the best life you could live and then I fucked it all up right at the end.

I dont want to hear any more of this nonsense.

Surprise, surprise. *Tell me what happened*, I mocked.

She turned again to the window and rubbed her big belly like she was soothing a pet. When she finally spoke, it was in a quiet voice that I could barely hear. Tell me the rest.

Like hell, I thought. But till Linda got back from the next rest stop, my gums were beating again.

You know how Mom was, even before Dad died, I said. She laid in the bed all day while I shopped and cleaned and worked the garden. Dad tried cooking but it was easier for me to cook than to clean up his dishes. One time I took the skillet out and beat it over a fencepost till I thought I had the burned grease hammered out but when I put it on the stove it melted. I'd wore the skillet off and left the grease. And without Bunk's tractor and chain I never would have got the weeds pulled out of the garden.

Linda smiled. Dont get caught up in your storytelling. I thought your mom was getting better. She'd quit smoking and even started going to church. I remember her singing one evening out on the edge of the porch.

She got better but she got over that quick.

I never understood why you ran off. It doesnt make sense to go turn into a woods animal just because your mom's depressed.

Depressed aint the word for it. She slid into a septic tank and tried to drag me in with her. (*Tried?* Maybe I shouldnt of put that word in.) But you're right. That's not why I went out and lived in the State Forest for a spell.

Like the memory had swirled up out of the defroster and I'd sucked it up my nose, I recalled a tourist stopping to ask Bunk Reddy how to get to the State Forest. Bunk said, Go on to the road fork. If you turn right you'll see a old broke-down silo in a apple orchard and past that you cross Gandy's Fork and then watch close on the uphill side for a graveyard growed over in briars. Half a mile past that—before that big string of woods with NO TRESPASSING posters—they's a crossroads.

Bunk raised his eyebrows and both the man and the woman nodded. Well dont go that way, Bunk said. That there's the wrong road. Take that other fork and the State Forest is just hair near everwhere you look. Big trees and stuff. Yeller paint on the trees.

Somehow Mom figured out about Matt, I said. Either Dad told her or she wooled it out on her own. But just about every day she'd say, Andy, tell me what really happened. I wanted to tell her bad but I couldnt.

I know. Linda's voice as soft as it ever got. It was my secret, too.

But there wasnt someone trying to lever it out of you every day. She was like a extra conscience. I had to get away from it. All the time I packed my camping gear she followed me around the house whining like a pup. I could hear her a hundred yards down the road as I went walkabout. I could *still* hear her. And you didnt help none. I mimicked Linda's nagging: *You better keep your nose clean. They're watching you.* Linda's face closed down but she asked for it. You wanted to hear some stuff, I got some to give you.

CHAPTER 15

The night had been hard and brittle. Ice crunched in the creek's edge where I squatted to drink. Smoke curled from my bullheaded fire and turned my fingers black but not warm. My month-old beard scratched my throat like a rake made of icicles and my broken nails were dirt-rimmed and I hadnt had a bath since the creek got more cold than my stink was strong. But my mind was firing again. At least on a couple of cylinders.

I blew on the fire and fed twigs till it strengthened and when my hands were warm I straddled the flames with my feet. My dirty foot showed where the sole had peeled away from the upper. There wasnt much left of the sock.

You are one cold miserable empty-headed waste of good air, I said. Out loud like I'd done since I'd turned into an animal.

For a while I'd talked mostly to Matt: the lines of his poems I could remember, conversations rehashed and improved. Sometimes at night I'd raise my head and look across the fire for his sleepingbag. I'd rattled on to Dad some, too. And now I was down to talking to myself. About going home. I fingered the four .22 shells left in my pocket and yearned for a bath and a hot meal and for pencil and paper. Toilet paper.

The trees stood black and bare and the vines and briars were dead.

What you say we go home? Like the idea had just popped up.

I hatcheted a hole in the rocky dirt and buried my empty cans and the half-gallon whiskey bottle I'd used for a water jug when the liquor was gone. I gathered the rifle and the tent and the sleepingbag and the frypan and started from the State Forest toward home.

I already knew what I'd say to Mom. *You believe what you want. I had nothing to do with Matt. And that there's the God-strike-me-down-dead truth.* Then I'd wait for the new hope in her eyes.

Snow pricked my skin and the western sky was heavy with more. It was a good time to go home. The road was even whiter than the forest and the lone car that passed drifted and then spun as the driver studied me in the mirror.

The riffles of snow in our driveway were unmarked. No smoke drifted from the chimney. The door was locked and the dog was gone. I found the key atop the back-porch rafter. Mom's note was on the kitchen table. *I kind of believed you till you ran off.*

That's okay. You'll come back. Or I'll find you. Either way, I'll convince you.

When the kindling was roaring I loaded heavier wood and shoveled coal into the furnace and soon the smell of hot sulfur nosed through the house and the iron grates popped as the air warmed. I was drinking my fourth or fifth cup of coffee and scratching my cheek when I looked out the kitchen window and saw what I'd missed earlier.

A leg protruded from behind the doghouse like a gnarled stick thrust into the frozen mud. I stopped on the back porch and groaned and hobbled barefoot across the lawn to see what I already knew. A possum had been at Fiddler, or rats. Hair tore loose when I prized him loose from the ground, and the chewed remains of his plastic bowl came with him. I held him in my arms and tried to comprehend what had happened. I looked across the field and into the woods and toward the mailbox at the end of the long lane and at the turnaround where the meter reader would have parked—all too far away to notice an abandoned dog.

How could you, Mom? I'd never hated more. Nobody had.

Two hours later, when I'd finally chipped away enough frozen ground, I placed Fiddler's body in the jagged hole and covered him with nuggets of muddy ice. You deserve better. That's all I said.

Snow turned to sleet as Linda and I got closer home. Ice made pretty velvet antlers out of the oak limbs and signposts and then smashed them to earth. Linda broke the long silence that had followed my outburst of ancient history. Help me understand why you were still going to lie about what happened. Even after they knew.

It wasnt for my benefit. I cant change what happened. But I could give her some peace about it. (It felt reasonable till I said it out loud.)

Linda raised her hand like I'd threatened to hit her. I'm not accusing you. Just trying to make sense of it.

Taillights lit the snow ahead again and I pumped the brakes and watched the mirror. Traffic was backed past our exit but I crunched past on the shoulder. Well? Dont it make sense?

Several times her lips parted, but it took a while for her to get it out: The truth can be nasty. Sometimes you cant stand it but you cant stand to get rid of it either.

You got that right.

She put her hand on my arm like I'd interrupted, but she'd got it exactly right. Mom couldnt of stood the truth, I said. She couldnt handle her own problems much less get saddled with mine.

That's not what I mean. Even when you have the best of reasons to lie the truth just keeps rotting and festering and when it finally comes out—and it does, it *always* does—it's even worse than it was to start with. Like Vienna sausages gone bad. Canned hate.

You want to talk about hate? What if I tied up Funky and left her to starve? Then you'd get some grip on what hate is. Then you wouldnt be acting like The Truth was a crossword puzzle with just one right answer.

You left the dog there too, Andy. That's not why you hated your mom.

I wasnt the last one . . .

You hated your mom because you thought she knew you. The same reason you hate yourself.

Within a mile of slamming my frustrations out on the poor old Subaru, my hand had quit hurting to where I could tell it wasnt broken. The dashboard didnt fare that good. Linda touched my leg and a while later my hand wandered over and touched hers. Whatever that meant.

Route 29 was splashed half dry but the side roads close to home were glassy. Traffic oozed in the glittery gloom.

Linda couldnt leave it alone. Your Mom *tried* to make up with you. She wrote but you threw it in the trash and never answered.

One smartalecky birthday card.

I didnt read it that way. I thought the barb was at her, not you. An apology.

What. You snoop through my trash now?

When I have to.

Hell's bells. I guess I'll have to start burning it.

Good. Run the vacuum too while you're at it.

Some conversations are like catching bobcats. It aint that hard to get one cornered but sometimes there's a measure of difficulty in turning it loose again. Dad aint hardly dead till she shacks up with somebody I never even heard of, I said. One birthday card wipes all that out?

Two years? Not hardly dead? And what does it matter if you knew him or not?

The car drifted on the next turn because I was running too fast and didnt care. You dont know anything about it.

Linda unsnapped her seatbelt and leaned the seat back and groaned and massaged her back. I probably know more than I want to. She shook her head. Thank you for sharing.

You asked for it.

Yes. I did.

I downshifted and turned up Hungry Holler Road. Almost home. Well I'll tell you what. I'm glad she's dead. *She's* most likely tickled about it. (Maybe I'd been sad for a minute when Alison Reddy called and said she was in intensive care with a stroke. And yes, I did cry a couple of hours later when I heard she didnt make it. But you know how drunks are. They'll sing "Amazing Grace" around a case of beer and bust out bawling over a dead miller and then back up to finish off a cat they ran over on their way to fornicate with their cousin. By the time Linda and I had gotten there—too late for the viewing and I sure didnt request a private show—I'd got to the cat-killing stage. Just once I wish I could get shut of a hangover that easy.

Nobody'd told me that the church had shut down. They opened it up just for her funeral—I reckon no place else would have her—and it smelled of bat manure and mildew. I had to admit she was pretty stretched out peaceful and still. Some preacher I'd never heard of dripped snot and tears and talked like they were best of friends but he had no clue what she was really like. Linda bawled and whimpered but I beat back any such nonsense by thinking about my dad and my old dog Fiddler.

At the graveside service I waited beside Dad's headstone while the people took one last chance to throw dirt on her. More of them than I'd expected.

When Linda drove us past the old home place I looked in the other direction, over toward the State Forest. We went into Hardly and parleyed with the lawyer and then a Realtor and it wasnt a week till I got a call that we had an offer. I was tickled that Bunk and Alison were getting the place and not some touron but I was even gladder a couple months later when the check came. It was enough money for us to move out of our mean little apartment and into a squalid little place of our own. I probably drank up what was left, not that there was that much.

The iced-over trailer park looked like gilded rubble. A king's junkyard. Getting out of the world of four-lane highways was good but I wasnt all fired up to get back into this one. I sat in the Subaru after Linda got out.

She rapped on the window. Help me carry stuff in.

Go on fore you turn your panties yeller. I'll get it. There wasnt much: two tattered suitcases and a cardboard box of gifts and a bag of apples. The power had gone out, though the lights were working again now, and the trailer was a dank, clammy tomb.

Funky scattered pups everywhere as she dashed back and forth and acted happy to see us. Keepers of the food. Linda reset the clock and then we snuggled on the couch under a blanket and waited for the heat to come up. Funky gave up after I pushed her off the third time and sprawled to let the pups take tittie.

Look there at that one pup, I said. What's amatter with him?

One puppy had gotten confused by the maze of table and chair legs and stood whining and smelling. He squirmed once when I picked him up but then hung possum-like in my hand. Linda stroked his nose with one finger and his little tail fired up like a windshield wiper. His eyes were cloudy and unfocused and didnt track my hand. I slapped at his face without touching him. He didnt blink.

Dont hurt him.

I aint. I think he's blind. I batted at him again with the same results.

Poor baby. She cuddled him against her neck and he discovered her earlobe and suckled. She closed her eyes for a minute and let him suck before she hauled him away. You wont find milk there, puppy. She uncoupled one of the bigger pups from one of Funky's front-row tits and attached the blind one in its place.

We ought to name them. Or shoot them, one. It aint good for them to be without proper identification. How they going to know which one I'm cussing?

The blind one's so much like you he's just got to be Junior.

Show one patch of skin through a chink in your armor and they got a switchblade buried in it. I considered arguing that the blind puny ignorant wormy soon-to-be castrated mutt of questionable lineage was nothing like me but decided I didnt want to tackle the argument unprepared. We going to name that fat one Linda, then?

I'm just *temporarily* fat. It's getting a *permanent* name. She picked one up and turned it upside down like she was inspecting a pear for rotten spots. Marybelle. Each one she named like this then put it back on its tit.

Alice.

Snoot.

Aw, that's a ugly name.

It's a male.

They just dont make armor that fits anymore.

Belinda. Prissy. And Junior. Discussion over.

She crawled back under the covers with me and as the sun went down the heat came up and I slid off into a doze.

She stirred and said, I love you.

Mmmm, I said on the off chance she was talking to me.

She kissed me and rubbed my cheek and nuzzled into the hollow of my neck and shoulder. Why does truth scare us so? she said. I dont just mean people like us who have something to hide, either. Everybody's afraid of it. She sighed and went to sleep.

You ever notice that? How women hand off crap that would turn Rip Van Winkle into an insomniac and then instantly fall asleep. Like Rip said, the tongue is the only edge tool that grows keener from constant use.

She snored. I bumbled around in the past like a blind dog on the freeway.

I'd buried Fiddler and stuffed clothing and what money and valuables I could find in a gym bag and thumbed south. Toward Alabama, though I never figured out why. Maybe I figured there was someone there lower than me on the food chain. Do they still got slaves? But I didnt get there. I hung up on a liquor store before I even got loose of West Virginia.

Linda found me in the Ransom Mini-Mall one Saturday morning three months later. My room smelled like a pigsty and the wind had teeth so I sprawled on a short bench just inside the door.

Hi Andy, this woman said. You running from me? She stood at parade rest and bounced on her toes. The corners of her eyes were wrinkled like apples that had got lost in the produce drawer and her yellow blouse had a coffee-colored Rorschach on one breast. A buzzard eatin rutabakers it looked like to me.

Looking up made my stomach roll so I looked somewhere else. At a fat woman in chartreuse stretch pants. An old man inch-worming on a four-footed cane.

No security guards, though. I ducked inside my jacket for my bottle and a blast of warm wind swept the dandelion fluff from my head and I knew this woman. Linda. Linda . . . Lawton.

After five minutes or an hour or so I said, Hi, and it sounded like the crotch tearing out of my pants. Maybe I should of said, How are you? or something along those lines but instead I said, What in jumpin up hell do you want?

Not happy to see me? Words like a warning shot that catches you squarely between the eyes. Colorless lips.

Something was gnawing in my armpit but I couldnt find it. I steadied myself on the edge of the bench and gathered my feet under me.

No you dont, she said. I'm sick of chasing after you. She was sitting beside me then rubbing circles on my back but her other hand had fast of my belt.

You leave me be.

My my. Sounds like somebody's memory got in gear.

I leaned back and mashed her hand between my back and the seat but she didnt loosen her grip.

I think we need to talk about it, she said.

I got nothing to talk about.

Not even about Matt?

Matt. The name was in my brain like a workboot in a clothes drier. Get away from me. I hove up and my foot slithered on the tile floor and I did a pirouette like a one-legged duck and missed the armrest and my arm jammed through the hole under it and my mouth rattled against the edge and the taste of a copper penny filled my mouth. Now look what you done. I sat back down and looked at the blood on my fingers.

Shhh. Settle down. Her hair flicked across my face as she glanced around. Dont get all wound up. She touched my broken lip and her sweet earthy smell made me gag but there was nothing in me but liquor and I wasnt about to turn that loose.

I sat there with my head between my knees and wondered where I'd gotten red sneakers. Footsteps clomped my way and a polished black brogan and a blue pantsleg with a khaki stripe horned into the picture.

It's okay, Linda said. He's not well. I'm here to take him home.

Get him out of here, the security guard said. I've warned him before.

She kissed the back of my neck and I gagged again and the shoes went away. Come on, she said. We have to move. She had her fingernails in my arm and I didnt have the intestinal fortitude to hang back.

Sorry I make you sick, she said when the security guard fell out of sight. Not sounding sorry a-tall. I was half aware of going into the Hardee's at the off-end of the mall and then she was gone again and I put my head down and slept a little. The sun had shifted around the corner of the skylight to warm my arm before I heard her again: Sit up and eat.

I dont want nothing. I pushed the burger and fries away but drank of the Coke and the bubbles went up my nose and made me cough.

She bit into her sandwich like she was good and ready to bite one and she auger-eyed me the whole time. So. Who all have you told about Matt?

Matt. Matt Tamper. Nobody, I said. That dead boy. I aint *clear* stupid, I said. Just relatively.

She chewed and drank and belched into her napkin. You're not too good at keeping your mouth shut. Or remembering if you did.

I aint talked to anyone *period* other than to pay the rent and whatnot. The hot grease smells were making me both pukid and hungry. I took a fry and wooled it in my mouth.

Eat up, she said. I'll be right back.

When she turned the corner to the bathroom I grabbed the burger and lurched up out of the chair and got on with my life. The janitor's closet in the bathroom was unlocked till I got in it. I sat on a scrub bucket and chewed the burger. Stall doors flapped and the doorknob rattled and a man said, What the bloomin hell, lady, and then the racket went away where it belonged.

I finished the sandwich and gave her time to get clear gone before I headed for the exit but she squirted out of the used bookstore like a running back trying to turn the corner and I dodged into the His-n-Hers with her hollering behind and ducked under a rack of lingerie and a red-faced woman took up the chase and the caress of silk and the smell of women's things got something to working in me that I thought was dead. Some blue slinky thing caught on my jacket button and tore loose from the hanger and followed me like a bad dream out the back door into the parking lot before I could get shed of it. It wasnt but twenty yards to where the pavement fell off to scrubby woods and she went the other way toward a rusted Dumpster and that was all the chance I needed to get gone. Ransom had more dogs than showed up on the census but after a long trial of backyards and chain-link fences I found an alley that took me to a street and the street took me to Rim Road and that took me to my room.

While I fumbled with the key the door of an old Dodge Dart with rusted quarter panels creaked open and she got out and stretched like we'd just come home from a long drive.

She didnt knock long, hardly even an hour. I dozed but woke up each time she started the old slant-six to run the heater. The valves clattered and if it had an exhaust system it was well concealed. I wouldnt hear it for a while and I'd think that she'd vamoosed but then it would rattle and roar again. Late in the afternoon the knocking started again and went on and on until I jerked the door open to cuss her and she crowded past and said, Get out of the way, I got to pee.

I heard her say, Yuck. When she came out she said, Where's your broom?

She swept the room and the bathroom and by then she knew that I didnt have a dustpan or a trashcan so she left the dirt in a pile next to the wall and sat down on the edge of the bed. I dont care for unfinished business, she said.

You ought not of started then. The maid's due in tomorrow.

I'm not talking about cleaning and you know it.

I didnt know anything. That's the only thing I knew for sure.

She went to call her folks and I left the door unlocked because it wouldnt take another siege like the last one. Some of the mean had run out of her and a tired look had taken over. She ordered pizza and ate most of it herself including the onions I picked off my slice and then she wondered could she take a nap before she headed back and I waved at the bed and told her to rip on it. She started snoring almost before her eyes went shut.

I swept the pile of dirt she'd made into the pizza box and took it out and put it in the neighbor's trashcan and sat on the curb in the pale early-afternoon sun till I got chilled and then went inside and sat against the wall and watched her sleep and after a while I nodded off myself.

When I woke she was sitting on the corner of the bed watching me with her hands like kittens sleeping in her lap. The sun raked low through the crack under the door and my back felt broken. I got things rowed up in my mind and said, How'd you find me?

I showed your picture at liquor stores.

Try that on for size sometime and see how it feels.

You made it farther than I figured, she said.

Why'd you bother?

Like I said, I dont like unfinished business. She stood and looked down at me and I could see inside her nose and she sat again but her hands argued and squirmed. I need to tell you something.

She sat staring at her hands and while she did two black bars appeared in the crack of sunlight under the door and a voice said, Linda? and she looked at me and said, Who's that? and in a bigger voice, Hello, and the shadows retreated and then the unlocked door bowed in and splinters flew from the jamb and the door flew back against the wall and a short muscular man staggered through the door and stood blinking and his eyes found me and before I could get up he kicked me in the side and my guts and my wind tangled up and he kicked me on the shoulder and his heel skittered into my throat and right then I knew I was going to die.

Linda was on him with fingernails and teeth and while he was shaking her off I dragged up onto the edge of the bed so I wouldnt get kicked to death but his fists were harder than his feet and smelled of snuff and a shower of sparks flared behind my eyes and I went down on the bed and pulled the pillow over my head and he started pounding me in the kidneys, the same place over and over again till I rolled away and felt my ribs cave in and then he grunted and cursed and said, You little whore, and I slithered off the far side of the bed and pulled the little end table down on top of me and it was quiet for a second and then the table blew up and a jagged splinter appeared in the web of my thumb and forefinger like it had grown there and things started to go gray as my throat thrashed against the plug that had been driven tight inside.

Damn you, he said and grunted again and there was scuffling and a whimpering, the same sound over and over like a dog that's hurt bad, and the door banged against the wall again and feet slid in the gravel outside and a fender popped and a door opened and after a moment closed and a motor started and tires squalled out onto the highway.

My air came back like I was breathing through a swizzle stick at first and then through a straw and finally in gulps that tore through my throat like coils of barbwire. I crawled under the bed as far as I could get and I remember thinking I wished they'd closed the door and then the day folded down around me like a dark, cold cocoon.

I heard her sniffles first and then the door closed and she said, Andy? Oh God, Andy.

I spoke out when her hand touched my back and I felt the bed's pressure lessen and the legs groaned on the floor as she slid it over against the wall. She rolled me over and I made another sound and opened my eyes but only one would open. A dark red dirty welt sliced down her cheek like an Indian's warpaint and her bra showed where the flap torn from her blouse folded down against her belly. One of the fingernails on the hand that felt of my face was torn loose and bleeding.

I examined the three-inch splinter through my hand and put the big end of it between my teeth and pulled it out. It tasted like soap and felt like a string being pulled through the hole. She disappeared and the faucet ran and she came back with a wad of wet toilet paper and touched it here and there to my face. She lifted my lips one at a time. I dont think he broke any teeth.

I tried to talk and coughed and she helped me sit up and I said, I always been lucky like that.

Can you walk?

I mostly always have been able to. I just aint all that anxious to do it right now. Only enough air would come in at one shot to get out two or three words.

She laughed and shook her head and dabbed at her fingernail with the bloody toilet paper. If you can still joke you must not be as bad as you look.

I inventoried all the things inside me that were either afire or located where something else ought to be. Is he gone?

I think so. He tried to take me home but I got loose and jumped out at the first stopsign. I dont think he'll come back. He's scared of how bad he hurt you.

The coward, I said. I stirred what I knew until it started to make sense. Your brother.

Slick.

You called home. Told them where you were.

I'm sorry. I had no idea.

I tried to get to my feet but a red fog built in my head and I lay over on my side on the bed. Thanks for your help, I said when I got my air gathered up again. A fire had been kindling in my lower back and was trickling down to my groin and I got onto my knees and Linda helped me to the bathroom and I sat there until I couldnt stand it any longer and tried not to look at the red clotted water that spiraled down the drain.

I ought to be going, she said when I opened the door. Will you be all right?

Never been better. I sat on the edge of the bed and tried not to move anything.

She went in the bathroom and closed the door and opened it and said, There's blood in the toilet.

Dont worry about it. Like I said, the maid will get it in the morning. Her and the butler took a day off.

She looked back at the toilet that didnt flush as good as it ought to and she shut the door again and when she came back out her blouse was gone. Her bra was bigger than her boobs and puckered where it shouldnt of. Do you have a shirt I can wear? She sorted through what I had on the closet shelf and chose a T-shirt and turned her back and tucked it into her pants and then she got me under the arms and said, Come on.

I wasnt in much shape to fight so I let her help me out to her car. She stopped at a Shell station for directions and after a couple of wrong turns we parked in front of a white aluminum-siding ranchhouse with double glass doors in the front. A man in a blue jumpsuit came out with her and they helped me inside and he squeezed and prodded everywhere and looked into my eyes and at my hand and said that I had to go up to the hospital at Clarksburg. I said I wouldnt and he couldnt make me.

He shrugged and looked at Linda and she shrugged. He bandaged my hand and told me to breathe deep till my ribs knitted and wrote prescriptions to stop infection and to help my bones grow together and one that made me feel so daggoned good about the whole deal that I was hopped up ready to do it all again.

I woke in the middle of the night and listened to her breathe and found the pill bottle without waking her and held it in my hand without opening it. I felt my forehead and it felt hot and felt my hand and that felt hot and after a while I dozed off.

My fever dropped the following Thursday and she went home but came back on Sunday with a cardboard box full of clothes and another of cleaning supplies and vitamin pills and a little radio. After a while I got used to her and quit marveling each time I realized she was there. I still stopped to listen every time I heard tires crunch in the graveled parking lot but Slick never came back.

Every day she changed my dressing and worried at my sore muscles and made me eat. She talked and laughed and I mostly listened and a couple of weeks later when I could stand up straight without my breath hanging up on the jaggers of my broken ribs we both stood up straight in front of the Justice of the Peace and said our vows again for the record.

When my body had healed all it was going to she went to work on the rest of me. Something was missing, though: some three-cent part that made me crap out every time she started to depend on me. But she kept fixing with tape and wire and baler twine the way women repair stuff. I reckon I should of been grateful.

Lying on the couch all these years later with my arm pinned under her warmth, listening to the petty complaints of feeding puppies and thinking about my baby growing inside my woman, I got blindsided so slick that I didnt even have time to blink before a tear streaked down my cheek.

My lengthy career at Workman's had accrued one whole day of vacation that I had to take or lose, so Linda took an extra day off, too. The sleet had shot its wad and by afternoon the temperature had niggled up and the ice rattled from the trees like a rockslide from heaven. Salt and road grime from the car made a gray lava flow down the driveway from where I washed the Subaru. As rotten as the talk had been the day before, I'd never slept better and I felt as complete as I ever had. Like my two lives—the one right now that made me so happy I cried and the one from before that trailed like a half-shat tapeworm—finally had some relationship. Third cousins maybe.

I had energy to splurge even after I'd washed the car so I lit into cleaning the shed. But I hardly got started till I rolled back a dirty rag and found two cans of beer nesting like mice in the bottom of a five-gallon bucket. They were hard and real and mean like a devil's touchstones. I crammed the junk back into the shed and locked the door and changed clothes without interrupting Linda's nap and then I pounded long and hard into a north wind that warmed as I ran.

CHAPTER 16

Linda's contentment puffed up along with her belly till my cynicism was outgunned. We considered a sonogram but decided to be surprised. Too much like opening your presents before Christmas. The doc said everything was normal and I always did say if it aint broke leave it the hell alone. Or it will be.

New construction froze solid in January and Workman's business was as sluggish as the sink drain. I asked Ken for something extra to do so I wouldnt get laid up with boredom so he put me to counting inventory and showed me how to punch the numbers into the computer. I wont suggest that didnt make me feel important.

Neither will I claim that alcohol didnt feel me up in the middle of the night and on lonely days in the cold warehouse. But I slapped its hand one flirtation at a time and each time gave me a little extra horsepower for the next. If I'd look crosseyed at my life I could almost see a normal one. Like an impressionist painting. Up close something you'd whack the dog for but from the right distance pretty as a bucket of boobs.

But even I'm not stupid enough to expect it to last.

One night when I walked into the driveway it was empty and the trailer was dark and still. No note. Funky bared her teeth at me. I sat at the kitchen table with my forehead on my arms and let my fear and hunger churn together into one feeling I knew but couldnt call by name. Dreading its approach. Welcoming its arrival. I saw Linda laid open like a field-dressed deer on an operating table somewhere. Tasted whiskey. Felt it in my stomach and veins and tongue.

Then I heard the bumblebee-in-a-tin-can rattle of the Subaru and the crunch of her tires. When I met her at the door I was breathing hard. Where you been anyway?

Carry that stuff in for me. She kissed my forehead and crowded past me and disappeared into the bathroom.

She was in there long enough for me to carry in the boxes and to get excited about what was in them and to work up a halfway-decent mad. When she emerged from the bathroom I was rapping my knuckles on the biggest box that held the monitor. Just who's gonna pay for this?

It's paid for. I laid back a little bit each week for a long time.

I kicked at a smaller box, not hard enough to hurt it but close. You held back *our* money while *I'm* trying to get out of debt. That's just wrong.

Right there's where her voice would always go serrated and I'd get madder and bust a hole in the wall and she'd lock herself in the bedroom and I'd go to The Hole.

It was just my insurance policy for when you broke worthless again. She sawed at the cardboard with a butcher knife.

I came at it from the other end: Well, what happens if I screw up now? Since you spent the insurance money on a playtoy?

I dont need it anymore. Lift that thing out of there.

She didnt say another word until we'd connected the cables and plugged everything in. Do I click on this? she said. I'm scared to do anything.

I sat beside her and put my hand over hers and mashed her finger down onto the mouse button like I knew what I was doing. You're not as scared as I was. I thought something bad had happened to you.

She grabbed me by the point of the chin and shook it. Nothing. Is. Going. To. Happen.

The next few evenings were some of the best I can remember. We sat side by side and heat leaked into me from her gentle furnace and our hands nestled over the mouse and everything was as new and exciting as a tent revival.

I hope you didnt buy this just for me, I said. Just because I like the one at work.

I bought it because the place I'm working is going out of business and I'll have to know how to use a computer to get another job.

Aw. Not trying to keep the disappointment out of my voice as hard as I should.

She made a screensaver that scrolled *I love Andrew Price, a friend of mine* over and over like she was chanting it. I thought about making her one but you can only have one.

So maybe we did argue some. When you look back you have to wonder just how good life is if you're fighting over a mouse.

And right about then's when the wheels started to shimmy.

An old Pontiac Tempest with a bad case of the mange coughed into Workman's yard like it had emphysema as bad as the driver. The window skreeked down and a pasty-faced woman with black sunglasses said, Hey.

Howdy do. What can I get for you?

She passed over a pick ticket for two pieces of pine.

Pull down to door number four, please. Right on the other side of that yeller forklift.

She was standing outside the car smoking a cigarette when I returned and together we finagled the boards through the passenger-side window and lassoed them to the mirror. Something about her was familiar. Do I know you from somewhere? I said.

I cant imagine it. She removed her glasses and looked at me the way you'd look at a condom in a bowl of chili. Her plastic nametag said Beverly and her generic white pants and blouse said waitress or maybe cashier. Worn out and skinny like ten thousand others around. She broke down in a fit of coughing and ground out the butt under a dirty white tennis shoe and got in and revved the Tempest and was gone. I looked for a name on the pick ticket but it said *Cash Customer*. I spiked it on the board inside the warehouse and didnt think much more about her.

Three days later I heard her coming before I saw her. The sound of the Tempest's engine depressed me in a way I couldnt find a handle on. She was polite while I loaded a bag of cement into the rust-holed trunk but she put me in a surly and short-tempered frame of mind that hung on like a mosquito bite.

Ken had a big push on to finish the inventory, so the following day he moved me inside to punch inventory into the computer while the other yard apes counted. He watched and slurped coffee behind my shoulder for a while and then touched me on the shoulder and left me to it.

I brushed a wet strand of hair from Linda's face and pulled her down on the couch with me. You knew the rental store was closing. You been saying it for months.

But I hoped they'd hang on till the baby came.

It'll be all right. We can get by on what I make.

She reached across me for a tissue and wiped at her eyes. It's the insurance I'm worried about. What if something goes wrong?

They talk about some kind of COBRA thing at work where they got to keep you on insurance for eighteen months after you're gone.

But we'd have to pay for it. And I already checked how much it would be. She threw her tissue at the trashcan by the door but didnt come close. It's almost $600 a month.

Bag that. I'd never worried too much about paying doctors anyway. Or lawyers. Bottom feeders. Maybe I can get Ken to put me on Workman's insurance. I think you're supposed to work there six months first but he can make it happen if he wants to.

Will you? For sure?

What do I got to lose?

Some dude in a three-piece suit had taken over Ken's office with a laptop computer and stacks of yellow pads and ledgers and rolls of register tapes. I found Ken leaning against a kitchen cabinet display chewing on his fingernails and looking like he'd swallowed a termite.

I reckon anyone with a thimbleful of brains would have come back some other time. But you'd have to ask someone besides me if you wanted to know for sure.

Hey, Ken, I said. Looks like you got run out of your office.

Yeah. The accountant took it over.

Aw. Common sense flared up like a match and died just as quick. Well, you should have done good last year. It's slow now but we had a magnacious fall.

You cant win either way. If you made money, now's the time you send it all in.

Aint that the way. (Like I'd paid taxes before, too.)

What's up?

I need you to slip me onto your insurance. My wife just lost her job and we got a kid on the way.

Sorry. There's nothing I can do about that. You have to be here thirteen full pays before I can put you on. And even then I couldnt if she was already pregnant. That's a pre-existing condition.

I glanced around and eased close and lowered my voice. This here's ole Andrew Price you're talking to, Ken. I aint going to tell stuff around. I known you got rules to follow but I never seen one that didnt have some give to it. We need a little help here.

His features scooted in till they didnt use up so much of his face. They're not my rules and I wouldnt break them if they were. Especially if they were.

There aint nothing anymore fun than rules to break. Dishes or clay pigeons dont even come close.

He focused on me in a way I didnt care for. Like he'd touched me where I dont hardly even touch myself. Dont you have some work to do?

All right, all right. I know you aint had a good day. The taxman cometh and all that. But you think about it and I'll check back with you later.

No, dont you do that. I told you how it is.

Good deal, buddy, I said and patted him on the shoulder and winked at him like he'd said just the other. I appreciate it.

From the look on his face I could see it wasnt going to happen. But I give it a shot anyway.

The next morning I almost called in sick. The wet and chill had worked into my bones and I woke with a fever and a briary throat. And I was on Ken's list anyway.

But I'm not that smart.

I watched Linda while she slept. I held my hand just away from her mouth and felt her breathing and touched her hair and then I rested my hand on her belly ever so lightly and after a few seconds something moved inside and then was still again. I kissed her on the cheek without waking her and dressed and shaved and kicked Funky out of the way and walked down the hill to catch my ride.

CHAPTER 17

The air was as damp and uncomfortable as a wool bathing suit as I left the trailer park. Dirty clouds rolled over the treetops and the air stunk of the papermill forty miles away. A skinny calico one-eared cat crouched beside a guardrail post and tensed but didnt run when I hawked and spat its way. I shivered and felt like I had a hairball caught in my throat.

Doug was late picking me up at The Hole and then bitchy about stopping at Revco long enough for me to buy cough syrup.

Ken hadnt invited me inside since the inventory was finished and with business so slow I was running out of things to do between customers. The lumber was stacked and the trash was picked up and the floors were suitable for fine dining so that morning I mostly leaned on my broom and coughed and watched the rain fall. Two doses of cough syrup a half-hour apart didnt budge the hairball in my throat so I took a horse dose that nearly emptied the bottle and then felt dopey and pukid. I looked at my watch and calculated how long it would be until Linda was home from her doctor appointment and could come take me home.

Then that same old Tempest came glug-glugging into the loading area. I was hidden in the warehouse gloom so the woman just sat and dead-eyed out the window and waited. Framed in the glass with that faraway look she was someone I knew. She was Lilo's skinny woman.

The whole scene slopped back over me: the skin stuck fast to the chair and the air bubbles floating up slow in the thick fish-tank water and the names on the envelopes on the bedroom dresser: Walter and Beverly Fraley. Mrs. Lilo.

She honked the horn but I just stood and stared. I didnt hear Ken come into the warehouse so I dont know how long he'd watched me. His voice made me jump. Load the damn customers, Tuesday. Dont just stand there and admire them.

Sorry, sir. I scampered out into the rain and the window dropped just enough for the pick ticket to slide out. Stale smoke puked out with it.

I wrapped her stuff in plastic and tied it on top of the car and rapped on her window till it eased down an inch or so. You're Beverly Fraley aint you.

The window screeched all the way down and she brayed at me like I was standing on the far side of the yard: Look. You dont know me and I dont know you. I moved here from Iowa for the express fucking purpose of getting away from assholes like you. So back off and stay off.

Straight on and up close she didnt look at all like Beverly Fraley.

Sorry, I said, but the half-muffled engine roared and the tires whistled on the wet pavement and hosed water up the side of my pantsleg. Ken shook his head and wheeled and disappeared and the warehouse door slammed back in the gloom.

No way was I going to ask for a sick day now. The rest of the morning I invented work where there wasnt any and greeted customers before they rolled to a stop. I cut my lunch break short and worked in the rain around the lumber piles, picking up metal bands that should have waited for better weather. It wasnt even my area to police. It was Tony's, and in a better world he'd have waited on the next customer.

I didnt hear the big pickup until it was right beside me. Well, what do you know, this voice I knew too well said. Tuesday Price working in the rain.

I glanced at the lawyer I'd owed money to forever and then turned back to the band I was trying to work loose from under a fallen stack of lumber. Some of us got to work even when it aint fit, Mr. McKevey.

How long have you been working here?

A while. What can I get for you?

What he wanted was to worry the bone he'd gotten hold of. Then you're getting a regular paycheck. I'm kind of surprised none of it's come my way.

I'll get you paid. There's just some other things I got to take care of first.

What do you think? Maybe the first of next month? How's a hundred dollars sound for a starter? That shouldnt break your budget. He'd never dunned me this way and I didnt much care for it. All he'd done was keep me out of jail for stealing some little bit of nothing that wouldnt have mattered if I *had* stole it. I shouldnt have even needed a lawyer.

I'll pay you when I can, I said. Now what do you need?

Seven treated two-by-sixes, eight feet long. His nose hairs showed when he showed me the invoice from the cab of his highdollar truck.

Third row on the left, second pile. He idled along behind me to the pile and then stayed in the cab while I slid wet lumber into the bed of his truck. I didnt really make a decision or even think about it but I loaded fifteen boards—eight extra—and then waited alongside until he rolled down the window. Right there's your first payment.

He looked in the mirror and then opened the door and slid down. You drinking? He sniffed the air and zipped up a jacket that cost more than my house.

The rain felt like it was sizzling on my face. Hey, stay in. I was just fooling. I just wanted to see how crooked lawyers really are.

You go on about your work. He stacked the extra lumber back onto the pile while the rain plastered his possum hair down to his head.

You're no better than I am, you bastard. You just know how to steal legal. Sounding like I loaded extra materials every day.

You might be right. But I surely hope not.

I expected him to gun the big engine and hose water off the tires onto me like Beverly did but he eased out of the lot like he had a cup of coffee on the dashboard. Well, I screwed the pooch for sure that time, I said and went back to the warehouse and drank the rest of the cough syrup.

About a half-hour later Ken called me to his office. I stood and dripped water on the floor while he signed a check and put it in an envelope and handed it to me.

This aint payday, I said.

It is for you. It's your last one.

Listen . . . Desperate, and sounding like it.

If there's one thing I wont abide it's a thief.

I didnt steal one thing from you. Not one single damn thing. Not ever.

You've paid your last bill with my materials. Now you get off my property and dont come back. Not even to buy something.

Ken . . .

What really pisses me off is how stupid I am. I knew what you were when you came here but I let being busy override my judgment. Now are you going to get out or do you want me to have you thrown out?

I called Linda from the first pay phone but she wasnt home yet. I walked backwards into the rain with my thumb high but nobody ever picks up a wet man. I stopped at the bank in the shopping center and cashed my check and bought a pint of cinnamon schnapps at the liquor store across the way and then slogged back onto the highway. The red liquor disappeared but my guts got colder and harder like the rain that had turned to sleet. The bottle was empty when I got to The Hole but I was as sober as I've ever been. The bar was deserted except for Ace and one old guy parked under the TV with his mouth open like a baby bird. Well look at the muskrat, Ace said. Beer?

I want to pay my bill.

He looked at me hard for a moment and then got his book from beneath the cash register. Eighteen dollars and you're all clear.

The wet bills in the bank envelope stuck together but my hands were too numb to separate two twenties so I handed both to Ace.

He didnt look at them. What the hell's going on now?

I tried to speak and couldnt so I just raised my hand in a little wave and turned and headed for the door.

Hold up. You give me too much money.

I shut the door behind me and stepped down off the cement slab and my feet slithered on the ice and the hardtop jumped up and clewed me on the forehead. When I hit, something broke loose inside me and the alcohol and cough syrup kicked in all at once and time skittered sideways and somehow it seemed that all the screwups and dead people hadnt happened yet but it was all coming down right now and I couldnt do a thing to stop it except lay there on the ice and try to die before it happened.

Then Ace was there trying to help me up and I said, Just leave me alone. There aint no cause for anyone else to die.

He picked me up and dragged me inside and my elbow bounced off the doorjamb and he sat me on a barstool and said, You think you can set there by yourself like a big boy? I'll call Linda to come after you but I got to spread a little salt first.

Dont let her get sucked into this.

Ace shook his head. If you was trying to get drunk you done it. A number one piscutter. Cant even talk. He went outside with a red bucket and I remembered the emergency vehicles where the wreck was and hollered out a warning but he was already gone and the world had gone tilty and I put my head on the bar and chucked it level with my arms. Just till it settled. Just for a minute.

When I looked up again the old guy under the TV was gone and two chapped-face construction workers were where he'd been and Ace was behind the bar again. He got off his stool and came down and looked at my forehead and said, You'll be all right. It aint but a bump.

I rubbed where I'd fallen and looked at my fingers and wiped them on my pants. Dont tell Linda about this.

His eyes shifted over my shoulder and he nodded toward where he was looking.

Linda sat at the table just behind me with her eyes big and wet. You ready to go home?

I turned back to the bar and she came alongside and lifted her belly with her hand while she edged up onto the stool. Why? she said.

I shrugged.

She looked at me for maybe ten seconds and slid off the stool and headed for the door.

I got fired. For stealing.

She stopped and turned and looked me over head to toe and back again, and said, Damn you. Not a curse but a judgment. The door grated shut behind her and an ashtray broke against it and I looked at my hand and Ace said, Now by hell that there does it.

So it took a while to get Ace simmered down and I drank a cup of coffee with a snort of brandy in it to keep from freezing on the way home and I fell down twice getting there and I missed her. Junior, the blind pup, stood in the open front door and whined. He must of been off in his own world when she hauled out with the rest of the dogs.

The neighbor opened his door and said, Dont be mad at me for helping her. Someone had to do it. Knocked up as she is.

Aint I lucky you were there, I said. Junior followed me inside and drank from the puddle where I shed my clothes and wagged his tail the whole time. The trailer looked raped. Dresser drawers open and empty. Her toothbrush and hair stuff gone from the bathroom.

I slumped at the kitchen table naked and cold and drunk. Junior smelled at my leg and I kicked at him but got the table instead. Where *I love Andrew Price, a friend of mine* had scrolled across a screen just a few hours before I laid my gravelly forehead down and cried.

CHAPTER 18

Next morning I leafed halfhearted through the yellow pages and just sat and stared out the window. I'd seen worse places in *National Geographic* and I wished I could go to one of them. Either I stood there for a long time or got up later than I thought because after a while it was afternoon and I had to get away.

Already the floor was littered with dirty clothing and the place smelled musty. I changed into running clothes and stretched against the shed and then loped off and without thinking I turned out toward the lake houses and then up the narrow road with winter-dead grass in the middle. When I rounded the turn at Lilo's the house was gone. So were the piles of dirt. Bright green ryegrass stood ankle tall in a little meadow surrounded by a sea of dead brown weeds. I kicked through the grass for some sign that Lilo and Beverly had ever been there but there was not a scrap of pipe or wire or concrete block anywhere. The transformer was gone from the utility pole.

When I left I stopped to look one last time at the empty field. Just before I reached the hard road again there came the long low lonely cry of a dog from back where I'd been. I stopped and listened to the moan of an old coon dog that had been skunk sprayed and had felt teeth tear his ears and briars rip his lips as he ran blind through the night. He bayed one more time and was silent. That gut-born howl worked on me as I ran back to the trailer and made me as lonesome and hopeless as I'd ever been. About halfway back I admitted to myself that I was running toward a drink. My pace picked up and all my empty places filled with thirst.

A black Toyota pickup was parked in my driveway. Linda's brother Slick rolled off the seat and closed the door behind him. I should of finished what I started last time, sleazeball. He was my height but broad and formidable in spite of the paunch that draped over his belt.

I understood full well what was coming and I didnt care. You drove all the way from Cincinnati to reminisce?

He spat in the gravel. No, I come to kill your sorry ass.

Well thank God for that. I was afraid you was after my head this time.

He pushed himself away from the truck. You think you can knock my sister up and then throw her out on the street? That's all the talk there was and then he came fast and hard.

I threw a punch full of new muscle and failure and frustration that caught him square in the face but he came over me in a rush and gravel bit into my back. The rest was discombobulated sensations of the taste of sweat and blood and grunts and thuds and the whistle of breath through clenched teeth and vague impressions of impact. It may have gone on for an hour or for a minute. He rolled away and I kicked him in the ear and we struggled to our feet and stood wheezing and shaking with adrenaline. Slick had a cut over his eye and the side of his face was red and muddy and someone had put teethmarks on his arm. His shirt pocket hung down just like his ear. There was blood—his or mine—where missing buttons had exposed his T-shirt. My nose had grown shut till I couldnt breathe through it and the fire under my ribs flared up each time I breathed.

She left *me*, I said in little jerks when there was air enough.

You calling my sister a liar? His voice shook worse than mine.

I'm telling you what happened.

He was getting ready to come again.

Come on then, I said. I'll haul my coat anytime you want.

We stood squared off and ready while our adrenaline drained away and the pain started to sink in. He blew bloody snot out the side of his nose and wiped his thumb on his jeans. You've done enough to that girl.

That's between me and her. We'll decide when we're done doin each other.

You talk big all of a sudden. But it dont make any difference. You leave her alone.

As we glared at each other and shivered in the cold air we ran out of fuel. He cursed under his breath as he stepped up into the pickup and then spat out the window as he backed out. The bloody string straggled down the truck's door.

Not until I'd stuffed cotton up my nose and dug hunks of gravel out of my skin did I realize that my thirst was gone. If Slick hadnt been waiting

I'd have been working on a worldclass drunk by now. The thought lay sick inside like worms.

Junior licked at a bloody place on my knuckles when I bent to pet him. When I checked my face in the mirror the bruised flesh was that of someone who'd fought back. The idea scared me a little.

That evening Dave's truck rumbled into the driveway. Dave and Mike tramped in without knocking. We heard it was party time, Dave said and plunked a six-pack of Bud on the table. Streamers of cigar smoke wound behind them like squirrel tails on an antenna. Swooping in like vultures in hard times fighting in the middle of the road over a broken fan belt.

Godamighty, Dave said when he got a better look at my face. We heard you made a new pothole with your head but nobody told us a truck backed over you while you was down.

My shrug said everything I needed to say.

Maybe we need to call you Hammer Head. Get you on the WWF. Have a beer, little buddy. You'll feel better. Dave tilted a can from the plastic holder and slid it across the table.

I pushed it back. I dont want it. I dont even want it around.

Well, aint you in a mood.

One wont hurt you, will it? Mike said.

Dave wiped spilled ashes from the table onto the floor and leaned back on two legs and squinted through his smoke. Why dont you come right out and say what you mean here. Quit beatin around the bush.

Dont bring drinks in my house.

He stood up and let the chair fall over backwards and didnt bother to right it. Tell you what, you little asshole. It'll most likely be a long time before anyone buys you a drink again. So you enjoy these here. He pushed the six-pack to the center of the table and turned and walked out the door. Mike shrugged and winked and followed him out and shut the door behind him.

I didnt realize that Junior was barking until he quit.

I carried the six-pack like a road-killed possum and threw it in the outside garbage can. Two pimple-faced kids cruised by on their bikes looking redneck and poor in their big coats and stocking caps. The bikes wobbled on the icy patches that glittered under the streetlights. Hey, beer breath! one of them yelled.

I swept up the ashes and dirt and put in a load of wash and straightened the mess Linda had made as she packed. Then I sat in my chair and brooded until the front door jumped under someone's crashing fist.

Get your ass out here, dirt bag. You gone too far this time. My neighbor had to back down the stairs before I could open the door. His pants were unbuttoned and held up with ragged blue suspenders. No shirt. You're going to jail. The finger that pointed in my face was nicotine stained brown like a fat sausage.

What's the problem now?

You know what you done. You give beer to them boys and now they're drunk as polecats. They aint even in high school yet.

I leaned forward and looked at the trashcan, at the lid on the ground. They even steal out of the garbage. I pushed down past him and looked in the can and replaced the lid. There's some cheese in there if they want it. It's a little moldy but they can whittle the green off.

He looked away and hitched his pants. My kid dont steal. You give it to them.

You think what you want. Do whatever you want to about it. I dont much care.

He was still standing there when I shut the door. Looking as old and tired as I felt.

The following morning I found a scrap of plywood and a can of black paint in the shed. A hard scum had crusted the paint but I broke through it with a screwdriver and poured the thick liquid into a butterbowl. The painted letters ran a little bit but they were readable: FOR SALE BY OWNER. I nailed it fast to a stake and drove it in the rocky dirt by the driveway.

I worked for four days cleaning and patching and painting and raking dead grass and dry leaves. Then on Tuesday afternoon a rattling Ford wagon pulled into the drive. A used-up man and a tired woman peered crane-necked through a cracked windshield. Two ragged kids hung over the seat. Wornout fluid of some kind dripped from the motor. The man balanced a can of Milwaukee's Best on the dash and got out and flipped a cigarette butt into the street. Old olive-brown work pants and shirt and a frayed baseball cap set crooked on a lopsided head. The woman busting out all over from hot-pink sweatpants. The kids mostly dressed in dirt. How much? he said without preamble.

Twelve thousand. That's a bargain, but I've got to sell.

Dont sound like no bargain, he said, but his eyes glittered. Can we look at the inside?

No. I aint selling that part of it. Just the out. He looked at his woman and I laughed and said, Sure. Come on in.

The kids turned on the television and the woman looked through the closets. The furniture comes with it, I said.

The TV, too? the woman said.

Yep. You can even have the pots and pans.

The man's phlegmy cough was like a merit badge in smoking. She prowled inside while I unscrewed the underpinning and let him look up underneath.

Does it got a clear title?

I assured him that it was all paid for.

He twirled his cap on the end of his finger. Brown spots showed through his thin hair. We'll think on it.

All right. But it goes to the first one with the cash.

He herded the family into the car and started the engine and I realized I hadnt gotten his name. Your name isnt Wednesday is it?

No, it's Harvey Henchport. My cousin Alvin lives at the end of the street. Why in blazes would you think my name is Wednesday? The cigarette lighter popped and he lit a new cigarette.

I dont know. It was just a thought.

He returned that evening with ten one-hundred-dollar bills. It'll take a couple of days to get the rest of it together.

All right. I wrote a receipt on a piece of notebook paper.

He brought a cashier's check for the balance on Friday morning. By early afternoon my utilities were cut off and I was packed to go. My gym bag held my few clean clothes and my old copy of *Moby Dick*. I looked through our scattered paraphernalia without interest and pocketed only the pretty barrette I'd found at Lilo's.

I knocked on my neighbor's door and he yelled, What, dirtbag? I waited until the door opened and he filled the space.

I just wanted to say goodbye.

Why, you leaving?

I bit back my smart reply and said, Yeah. You take care.

He scratched his head and looked confused. Where you goin?

Up north somewhere.

For good? You aint comin back?

No. I'm going for good.

Oh.

I held out my hand and shook with him for the first time ever. His fat fingers were as hard and rough as a brick. Well. Good luck.

You too.

When I looked back from the end of the drive he was still there. We waved. Junior, with his head sticking out of my coat, whined and adjusted his feet against my chest.

I cashed Harvey's check and bought two money orders—one to the lawyer Phil McKevey and the other to Linda's dad to pay off the car loan—and changed most of the balance of the money into traveler's checks. McKevey's check went into the mailbox, Homer Lawton's into my shirt pocket.

The Ace in the Hole was rocking with the Friday night crowd. Ace looked at the pup sticking out of my jacket and said, Get that stinkin thing out of here.

I aint going to be but a minute, I said.

Mike patted Junior's head. Where'd you get that sorry looking thing?

With my fingers I moved the pup's lips like he was talking and said without hardly moving my lips, It started out as a wart on my butt.

Mike laughed and said, I thought it was the frog sittin on the Polack's head that said that.

Yeah. Ole Junior probly read it in a joke book or something. He's right smart. That's why I'm taking him with me.

Dave finally turned on his stool to acknowledge me. With you where?

North somewhere. I aint sure.

You'll be back fore dark, Dave said. He gave my hand one quick hard shake and turned again to his beer.

I said goodbye to Mike and he followed me outside. You coming back a-tall? He looked like an old basset hound.

No, Mike. I'm out of here.

Gonna try to get back together with Linda?

I shrugged. She's had enough of me I reckon. I aint real sure what I'm doing.

He drew hard on his cigarette and scuffed his foot on the pavement. I aint trying to talk you out of doing what you got to do but the door's always open at my place. Should you decide to come back.

That's mighty white of you, Mike.

We shook hands and he flipped his cigarette away and wrapped me in a smoky, beery hug. Junior licked his fingers as his hand trailed across my chest. We gripped each other's arms, both of us blinking way too much, then I turned and walked away. Mike coughed behind me and I knew he was watching and smoking, anxious to go inside but wanting to leave with me. I thought I was beyond hearing the puff of bar sounds as the door opened and closed as he went back inside.

Two miles down the road I discovered a ten and a five and three ones in the jacket pocket that had been on Dave's side. I fondled them as if they were pearls, and as puzzled as if that was what I'd found there.

CHAPTER 19

I had to walk all the way to Route 29 but then within minutes one truck from the long line grinding up and down the mountains flipped its lights on high beam and air brakes cycled and a maroon-and-chrome rig eased over onto the shoulder. I ran to catch up and jumped up on the fuel tank and gave the driver a quick check-out and threw my bag onto the floor and hauled myself up onto the high seat. Junior squirmed once and settled against my belly.

Instruments enough for a spaceship cast the driver in a soft green hue. A porkpie hat pinched onto a squat head and wide red suspenders stretched tight around a big belly. A down-home face that had seen hard use. Someone who should have been selling apples from the back of a rusted pickup instead of shuffling the gears of a hundred-thousand-dollar rig.

Where you headed to, buddy?

North.

That's a right general destination.

Up near the Maryland line. Union County. Little place called Hardly. Until I said it out loud I wasnt sure.

Yeah. I been through it. Purty little town. You got kin there?

Not anymore.

There's probly some jobs up there but not too many. Woods work. Cuttin pulpwood and whatnot. I dont know of no mines close around.

I'm not looking for work. Especially.

His eyebrows slid high up on his forehead and he looked at me while he worked down through the gears on a steeper grade.

Things have just went to hell so bad here I thought I'd give it a try somewhere else for a spell.

He leaned forward and rocked like he could nudge the truck along a little bit faster. You aint got no family a-tall?

I got a woman. And a baby on the way. He was one of those nosy people so open and bold you just couldnt get resentful. But she left me.

He touched his face in the same locations as my yellowing bruises. It dont look like it was because *you* was thumping on *her*.

I grinned. Naw. It wasnt nothing like that.

The CB crackled and he cocked his head and picked up the mike and spoke close and low into it and laughed and I settled down in my seat and closed my eyes and let the diesel roar and the tire's whine become just another type of silence.

When I opened them again he said, I got to tell you about my Jesus. He dont give me no other option.

I shifted to get more comfortable. I aint overanxious for you to do it but I guess it beats walking.

It wasnt a bad story. Drugs at first just something to keep him awake. Then later to feel better. Then sex while he was lonesome and screwed up. A wife that died before he could get it back together. And then Jesus come along and fixed him. He told it so that I could feel the hurt and hopelessness and even his new peace. And then just when he was ready to close the deal and welcome me into the fold, as we were passing a lighted exit, Junior stuck his head up out of my jacket.

Porkpie was looking at me—he didnt ever seem to watch the road—and he yelled Yahhh and the rig swerved but he was pro enough to pull it back under control.

It's just a puppy, I said.

He slumped in his seat and held one hand on his chest. You just about done me in, boy. When that black head come a-slitherin out of there all I could think was serpent.

Then durned if he didnt segue straight into the Garden of Eden and from there right back to me. Just ask and believe and He'll forgive you.

Dad would have been proud of him.

What's your name? he said when I didnt respond.

I go by Tuesday.

Tuesday, would you like to make Jesus your friend?

You left out the speaking-in-tongues paragraph.

He laughed easy and short. I reckon you done heard it all then.

A time or two. My pap was a Pentecostal preacher.

I sure hope you listened. And believe.

I might lay claim to parts of it. But not all. I tried it and come up short.

He shook his head and didnt say anything back and I drifted off again into the whining silence of the highway. I'd just about dozed off when he said, I'm gonna pray for you.

Let er rip. We were north of Jane Lew, so it couldnt last much longer.

Not right now. You aint ready yet. But I'm gonna pray for you every day. And when your heart's right Jesus will take you in.

He let me out at the Route 50 interchange but not before he gave me a Bible the size of a deck of playing cards. He gripped my arm before I climbed down from the cab. Take care, Mr. Tuesday. I thanked him for the ride. My arm burned where he'd touched me. I smelled it to see if it had diesel fuel on it. It just smelled like me.

Junior and I shared a burger and watered a tree together and then slept on a row of seats in the little Clarksburg airport. The place was deserted. The US Airways luggage tag that I'd fastened to my gym bag made it look like we had business there. The college student that scrubbed the floors didnt bother us.

The sun was well over the trees by the time I knocked on Homer Lawton's door. Freda spoke through a narrow gap. She's not here.

Do you know where she is?

Yes.

I waited a while. Will you tell me?

No.

The crack between door and jamb was shrinking.

I need to talk to Homer before I go.

The door closed and after a minute or so swung wide. Hostility dripped from his expression and from his stance and from his voice. What do you want?

I handed him the money order I'd purchased in Ransom. Thanks for the loan. I really do appreciate it. Something changed in his eyes but the door closed anyway.

This time the air was warmer as I walked up the lane to the old home place. More winter would come but not today. Hard lumpy pillows of dirty snow still marked the edges of hollows and cutbanks. The house looked worse than it had at Christmas. Then snow had hidden the sagging roof and missing shingles, but now the late February sun had worried it away. Junior stumbled over the rough ground and made puddles and piles everywhere.

The edge of the back porch where I rested was smooth from the thousands of times a tennis shoe had skidded off the edge. I sat there and stared at the old Dodge abandoned near the woods but before I could sink into the past the jingle of dog tags hauled me back. A rangy coonhound with a high-hipped stride loped from the woods. He stopped and stared and then came straight to Junior and then sniffed my shoe and sneezed. I let him sniff my fingers and then I scratched behind his ears. His white and brown and black patches were sharp and equal and his big feet and floppy ears came from good Walker bloodlines.

He jerked his head away and looked back the way he'd come and wheeled and bowled over Junior and disappeared into the woods. An orange hat flickered through the trees and then I heard the galump of rubber boots. A tall loose-jointed man clumped out of the woods. When he saw me sitting there he turned back quick and then stopped and stared with a hand shielding his eyes. Well hello. He raised his hand and I nodded.

Before he reached me I placed him as the man who'd known my name when I'd turned around at the church. The unbuckled earflaps of his hat bounced as he walked. Curlicues of steel-wool hair crawled from the neck of a ragged Promise Keeper's T-shirt, though the air was snow-chilled. We stared for a spell before he spoke. Has spring sprung do you think? He swept his arm like he'd spoken the sunshine into being.

There'll be more bad weather yet. The dog high-nosed away into the wind. Maybe tonight, I said.

He examined me without apology until I said, Who are you anyhow?

I'm Grover Dulaney. That's my dog Hobo. We live back over the hill a piece. A big gesture again toward what used to be the old Scott place.

How do you know me?

He shook his head. How you know I do?

I leaned forward and spat between my feet and pushed Junior away from licking where it had landed. You called me by name when I turned around at the church. At Christmastime.

Christmas, he said. His voice was a lot like the locals' but with an undertone of an accent I couldnt place. You werent quite so beat up then.

None of his business. I didnt respond.

He coughed and his google worked like a peach pit in his throat. I talked to you at Jasmine Price's funeral.

No you didnt. I'd brushed off every conversation. Every one.

I didnt say you talked back.

I stared at him and held him up beside everyone who'd been there till I found a match. You're the preacher.

Not anymore.

Reverend Dulaney.

Just Grover. And you're Andy Price.

I most generally go by Tuesday. His hand was thin and bony but firm and calloused.

Your speech is so much different than your mother's was.

You mean this here redneck hog-ranger patois I got?

He nodded and smiled.

I reckon I started talking this away when I was a kid cause I was so enamored with ole Bunker Reddy that lived yonder. He knowed all the kinds of stuff I wanted to know like how to grow sang and get a rototiller to run and weld a busted spring shackle. All Dad knowed was how to spout hellfire and damnation. And then when I got in school I done it so I'd be different than the church folks and then down in Green County where I lived since my buddies all talked like that so I done it too. And it's like your mama warned you about crossing your eyes. After a spell it stuck and I couldnt talk no other way. Or maybe I just didnt want to.

I wasnt being critical. Just curious.

I knowed that or I wouldnt of answered you.

Hobo returned from wherever his nose had taken him and lapped water at the springhouse drain. I'm going to get a draught of that myself if you dont care.

Go ahead. It dont belong to me and I doubt you can use it up.

He squatted and set his gold-rimmed glasses on the crumbled concrete reservoir and cupped his hands under the outflow. Earflaps hiding his face and boot tops gaped wide. Water from each handful running from his elbow into his boot until he jerked and said Arghhh and laughed along with me.

Chilly, aint it, I said.

Yeah. It's a shame it has so much iron in it.

I kind of like it, I said as we traded places. The iron bit my tongue, squeaked in my mouth. I grew up thinking that's what good water tasted like. The hound walked between us with Junior scrabbling between his legs as we walked to the porch.

We sat on the porch and he said, That's a cute pup.

That there's Junior. He's blind as a ballpeen hammer. I batted at his eyes and he blinked the way dogs and women do just to prove you wrong.

I thought maybe he was. But I didnt say anything. Grover glanced at an oversize kid's sports watch that somehow went okay with the hat. You visiting close by or just passing through?

Neither one I dont reckon. If I can find a place to stay I'm going to move back around.

Well, I hope you find something. Like I said, I'm back at the old Scott place. I guess it sounded too much like an invitation because he shook his head and added: It's a mess but it's home.

After I get settled maybe I'll swing by.

You do that.

We shook with spring-chilled hands. Your mother was one fine woman, Andy. I miss her a lot.

Yeah. He should of known her a little better.

He turned at the edge of the woods and waved and disappeared. Junior sniffed the air and whined.

CHAPTER 20

A short walk took me to the Reddys'. Their place was run down, too. The garage leaned toward Jesus and slats were missing from the yard fence and weeds snaked high around the house foundation and the paint was peeling on the sunny side. A yellow cat crouched in a basement window looked too old and sick to move. I latched the yard gap and climbed the sagging stairs and the door opened and Alison was there. Old as Methuselah with wrinkles and gray hair and a face that had collapsed around missing teeth, though she had them in now. What you need? The voice thin as her frame.

Well, hi Mrs. Reddy. Like I was surprised to find her there.

What do you want, Andy?

I scratched the back of my head. How you been anyhow?

She looked me over good and said, Come on in then if you aint going to go away. Wipe them feet.

I dug Junior from my jacket and set him down on the porch floor.

Bring it in with you. It's so scrawny the cat's likely to eat it.

The house felt fresher inside. White paint mostly covering the dark paneling. Worn vinyl on what used to be a scarred wooden kitchen floor. A flower in a windowsill. Coffee? she said.

I sat at the kitchen table while she struck a wooden match to light a gas fire under the tarnished aluminum percolator. Where's your woman at?

I looked at the floor and then at the clock and at the floor again.

We aint to talk about her?

I'd ruther not.

Well. That's your lookout then. See that you dont go back on it. She slipped into her chair like she might fall apart if she took too much of a jar.

How's Bunk been? I said.

I dont reckon he's changed much lately seeing he's been dead better'n three years.

Aw, I said. I never heard. That's awful. I looked around like he might jump out of a closet and bray at the expression on my face. The way he did.

She left the kitchen without saying anything and boards creaked down the hallway and up the stairs and then overhead and after a while a toilet flushed loud and water gurgled above the ceiling and inside the wall behind me. She was limping and holding her hip when she returned. She slid a mug of black coffee my way and poured one for herself and sat without offering cream or sugar and then sat and took a spoon and swiddled the coffee anyway. Bunk said you'd be wantin the homeplace back someday. So I guess that's why you're here.

I leaned down and unhooked Junior's teeth from my shoestrings and tried not to see her legs. Thin and scabrous as raspberry canes. Just the house maybe. And enough ground for it to sit on.

I wished we'd never of bought it. The last thing we needed was more ground for Bunk to work. But you couldnt tell him nothing. You never could.

The coffee had cooled to where I could stand it and it was coarse and bitter and good.

I aint sure I want you for a neighbor though. I'd be right cautious of that.

I sipped my coffee and let her work through it.

I dont recall you being of much account. Not so that you'd notice.

It's up to you. Wont be the end of the world if you decide you want to hang on to it. Sensing the sale. Working on the price. I'll find some other place.

Can you change oil? Or put in a fuse when one blows?

Oh yeah.

Well I cant, she said before I could offer more. I dont know how to do one blessed thing once I get out of the kitchen. Bunk done everything there was and never taught me nothing and then he up and died on me.

She got up and limped to the door and held to the jamb with a pale bony hand and said, Where you staying at?

I hadnt really thought that far ahead. In town, I reckon. The Brays still got that motel dont they?

She snorted. Paul died in '92 or maybe '90 and Alice been in the old-folks home since afore that. She creaked down the hallway and said as she started up the stairs, But the motel's still there. What's left of it.

She stopped again at the top. Her voice shaking from her effort to be heard. You come back tomorrow. I got to think on it. And leave that dog here. Them new people dont allow no pets. That's what people says. And get you a piece of liver and soak them face bruises again it. You look like death a-walkin.

I finished my coffee and after a while I patted Junior on the head and let myself out and set off toward Hardly.

The girl at the desk of the Slumberland Motel had a ring through her eyebrow and a cellphone in her ear. A cigarette with an inch-long ash smoldered in a red plastic ashtray. A fat dog of no particular breed or color raised its head and snuffled and sneezed and stood and made a circle and laid back down. The girl said I know I know I know into the phone. She looked at me and raised one finger and both eyebrows and I nodded and she wrote $29.95 + *tax* on a pad and turned it toward me and I nodded and filled out the register and she slid forward a key on a big plastic tag and tapped a sign on the wall behind her that said CHECKOUT 10 A.M. and I made a circle of thumb and forefinger and went out and down the cracked walkway to my room.

I should have been hungry but I wasnt. I sat on a bed that smelled like garlic. But not. The TV remote was epoxied to a chain fastened to the wall and I looked at the buttons and put it back on the nightstand and laid on the bed and listened to the icemaker in the cubbyhole between my room and the next.

I was awake before 5:00 A.M. In a dusty desk drawer I found a yellowed envelope and I put the key and a twenty and a ten and three ones inside and dropped it inside the key box outside the office door and walked toward the other side of town till I found a diner with the lights on and pickups in the lot. Not a single familiar face.

I took my time with eggs and bacon and coffee. When I stepped out into a morning heavy with hot grease from the diner and diesel fumes from a bobtailed semi idling along the side of the parking lot the pole lights were off and the crows were cussing overhead.

At the hardware store I traded a traveler's check for a Carhartt barn coat with a heavy hood and a sleepingbag and a camp cookset and a bicycle with balloon tires and enough sprockets to gear up a dragline. By then the sky had lowered and darkened and snow pricked my face as I pedaled back the way I'd walked the evening before. All I owned on my back and in my pockets.

CHAPTER 21

Alison opened the door before I knocked and turned and walked back to the kitchen without saying a word. I followed her into the smells of baking and Junior got up from a rug in front of the sink and smelled my shoe and when Alison had poured coffee and sat he snuggled next to her foot.

You sleep good? I said.

I'm eighty-four years old. I dont even recollect sleepin good.

She looked at the clock and hobbled over and opened the oven door and looked in and gathered her dress in her hand for a potholder and withdrew a tin of cornbread muffins. She upended the tin over the counter and when the golden lumps had all fallen forth she collected them into a wooden bowl and set them between us. If I remember right you like pone without nothing on it.

Yes maam. The bread was grainy and sweet and better than anything I'd eaten in years. I leaned over the table to limit the spread of crumbs but I felt Junior browsing among my legs.

How much money you got?

I drank of the coffee. I dont like to say. It aint a good way to dicker.

We aint dickerin. I'm cuttin a deal and you can either jump on it or leave it go.

All I got's not spendable. I need some left to live on and stuff.

She picked up a muffin and smelled it and touched her tongue to its top and set it beside her coffee cup. How much of it can you part with?

I did some calculating and threw her a lowball. Four maybe. That'd be pushing it.

Four what?

I didnt care for the way this was going and I could feel the heat in my face. Thousand.

Dollars? Four thousand dollars?

I nodded.

You sure aint bought no property lately have you.

No maam. I'm just telling you how much I got. I dont know if it's enough or not.

It aint too much. I can tell you that with a good measure of confidence.

Probly not.

She took the muffin and placed it on the floor and said, If you make a mess down there I'll show you what the pointy end of a broom feels like you worthless little heathen mongrel mutt. Junior's toenails clattered on the vinyl as he went after it.

She grimaced and arched her back the wrong way. I used to could run into town and back without sweatin or breathin hard. Now there aint a place on me dont hurt this time of year. She leaned toward the stove and said, Look there. I left the oven on and gas high as it is.

I'll get it, I said. The stove was old with massive burners and the knob warm and heavy.

Here's the deal, she said.

I turned and leaned back against the countertop and crossed my arms.

Set down. I aint about to crane up at you all the time we talk.

So I sat and she got up and poured more coffee into my cup and then stood where I'd just been. You say four cause then you think I'll say six and then we'll split the difference at five. But I aint about to sell you no house and land for six thousand dollars. I aint clear ignorant. But six aint a bad place to work from.

There's no way in the world I could go any higher than five. No way.

That ground alone's worth twenty. Maybe more. Anyhow, if I sell it to you right out I'll never lay eyes on you again. So you give me your six thousand dollars and I'll lay it away somewhere. And then I want you over here every week. Bright-eyed and ready to work. And I'll put half your wage with the other and give you the balance to spend. And in the meantime you work on that old dump when you can. And when there gets to be enough money and the work gets caught up around here and that house gets patched up to my satisfaction maybe then I'll put the money over in my pocket and we'll talk about whose name ought to be on the deed.

It was so audacious I had to laugh. I cant wait to read the fine print on this deal.

There aint gonna be no print. Coarse or fine neither one. I never seen the need to reinforce a good solid word with a piece of paper.

I considered it. When would the money be enough? And the work be done?

After a spell. When I said.

How do I know you wont just spend up my money and never sign over the place?

The trouble in my back aint come from carryin bales of money around but I got all I need. What I dont got is someone to work that dont steal me blind and break up more than he fixes. Your money'll be there.

I crossed over and shook the coffee pot and found it empty and sat again. How many days a week do I have to come here?

I was thinkin four. That leaves you three to worry at the other.

One. That old house needs a pile of fixing.

Three then.

Two.

They best be good fat days. I mean biguns.

How much a hour?

Four dollars.

Each half I hope you mean.

Eight dollars a hour? I never in my life made that kind of a wage.

You sure aint paid no wages lately have you. Making my voice hoarse and shaky like hers.

She laughed out loud and said, Do that again.

Do what?

Sound like me.

So I said it again but not as good since I was really trying and she cackled and slapped the table and said, That right there was worth eight dollars.

I took that for an agreement. How much ground goes in the deal?

You stake you off a patch and I'll see if it suits. I dont see that it makes no difference since I aint decided what you're gonna pay for it yet.

What if something happens to you?

Well then you'd best be pretty slick at findin where I've hid stuff. And you best be better at makin deals with the next owner than you showed today.

I shook my head. Amazed. As much at myself for considering Alison's offer as at her for making it. Let me think on it.

That's today's deal. It most likely wont be available tomorrow. Besides,

I cant get the water in the barn to shut off and I done thawed out four pork chops for supper. And I cant eat but one.

Fried?

I figured to bake em in milk with new red potatoes.

I picked Junior up and scratched behind his ears while he licked my chin. Where's that leak at in the barn? In the calf pen or the milkhouse?

I figger even you can find it. Its runnin out under the door.

I looked up at the heavens and said, She sure drives a hard bargain dont she, Bunk?

He's deaf as a post. You got to look at him when you talk. She pointed at the floor.

That night I scraped the trash from a grave-sized plot on my childhood bedroom floor and unrolled my sleepingbag onto the damp pine planks and spread an old blanket Alison had given me for Junior. Home again. Even if it felt more like going back to hell. Ghosts lamented and rattled through the hallways either of the house or of my mind. In the dark it's hard to tell. Junior slept good.

Alison's labor stood in line ahead of mine—no great surprise—so the following morning after I'd signed six grand worth of traveler's checks I found myself gouging a half-decade of gunk from the gutters. Glazing a new glass pane into a basement sash. Replacing a rat-chewed header over the coal bin door. Hanging from a crude, weathered whiteoak ladder tied to its mate and slung over the barn roof ridge while I nailed corrugated steel flapped loose by the wind.

Eating.

After a supper of fried mush and soup beans over fresh-baked bread caked with real creamery butter and blueberry cobbler, Alison said, Was you to bed down here tonight you could get a quicker start tomorrow. And I reckon you're fond of warshin in the crick but that cold water aint clear cut the sweat loose from you. A hot bath'd not hurt you any.

So two nights a week I slept in her back room on a steel-sprung cot that cried for mercy at the slightest motion. Bathed earhole-deep in an iron-stained clawfoot tub. Watched TV with the sound off while Alison ordered her life into rows and columns of memories and words. Fell into the sleep of the bone weary and clean of heart.

Then there were the other five days. And nights.

I started with a scoop shovel, Junior sniffing every new layer of filth and rot. When I could see the floor in most places I switched to a crowbar more suited to waterbagged ceilings and mouse-chewed closet shelving and rotted floorboards. The more I tore away the more remained to be torn. But sometime during the second week I swept the entire house, top to bottom, and moved outside into weather turned fresh and balmy.

Five days alone got wearisome but Alison rejected my suggestion to distribute her two days labor across the week. What if somethin was to happen to you and you never got back for the second day? she said.

You'll always be ahead.

What if I have a job you cant get done in a solitary day?

Forget I asked. It aint no big deal.

Grover Dulaney's dog Hobo wandered by every few days but the old preacher hadnt come by since the first day I'd been back. So when the jingle of dog tags was joined with the clump of unbuckled arctics I wasnt disappointed. At least he'd given up the orange hound-dog hat for the summer. I offered a howdy and threw my crowbar onto the nail-studded pile of porch boards and we sat on the stoop. I mopped sweat from my face while Grover scratched behind Junior's ears. It's hard to believe how fast a pup can grow, isnt it? He doesnt even look like the same dog.

I reckon. I just dont notice it because I see him all the time. The dogs rambled away behind the house and he scratched the top of his own head and finger-combed his thin hair and nodded toward the pile of debris I'd dumped over the bank toward the creek. Does Alison Reddy know about this?

Who's that?

She's the . . . you know who she is.

I grinned. Yeah. She knows all about it.

You renting the place?

Nope. I bought it.

Oh. Not a lot of joy in it. I let the idea rest on him like a yellowjacket without shooing it away and after a while he stuck out his hand and said, Welcome to the neighborhood.

Thank you.

Hobo and Junior came skidding around the corner with Junior not a pace behind running splay-legged like he'd learned to do.

You sure that dog's completely blind?

He cant differentiate the sun from the coal pile near as I can tell. He's just learned to get by.

Well he does pretty durn good.

Once in a while he gets in a pickle. Tied into a watersnake a couple of days back but he was straddle of it and paying attention to the wrong end. The snake was trying to fang him in the bunghole but Junior's tail was beating him clear to death. They got enough licks in to part both thinking they'd licked the other one.

I guess he was the kind of preacher who didnt tolerate such language as bunghole. He didnt smile at the story but looked troubled at the trash I'd dumped over the hill. I guess you know there's an ordinance against that dont you?

A dadblamed tree hugger. Just what I needed. There aint nothing harmful in it. Just wood and plaster and stuff that'll rot up and make good compost in a couple years. And you cant see it from the road.

It wasnt my intent to give you a sermon. I was just telling you so you knew.

All right. I'll write that down and put it in the file.

Dont get me wrong. A fellow ought to be able to do whatever he wants with his property. Without the government nosing into everything.

That's the way I see it.

I wont mention building permits then. He grinned and was hard not to like.

That'd be a courtesy.

You done much inside?

Come on. I'll show you. I catwalked across the open porch joists and paused to mash over a nail with my heel. The framing is hair near all oak and the sheathing is chestnut except for a little poplar here and again. It's still solid.

He stooped through the doorway the way tall men do even when they dont need to and stood blinking and shading his eyes. Sun streamed through the windows but the dark wood swallowed the light. Just inside the door was a box where I'd stowed the few mementos I'd scavenged: Dad's seminary graduation picture and a *Pentecostal Minister* calendar doodled up with notes and appointments in his hand and a coffee cup that said *Know ye not that your body is the temple of the Holy Ghost—I Corinthians 6:19* and an Old Timer pocketknife with a single locking broken blade and thirteen damp-swelled spiral binders full of sermon notes and a sheaf of papers concerning Mom's garden. Grover stooped and leaned forward to read the calendar.

That was Dad's, I said.

He didnt respond but seemed to stare through the floorboards to something only he could see.

You know this is my home place dont you?

He roused himself from wherever he'd gone. Yeah. I know that.

There aint much left. Hardly anything a-tall of Mom's. I got these couple sketches of her garden layout. But she must of throwed everything else away. Pictures and all. Down in the mollygrubs like she was all the time she'd of done that.

Grover slid the papers from the bag and leafed through them and grunted and shook his head and put them back inside the plastic and returned them to the box. Not all the time she wasnt, he said. He picked up the copy of *Moby Dick* that I'd put in the box with the other things and replaced it as soon as he saw the title.

That's mine. It didnt belong to my folks.

It didnt look like something your parents would read. Dismissive.

Butthead, I thought. Matter of fact Dad got a lot out of that book, I said. The last talk we had fore he died was about it. Probly why I've hung onto it. Though I hadnt realized that before.

He tried the book again and fanned the pages and stopped here and there to read a line or two.

Dad made up his own mind about stuff. If he wanted to read Melville he did.

I'm sure he did. He looked at the garden papers again and then stood and brushed off his pants. I ought to be going.

You want to see the rest of the house?

Another time. He left without saying goodbye. I heard him whistle up the dog and then he was gone.

That night I raised my head from my sleepingbag to listen. I'd dreamed of wintertime so real I could still smell the brimstone shook down from the furnace grates. Somewhere the echo of their clanking gone but lingering on the heavy night air.

Grover came around a week later with an aluminum piepan filled with black walnut and cranberry cookies. It was enough peace offering for me.

We sat together on the basement stairs where I'd went to rest for a spell in the cool dank air that leaked out. Today he wore knee-length black shorts and a woreout white short-sleeved dress shirt and battered leather moccasins. Like a uptight preacher trying to go casual would.

I never ate a better cookie than this kind, I said after I'd swallowed three or four. I never knowed anyone to make them but Mom.

Me either, he said.

I looked at him hard till I realized he was talking about the cookies.

You find any more artifacts in your digging?

No. I aint worked inside hardly a-tall. I been working on the eaves where the ice has backed up and rotted the rafter tails.

Dont be bashful on those cookies. I've had my fill.

All right, I said and picked the last two from the pan. Junior's even got into the box of stuff I already found. That old plastic bag with Mom's garden stuff in it is gone. I aint found what he did with it but when I do I'm gonna warp his tail till his nose bleeds. I laughed to let him know it wasnt so. It aint that I care about them old papers but he's took to chewing everything he can get ahold of. I indicated where sock showed through my running shoe. Like this.

Dont be too hard on him. He's growing up, but he's just a pup inside. Pups chew.

He's just lucky he didnt get hold of any of Dad's things. I *would* of killed him then.

Grover scratched his chest with two fingers inside his shirt then the back of his knee like he'd drove his itch under just to break out in a new place. You ought to value her things as much as you do your father's. Maybe more since there are so few of them.

Yeah right. As much sarcasm as I could load into it.

There I go preaching again. Sorry.

Aw, looky here, I said. I looked close and pulled at the end of a leather shoestring caught in the crack between tread and riser. Drew it forth with the same care I'd apply to a hair between my teeth.

He looked on without interest. What is it?

I think it's Mom's old gotcher cord. The far end came free and I pulled it taught between my spread hands and smelled of its center. I believe it is. I sniffed down its length with my eyes closed. I'll be go to Kansas.

He leaned forward and fingered the dry, dirt-stiffened leather. What did she use it for?

I thought and shook my head and said, It's probly easier to show you than to try to tell. I looped it around one thumb and fumbled with the other like I was trying to tie a one-handed knot and started to put the end between my teeth and made a face and pulled it away. I aint as good at this as she was. I cant get it set up by myself. I looked at the string and let it fall back onto the step. It aint nothing anyway.

Can I help?

I dont know. I doubt it will work that way. But I'll try it. I picked up the leather cord and tested its mettle and said, Hold out one thumb and your index finger. No, on the same hand.

I frowned and made and adjusted a loop around his extended fingers and then held both free ends in my hands and jerked the ends. Dirt flew from the dry-rotted string and his fingers slammed together and he grunted before it broke into three pieces. Gotcher, I hollered and let go the laughter I'd been holding.

He unwrapped the shoestring and looked at his fingers from all sides and picked up the two pieces I'd dropped and said, Yes you did. You got me good. Mad and trying to hide it. He stood and dropped the pieces in his pocket and walked up the steps.

It was just a joke.

He stopped at the top and looked back, a slim silhouette against the light beyond. Your mother teach you that?

If she'd learned me anything with a rope it would have been how to hang myself.

I'm not so sure you knew your mother as well as you think you did.

I thought that over for a long time after he was gone. Not about how much I knew her, but how much he did.

That afternoon I went for the first run since I left out of Ransom. I shut Junior in the house and stretched against an apple tree in the front yard. For the first quarter-mile I held it to a slow trot and then eased into a hard steady run. The flap of asphalt against my shoes was like a backslap from an old friend. My breath whistled hard but not hard enough to stop me from clearing the long grade between my lane and the Reddys' without walking. About a mile out just when my pulse and breathing and stride started to sync up to a second wind a car came up from behind and slowed down to my speed.

I dodged over onto the berm and waved it around but it hung right there on my tail. I couldnt look away from the broke-up ground without turning an ankle and I didnt want to stop. Then the engine whined and a white official-looking car accelerated past. Inside Jenny Yunker stared straight ahead grim as a July frost. Her red hair hadnt changed over the years. Same freckled forearms. Same expression. Like she had a mouthful of cow pie and no place to spit.

I walked back home cramped and winded and didnt run again.

CHAPTER 22

Grover didnt come around for weeks, till way up in May. Long enough to make me wonder why I'd ticked off the only human being in the county willing to make a neighbor-move in my direction. Not long enough for me to change my behavior.

Alison Reddy's work had slid from the emergencies of leaks and collapse and failed mechanical parts to that just threatening to do the same. Some of the know-how I needed to do the work I found in the metal file drawer where Bunker had hoarded every owner's manual and parts list he'd ever got his hands on. More came from an old codger named Glen that worked at the Hardly Hardware and Farm Supply. I could sell you this thirty-dollar spring tool but you can do the same thing with the pair of vise grips you already got, he'd say. Just make sure you get the jaws set square on it and wear some safety glasses. And if it does fly dont be cussin right off—listen close for where it lands so you can find it again. Then you can blaspheme it all you've a mind to.

So I found myself headed for Hardly in Alison's old Ford pickup just about every day for either materials or advice. I even bought an old bed-frame and a mattress and a rocking chair at an auction. As summer creeped up Alison's share of the load had petered out but mine had swelled up in a right satisfying way. The old home place was coming along.

The spring had been milder than some and wet but the rains came mostly at night. I worked out and saved the inside fixing for catchy weather. The day Grover returned was a mean edgy day neither hot nor cold but either at the slightest provoking. The sky sat low and flat and hard as a stove lid and pollen hung like mist and the air stunk of tar.

I heard dog tags and a low whistle. I leaned into the scraper and sent another long curl of yellowed paint windmilling down to lace the high weeds around the foundation. There was the swish of shoes in grass and the sawhorse creaked as Grover eased down onto it. I scraped what I could reach and snared the ball of glazing compound from my shirt pocket and puttied a knothole before I spread primer from the bucket that hung from a ladder rung. They say a bat can wiggle through a hole the size of a pencil, I said.

Either you've taken up talking to yourself or I wasnt as quiet as I thought.

The Bible talks about poking a camel through the eye of a needle. It got anything to say about bat control? I cant keep them out.

Bats are good to have around. They eat a lot of mosquitos.

And they fill up the attic with gu-a-no and carry rabies and squeak and thump and carry on till a dead man couldnt take a nap. And they give me the fantods. I'll take skeeters any day.

I wouldnt know how to keep them out.

I climbed down the ladder and shuffled it down the wall and then turned to him. He wore jeans and sneakers and a plain gray T-shirt and a Nike ball-cap. Made suntanned and trim and manlike by the right mix of clothing.

Sorry if I ticked you off last time, I said. It was just a joke.

No apology's necessary. It was childish of me to take offense. He offered his hand.

I got paint on my hands.

I dont care.

He shook my hand hard and firm and then we both had paint on our hands and I wiggled the ladder onto firm footing and went back to my scraping.

It's good to see you're doing the job right, he said. Scraping and priming and all.

Here came the preacher cropping out in him. They cant help it.

If you dont fix the inside parts it will leak through to the external.

Whitewashed sepulchers, I said. That there's most likely the analogy you're looking for.

After a bit he laughed. Am I that predictable? I suppose I am.

You're a preacher aint you?

No. Not anymore. Not really.

I jiggled the top of the ladder sideways so that I could reach all the way to a window. Dont tell me to be careful, I said. I know you're dying to.

Fear not them which kill the body, but are not able to kill the soul: but rather fear him which is able to destroy both soul and body in hell.

It was my turn to laugh. That was pretty good for off the cuff. I took the brush and made a vertical mark on the siding. One for you. Just then the dogs came tearing through and Junior bounced off the ladder and it slid over a tad more than I'd intended and I scampered down fast like that was my plan all along.

Hows come you quit preaching?

He looked into his lap and then up at me with raised eyebrows. You dont know?

No. I guess it wasnt my day to keep track of preachers when you quit.

He scratched behind both dogs' ears. I guess my personal life got ahead of my calling.

I didnt need any details of his personal life. What do you do now?

I sell sermons.

If he was joking I couldnt see the evidence. You sell sermons.

Over the Internet.

To who? Who in hell would buy a sermon?

Most anybody in hell would, he said and laughed. But it's too late then.

You're kidding me, right?

Not at all. I sell sermons to ministers.

I was struck dumb and fooled with plumbing the ladder in a new out-of-level place while I blew on my spark of mad. I saw Dad poring long hours over his notes preparing his preachings. That's just about the most pathetic thing I've ever heard. Sermons come from God. They're not like some toy you pull out of a Cracker Jack box.

He stood and came to me and said, Here. Let me steady that for you. He already had his skinny claws clamped onto the ladder, too late to turn down his help. What do you think your father sold? Used cars?

He didnt sell anything. He brought God to these folks around here and they paid him a living so he could do it. So he *wouldnt* have to sell used cars on the side. I'd reached the top and I rained paint shavings down onto his head so hard that I left gouges in the wood.

He sold his time.

It was time spent with God if he did. I could feel the ladder trembling with my legs but I couldnt make them stop.

Come on back down here. I can tell I've made you mad. It's not safe for you to be up there in that kind of a state.

When I reached the ground I held the scraper just under his chin. Dont ever say anything about my dad. Or I'll ream your stinking noseholes out.

He didnt back away or look at the scraper. Just straight into my eyes. I wasnt criticizing him, Andy. I was just making a point.

I jammed the scraper into my pocket and wiped the paint from the groove around the top of the can and hammered the lid shut.

In my experience, Grover said, preachers either deliver good sermons because they've applied the necessary effort or they dont because they havent. Darrell Price was of the first persuasion. Grover Dulaney wasnt.

So now you sell your sorry-assed sermons to preachers too dilitary to even work up a bad one.

I have time now to prepare. My sermons are good. I've thought them out. Prayed over them. Backed them up with scripture so they'll stand up to questions. Like any sermon should.

Well what kept you so busy back then when you was preaching? You too busy counting the offering? Or maybe hanging out with the widow women?

He looked at me for what felt like a long time. A good minister fulfills two jobs: he brings the word of God and he shepherds and nurtures his flock. Very few strike a balance. This flock was hurting. I spent too much time on individual needs. Counseling. Listening. Listening some more. And then some more.

I lowered the ladder and stowed it against the foundation. You saying Dad left this congregation in bad shape?

Not at all. It's just that he swung to the other side of center.

I gathered my paint and tools and went down the outside stairs into the basement where I stored them and he followed without being invited.

His preaching was superb. Mine wasnt. I lost my focus. My balance. The time I spent with individuals came at the expense of the whole. I let the church wither and die. His voice echoed inside the basement walls. There're other preachers making the same mistake. My sermons can help. They're not lofty theological treatises. Just down-home country good Godly ideas. And they're just that: Ideas. Outlines. Starting points. Some of them are custom-made for a particular church and situation. If I make enough to live on from that, I'm not apologetic.

I hawked the pollen and coal dust from my throat and spat it away into the dark. How much you knocking down doing this?

I didnt pay any taxes last year. And I keep honest books.

Behind a cement ledge that held back icy water that trickled along the basement wall I kept a line of Cokes. I felt for and removed two and passed one to Grover. I guess that aint as bad as it sounded at first.

I do some counseling, too. But I dont charge for that.

Come out here, I said. I want to show you something.

That anger you have toward your mother—you're going to have to deal with that at some point.

Some things can be forgave but there's others that cant.

He said nothing but put his hand on my shoulder as we went up the stairs together.

What she did to herself, that's her business. But when she disrespected Dad and shacked up with some butthole before he was hardly in the ground and pretending to be happy after all the miserable hell she put him through… that's a different matter. We stood blinking and shielding our eyes after the basement's gloom.

What if she wasnt pretending? Was really happy?

Then she should of pretended not to be. After all them years.

I shook free of his hand and pointed at the house's roof. You got any idea what you could do to fix that?

You could put new shingles on. But those dont look too bad.

No. I mean that sag in the ridge. Looks like the whole thing's gonna collapse.

He cupped the bill of his cap over his eyes and stepped back a few paces. Just about every house around looks the same way. All the old ones.

Well I dont want this one to. I thought maybe you'd know.

I know people. Not wood.

Well. So much for that.

Have you looked in the attic?

No. I aint overfond of those kind of places. They give me the hobgoblins.

Let's check it out. I'll help you.

It'll be too hot up there.

This might be the coolest day you'll get for a while. Cloudy. There's some breeze. But I can understand if you're afraid . . .

Wasps snarled above my head and old rockwool insulation fibers clawed at my belly where my shirt had slid up. Sweat already dripped from my nose.

You see anything? Grover's voice was muffled though his head poked through the scuttlehole just a few feet away. Junior whined from where we'd left him, as though he were worried for us.

You got the light right in my eyes.

The spot of light caromed away toward the corners. Any artifacts up here?

Oh, here's some now, I said. The light blinded me again. Some prehistoric saber-toothed bat droppings.

Do you ever think maybe it's not your mother you're really mad at? That maybe you're angry at the man who made her happy?

Well of course I'm mad at him. He'd just as well of took advantage of a retard.

The beam stilled on a place just ahead and to my right. Is that rafter cracked? Right there?

I ran my fingers across the jagged diagonal line and wiped them on my pants. No. It's just pitch or tar or something that's run down the side of it. The feel of it filled me with an unease I couldnt hang a hat on. I dont see nothing wrong. Let's get down out of here.

He'd moved up the ladder and was picking overhead with his pocketknife. It all feels solid. He leaned out and poked down at the ceiling joists. Your mother's gone, but what if you had the opportunity to meet that man? What would you do?

Beside my ear a wasp buzzed and brushed against my hair and I froze with my head down. I could feel the rockwool fibers hanging up in my nose and in my lungs. Get out the way. I'm coming out of here. I'd gotten turned and the daylight leaking around him was like a homing beacon.

His light probed close beside him. Wait. I see the problem. The light bobbed back and forth from one side of a pair of spliced joist to the other. The nail heads go in here—he touched one side—but come out way over here.

I glanced at what he'd discovered and put my hand on his shoulder and tried to cram him down the hole. They're just drove crooked.

No they're not, he said, but he backed down. Fresh cool air swept upward as my feet found the rungs. The heads arent angled. They're flush and square. And there's lighter colored wood where the splice has slid apart.

Something rustled under the insulation not far from my hand and I nearly fell down the ladder in my hurry to get away from whatever it was.

We sat on the floor with our shirts sweat-stuck to the wall and wiped at our faces with our sleeves. If I met the man that shacked up with Mom I'd likely nail his bag to that big old wood table downstairs, I said when my pulse had settled. And then I'd give him a dull butcher knife and set the house afire.

He leaned back with his eyes closed and gave me an opportunity to study the strength of his jaw and the hard angle of his nose and the gray stubble that gave away his years. Green wood, he said.

Green wood. The table green wood? The house?

All these roofs were framed with green wood. When it dried it shrank but the nails didnt. And then the joists spread under the weight of snow till the nails pulled tight again. But by then it had a sag. Because the ends couldnt spread. They were held up by the gable framing.

It made sense after I'd thought about it for a while.

What if he turned out to be someone you knew? he said. Someone you liked?

How would you go about fixing it, do you think?

I doubt you can. Not without tearing off the whole roof. Rafters and all. Maybe you could reinforce it somehow.

After a while I thought I had it figured out. I think I'd take away the butcher knife and give him a pair of fingernail clippers.

Then it got so still that the sounds of our breathing strove each against the other and then gradually pulled into sync.

When you start fixing inside—that's when it gets interesting, he said when I thought he'd fallen asleep.

Is that another daggoned analogy? Is it gonna be like this the whole time with you? No rancor in my thoughts or in my voice.

No. I'm talking about wiring and drywall and plumbing and such. He stirred and stood and stretched and looked at his watch. You ever wonder whether our lives just naturally boil down to fulfill some analogy? Or do we each subconsciously choose some random analogy and grow into it? Maybe one from a children's book, or from literature, or a movie. That might make a good sermon.

I aint sure it's either one, I said after a while. Mostly people make up analogies special so they dont have to look square on at the real thing. But he'd slipped away, and I let the thoughts I'd been entertaining go with him. So I'd have to deal with neither one.

———————

I borrowed Alison's pickup and her cordless drill and drove to Hardly Hardware for carriage bolts and nuts and washers. Then I drank two cold Cokes and took a deep breath and climbed back into the attic. I bored half-inch holes through the joist plices until the battery died—two through all of them and three through some—and drew the nuts down against the washers till my arm shivered with strain. I tried not to think of the dark spaces past my light and under the insulation and behind my back. Or of the things in them.

A rope tied to a short board that spanned a second-floor window held the bottom of the ladder from sliding off the porch roof. I eased up onto the upper roof and scrabbled to the ridge and found my feet and stood crouched and unsure. I gave a iffy jump and then one harder as I gathered my balance. Solid as a whiteoak stump.

From the ground against the setting sun my sagging ridge said not weakness but character.

On the second Saturday in June I leaned against the front-yard apple tree and admired the new glass windowpanes and the flue I'd laid up from old reclaimed bricks around new terra-cotta liners and the new paint that glittered on the siding and soffit and the aluminum covering that hid the weathered fascia and the bright hit-and-miss board patches in the porch and stairs that were already headed toward a match with the weathered ones. Nothing perfect. Just daggoned good.

Analogy and allegory and metaphor and simile and nosy washed-up write-for-food preachers be dogged, it was time to go to work inside. I felt ready.

CHAPTER 23

If I'd just stripped the worst spots and fished wiring through the walls like Dad had done upstairs I'd of been okay. But I stood there and thought about how good the outside looked and I rammed the wrecking bar through the old horsehair plaster directly into hell.

From then on I never enjoyed a moment without dust in my lungs or grit in my eyes or splinters in my fingers. How white plaster could make so much black filth was beyond my ken. The pile of rubble spilled into the creek like mine tailings and the little backyard burn pile of damaged siding and rotten porch boards grew into a scraggly hill of wood lath.

Grover yelled once into the cloud of dust but was gone before I could find my way outside. Preach on that for a spell oh bearer of the light.

One short wall at the end of the downstairs hallway gave me pause and a dark blotch halfway up gave me the jimjams. Maybe because while stripping plaster from the ceiling just above I thought I heard movement behind the stain. Excuse enough for not tearing it out was cheap: The house's single big cold-air-return register centered along the bottom would need tinsmithing to keep it from sticking out if I stripped that wall.

Some things are better off left alone.

Five days later I swept the last of the plaster into a shovel and dumped it over the hill and drove to Alison's for a shower and a meal and to put mustard plasters on her latest emergencies. Change them to *pending* disasters.

One day late.

Where you been? she said. Her eyes traced the filthy lines at the corners of my eyes and in the crooks of my elbows. You layin out havin a bigeyed time at my expense?

I took a little trip to hell. That's what it seemed like anyhow. I'd scrubbed in the creek and changed into cleaner clothes but still felt like a coal-miner at a wedding. I looked around the kitchen for a safe place to sit and decided to stand. The smells of frying fat and hot flour drew a groan from my belly.

That aint no excuse. I've half a mind to tear up our agreement. If you're not gonna bother to keep it. Put you out on your butt. Pretending to be mad but not pulling it off with one hand patting Junior on the head.

Aw, get down off your high horse. You never wrote down any agreement. I explained what I'd been doing and why I wanted to finish before I came. I wouldnt of had the heart to crawl back in that mess if I'd of left it for a couple days. I was in hell for sure.

What was Bunk wearin? You tell me that and maybe I'll believe you was there.

I scratched my head and dirt filtered down over my face. I wish you wouldnt talk that way.

I'll talk any way I take a notion to. Now you either git in the tub or to the barn one. And scrub it out when you're done. Or I'll scrub it with you. And then git out here and eat.

I neednt have worried about the wiring. I stripped out all the mouse-chewed wires and rusted undersized electrical boxes from the exposed framing and then tacked bright blue plastic boxes to the studs and strung new cable through the holes. Just like the sketches Hardly Hardware Glen drew with a felt marker on brown paper bags. I even rough-wired a three-way switch in the kitchen just to show off. *Just bug the whites together and put that there black'n under the funny colored screw. Make er a four-way or a five-way or a fifteen-way if you want to; just keep stickin' four-way switches in a line between them two three-ways.* Glen touched fingers together to show what the switches did inside. The main panel was no harder once he explained its simple division of hot wires and ground and neutral.

On July 2, just in time for the holiday, a white power company truck growled up the driveway to turn on the juice. That evening for the first time in decades bare bulbs dangling from temporary pigtails cast light into the night.

Grover appeared like he'd popped out of one of the sockets. He walked around the house without speaking and stopped at the short stained wall I hadnt stripped. You need a receptacle there, he said.

You cant set nothing there. It'd be on top the register.

What if someone puts in different heat? Hot water or something?

Then they can string a receptacle while they're at it. His attitude found purchase under my hide. Is that all you come for? To find fault and mounce on my work?

He shook his head. No, I'm sorry. It just stood out. That's all.

Well. It'll have to keep standing out. Cause tomorrow I start the plumbing.

This I got to see.

Then you better be here more than you was during the wiring. Dont show up after it's done to tell me what I did wrong.

Probably be better if I stayed home and prayed for you.

You do whatever floats your boat.

That's kind of what I had in mind: Boats. Water. Lots of water. He grinned.

This old boy didnt need no steenking prayers just to run a couple water lines. Not even if Glen wasnt there to tell me what to do when I picked up materials from Hardly Hardware. Years ago I'd watched Bunk Reddy fix frozen pipes in the milkhouse and there was nothing to it. My pipe runs were so gun-barrel straight I could see through the holes from one end of the basement to the other.

The PVC drainpipes were easy as buttering a corncob and the cleaner and solvent gave me a dandy buzz that hung on while I scrubbed the box of copper fittings with steel wool. Grover poked his head in the basement door and said, Wheww. That's going to rot your brain.

Brain rot can be a right likeable occurrence, I said, but I took the fittings out onto the stairs so I'd have someone to talk to.

How about the pump? You going to have to put a new one in?

I hope not. It's a submersible and I didnt pull it out of the spring to check it out. But it looks okay.

It's got to be getting old.

Dad put it in right before he died. Took out a old piston pump that was evermore waterlogged or airlocked one. And it's had a good long rest laying there in the spring. Ought to be anxious to go.

He set his chin into his hand and looked off into nowhere.

I smell another sermon a-cooking. You think rest wont be good for it.

He grinned. I'm getting too predictable.

You ought to at least wait and see whether it pumps. That might make a difference in your sermon. Or not. I never seen much effect of real life on one. But I could see he had the sermon wheels grinding, and wasnt paying much attention to me. I scoured the fittings new-penny bright and then cleaned them some more.

You had a wife, he said.

I gathered the fittings tinkling into the bag and stood and stuffed the steel wool in my hip pocket. And you had some sense, I thought. At least for a preacher. Now you've went to meddling, I said.

Grover stroked Junior's belly with his foot, and Hobo crowded in, jealous. A pretty girl. She had that pleasant open face I always liked. Like I hadnt spoken.

Grover. I waited till the tone of my voice brought him to full attention. I'm starting to like you. But keep your nose out of where it dont belong.

He levered up and put both hands on my shoulders and peered like he could see movement behind my eyes. His breath like new-mown hay. You have so much pent-up anger and aggression. You need to release it. Before it destroys you.

What I need—I lifted one of his hands away and wheeled out from under the other—is get these water lines run.

He followed me inside and watched for a while as I measured and spun the tubing cutter and brushed flux on pipe and fittings and fitted the network together. When do you solder the joints? he said.

After it's all pieced together. Then you do them all at once. It'll probly be tomorrow sometime.

You act like you know what you're doing.

I know all a plumber's got to know: hot's on the left and cold's on the right and shit dont run uphill. It's just barely harder than preaching.

So tomorrow you put water in the pipes?

No. I still got to hook up the toilet and the sinks and stuff. Be more like Thursday.

Tell me some more about your mother.

I measured and cut and fluxed and fit and after a while he went away.

I made one last pass over the fittings to make sure I'd soldered every one and that each line terminated in a fixture. Whaddya think?

Looks like a good job to me, Grover said.

I took a deep breath and flipped the water-pump breaker and the pressure switch clicked but nothing else happened. We stood and listened and watched each other like I imagined people in a fallout shelter would while the bombs rained down outside.

I wondered, Grover said. It's been a long time since that pump's been turned on.

Then both dogs perked their ears and the pressure tank moaned and I looked at the gauge and saw the needle creeping up. Sweat beaded on the inlet pipe. I pointed and Grover nodded that he'd heard and seen. We watched fascinated till the needle quit trembling and the switch clicked off.

All right. Let there be water. I cracked open the main valve and released pressure into the pipes. Copper rattled against wood as the pipes took up the load. A few more creaks, then all was still again. I released the breath I'd been holding. Oh mighty prophet, wherefore art thy need for thy boat for to float on thy waters whom hath not been forthcoming?

When Grover raised his palm to give me a high-five a drop of water fell between us. We looked at the floor and then up at the fitting where another drop was forming. A drop hit my shoulder and others twinkled behind Grover.

Helly kerdam, I got a leak. I flipped off the pump breaker and opened the drain bibb and blew away the pressure into the floor trap.

More than one, Grover said. I saw another one over there.

No, I dont think so. That was probly just condensation. Like on the tank here.

Put the pressure back on and I'll help you find them mark them so you can fix them.

Like heck he'd see how many there were. Not today. I'm clear tuckered out. I hustled him toward the door. I'm gonna get cleaned up and get a bite to eat and turn in.

I'll be over in the morning to help. I think you've got a mess on your hands now.

All right. That would be good.

I sat on the front porch stoop till he was gone and then hurried back into the basement. Seven wet spots on the concrete. I marked each with a pebble so I wouldnt lose track of them and fired up the torch and drug a smear of flux onto the end of the solder and heated the joint and waited for the solder to melt. And waited.

I touched the end of my solder to the end of the flame like it might be defective and a shiny BB skittered down my arm and the smell of burning hair singed my nose. Two minutes more of heating did nothing to melt the joint. I touched the pipe a foot from the flame and skin sizzled like a grilled steak and I dropped the torch and it bounced and touched off borehole shavings that smoldered and stunk after I'd stomped them out. Junior watched from the doorway, where he'd retreated, and then wandered away out of sight.

I remembered something Bunk Reddy had said: *One little dab of water in the pipe, she wont melt. Fills the pipe with steam, keeps her too cool to melt solder.* Water in the pipe. Of course.

What had Bunk done? I remembered steam blowing from the pipe. Downward. From a hole. I found my littlest bit and drilled a hole through the fitting and flinched away from the hot water that spattered my arms when it broke through the copper.

Solder melted right off in that fitting and the next and after I'd bored two more holes the pipes were empty and soon new fittings were scoured and flux balmed onto the new-bright metal and the job was finished. The pipes rattled and groaned as the pressure came up but no water dropped from the joints.

What a day. I whistled Junior down off the porch and held him on my lap and scratched under his collar and under his chin. I found a tick under his ear and he stiffed up and hauled against the collar when I pulled it loose and kept lunging and I laughed and said, It cant hurt that bad, and he pulled loose and tore off toward the edge of the yard and I saw a groundhog dip back into the brush with Junior right behind it.

He came hounding back for approval with his tongue hanging back with his ears. I called him a humungous fine dog and rassled with him till he wearied of it. How's a blind dog know what he's after? He shook his head and worried his ear with a hind foot. How you know it aint a thing that figures to eat you? Something after you instead? He sneezed and trotted back to his front-porch rug.

I yawned and breathed deep the liquor of new growth that hung keen on the late air and went back inside the basement.

Where it was raining. Everywhere.

———

I picked a blob of solder from my watch face and shook the almost empty propane tank. Thirty-seven minutes till the hardware store closed. Stay, you worthless little flea farm, I hollered at Junior as I pedaled away on my bike.

Alison passed the keys out the door. Dont you be drivin my truck like you do that bike. And you best put some gas in it for oncet.

When I roared past the Citgo station the needle hung ten cents below empty and fell way down when I rapped on it. Come on, come on.

The same pimply-faced clerk was at the door with a handful of keys when I got to Hardly Hardware. We're closing, he said, but I crowded past him.

You're gonna have to hold your tater for a minute. I just need one dad-blamed thing. The main lighting was already turned off but I knew where the propane was.

I already counted the cash and put it away, he said. You'll have to come back tomorrow.

Where's Glen at, anyhow? I got in the wrong aisle and backtracked and toed a spool of wire and a half bushel of electrical parts fell off the shelf when I caught myself. Aint there somebody around can give me a hand?

I told you we're closed. I'm the only one working tonight.

I looked at the wall clock. That there sign on the door says it'll be locked at eight o'clock. That's two minutes yet. If you can wake up long enough to wait on me I'll be out of here by then.

He was right behind me. You want me to call the cops?

I wheeled so quick his face was in mine before he could stop. Yeah. Call em. Call your boss, too. You want to make a scene let's make her a ring-tailed dandy.

He backed away. Come on, man. I just want to get out of here.

The tank I grabbed felt light so I traded it for another one. My juices pumping now. I need some couplings, too, and a tee. And some solder and flux. The bins were dark so I pulled handfuls of fittings out till I found the right ones. Some tinkled on the floor and some went back in the wrong place.

Why does this always happen to me? the clerk said.

I gathered my stuff against my chest and headed for the checkout.

Just take the damn stuff, the kid said. I already put the money away and I cant open the safe again. The cash register drawer hung open and the tray was gone.

I blew air through puffed cheeks. Look, I'm sorry. I aint trying to bust your hump. I just got a mess at the house that I got to get fixed. Let me give you some money.

He looked at the clock. At the open empty cash drawer. All right.

How much you figure?

His lips moved as he shuffled items from one pile to another. At the flux he stopped and held it up to the light and said, You got the wrong flux. This is acid flux. For leaded solder. We cant even sell that stuff anymore.

What's the difference?

Not a thing, if you dont mind leaks. It just dont work with lead-free solder. He came around the counter and went back into the dark and came out with a different can and finished shuffling the items and said, I dont know. Give me twenty bucks and we'll call it square.

You little shitass.

That's about what it adds up to. Real close.

You couldnt of told me about that flux the other day? When I bought all that stuff.

In the scattered dim lighting his face flushed dark. I'm not your mother. If you dont know what you're doing it's not my fault.

I glared at him till he looked away. Add it up.

I told you. Twenty dollars.

No. Add it up right.

I'm not cheating you. You'll see. On a paper bag he jotted the figures and added them and drew a double line under the sum. It's $19.61. Plus tax.

Put it on there.

He shrugged. Just give me the twenty. It's a better deal. He looked at me and shrugged and calculated and when he'd finished I gave him a twenty and three quarters and a nickel. He put it into the empty drawer and pushed it closed.

You owe me a penny, I said.

You got to be kidding me. He looked at me again and got a penny from his own pocket and slapped it down hard onto the counter.

I picked it up and threw it into the get-a-penny dish and said, Tomorrow morning you ring that sale into the register. You dont, I'll see that your ass gets fired. You understand what I'm telling you? If there's one thing I cant abide it's a daggone thief.

Yeah, yeah.

———

The pickup choked and sputtered and died and lurched to a halt on the shoulder. So close to the Citgo station I could almost read the gas price. I slammed the door and set off walking and right off an old Chevelle with a high rump and cancers of bondo and primer rumbled up alongside. Having trouble? A voice I knowed from somewhere.

Yeah, I am, I said. I run out of gas. I bent to look in the open window.

There is a God, said the pimply hardware clerk. He dumped the clutch and the tires smoked past my toes and his turn signal came on and he turned into the gas station.

When I got there, he was leaning against the icecream case drinking a Dr Pepper. I ignored him and went to the checkout counter. The cashier looked up from reading his paper and raised his eyebrows.

I ran out of gas. You got a can I can borry for a minute?

Nope. People never bring them back.

I'm just right there. I leaned back so he could see past me but he looked back into his paper.

We dont have a loaner.

Well hell. I wheeled and found the short aisle with oil and transmission fluid and fuses. And an empty spot where the gas cans used to be. Clean square patches on the dusty shelves. I went back to the counter and reached across and folded his paper closed. He slid his stool back where I couldnt reach him and glanced up at the security monitor. In it I saw the hardware clerk move closer behind me. I reckon you just sold out.

Ten minutes ago. He stood and leaned back against the cigarette rack. Right after the hardware store closed.

I turned and looked at the hardware store clerk. You guys sleep together too? He was breathing even harder than I was. Punk. I turned my back on him. How about I look in your back room for one.

His freckles looked flighty on his pale face, like they could be knocked loose. Customers cant go in there.

Hows about you fetch me one, then.

But it wasnt a good choice of verbs. And my voice shook when I said it. I watched the steel return to him. Hows about you kiss my ass.

I looked at the monitor and saw in black and white how it would really go down. How it would look on the magnetic tape. They laughed before the door closed all the way.

———

It was a mile to the other side of town and the Sunoco station. Then another one back leaning against the weight of the can. Gas burned both legs where it had slopped from the leaky lid. I forgot to save a splash to prime the carburetor and the battery was near dead when the engine finally fired. When I returned the can to the Sunoco station I tipped the clerk five bucks. The bill disappeared into her jeans and her eyes went back to the TV she'd been watching.

You're welcome.

No problem. She laughed at something on the screen.

I knew better but the pickup didnt. It steered back into the Citgo lot and bumped hard against the curbstop.

He got off at nine, said the clerk. A heavy old man that I didnt recognize.

He glanced at my face and eased back toward the cigarettes the same way the freckled punk had. You need something?

I made my fingernails quit against the countertop. Yeah. Matter of fact I do.

Dont worry. I aint going to drink it, I said to Junior later that night. I dont even know why I bought it. Sometime around 3:00 A.M. just after I was done with cleaning and re-soldering all the joints I hid the six-pack on a shelf behind old canned goods and empty fruit jars and joints of stovepipe. Unopened.

I would have slept in till noon but the drywall and insulation I'd ordered two days before showed up just after 8:00. After we horsed the pile of four-by-twelve-foot sheets inside I took Alison's pickup back. When Grover showed up about 11:00 I was finishing a bowl of Wheaties.

Sorry I'm late, he said. Late breakfast?

Early dinner, I said like I'd had breakfast in the dark. If I waited for the retirees and retards to show up there wouldnt much get done.

Eat up and we'll fix those leaks.

They're done.

All of them?

There wasnt but one. I told you that.

If you only fixed one, it still leaks. I'd bet on that.

You got a dollar to back that up, Bible breath?

Well. He thought and dug for his wallet. That's not even gambling.

We went down the stairs to the basement and I didnt tell him to watch his head till I heard it bonk like a rotten pumpkin. I pulled all the light chains and opened the door to let in some extra and opened the main valve. See. I waved my hand and a drop of water fell not a foot from his ugly nearsighted face.

A gold filling I'd never seen before twinkled at the corner of his smile.

I screwed the valve shut and dug a dollar from my jeans and shoved it into his shirtpocket as I pushed past him and went upstairs for my plumbing tools.

It wasnt a bet, he said when I came back. I dont want your money.

He didnt say anything while I drilled another hole to let the water drain and sweated the old fitting loose and polished a new one. That's the problem with gambling, he said. Someone has to lose.

Leave it alone.

He stuffed the dollar in my hip pocket. I dont gamble.

My hand shook as I fed solder into the joint.

I wish I'd have lost.

Yeah. And I wish I'd of been born dead or aborted or put in a sack and drownded. Then life would be just hair-near perfect. For somebody at least.

Oh. Andy.

I wiped the joint with steel wool and closed the torch valve and looked the joint over good and turned on the water and waited and watched.

You have to get some of that stuff out of you.

He was right about that. There was stuff that needed to come out, and I was ready to turn it loose. I spun and lammed the propane tank against the wall and the neck broke below the valve and the cylinder went spinning *pshew pshew pshew* across the floor and the basement stunk of propane and echoed with curses and with the most lonesome sound there is: the soft click of a closing door.

Putting up insulation is side meat all the way if you got three arms: one to staple and two to scratch with. Fiberglass bored under my skin like new-mowed hair and crawled up my nose and took root in the corners of my eyes. As the wall cavities filled, sound got muffled and my cussing sounded far off and impersonal like a fight at the neighbors' place.

When the insulation was done I lifted the end of a sheet of drywall and reckoned it was time to apologize to Grover. But he wasnt there to take it so the heck with him. The closets and short ceilings I could handle by myself. But then they got finished and I was still on my own.

The ceilings had to go up first. That much I knowed from helping Dad. I studied at it for a while and then measured from floor to ceiling and nailed together a two-by-four tee just an inch shorter. I dragged a sheet into an empty room and finagled one end of the sheet onto the tee and staggered onto the sawhorse with the other. I stood on tiptoes with my head jammed against the drywall and fumbled for my hammer and nails and when I had them I tried to start a nail in the end of the sheet but couldnt quite reach. When I shifted closer the sheet bagged in the middle and the end pulled short and popped up over the edge of the joist. If I pushed up in the middle it jammed tighter, and if I eased off it bagged further. Then I felt the prop start to shift to one side and I grabbed back toward the middle and the sheet cracked half in two and one half folded down across my face and smacked across my legs and knocked me off balance and the tee went down with a crash and the back half slapped down and I was caught in the inverted vee and couldnt move my feet and I leaned over slow like a tree starting to fall and went down the same way in a crash of dust and busted gypsum.

I laid there and inventoried all my parts and then I found my hammer and worked it from under my hip and beat a hole through the drywall and with a nice even swing I reamed it out till it was big enough for me to get loose and I worked on it some more and a little extra. I was whistling when I stood up and brushed myself off. The sheet was so broke up that it was hard to prop up with one end against the sawhorse and the other against the doorjamb. But I got it done and then I took up the hammer and worked it down to rubble about the size of gnat droppings.

I sat on the front porch steps and pondered everything but the six-pack in the basement. I was diligent not to think there. Junior nosed my ear and whined but I kept rocking up and back with my head down and my hands clinched behind my knees and listened to a whippoorwill. The first one I'd heard for years.

After a while it was black dark though it wasnt possible yet and I got up and peed off the porch and felt my way to the bedroom and stretched out on the bed. Junior horned in beside me and for once I didnt chase him to his rug but hauled him close and stared through the tall naked window into a sky that had exploded with stars. I went out through them feeling for the hollowness and the fullness of that unfenced space. After a spell I felt myself slipping away, creeping through an untold expanse at speeds I couldnt fathom, out where I was a microscopic flake of an atom on a speck of dust in a sea of snowflakes that used to be stars and worlds. All around tiny galaxies blossomed and died and toy suns flared and fizzled and dust-sized rocks elbowed for room. Dimensions turned worthless till everything lay ahead and nothing behind. Zooming and zooming and making even more space as I diminished, I fashioned empty universes among galaxies and within worlds and between particles and in the midst of light till I rested in white all sated and spent and filled with nothing. Like God must of felt at the end of a hard week.

Far off beyond my reckoning people laughed and cried and birthed and died and flourished and perished.

I woke a broken old man lying alone on a lumpy mattress in a sagging house, blind and helpless as the dog that snuffled on the floor. Outside, young crows that had not yet learned the art of cawing gargled at the morning. I also woke up with the knowledge that by now I must be a father.

Jesus wept. So why shouldnt I have a go at it.

CHAPTER 2 4

The next day belonged to Alison. You look like you got the scurvy, she said instead of hello. What you been eatin, anyhow?

Dont start on me. Just tell me what you want done.

I think you best go work for yourself today. Give me one when you aint in such a mood.

No, I'm working here. My cash money is getting low, and I cant stand to lose a day. Even if you dont pay hardly anything. And besides, I got to find some help to hang the drywall before I can do anything more at my place.

Get Dulaney to help you. He's always hangin round, aint he? Put him to work.

That gimletass dont do anything but tell me what I done wrong. I'll find somebody.

If there was anybody around here worth the air they sully up pantin everytime they even think about work I'd hire them instead of you. So lots of luck.

What you need done?

Git in here and eat. I went to the trouble to fix and you're gonna eat it.

I aint all that hungry.

I didnt ask was you hungry. She stomped off toward the kitchen without telling me what work to do and I heard batter sizzle on the griddle and caught the hot smart stink of buckwheat flour and I let myself be drawn in.

Part way through my fifth cake she said, So what you two spattin about? I was commencin to think yous had made your peace.

I didnt know we had any peace to make.

She turned from the stove and looked hard at me and said, You want any more?

Maybe one.

Batter hissed and the dipper clattered in the sink. Git it eat and run in town and get what boards you need to fix the yard fence. And some white paint. Not that water-based stuff. Use hot dipped nails. You'll find them overhead along the garage wall.

Shortly after I returned from Hardly she limped from the house and ratcheted herself up into the pickup and lurched from the driveway slipping the clutch and raking the gears.

I pushed away the dinner plate and pulled my coffee cup into its place. That fence suit?

It'll do till someone comes by knows how to do it right.

What's on the chalkboard for tomorrow?

I'll not be here tomorrow. I got a doctor appointment.

She limped around gathering dishes and scraped them into the compost bucket. There better be some gas in the truck for oncet.

You drove it last.

I dont care who run it last. There just better be gas in it.

What you want me to do while you're gone?

I dont want you around here when I aint. Dulaney's gonna be at your place at 8:00. Go get your sheetrock done.

I carried my coffee cup to the drainboard and set it down harder than I intended. You, maam, are one meddlin bitch.

She picked up the cup and examined the bottom and let it go into the dishwater. The taste of Octagon soap one that's familiar to you?

I paused in the doorway without answering.

You dont clean up your trash mouth I can guarantee you it will be.

Sweat coursed like limed-field runoff down Grover's gypsum-whited face. All you had to do was ask. You dont need to send Mrs. Reddy to smoke my ears.

Come my way just a little. Little bit. The sheet bumped into place and I drove the nail home and reached for another. I never sent that viperous old bag to do nothing. You can get that notion out of your head right off. Ignorant heathen busybody.

Grover laughed. We must be talking about different women. The Alison Reddy I know is smart and a devout believer and tends to her own business unless she sees a pressing need to do otherwise.

You're talking about someone else. This one has a pressing need to get her head pressed in a vise. Shut her daggone mouth.

We heaved the next sheet overhead in a fit of grunts and muttered advice. When I had it tacked fast he wiped his face on his sleeve and said, You ever see *Cool Hand Luke*?

That the one where the dude cut the parking meters off? Ate all them eggs?

Yeah. Paul Newman. Jack Kennedy. Strother Martin's the one I remember best.

I dont think I know him.

What we've got here is a failure to communicate. Remember that?

His nasal, whining impersonation was so right-on and brought back such a clean shot of the movie that I had to laugh and give it a try myself. A boy's mama dies, he gets rabbit in his blood. Luke, you get a night in the box.

You got it.

Yeah, but what's that got to do with anything?

You think we could take a break? I brought some cookies and a thermos of coffee.

I grumbled about wasting time but my muscles were singing with the strain of working overhead. We sat against the wall and he poured coffee into two enameled cups and unwrapped a foil packet. In the smells of cranberries and black walnuts and harsh black coffee, for one moment I could have been home again. These are still warm.

I baked them this morning, before I came over.

What time you get up?

He shook his head. Whenever I cant stand it anymore. I dont sleep very well.

The cookie melted away in the coffee and I swallowed the mouthful with my eyes closed. I never knew anyone but my mom to make that kind.

We need to talk about your mother. That's what Alison Reddy came to tell me.

My cookie crumbled and fell into the coffee cup and made a lumpy soup of what was left. Now *she's* starting. If you got to talk about someone's mother talk about your own. I tossed the mess in my cup onto the floor and Grover refilled it from his dented thermos.

All right. He stared at his feet for a minute. Mine grew up just outside of

Pittsburgh. Her name was Delores. I called her that since I can remember. Not Mom or Mother. Kind of blonde hair, a little bit on the heavy side. Brown eyes. She was a single mother. Paul—that was my father—remarried and moved to Meridian Mississippi. I never really knew him. She worked two jobs—some nights and weekends as a receptionist at Howard Johnson's and days at a printing store—T-shirts and hats, not books. She didnt have to. Paul paid support, as far as I know, and she kept the house when they divorced. Made decent money. She just liked to work.

There aint a thing wrong with that, I said. That's the way Dad was. Grover pushed the foil packet my way and I picked a cookie that showed lots of red. What happened to her?

Nothing. She's seventy-eight. She has diabetes but she still delivers meals on wheels and volunteers at the hospital. She's quite a gal.

How'd you get to be a preacher?

She didnt go to church, but she put me in a church-run daycare center. I guess the adults who had the most time to pay attention to and influence me were Christian folk. It rubbed off.

That's what happened to me. Only it was Mom rubbed off and not Dad. That's why I'm such a worthless turd. I got to my feet and brushed off my butt and tied the strings of my nail apron behind my back. Let's get the rest of this done up.

Your mother was a woman of immense worth. And so are you.

You dont know a thing about her or me either. So dont talk like you do.

He got up and tried to put his hand on my shoulder but I batted it away and got up on the sawhorse to measure the next sheet.

Let me tell you what I know and then see what you think.

No. I dont want to hear it. I do not want to hear it.

Well, I'm going to tell you anyway.

I extended my tape measure and poked it into his chest. I said I *dont* want to hear it.

If not now, when?

That's for me to know and you to find out. Now you can either heist up here and help me or you can skedaddle back over the hill.

I need to tell you.

Shut or git.

He shrugged and climbed up with me.

We finished that room and most of the next before our conversation wandered outside the fences of sixteenths of an inch and do you need nails while I'm getting some. You ever been married? I said.

He wet his lips and then wiped them with the back of his hand like it had been a mistake. No. Not technically.

Good. Then there's one more thing you dont know enough to talk about. So dont bring it up.

You're probably right. Why dont you tell me what it's like.

Why dont you shut up and pick up your end.

Work went along way better when we didnt waste our steam on gab.

I'll see you in the morning, he said when we'd finished for the day.

How much I owe you for today?

Not a thing. If your friend cant give you a hand once in a while without being paid, he's not much of a friend.

I thought about forcing money onto him and wasnt up to it. Look. We got the ceiling done and the biggest sheets on the wall. I can get the rest of it. You go do your God-for-cash deal.

I'll be more than happy to help.

Was there some piece of that you didnt understand?

He emptied his apron into the nail sack and wrapped it around his hammer and pencil and utility knife. No. That was pretty clear. Outside, he whistled up the dog and didnt stop at the edge of the woods to wave like he usually did.

I'd been the one to bring up being married but it didnt feel like I had.

Where was she? Boy or girl? Did it look like me? Even a little bit?

Help's way easier to get shed of than thoughts are.

CHAPTER 2 5

The next morning I found a sheaf of papers folded and held down with a brick beside the front door: instructions for finishing drywall downloaded from the Internet. Complete with pictures. At the end Grover had written: Call if I can help. I sat on the step and read them twice and tore them in half and sailed them over the pile of rubble into the creek.

When I came to the short wall with the dark stain I was tempted again to strip it down and see what was going on in there. But when I unscrewed the cold-air return grille along the bottom of the wall I could see if I tore away the inch of plaster and lath the register was going to stand proud of the wall. Cover it up.

I felt easier when my nails found solid wood on both sides of the stain. At least it wasnt rotted. My mood lightened a tad when the stain disappeared behind new gypsum.

Just before dark I nailed fast the last little piece of drywall. I slept like a hammer.

How'd you and Dulaney get along?

The edge had gone off my irk at Alison's meddling but it still prickled. I appreciate you thinking about me but you stay clear of my business. When I need help I'll get it on my own. You worry about your work and I'll handle mine.

She wheeled from the sink and for a second I thought she was going to throw either the potato or the paring knife at me. You talked about work?

I do believe that's what we was into. Like I was talking to a baby.

She turned to the sink and said, Jeeminy fires and hell and brimstone. After a bit the tightness went out of her shoulders and I could hear again the soft swipe of the knife.

What did the doctor say?

She peeled and quartered two more potatoes before she replied. What was that you said about tending your own business?

If there's one special time to be alone it's when you're making your first tries at taping and filling joints. When joint compound slops onto your face and down your shirtfront and in your hair and mouth. Everywhere but where it ought to. With nobody laughing at you you could almost hold your temper. Almost.

The feel of the motions came all at once like learning to ride a bike. All of a sudden the mud hung onto the trowel and wiped clean off the blade. Well, mostly hung. Kind of clean. The closets might need a extra shot of sanding but by the time I got out in the open my work was passable.

At the covered up wall I rubbed at a spot on the drywall and smelled it. Just dirt. I swiped the trowel across the splotch and wiped it back off and all was copacetic.

What seemed like a month of troweling and sanding and sweeping was actually just over a week. Rolling primer onto the smooth clean surfaces was like a day off after haymaking. So what if I'd wore out a wheelbarry load of sandpaper. It looked dern good.

I dont know what I said when I came to the wall I'd covered up but Junior hunkered and slunk off to the far end of the hallway. The faint shape of the stain was clear on the new drywall. It's just a stain I thought but my gut told me different.

I poured paint back into the can and wrapped the roller in plastic and drank a Coke and tried to come up with some route around tearing out my new work. Finally I took a deep breath and jammed my compass saw through the drywall and plaster and felt with the tip while I followed the stud down both sides. I sawed through the crack between two slats of lath across the top and then scored the bottom of the rectangle with my utility knife.

No blood ran out of the crack. No stink of decay and death.

I drove the claws of my hammer through the board and pulled the cut-out section from the hole.

A wave of black pulsing horror puked out over my face and arms foul and corrupt inside my mouth and nose choking my screams biting crawling inside my shirt and tunneling through my hair and chewing inside my ears down my back and my foot slipped in some crunchy paste and I fell into the black seething pool that swept across the floor toward Junior and he yelped and his toenails clattered away and left me floundering in a cesspool of what finally sunk in were ants—millions of giant ants with white egg cases that churned in the waves like maggots—and that realization did nothing to quench the fire of my panic.

I fought up to my knees and scraped at my face and hair and spit and gagged and tore at my shirt buttons and shoes and when I could think again I was shivering naked at the end of the hallway and still shying from the black pool that contracted and expanded like it was breathing and more poured from the wall like I'd hit an artesian well of black water. I felt millions of feet on bare skin and swatted where nothing crawled. My skin was as alive as the swarm.

Then fingers came from the mass and felt for new territory. I shook out my pants and shirt and jammed my feet into untied shoes and found my scoop shovel and a box of garbage bags. Ants swarmed out faster than I could shovel them in until I clutched the bag with one hand and gritted my teeth against the tiny bites that in sum felt like flesh tearing while I scraped the fluid wash into putrid piles and released the top of the bag just long enough to shovel them in. As the corporate foulness gradually became a multitude of individual insects I became the aggressor.

When I was finished four green plastic bags with a gallon or two of ants inside pulsed on the floor like dinosaur hearts. Junior sniffed and snapped at stragglers and yipped when he got nipped.

I carried the bags to the backyard and the pile of clapboard siding and wood lath. My shaking hands struck several matches before the splinters caught and wormed crackling through the pile. When the blaze was so hot that I had to hold my arm in front of my face to come close I lobbed the bags into the fire. Plastic writhed and the ants spilled out in a crackling rush and a dense cloud of smoke belched upward and then dived at me in a gust of wind. I cussed and ducked and ran back to the house.

The six-pack of beer was behind the fruit jars where I'd left it. When I felt for it I knocked a length of galvanized stovepipe onto the floor and the racket beat at my head and I leaned it against the dusty shelf until my breathing slowed. After a spell I pulled my hand away empty and took up the joint of stovepipe and went upstairs.

When I'd cleaned the wall cavity and stuffed it with insulation I cut the hole back to the center of the studs. I flattened the stovepipe and folded the edges back until it would fit and nailed it fast and installed a new drywall patch over it. Bleed through that, I said. My hand shook when I filled the patch so that the joint looked like it was covered with feathers, or waves.

I didnt have a deadline but somehow I felt far behind some shifting point in time when my work must be complete. I worked that night till way past dark when I was too tired to do more and then stretched out on my bed without washing up or eating. My skin was gritty and my ears rang and I tossed and turned till Junior came and his nose touched my knee and my chest and my ear. Then he whined and went back to his rug.

I felt my way to the kitchen and listened at the basement door and drew a glass of iron-sharp water. Dawn found me asleep on the bare living room floor. I didnt remember lying down there.

Flecks of paint flew from the roller and I was missing spots that I had to go back and retouch but I couldnt make myself slow down. Where I didnt take time to roll it out right the paint ran and dripped down the wall. I had to stop. Before I went nuts.

My fingers steadied when they touched the cool cans on the basement shelf. I sat with the unopened six-pack at the top of the stairs and rocked in and out between the dark basement and the bright upstairs like a mother rocking a child. Junior nosed at my arm and the side of my face until I put him outside and shut the door behind him.

I eased a can from the holder and ran my finger along the top of the rim and slid my nail under the tab. The beer sighed and that flat sharp yeasty smell of fermentation poured out. I touched the hole with my tongue and tasted the same well water that stained the kitchen sink's porcelain finish.

Junior barked and his toenails skritched down the front door and I jerked it open and hollered at him and he hunkered and whined till I stooped and touched his head. You cant tear up the house, dummy. He nosed up and licked at my face and his pink tongue slid across the top of the open beer.

You little jerk. I smelled the can and poured it down the sink and took the six-pack out to the rubble pile that tailed down into the creek and one to a throw I lobbed the cans down onto the pile. The burn pile was still glowing with coals and flared up around the plastic holder and died again.

I started over and as steady and methodical as a Sunday-night sermon recoated all the walls. My hands shaking hardly at all.

After I put away the painting tools I ran the old cast-iron bathtub full enough that I could slide my ears under the water. Far away the pipes clunked and groaned in some struggle I wasnt privy to. I slid lower until only my nose cleared the soapsuds. The warm water soothed lids gritty from lack of sleep. Air rushed through my sinuses like fans in a vast empty hall. I rested there for a while.

At the far end of the hall was a door or a window. A light. I moved away from it but every time I looked it was closer. I started to jog but I felt breath behind me and I yelled and fingers slipped around my face and through my lips and down my throat.

I gagged and blew up out of the cooling water and blinked at the orange greasy ring that had been soapsuds. My skin felt waxy and clammed even after I buffed it red with a coarse towel.

It was almost dark. The frantic scrabbling rush toward some deadline had been replaced with a laid-back thoughtlessness.

I shaved and put on clean clothes and walked outside and slid down the trash pile to where I'd thrown the cans. One had punctured and the beer left in it was flat and stale but drinkable. The others were warm and fizzy like carbonated tea. It aint like I'm going to get drunk on five cans, I said to Junior. Four and a half.

The evening was mild and quiet. I sat in the rubble and drank just as I'd painted, patient and determined. Junior's head across my leg leaked warm slobber. While I was taking a long drink I heard someone spitting and I started but Junior didnt move. When I heard it again I shook my head and pounded the heel of my palm against my ear to knock the bathwater free but that made it sound like someone laughing.

Junior got up and walked to the house and I heard his toenails click across the porch to his rug beside the door.

I sat there even after the beer was gone till the night was fullblown and I was chilled and resentful of the dark. I eased to the house and found Junior stretched like an old-testament shepherd across the front door and he growled when I nudged the door against him and I backed off to where I could get my leg into a kick. His dogtags tinkled when he raised his head and I stood there for what felt like a long time till I said, Well excuse me all to thunder.

I turned away from house and bed and felt along the foundation for my bicycle.

Pedaling into the dark couldnt be any harder than a blind dog running into the daylight. The chain rattled and the tires hissed in the gravel when I wandered off either side of the road and I veered back onto the hardtop and pedaled harder. Daring the night to reach out and touch me.

I was sweating hard when Hardly's lights struck a faint horizon through night's black shroud. I stopped short of the Citgo station and found a potato-sized rock just right for breaking freckled heads.

The rock bulged in my pocket like a hard-on in the wrong place. The unfamiliar clerk couldnt keep her eyes off it as she rang up my beer. I threw the loose change quarters and all, into the penny bowl and opened a can before I even left the store and chugged it and set it on the cement ledge below the window.

I couldnt drink and drive but after I tied the thirty-pack to the seat with my belt I could drink and push the bike.

I remember arriving home but not when the destruction started.

The beer ran out before the anger and loneliness did. The night's sounds were splintering wood and breaking glass.

Grover would pick the next morning to show up again. When I heard Hobo's tags jingling I didnt even look up from where I sat on the porch with my head in my hands. Grover whistled and said, Holy cow. I felt his hand on my shoulder and he said, What happened here?

I opened my eyes and surveyed one by one the scattered cans and the splintered doorjamb and the dangling latch and the broken window. Wasted dollars I couldnt afford.

You threw one of your fits.

Is a lie that flows forth without thought a lie? No. I didnt. I didnt care what he thought, so I guess I was trying to convince myself. I no sooner than laid down last night when this car pulled into the driveway. I figured it was just someone turning around but then I heard footsteps on the porch. And then just as I got to the upstairs hallway the front door blowed off the jamb and glass and splinters flew everywhere.

I could see it all as stark and plain as any memory I'd ever had.

I dodged back in my room and grabbed my crowbar and a light and when I got out to the head of the stairs there was three guys and a girl looking up at me. College types. And they had beer and blankets. And a boom box, I think. Yeah, they did. I didnt have a name for the color of the biggest kid's hair but I could see it now in my mind.

So I hollered, Get out. This is private property.

And the girl and two of the guys backed right off, but the big kid set his beer on the step and he said something about this being his party house, and I said, I'll by god show you whose house this is and I started down the stairs and he had this big long flashlight that he drew back like a club and I smashed it with the crowbar just to show him I was serious and then he said they was out of here, to cool my tool and all. And they took off but he left the beer there.

I followed as far as the porch but then their headlights blinded me and one of them threw a rock that went a-whistling past my ear and busted the window. They stopped out there and yelled back cusswords and took off. And I thought they were gone.

Man oh man, Grover said.

I carried their beer out here and set it on the porch and was gonna throw it away today. But they must of come back. Good god, they was out here all night it looks like. I stared around at the scattered cans. Aw no, look what they even done to my bike. I stood the bent frame up but the wheels were too twisted to turn. There just aint no call for this.

Grover went inside and came back out and said, What did Junior do while all of this was going on?

I scratched my forehead, trying to remember. He barked some. But I dont think he went after any of them. Not that I remember, anyhow. He might of, though.

We need to call the sheriff. This kind of thing cant be gotten away with.

I chewed on my lip. We ought to. But I dont know. I didnt get any permits or nothing for this work. I dont want to get in trouble my own self.

Trespassing is one thing, but violence is another. You need to report this.

No. I got too much to lose. They'll end up locking me up for something. And they never catch anyone nohow.

He disappeared inside and after a while he hollered out, Did you break that flashlight?

Yeah. I smashed it to the dickens.

I cant see any trace of it. Or of a rock. All the window glass went out the other way.

I went and stood in the doorway. What is it just exactly you're trying to say here, Grover?

Nothing. But I'm not sure this happened just the way you said.

You got one hell of a nerve. After all this.

He sat on the steps to the upstairs and ran his fingers through his hair and finally met my eyes again. No. That's one thing you cant accuse me of. He pushed past me and was gone.

I was half spooked the whole time I cleaned up the mess. Half expecting those college punks to jump out of the bushes. The water in my ear kept making that spitting sound. And my peripheral vision was full of jumpy figures the way it gets after a real bad drunk.

A hangover was something I thought I knew all about but this was a brand new experience.

CHAPTER 26

Monday morning, while I tore up the old linoleum in the kitchen so I could sand the wood floor underneath, my eyes were still giving me fits. There was forever someone standing there on one side or the other but when I looked they were gone. And the water had really messed up my ears. Maybe the iron in it had done something. Even when I stuck my fingers in my ears I could hear sounds like someone grousing and muttering and then that night it sounded like two people arguing.

The roar of the floor sander I'd rented helped with the sounds but it made my seeing worse. It didnt matter whether I drank from the half-gallon bottle of gin I'd bought on Saturday night or not. Whatever the trouble was it wasnt from the liquor. By Friday night the floor was slick and warm under a satin finish and I was a wreck.

What you doing here on a Saturday? Alison said. I didnt contract for no three days a week. She sniffed the air. Is your bathtub broke?

I sniffed my arm where old alcohol and cold sweat rotted in the pores. I dont know what I got into but I cant get it off. Some kind of weed maybe.

It dont smell like no weed to me.

Well, hey. I thought I'd just drop by for to visit. Aside from work.

Come on. She led the way down the now-familiar hallway, her body just bones that poked here and there at her dress as she limped along.

So how you been?

She eased into the seat across from mine with a frown. Was you makin a swing at small talk or you wantin to know how I am.

I want to know.

Well. She pulled a rumpled lacy hanky from somewhere in her dress and dabbed at the back of her hand. What do doctors know. They die off just as hard as the rest of us.

I rested my fingers on her arm firm enough that she couldnt feel the drinking tremors. What are you telling me? Is there something bad wrong?

They're wantin to bore holes in me and take samples. Like I was a oak tree or somethin. But I aint going to allow it.

Samples for what? You mean like a biopsy or something?

I think that's what they called it.

You dont have . . .?

They dont know what's a-wrong. They dont know much of anything.

Somehow I'd always thought of her as just always being there. Always the same. But then I'd thought the same way about Bunk. Now look here, Alison. You got to do what you can. You cant just sit and let whatever's wrong get worse. If you had kids they'd tell you the same thing.

She looked at me like I was something she hadnt seen before and then she shook her head like she wished she still hadnt seen it. When you got to the edge of your belly button you thought you'd found the property line at the far end of the universe, didnt you.

I'm sure that was supposed to mean something but it got past clean.

Even a slug's curious about what's on the other side of the spinach. But you're just about the most self-centered beast I've yet encountered.

I crossed over and felt the coffee pot and found it cold and empty. She didnt offer to make any. I know I either said or did something to bring that on. But I dont know what it was.

How in the world you could not know that I got kids is beyond me. Who do you think that is in them pictures? She waved her hand and everywhere it pointed pictures of vaguely familiar faces jumped up where there hadnt been any before: On the wall. In the windowsill. Stuck fast to the refrigerator with fruit-shaped magnets. Right there's Lawrence and his wife Judy and my grandkids Dink and Tyler and Sissy. And that right there's Mandy.

If there's some way to respond to that I dont know what it is. Beside the kitchen window hung a padded heart with a short handle and an embroidered logo that said GRANDMA'S PADDLE. Her coffee cup said MOM.

Well. Where are they?

Kansas. And Mandy's in Warshington DC.

I guess they was gone before I was big enough to remember.

Maybe so.

What do they say about having tests to see what's wrong with you?

I aint told them. And I aint going to.

How are people supposed to know stuff if you wont tell them?

You ask questions. If you dont care enough to ask, you dont care enough to know.

The ticking of the clock over the cabinets was way louder than usual and when Alison shifted in her seat I could almost imagine I could hear the linings of her joints rubbing together. This might sound less than sincere, coming right now. But I'd like to know about your family. And about how Bunk died.

I aint up to talkin about it. She picked at her bra strap like it was gnawing on her. The work's just about caught up around here. So how about you dont come for a couple of weeks. And then just for a day.

Tell you the truth, I cant get by on no more money than that.

Then get a job. I cant work you till Jesus comes. This wasnt no permanent arrangement we had. Just while you was fixin' up the house. Just till you earned enough money to pay for the place.

When's that gonna be?

Like I said. When I say.

Well, I got a lot of money into it by now. We need to come to some kind of an agreement because I dont want all my time and money to go to waste. For somebody else.

I started listing the work I'd done but she held up her skinny hand to cut me off.

I know what you've done. Probly better than you do.

Well how would you know that? I havent told you what I was doing.

I ask questions.

There just wasnt any way to get around her. I really do want to know about your family.

You go find out about your own first and then maybe I'll share a piece of mine. Now you go on home. I feel like laying down for a spell.

As I climbed up the stairs to my place it felt like a lead blanket settled over my shoulders. I stayed sober and filled nailholes in the trim until dark then went to bed and fell asleep before the old worry mill got to grinding.

Just after midnight I woke to the chokey glug of Beverly whoever's old Pontiac Tempest in the driveway and smelled the sour smoke that puked from the rusted tailpipe. I sat straight up in bed but Junior didnt stir and the sound faded away but there was no crunch of gravel or flash of headlights. I felt my way to the kitchen and found my bottle and sat at the table until daylight.

Two nights later it was Lilo's cornhusk voice that dragged me up from a dreamless hole. *Get down, get down!* Then the rattle of old Fiddler's chain through the doghouse door and his low whuff as he smelled something strange or interesting. Even when I clutched the covers over my head I could hear aluminum cans rattle in the pickup's bed when Lilo shifted on the seat. I burrowed deeper until I could hear only my own shallow breathing and smell only my own fear.

But when the unmistakable clatter of Linda's Subaru came I ripped open my bag and jumped to the window. Nothing.

The next day I sat on the porch swing I'd repaired and rehung and stared at nothing. The sky was high and indistinct and air was keen with faraway woodsmoke and the drone of locusts numbed the mind. A green apple fell from the front-yard tree and Junior raised his head and trotted there and looked and smelled. He'd grown to a lanky muscular grace, his back higher than my knee. He selected a hard green globe and tossed it in his teeth and caught it and loped back and laid his head on my knee. Wanting me to throw it but not wishing to give it up. Apple juice ran through my fingers and my memory.

On the Fourth of July of the year Dad finished seminary we went on the only picnic I remember. While he put away the scythe and the handsaw and the hammer Mom packed cold chicken and dill pickles and crusty bread and a half-gallon jar of Kool-Aid into an empty drywall bucket and we walked up along the creek to a rundown apple orchard. She spread an old blanket on the ground and we all ate too much and Mom stretched out and slid off to sleep.

You want to play ball? Dad said.

Yeah. But we didnt bring no ball or bat. By the time I'd run get them he'd change his mind. Or be asleep beside Mom.

Let's see what God's got that we might use. He levered himself up and twisted a dead branch in the crotch of a tree until it broke and tested it for size and picked a green apple from the grass and tossed it up and swung and missed and looked stupid and girlish.

Let me try. You throw to me.

He gathered an armload of apples and walked away but not far enough and lobbed one back and I broke it and he threw a little harder and I smashed that one and a blob of it landed on his shirt and he dumped his armload of apples and spit on his handkerchief and dabbed at his shirt.

Leave it alone. It'll wash out. Mom was sitting hugging her knees. Her big dark eyes like pools of maple syrup.

Dad made an underhand toss that landed short and I said, C'mon, put the pepper to it. He threw overhand and I bowed forward in the middle and let it go behind me and he looked embarrassed and red-faced and Mom laughed and then he really fired one right down the middle that caught me by surprise and I swung a mile behind it and she laughed again.

Dad rubbed his arm. I should have warmed up first. I'll be sore tomorrow.

Fraidy cat, I said. Fraid you'll get your shirt dirty.

He fingered an apple like he was feeling for the stitches on a baseball. Are you going to be mad if I strike you out?

You cant do it so it dont matter.

No. I'd better not.

Throw the apple, Darrell. I looked at Mom and she was no longer smiling. But not sad.

The apple came slicing in and I just brushed it with a bat. A clean miss on the next and then the next one turned into a green mist that burned my eyes and left a tang on my lips.

Dad paused and unbuttoned his sleeves and rolled them above his elbows. His face was already red and sweat coursed just ahead of his sideburns. He hitched his pants and shuffled his feet to a place he found suitable. You better be ready to swing.

I waved the bat where I wanted the apple and it came there so fast that it moaned in passing and I heard it rip through the grass behind me before I'd hardly started my swing.

No fair. I wasnt ready.

I got set and he threw again but now I was afraid of being hit and I shied away even though the ball was right where it should have been. I determined to hang in and stay ahead of the next but it came drifting in like milkweed fuzz in the breeze and my swing nearly tore my arms from the socket and then I swung backhanded and missed as it finally went by.

That's three strikes. You're out.

I looked at Mom and her eyes were saying something that I couldnt understand. You're too close. Back off some.

No. I didnt say I'd play all day.

Just a little bit more.

All right. Just a little. He backed off and it made the balls seem a lot slower and I broke them and crushed them and demolished them and when I looked back at Mom she smiled and I felt like the king of the world.

I carried the bucket when we walked back down the hollow to home with Mom right behind and Dad in the rear. It wasnt no fair that you struck me out, I said over my shoulder. You never told me that you knowed how to throw.

You never asked.

Mom's footsteps stopped and she said, You've got apple on your lip, and when I turned she'd leaned up and kissed him on the mouth.

I said, Awww, and wheeled away so I wouldnt have to look.

We rocked in the porch swing for just a little bit and Mom said, Andy, I'm out of eggs and I'd like to make a pudding pie. How about you run over to the Reddys' and get a dozen.

Give me the money.

Dad dug two quarters from his pocket. Dont take any change. Make them take it all.

I know. I started for the shed and Mom yelled, Not on the bike. You'll break the eggs.

I get them that way all the time.

You break them sometimes too.

It wont hurt you to walk, Dad said.

With both of them on the same side it was no use to argue. You better not do anything without me.

Alison fed me pie and Bunk showed me the baby ducks and when I came home with the eggs they were wearing different outfits. How's come you changed clothes in the middle of the day?

I got sweated up playing ball, Dad said. But Mom hadnt played.

You got a whole bunch of eggs in the frigerator, I said when I came back out.

I must have misfigured, Mom said.

Well you better make two pies then.

I sat here and got tired. Maybe I'll make one another day.

———

I prized the apple loose from Junior's teeth and threw it and heard it splash in the creek. Now we'll see if you find it, I said as he scrabbled off the porch after it.

As nearly as I can remember, those were the last words I spoke for several days. Not even to Junior or to the haunts that danced in the corners of my sight and groaned and argued and mumbled throughout the night. Even when I hit my thumbnail while tacking up a piece of crown moulding I dont recall commenting on it.

Whatever was in me that was wanting out, I was going to be empty when it was gone.

I wasnt drunk but it wasnt because I didnt try, at least for a while.

One morning—I dont know if it was one or five days later—after a night that crawled with sounds and voices and smells, I walked through the dew-bent grass to where the path to Grover Dulaney's split the woods. Daylight had spilled into the meadow but the forest squatted dark and hollow and impenetrable.

I returned to the house and made coffee and sat on the porch swing and waited for full daylight. The night was a dirty blanket—cold and wet and used. Then a warbler trilled and a rooster crowed far away and a cow bellowed forth the agony of a full udder.

I tossed the dregs of my coffee into the grass and set off down the driveway with Junior brushing against my leg to keep me located. I turned right at the mailbox and when the sun caught me at the open field where Dad had died, I stood and let it soak deep inside.

Until I waded through the waist-high grass behind the old church I wasnt sure where I was headed. Then I knew I'd been aimed in this direction for a long time. Junior thrashed through the wet grass and nosed impatient at the gate. I forced it back through goldenrod and thistle and stood among gray tombstones lurking like woreout cars up on cinderblocks.

One small stone deep in a back corner marked where both Dad and Mom slept in the yellow clay. I stomped the weeds down till I could see and then gathered Junior between my legs and sat on the stone of someone I never knew. The marble was warm against my wet jeans.

The graves were uneven, Dad's side bloated and Mom's shrunken. The single stone just had the names and dates and at the bottom one word—*Together*.

My jeans were almost dry when I spoke. Who are you? Junior lunged up and licked at my mouth, his breath tarnished with something I didnt want to consider in a graveyard, and I spat to the side, careful not to hit anyone.

The graves sucked away my energy. I edged the dog away and slid to the ground and leaned against the stone. Junior leaned his head back to nuzzle my ear. I was staring into his sightless eyes and I could see inside as though it was installed backward. He was soft and warm and kind to the core but then he jerked his head and his skull whacked my nose and I said, You little bastard. I pulled him tight and he wiggled into place and stilled.

Junior was gone when I woke and the grass was dry and I was bewildered. I read the names and felt that some part of me had joined the dead while I'd dozed.

I got to my feet and whistled for Junior and when he came we walked stiff-legged to Matt's grave. I dont know how long I stood there.

The gate screeched when I forced it shut, loud enough to drive a man crazy. Loud enough to wake the dead.

CHAPTER 27

The house was finished but for the odds and ends that never get completed: a piece of trim missing over the inside of a closet door and a few missed nail holes needing putty and a pull on a cabinet drawer. Final jobs I lacked money and energy to finish. The house felt like a tomb not for bodies but for wasted days and months and years. I swung on the porch for a while and then wandered around the overgrown clearing.

At the old Dodge I stopped to pick with a fingernail at the peeling paint and kick at cracked tires sunk deep in the dirt, then continued my circuit to where the weeds were divided by the path to Grover Dulaney's. It was smooth-worn as though by generations of bare feet. Come on, dog. Junior padded behind as we set out up the hill. I paused at the crest to catch my breath.

I wouldnt go down there if I was you, said a cornstalk voice that filled my mouth with litter.

Junior looked the other way as though he hadnt heard. Or had heard something more important.

I closed my eyes for a second and then looked to where Lilo sat on a rotted stump, all stick-limbs and sagging clothing—nothing new. He grinned and revealed inside the luminous green of months-old cheese. I'm warnin you.

He said something else but it was lost in the roar of blood in my ears and the pounding of my feet back down the path to home.

When Junior emerged from the woods, Lilo limped behind. Leaned on a crooked walking stick like he'd come a great piece. He waved and shaded his eyes and peered around the clearing and waded through the goldenrod to the old Dodge. Even from where I cowered inside the screen door I could hear the door's soft click and see the green flicker of his grin behind the sun-scalded glass. He was still there when I peeked out just before dark.

And the next morning.

You aint got the worms do you? You look clear hollered out. Alison didnt look any better. Hair like dead cornsilk. Putrescent oysters beneath her eyes. Her teeth still in a glass somewhere. Bare feet and legs hanging like dry branches beneath a tattered housecoat.

Top of the morning to you too.

Dont hammer the door down while I'm sleepin and expect sunshine and sweet potatoes.

I combed my hair with the fingers of both hands. Look, I'm sorry I woke you up. Can I come in for a cup of coffee? I need to talk to you.

It aint two weeks yet.

No, it aint. But I need to talk.

She backed away from the door and I stepped inside and she grasped the handrail and dragged herself up onto the first step toward the bedrooms. You make coffee while I get dressed.

I looked away before I had to watch her do another step.

She was gone a long time. I sipped from the steaming cup and examined her pictures. Her son and daughter—Lawrence and Mandy, she'd said—I might have seen before. Maybe at church where I didnt know who they were. Or maybe at the Reddys' where I'd mistook them for church people. The smaller kids were strangers but I could see Bunk in the girl's face.

In one picture Mandy stood with a girl of the same height. Their arms resting lightly on the other's hips. Mandy was Alison all over, just twenty-five years younger. The stance. Frame. Nose and eyes. Somehow very beautiful.

The stairs creaked a full minute before I heard Alison's slippers shuffling on the worn linoleum. I poured you a cup to cool, I said without looking at her.

I was comin to see you today but now I wont have to. Her hair was washed and pulled back wet into a hairstyle that had gone out in the '40s. A white blouse sharp-creased down the sleeves and navy-blue slacks. Her big brown purse replaced with a small tan clutch. Powder and a touch of lipstick. I'm goin away for a spell.

Well . . . where you going? Alison not being at the Reddy farm would be like the house not being there when I came. How long you going to be gone?

What you come to talk about?

I sat across from her at the table and tried not to let the cup clatter on the saucer. This hasnt worked out the way I thought it would. Fixing up the house and all.

That aint my fault.

I'm not saying it is. But I'm clear broke and I'm not as happy there as I thought I'd be. So I thought that maybe if you could just give me back the six thousand I gave you we could call it square. I wont charge you for the labor I did. And I'll eat the materials.

Backin out of our deal just when I need you.

You ought to be able to sell it easy now for way more than six. It's ready to go. At least give me part of it back. You got by far the shiny end of the stick.

That aint the catch. The point is keepin your word.

Let's talk about that. Keeping your word. I've done up the work here till you dont have anything left for me to do. And I've fixed the house all up. But it hasnt been enough. You're never gonna say that the deal's done.

She inspected the back of her hand and then chewed at the corner of a nail and inspected again. Some busybody's been tellin tales on me. Meddlin where he aint got no business.

I ran that one twice around and still came up empty. I havent told nobody one thing about you. I havent even seen anybody to tell anything.

Oh, get your nose out of your bellybutton. I didnt say it was you.

I thought we were talking about the house. About my money.

No, you was. I'm talkin about goin to Warshington and livin with Mandy while I get my boobs cut off. She met my eyes for the first time since she'd sat. Dont look at me that way. They aint nothin but reminders of what was there anyhow. Like raisins reminds you of grapes.

You got cancer?

Bunk said oncet that he was gonna try that streakin that was goin round back in the '70s. And I told him he ought to do it at the garden club cookout. That maybe he could take the prize for best dried arrangement. He didnt think that was very funny.

What did the doctor say?

Bunk never said it to the doctor. Just to me.

About your being sickly.

That dern Dulaney called up my kids and told em I was doctorin and now they're all in a froth about it. Now I got to let some sawbones butcher at me. Pump me full of chemicals.

Well good. I'm glad you're going to get it took care of.

She tasted my coffee and made a face and set it back on the table. Let me tell you, it's scary.

Anyone would be trepidatious about getting cut on.

Oh, I dont care nothing about that. It's goin to Warshington. Livin with two other women.

Mandy got a roommate?

They call em partners I think.

Heat built in my ears and I stared into my cup for another subject but saw only my own reflection. Holler looking like she'd said.

But we'll get by. She leaned forward and whispered, Mandy always was my favorite. Anyhow. I was plannin on you watchin over the place while I was gone. Keep the yard mowed. Make sure critters dont get into the house or nothing.

I been thinking about moving on. Maybe out to Akron. Somewhere I can get a job that pays decent. There's not much around here.

She groaned up out of her chair and opened a cabinet drawer and withdrew a manila envelope and slid it onto the table in front of me. See if this here changes your mind any.

Inside was a blue deed for the home place. In my name. And a stack of uncashed traveler's checks. I looked at all the papers and put them back into the envelope and closed it and then opened the clasp and took them out and looked at them again. Why?

Why not? Cause I felt like it.

This is no more right than not giving me anything at all. It's all lopsided.

Lopsided was when Bunk bought the place when I didnt care to cause we couldnt afford it. Up in your sixties aint no time to be borryin money. And I think it worried him to death. He never was content after he had holt of it. He couldnt leave it be. Had to be mowin and cuttin brush and fixin fence.

The place worked on Dad the same way.

Well. I'm glad to be shut of it.

I didnt know you were so hard up. That you had to borrow to buy it.

We wasnt hard up. But we didnt have money to be out buyin farms we didnt need. And he had a good insurance policy he bought way back in the '50s. So I'm set up fair now.

I walked to the window and looked out to hide the emotions that were leaking out of my face. I dont know what to say.

I only give you half the money back. You was three thousand worth of aggervation I figger. At least that much. And you done right smart of a pile of work this summer.

What all you want me to do while you're gone? I know the cat will need fed.

No. That's one of the first jobs I got on the list. Put that sorry old thing out of its misery. It's lived longer than it meant to.

When I hugged her as I was leaving I had the feeling it would be the last time I'd ever see her. With her ear against my chest she must of heard my thoughts. You aint gettin rid of me this easy. I'll be back. And the place better be in good shape. You aint too big to have a strip of harness leather wore out on your butt.

I didnt get a chance to check if Lilo was still in the Dodge when I returned home because Beverly was framed in the living-room window. Cigarette smoke boiled out when I slipped in the back door. Hello.

She coughed.

What are you doing in my house?

What do *you* want from *me*? I dont even know you.

I hid my envelope on top of the refrigerator and slipped down the hallway to where I could see her. Against the outside light there was nothing ghostly about her. Her breathing the soft rasp of tearing tissue.

I dont appreciate your coming in my house when I'm not here.

She turned to reveal eyes dim-lit from within like a jack-o-lantern with fireflies inside. The nametag on her server's uniform glowed too: LINDA. I covered my eyes and when I looked again she was gone.

The front door's latch clattered like ten-dollar teeth as I eased it shut. Junior looked in my general direction and thumped his tail against his rug. When I turned from the door Matt Tamper was stretching his muscles against the apple tree. The tree shook and a green apple thudded into the grass. Run with me, he said.

Junior stretched and closed his eyes and I wondered why a blind dog would close his eyes. That's when I knew I was crazy. The knowledge was a great comfort.

I cant. My voice was dry and deader than his. Junior slept on.

Scared you'll get run over?

Why not. I looked out the driveway, considering. Out by the mailbox someone lounged under a misshapen oak tree.

Who's that out there?

You coming?

Not till I find out who that is.

He straightened and shielded his eyes and faded and disappeared.

Lilo nodded and spread his moldy smile when I eased onto the Dodge's seat. Best set a spell, he said. He peered hard with clouded eyes. You look like hell.

You too. Junior lunged up onto the seat and sat facing Lilo like he was looking into his ear. I pulled the door closed and rolled down the window and looked out the windshield toward the house. Just like old times.

There aint no beer. Things is high and they cut off my checks soon as I croaked.

I slipped a pint of vodka from my hip pocket. I brought my own.

He laughed. Well by god. I thought I'd never see the day.

Junior sighed and sprawled on the seat with his nose occupying the same space as Lilo's spine. But I could see them both. I touched his shirt and sniffed the air. It felt like chambray and smelled like an old car and a wet dog. I stopped short of touching him. Lilo sniffed under his arm and shrugged.

You for real? I said.

Hell, I dont know nothing about that philosophical kind of stuff. I tole you that before. If Descartes never figgered it out dont look at me.

What's Beverly doing here? She aint dead.

Beverly who?

That woman in the house.

He shook his head.

Why's she got Linda's nametag?

Them's your people. I dont know nothing about em. Irritated.

I broke the bottle's seal with my fingernail and unscrewed the top and drank and coughed and drank again. You're talking.

I allus did talk. You just never bothered to listen.

The car rocked as Lilo shifted in his seat and tall weeds rustled against my elbow.

I'm ready to listen now.

What you want to know?

Whatever you got to tell me.

No. You got to ask. I cant volunteer no information. Them's the rules. He hawked and spat out the window and I turned my head so I wouldnt see.

Rules.

You made em. So dont go bitchin about em now. He looked down at the dog that shared his space and wrinkled his nose. That there's one stinkin dog. Course they all are.

I scratched Junior's belly and he hoed at the air with one hind foot but otherwise gave no indication of being awake. All right. Tell me about Mom and Dad.

Mine? I dont know a solitary thing bout yours.

Grover Dulaney.

Who?

I swallowed more vodka and searched for common ground. Linda?

The one you call Sweetpea. Heard lots about her. Never met her though.

I dont know what to ask.

Hows about that feller run down the road a bit ago.

Matt Tamper? I know daggone well he was dead a long time fore I met you.

He shrugged. You just as well go set in the house and feel sorry for yourself then. I'll just be on my way.

Then tell me about Matt, dammit.

I wasnt there. But I know someone that was.

All right. Who was that?

Lilo's skinny arm stretched from his sleeve like a snake's tongue and adjusted the rearview mirror. The lens was black-edged and cracked and threw back two out-of-kilter halves of my face. Lilo's green mouth was reflected in my eyes. Or was in them. Ask him.

I dont remember a thing. I never did.

Bullshit.

While I stared at my reflection years fell away from it and my eye swelled shut and my lip fattened and bruises welled on my cheeks. *The soft yet heavy thump of impact, the car slewing, seat fabric rasping at my face, the gritty floor-boards, my arm jammed under the seat and I claw my way up and it's Linda's face in the mirror wide eyed, I hit a deer, it's just a deer, go back to sleep it's okay, Andy . . .*

The backseat. I was in the backseat.

Lilo laughed. You done tole me that ten hundred times. Ever time you got your snoot full of drink. That aint no news.

Fingernails scratching at the door, slipping back and clawing up again and Linda crouched over a twisted body we have to get out of here now before some-one comes get in the car get in the damn car Andy get in the car now a car is coming we have to get out of here before someone sees us, get in the car, Andy, get in the car now, a car is coming, the engine revving and jerking against the clutch oh damn if they recognized us we're done for bouncing across ruts wheels spinning mud flying in my face Linda crying crying crying.

It was a accident. She never would of done it a-purpose. Not Linda.

Lilo waved his hand in a dismissive way. It dont make a rat's kazoodie to me. Tell Matt. He's the one got tire tracks up his bunghole. I aint got nothing in it. He laid his head back and closed his eyes and adjusted to a comfortable position. Though she might not be the girl you think she is. Seein as how she blamed it on you at her first chanst.

I ought to bust your filthy mouth.

He spread his lips and showed the green inside. Have at it. Not even opening his eyes to see if I would.

I didnt speak again until the bottle was empty. How could you of let that dog there to die. Just let him there where you could have got to him. Where you could have helped him. But you didnt lift a finger.

Lilo opened his eyes and lifted his head from the seatback and looked around like he'd been sleeping. You talkin to me?

You son of a bitch.

I see you done developed a fullblown terminal case of the self-righteous ass. His finger wagged just in front of my nose and for the first time anger tightened his voice. I aint never done one thing you aint done time and time and time again. Why in the hell you think I'm stuck paired up with you? So dont call me no sumbitch, you asshole.

I didnt leave Fiddler to die. Mom did that. I wasnt even there.

Dog? Dog! I aint talking about no dog. Dogs is expendable. They aint nothing. No more'n a acorn is.

I sailed the bottle out the open window and heard it break against a stone in the edge of the woods. Maybe I just give dead people more credit for making sense than I ought to.

Then I'll just list off some examples. Hows come your ole man croaked out in the middle of a field by hisself? And how'd your ma die? You dont even know cause you wasnt there, was you. He started ticking off his fingers. Where's your woman at? Aint you got no kids by now? Them fellers you hung with down there in Ransom—Dave Sinko and that there Mike somebody you allus yapped about? That old half-dead woman lives one farm over? The one you go gobble up her meals all the time. The preacher man lives back over the hill all by hisself that you treat like dogshit ever time he shows up to make friends with you? That feller Glen in at the hardware store that you wont even know now that you aint got no more use for them. Where they at? Where's a one of them at? You aint got the slightest clue cause you dont care. You just dont care. He crossed his arm and spit out the window like he'd filled up with venom. But them aint the ones that really chaps my ass. Nosiree bob. Not a-tall. Them's your own problems.

I reeled through the list and found nobody missing. My voice was small and belonged to someone I didnt care much for. You didnt miss anybody I can think of.

He wheeled and looked at me square on and a murky tear welled and spilled down his desiccated cheek. What about me? WHAT ABOUT ME?

Fifteen feet from the car I pulled up short at Junior's barking. Snotty swooshes trailed his nose across the glass and his toenails rattled on the door panel. I went back and opened the door and he jumped out with no way to judge where the ground was and piled up at my feet and stood up and shook.

I'm not like you, I said into the empty car. Not one bit. I went into the house and got another pint bottle and headed up the path to Grover Dulaney's.

CHAPTER 2 8

Thirty years ago the old Scott place had nestled in the hollow like an egg in a soft glove. Now the white German siding was psoriatic with peeling paint and straight lines of fence were sucked into the undertow of bramble and elderberry and collapsed outbuildings and the flotsam of discarded appliances. The rear of an old Chevy pickup protruded from a sagging garage. When I got closer I saw it had been cannibalized for wheels and bumper and glass.

In what would have been a front yard if it had grass instead of weeds stood a fifteen-foot-tall monstrosity made of what looked to be a truck front axle and an antique dump rake and a water heater and parts of a motorcycle and a bedframe welded together. A nightmare-induced sculpture of some sort.

Junior tried his feet on the rotting front stairs and then backed off and waited for me to lead the way. Dried flowerpots and a stained cardboard box filled a porch swing that hung akilter on rusty chains. The storm door was stuck halfway open on the heaving porch floor and paint-welded shutters buckled over smears of dark glass. Yellowjackets buzzed from a jagged hole in the porch floor. A vague path through the junk led around the corner to what was likely a kitchen door. Beside the door, chemical-red chunks spilled from a hole torn in a huge bag of Kennel Master dog food. A tarnished box lock secured the door.

I knocked knowing the house was empty. The door's glass was opaque with grime and nothing was visible through the antiquated keyhole but part of a white wooden chair. Above my head something scratched and fussed in a beaded porch ceiling that dangled strips of dingy paint. The bite of bat manure was heavy in the still air.

I sat on the listing stairs at the head of a ragged fan of bottles and cans tossed from the porch into the weeds. I got up and peered through a broken shutter slat and saw only my own eyeball reflected in dark glass. When I tugged at the hole the shutter collapsed over my head in a rockfall of coal dust and dead flies and I fell backwards and my heel broke through the boards.

When I'd brushed myself off and looked to make sure Grover wasnt coming, I shielded my eyes and looked in at a small tidy room—a desk and office chair and short stacks of tapes and disks and an oversized computer monitor with a screen saver building and collapsing.

On both sides of the monitor were pictures of my mom. I looked for a while and then sat on the steps again. From my hip pocket I took the unopened bottle of vodka and broke the seal and smelled it and held it to the light and screwed the cap back on and tossed it out into the grass.

Some time later came the rattle of loose parts and a faded red Chevy pickup wallowed over the rutted road into sight. Grover pulled up to the edge of the yard and Hobo jumped over the side of the bed and he and Junior touched noses and then tore around outside the house like puppies. Grover sat in the cab and looked at me for a while and then got out and went around to the other side and returned with a grocery bag.

Andy, he said. He stopped and considered the torn-loose shutter and then brushed by me up the steps trailing the smell of laundry detergent.

Hey.

Come on in.

Before I learn one other thing I got to know what that porkyakus right there is supposed to be. I nodded at the welded-together monument of junk.

Grover glanced at it and said, That's the Statue of Limitations. I built it to remind me that time changes things. And that even junk has value.

Only then did I realize how perfect it was.

His key rattled in the lock and the door groaned open and I followed him into a boar's nest of dishes and pans and books and newspapers and tools— nothing put away. Grover took what looked like a starter motor from a chair and set it on the swaybacked table and offered the chair to me. He shook a coffee pot and lit a burner with a wooden match and sat across from me.

Above the kitchen sink was a spray of dried wildflowers that had started to disintegrate. Something like it had hung in Mom's kitchen. On the windowsill was a misshapen blue vase I'd made in third-grade art class. On the wall hung other pictures of Mom that I remembered and some that were obviously taken later. Grover was in several of the pictures with her.

What are you thinking? he said.

I guess maybe I've known for a while. But I wouldnt let the thought take root.

He nodded as though that made perfect sense. What's it going to be? he said. A butcher knife or nail clippers?

I stood for a closer look at the pictures. You said you were never married.

No. He looked at the floor and at me and then at the floor again. She wouldnt. Said she'd changed her name once and that was enough.

She lived here with you?

The coffee was boiling and blowing steam but he made no move to shut it down. Yes.

I hope it didnt look like this then.

I've let it go.

Well. I guess that explains why you're self-employed now. Living in sin and preaching aint normally on the same line of the job application.

Yes. I had to choose.

Was it a hard choice?

Probably the easiest one I've ever made in my life.

You loved her then.

I cant tell you how much.

Did she love you?

As much as she could. She still loved your father.

I removed a picture from the wall and held it in better light. She looks happy.

He stood at my shoulder and looked at the picture. I think she was. Her depression was mostly a chemical imbalance. We got her on medication for a while and she learned to get lots of sunlight and exercise. Once in a while in the winter months she'd have to go back on the pills. But it was something we learned to live with.

Medication.

He nodded and shrugged. She had hypertension, too, and that added to her problems. High blood pressure.

I know what hypertension is. I just didnt know she had it.

She didnt either till I got her to see a doctor.

So her depression could of been fixed all along. Just take a pill.

It's not quite that simple. But yeah. Having someone to talk to helped.

And Dad prayed for her.

So did I.

I pushed past him and turned off the burner under the coffee pot and examined the cups on the counter and selected two and poured them full.

You still going to nail my bag to the table and set the house on fire?

The coffee was scalding and stale and good. Probly not. I got too much work into mine to burn it now. And I aint sure this rotted up place would burn.

Well. That's a relief.

But you could of told me.

You didnt make it easy.

I reckon there's that. I sat back in the chair and leaned back with my head against the wall and my eyes closed. I heard him leave the room and return and something flopped beside my elbow.

These are yours. It was wrong for me to have taken them.

He'd given me a plastic bag with Mom's garden plots inside. The ones I thought Junior had chewed up.

I was afraid you'd throw them away. They didnt seem to mean that much to you.

I took the papers out of the bag and leafed through them and put them back in. They didnt, when I thought the dog took them. When I find out you took them, I'm not so sure.

I just didnt want them thrown away.

I pushed it across to him. You keep them. But I'd like to get some pictures of Mom.

I could do that. Get some copies made.

Set down there for a little bit.

He refilled our coffee cups and sat and squared his chair to me.

It appears I dont know much about Mom. Or Dad. And half of what I did is wrong. You got time to enlighten me some?

I took a half hour of it before my head was spinning. I'll have to come back later, I said. But halfway home I sat on a rock for a spell and came back for another round. I never did get it all, not then. It was just more than I could swallow in one lump.

Back at my place, Dad's spiral-bound books of sermon notes reeked of decay with the peeling of each damp-stained page from the next. The books grew fatter as I leafed through them till they strained at the rusted wire spirals.

Not until partway through the second binder did I find a hint of support for what Grover was saying. In a sermon he was preparing about reaping and sowing he'd written *Thank God my wretched past has been cast into a sea of forgiveness.* Then he'd crossed out *my wretched past* and written in *our sins.*

Later in side notes not intended to be part of a sermon I read: *My joy at Harlan's death, my hope for Jasmine's healing; so wrong. Must convey human condition, uphold God's standards. Fine line brother's keeper. Reenter cesspool to save brother? Drown there? Unworthy, yet called. Absolutes elusive.*

Underneath Dad's unshakable righteousness and his patina of perfection I sensed the violence and wrecked lives and broken homes contained in the cryptic notes. His yearning to be understood but not at the price of his calling.

The next morning the mailbox held along with the usual junk an envelope from Alison Reddy. Inside was a picture of Alison and Mandy and her partner Sonia in front of the Lincoln memorial. All looking happy and hot. Her handwriting was not crabbed but that of a younger girl. Surgery the following week. The prognosis fair for remission. Dont forget about keeping up on her work. Feel free to use the pickup. The key is in the drawer under the spice rack. But there better be gas in it when she got home.

I pinned the picture to the wall where the ants had been hidden and stood back and looked at it and moved it to the wall over the kitchen table where there was more room.

Grover was disheveled and bleak-eyed. Obviously he'd been asleep though he was fully dressed in rumpled khakis and a worn dress shirt. I looked at my watch. Sorry.

It's all right. Come on in.

He fussed with the coffee and said, At night's when I do most of my work. I think better then.

I'll try to remember that.

No, you come whenever you want to.

I need to tell you something.

Yeah. You have that look.

I got a wife. Linda. We've been married fifteen years now. But she left me right before I come here.

I wondered.

I never beat her or fooled around on her or anything like that. It was my drinking that run her off.

All right.

Anyhow. She's pregnant with our first kid. Or was. She should of had it by now.

Where is she?

That's what I dont know. Can you find someone on that computer?

Maybe. Do you think she wants to be found?

I thought I had that all figured out but I went over it again till I was sure. If she doesnt I think she'd be awful disappointed if she didnt get to tell me personal.

That's convoluted thinking, he said after a while. But I guess it will fly.

How do you go about it?

Well, if she had e-mail, it would be easy. I'd just send her a message and if she wanted to be found she'd tell you where she was. But there's other ways.

She took the computer with her and she used to have a e-mail address. But now that she's moved it wont be the same.

Oh, yeah it will. Unless it was a really tiny little local domain.

Whatever that is.

What was her address?

sweetp@aol.com. All little letters.

It'll be easy. She wont have changed it.

Then I can just write to her? And she'll get it?

He linked his fingers behind his head and pursed his lips and thought for a while. I think it would be better if I wrote to her first. Maybe lay a little groundwork.

No, I dont want you writing to her. She needs to hear from me.

Do you know what you want to say?

Until that moment I though I had. I'll need to think on it for a spell.

I stepped lively back across the hill to home but skidded to a halt just into the field behind the house. Junior stopped and sniffed the air and the hair ridged up on his back.

A tall woman carrying an aluminum clipboard stood with Lilo in front of the old Dodge. Lilo was gesturing and waving and when she tossed her straight red hair over her shoulder I saw who it was. Jenny Yunker high-stepped through the weeds back to the house and stopped to brush her dark pants and peered in the door glass and wrote on her clipboard and stuck something on the door.

She glanced my way and disappeared around the house and gravel crunched under tires and a white car with a government plate backed into sight and then accelerated out the driveway. I realized I was squatted in the weeds holding Junior's muzzle. I released it and he barked.

Lilo met me and followed me to the house. The sticky note said CALL ME. JENNY YUNKER-COLLINS and a number and an extension.

Hee hee, Lilo said. You hit the big time now: a visit from the state's attorney. Mebby everybody else forgot old Matthew but she aint.

The paint thinner fumes were making me dizzy, but I kept scrubbing with the old toothbrush at every crease in the metal, every cranny that might hold a trace of Matt's DNA. So what did you tell her?

It dont matter; she wasnt paying no attention to me. Lilo squatted against the big red maple that overshadowed the car. You really give her a case of the backdoor trots. After I'd scrubbed for a while, he said, You ought to stand back a piece and take a gander at what you're doing.

The scrubbed front corner glared like a mismatched tooth crown. Lilo clapped his hands. *That* ought to slough off any suspicion. I guess it aint no use to be stupid if you dont show it.

I was out of paint thinner and didnt have any polishing compound or automotive wax and I didnt want to leave the car alone to go get some. So with a worn scouring pad and hot soapy water I returned the car to a uniform hue. In the last dregs of daylight it resembled the excoriated skin of a burn victim: bright and raw and ulcerous.

I like it, Lilo said. It's purty. His laughter still carried through the bedroom window an hour later.

From the same window the following morning, the car seemed to glow. As damning as a notarized confession. Jenny Yunker-Collins' note lay on the kitchen counter like an indictment.

The Dodge's tire's sidewalls were cracked and dry but they held air; the base of the old hand pump was too hot to touch when I finished airing them up. My breath whistled like the compressor I should of had.

They aint going to hold, Lilo said.

They'll stay up till I can tow it away. I already knew where it was going:

in the coalhole on the old Douglas place with the other tons of junk that had been deposited there over the years. I'd chain it to the back of Alison's pickup with an old tire stretched between the bumpers to take up the slack.

Why'ncha just torch it? They'll winch it back out of the coalhole.

Who said anything about a coalhole?

Lilo laughed and leaned his head back against the maple.

Then I'd have to explain why I burned it, I said.

I dont know what you're so worked up about. It aint your tit in the wringer. Linda's the one done it.

My voice trembled as I stood over him. I dont want to hear her name out of your rotten mouth again.

He peered up at me. You want a piece of me? Go ahead.

I was considering that when Grover spoke behind me. What in the world did you do to that car?

Grover's face was heavy-lined, his shoulders slumped. A missed button on his flannel shirt.

I'm done with the house. Thought I'd see if I could get this old wreck running again.

But why did you scour it like that?

Checking out the metal. Making sure it's solid enough to paint. I sure dont want to put a lot of work and money into something the body's gonna fall off of. Lame.

Grover shrugged. I sent a letter off to your wife. And it didnt bounce so she got it.

I told you not to do that. Dont you listen to nothing?

Not when it's stupid. If you just drop a bomb with your name on it, dont expect her to think it's a bouquet of roses. What I wrote was very innoculous, like I was the nosy preacher I am.

Damn you meddlers all to hell.

He grinned. Thank you. I figured you'd appreciate me.

You grow on a person. Like a hemorrhoid.

It's done. Whether you like it or not.

She didnt answer?

Not yet. I'll give her a day or two and if I dont hear I'll shoot off another one.

Dont you do it. Let me write to her.

No. Not yet. Not on my computer, anyway. Is there anything you want me to tell her?

You'll tell her what you want to anyway.

Maybe.

All right. Tell her this: Tell her I remember what happened and it's okay.

You remember. And that's okay. That's it?

For now.

He shook his head. And you dont understand why I wont let you write it.

You going to do it or not?

It took him a while to answer. If that's what you want to say, that's what it will be.

If that's all you came to tell me, I got work to do.

Are you still working for Alison Reddy?

She went down to DC to stay with her daughter. She has cancer.

I know that. She's a tough old bird. She'll pull through.

She did me a good turn before she left. That's for sure.

I know about that, too. She asked my opinion before she signed the deed over.

Well. Thank you for telling her to do it. After the way I've been to you.

I probably shouldnt even tell you this but I advised against it.

I scratched my head and hawked and spit over Lilo's way. I'm getting so far behind on things to thank you for, I'll never get caught up.

I'd best be going.

It wasnt just Mom's depression that got between us, I said. The big thing was when she tied up my dog and then left home. Left him there to starve.

Grover shook his head. She wouldnt have done that. She couldnt even kill spiders. Someone probably saw your dog running loose and tied him up as a favor. Like any good neighbor would.

Clear as this morning's sky I could see Bunk Reddy doing just that. Scolding the dog for his owners' carelessness: *You got to use some sense, dog, even if they aint got none. Now you stay home and dont be tormentin my cattle no more.*

As Grover watched my face, his changed as well. He lifted a hand and walked away.

————

A bead of sweat skated down the side of my nose and reminded me how hot it had gotten in the house. I'd worried the past like Bunk Reddy's collie dog had wooled a kitten—till it was a ball of hair and spit. I opened the windows and washed my face in the kitchen sink. I noticed that at least two of the Dodge's tires had gone flat but the scoured car was already coated with pollen and dripping sap. My urgency to get rid of it had withered in the heat.

The crunch of tires brought me to the front screen door. Jenny Yunker bent back into her government car and got her clipboard and shook out her long red hair and walked toward the house. She'd grown boobs. Still freckled and smooth faced and looking twenty-five years old. Thirty, I decided as she climbed the steps. Junior sniffed along in her wake.

Her hand was reaching to knock before she saw me standing behind the screen. She started but not much. Andy, she said. It's been a while.

Hello, Jenny.

With a long unpainted nail she divided her straight hair and flipped one half back over her shoulder. I remembered the gesture. I'd like to look around your house, she said.

My bare feet felt gelled against the wood floor. You got a warrant? The whiteness of her straight teeth sent my tongue across the outside of my own.

Well. I've never been asked *that* before. Her laugh hadnt changed. Still low and loose as a yellow-bellied woodpecker's song.

Keep her away from the car. Come in, I said, and pushed open the door.

Close, without the veil of the screen, tiny crows' feet lined her eyes. Under her slim jaw a second chin hinted. She extended her hand and I shook it. It's good to see you again, she said. A firm, cool hand.

You too.

May I? she said, gesturing toward the living room.

I shrugged.

You do nice work, she said as she opened the cover of her aluminum clipboard and began to shade boxes on a preprinted form. Dont look so worried. You'd be surprised how many people dont think to file a building notice before they remodel. There's no penalty, yet. But they're working on it. She held the pencil in her teeth and rubbed the first two fingers against her thumb. They're just worried about raising your taxes, collecting more money. The heading across the form said Union County Department of

Assessment and Taxation. Next year building codes go into effect. Then the process will be different.

You're the tax assessor.

Well, yeah. I assumed you knew that. She laughed again. Sorry.

You care for a bottle of pop? I said. I never seen it this hot.

She glanced at her watch. Yeah, why not. May I continue with this? I nodded and she wandered toward other rooms.

Floorboards creaked overhead while I broke cubes from the tray and she was back before I expected her. Alison Reddy can be glad you're getting the new assessment and not her. She grinned. But it wont be that bad.

She leaned against the doorjamb with the reflections of leaves outside the window dancing in her light-green eyes. I'm glad I caught up with you, she said. Did you find the note I left earlier?

Yeah. I just didnt get around to calling. I dont have a phone here.

Well. I'll be going.

All right. Be nice on those numbers.

I've been dreading this so much. Thank you for not being vindictive. Like you have every right to be.

Saying nothing pretty well summed up my thoughts.

When you werent here at my first visit, I was so relieved. I figured I'd just look in the windows and wouldnt have to square off with you. But then I saw that old car and knew that I'd have to face you sooner or later.

I'd missed something somewhere. Maybe a lot of somethings.

I dont think a day has passed that I havent been tormented by what I've done.

She had it rolling now and all I could do was try to keep my mouth shut and listen.

I had a crush on Matt that just *had* to be love. And then he got killed and they blamed you and I *wanted* it to be you. Someone I could strike out at. Someone to pay.

I didnt know that. That you had a crush on Matt. Scrawny, buck-toothed, flat-chested Jenny Yunker.

She was blushing, I realized, and I saw my own thoughts reflected in her eyes. He probably didnt know it either, she said.

Without warning it felt possible to like her. I was swirling ice and Coke and had been for a while and the fizz was gone. You dug up the dirt on Dad. That's what's stuck in your craw.

She hugged her clipboard to her chest and shook her head. He never tried to conceal anything. Not that I could see. I was in this journalism class and I just went down the checklist. After I got his address from his application to the church, I started making calls. All the drinking and fighting and weekends in jail was good stuff, but that's what salvation is all about. Putting that life behind you. And your father did that.

Yeah. He did. Never looked back once he laid his hand to the plow.

Just on a whim I checked your mother. At first I missed it that her husband was Harlan Price and not Darrell Price.

That got the job done. That would of got Jesus churched. Living with his brother's wife.

I wish I'd never have found out.

Someone would of. It was bound to come out.

Maybe. I wish it wasnt me.

She just came to get away from Harlan at first. That's what I hear. He beat her half to death. Dad took her in. And then somewhere along the line it turned into something else. I guess they figured there was too much to lose by then. Just left it go the way it was.

Inertia.

Something like that.

Did you know? Back then?

Not a clue. I didnt tell her that I hadnt known last *week*. They changed the subject any time I asked about anything before I was born. Till I learned not to ask. Or even wonder.

You cant blame them.

Probly not.

It took a lot of maturing for me to realize what a good man Reverend Price was. What a loss he was to the community.

I miss him. A lot.

I'm so sorry. I still feel responsible. Your life hasnt been easy. She blushed again. You just hear things.

I felt my words, rather than formed them: It wouldnt have mattered.

She picked up her glass and drank some ice that had melted.

You want some more?

No. I really have to be going.

Well.

Linda. Linda Lawton. What became of her?

I married her. But we're not together right now.

Her blushing was becoming as regular as my heartbeat.

Junior scratched at the door and I went to let him inside. Your note said Yunker-Collins, I said when I returned. You married?

I was. I just never changed the name back. It was on all my stationery and stuff. She squatted to pet Junior. When he tried to sniff her face his upthrust nose caught her face coming down. She recoiled and held her cheek.

He's blind, I said.

Aw, she said, and hugged him with more energy than he deserved. She looked at her watch and jumped to her feet. I really should be going.

I'm glad we talked, Jenny.

The woman that shook my hand was not the awkward Jenny Yunker I'd once known. Your father still inspires me. The changes he made to leave his old life behind. To become a minister. Sometimes when living the life seems too hard I think of that. He's a real example.

Someone told me once that I wasnt a total waste. That I could always serve as a bad example for someone else.

She laughed and petted Junior again. I dont believe that for a minute. Not as gracious as you've been about all of this. Your father's proud if he's watching.

I watched her down the walk and then yelled at her as she backed out to leave. Waited until her window came down. Those calls you made when you were looking for information on Dad. Where'd you call?

The usual places: the newspaper, the sheriff's office, the courthouse.

What town?

Maysville.

West Virginia?

She laughed like I was teasing. Kentucky, dummy. Where they came from.

She'd been gone for a while before I looked away from the spot where she'd disappeared.

CHAPTER 29

Days this hellish hot didnt show up in the hills but seldom. The breeze was dilitary and sulfurous and scorched away any new sprouts of ambition. Job-hunting on this kind of a day was as sensible as sled riding. The yard needed mowed but it wasnt going to get it.

The front-porch swing was the coolest place around but its chains creaked like a coffin lid flapping in the breeze so I gave it up and coursed through the house seeking some chore suitable for a day like this and got sweated wet in the looking and gave that up too.

I lay on the bed till it turned into a waterbed and then restacked the underwear and socks and snotrags I kept in a row along the baseboard. I picked through the butterbowl where I dumped junk from my pockets and found only junk: a red wire nut and an assortment of nails and a hair barrette and ragged shopping lists. I fanned one of Dad's journals and put it back on the pile.

The torn cover of *Moby Dick* curled in the wet air like it had been pan-fried. I read here and there and turned the book sidewards to read the notes I'd made years ago. Some of that made sense but I must of been drunk for the rest. But a hunger for the written word hove up in me and I took the book back out to the porch swing and began reading again.

Not till I'd dripped sweat into Ishmael's meeting with Queequeg did I realize that the overhang's shade had slid off and the afternoon sun was tattooing my neck. I slipped the book under my belt in the hollow of my back and stretched my legs around the yard. The old Dodge lurked under maple limbs that stretched far into the clearing and looked dark and cool inside. Lilo was nowhere around and somehow I didnt care if he was. With the windows rolled down the car was as comfortable as anywhere else. I stretched out on the seat and took up my book and read till I dozed off in the middle of Melville's sermon. Old habits.

When I rolled over, liquid gurgled like body fluids in the car's guts and the unfamiliar sound brought my eyes open. From there, with my eyes blurred with sleep and where I couldnt see the rusted and scoured exterior, the car looked just like it had so many years before. I wiped dust from the radio dial and touched the chrome horn ring. The key still hung in the switch though the blue rabbit's foot fob had gone to gray. Nothing happened when I twisted the key. I pushed the starter button and tried to remember how it sounded. I sat up and pushed the clutch. The column shifter was stiff but greasy machinations clunked under the floorboards. I leaned my head back against the prickly-soft upholstering and let the day peter away.

Just before dark I stirred and headed for the house. I stopped and looked back at the car and went back and popped the hood. Mouse nests of leaves and acorn hulls covered the flathead block. I brushed them away and greased the back of my hand. The fan cut into my fingers when I tried to turn the crankshaft over. I slammed the hood twice before it latched.

All night long I toyed with the idea of the car with a new paint job and wide whitewalls and clean glass. Parked in front of the house with Linda waiting in the passenger seat. Holding our baby. By daylight it still felt possible.

My head was deep in the engine compartment when someone spoke. It aint gonna run again. My head bonged on the hood like a potato chucked into an empty bucket. Lilo had claimed a spot at the base of the maple.

You're a automobile expert now.

He grinned.

It run when I parked it.

Lyndon Johnson still run when you parked it.

Speculate and pessimize. You dont do nothing but complain so you dont ever fail.

His grin widened. I aint gonna get mad at your sassing and go home, if that's what you're counting on. He puckered and shot spit my way. I kicked leaves over the iridescent glob.

You're gonna break it off. Then what? he said after I'd returned with wrenches and a quart of oil.

The rust-capped spark plug squalled as its threads broke loose and whined like a puppy as I threaded it from the head. I threw it toward Lilo.

That's one but you still got seven to go.

I buried his voice in the shriek of turning plugs.

After I poured oil in the plug holes I rethreaded the old plugs a turn or two to keep out dirt. When I retrieved the one I'd thrown Lilo puckered again.

You spit and I'll rub your nose in it, I said.

His Adam's apple worked and green flickered between his lips but he kept his phlegm to himself. She aint coming back. The kid neither.

You give up on cars?

His laugh was hearty. You're a funny little bastard when you lay your hand to it.

The bumper jack's ratchet made a good farm noise: *klik-k-k-k chuck klik-k-k-k chuck.* You were wrong about Jenny Yunker. Dead wrong. State's attorney you said.

Lilo shrugged. Maybe I was jerking your chain.

And maybe you dont know no more than I do. My conviction was growing.

The vehicle was in better shape underneath than I'd expected. There's something to be said for oil leaks. Both front wheels were froze up at first but spun slick enough once the brake shoes broke loose.

I wouldnt get my hopes up if I was you. Lilo had been getting antsy as the day dragged on.

Maybe you are me. Maybe you dont got a say in the matter.

I heard Grover coming and when his rubber-soled moccasins showed up I kept banging on the header pipe like I didnt know he was there. The feet roamed to the front of the car and around the side and when they got beside my head I said, Harya Grover.

You're really going to fix it up arent you. The sound of the gas cap opening. Whew. Did you smell that gas? Pure varnish.

I slid out and leaned against the door and kneaded my neck. I didnt think of that. It'll need a draining.

Figure on pulling the carb, too. Soak it in cleaner.

You hear from Linda?

I did.

My heart jumped time. What did she say?

She said she heard me the first time.

Maybe I best write to her.

That's the other thing she said. She said Andy will want to write and to tell you not to even think about it.

You tell her what I said? About remembering?

I did. She said you'll hear from her when she's ready.

I will hear? She said that?

I told you just exactly what she said.

Can I see what she wrote?

No. Because it has what I wrote on it too.

There's a special place in hell for the likes of you.

I'm counting on it.

What did you tell her? He looked off into the woods and whistled a hymn and I considered utilizing the hammer I still held on his head. That's all she said?

She said she was sorry she didnt send you anything for Father's Day.

I didnt trust myself to speak.

The tires had gone flat again. The old rims were rusted but sound and they didnt have a safety bead so I could pry the tires loose and slide new innertubes in place. Been a coon's age since I sold a tube, the man at the tire shop had said. You sure you cant use a couple more? His tongue worked in a toothless hole like fishworms in a tobacco can. After I sweated another half-hour over the hand pump the car stood up on its hind legs again.

When I undressed to shower I saw that my wallet was sweated wet. I spread my bills and papers along the baseboard to dry. Linda's graduation picture was stained and frayed along the edges. I leaned it against the butter-bowl of pocket droppings and propped the bottom with the little barrette and went to bed.

Every time I dozed off my dreams circled like a rabbit tormenting beagles. I was back at Lilo's doublewide and then in Dad's office the day before he died and then heading off to church with Linda. A barrette gleaming in her hair.

I felt my way to the light switch and waited for my eyes to adjust and then examined the barrette I'd found at Lilo's. One way I looked at it the ridge down the middle looked like a molding line but held in a different light it could have been a knife mark. It didnt smell like plastic but I didnt know if tortoise shell had a stink of its own. I couldnt tell if it was hand-made turtlehide or plastic and I couldnt remember why I'd brought it here. I turned off the light and went back to bed.

Lilo was waiting in the car the next morning just like I expected. I saw his green grin before I made him out. I ignored him while I scraped the terminals and drew down the clamps on a new battery. I tasted the tip of my finger and jerked my tongue away from the acid and headed back to the house to wash my hands in soda. Careful not to touch my clothes.

Lilo yelled behind my back, Hold a match to it. If it's plastic it'll burn. His voice sounded like something was working loose inside of him. But it wont. It's turtlehide. The one your Dad made.

Ow ow ow ow ow dogshitpeterbuttdamn, I hollered and ran toward the bathroom. Meteors of fire spattered onto the floor from the burning plastic barrette until I threw it in the toilet and flushed it away. You're lucky you didnt set the house afire.

You thought your woman had done me in too. Lilo's voice wormed through the firewall to where I worked. That's what you thought.

I kept on tightening the alternator against the new fan belt. But you knew she didnt.

Why in the blue blazes would she want to kill me? he said.

Look what you done to me, I said. I hadnt drunk for a long spell till I run into you. But it dont matter because she didnt. It wasnt her barrette I found in your house.

But what if it had been?

I laid my rag on the radiator and backed from the engine compartment. Lilo stared straight ahead over the steeringwheel. His profile was that of a younger man.

It dont matter. Whatever she's done I've got the big end of the deal. So shut your trap. I wondered what would happen if I smacked him with the wrench or set him afire with the gas I'd brought in a can. I surveyed around to make sure no witnesses were lurking and when I looked back again he was gone.

———

That evening I walked to Alison's and loaded a lawnmower and string trimmer and some hand tools into her pickup and drove to town for grass seed and stopped at the graveyard behind the church. I whacked and hauled away the weeds and mowed around the stones and shoveled extra dirt from Dad's side to fill Mom's. I planted grass on the raw soil and picked a spray of daisies and black-eyed Susies and leaned it against the stone. Something needed to be said but I didnt have the right words. After a while the need-to faded away.

Matt's grave was in good shape but his stone was too small. I wondered if they'd ever tracked down his father.

Some kind of night bird swooped through the stones as I toted the tools back to the truck and the first bats of the night dropped from the church eaves. A truck's Jakebrake clattered in the distance. I shivered at the gate's squeal and got a quart of oil from behind the seat and greased the hinges and latch until the gate clicked shut without such an argument. Just as I was reaching for the wheel to hoist myself into the cab, I froze. I knew Dad was right behind me, ready to speak. I even knew what he'd say: Go with God, Andy.

After a few seconds I pulled myself up and drove away and snickered at my imagination. But I didnt look in the mirror.

CHAPTER 30

I heard the vehicle stop at the end of the drive while I was eating dinner the next day but I figured it for the mail carrier. Then Junior whimpered and then barked and then howled and I stepped out onto the porch. The dog ran stumbling and spraddle-legged toward the four dogs that poured over the endgate of a red Dodge pickup. A pale woman in mismatched blue shorts and top and white shoes waved and the pickup pulled off and was gone. A lump the size of a workboot worked in my throat.

The dogs' confabulation faded out as I focused on Linda. Before I knew it my feet wasnt where they had been and we met in the driveway. One of her chicken-white legs had a grease smudge and her hair was dry and wind-frowlzed and a broken pursestrap was done up in a granny knot. A tight belt buckled a roll of leftover pregnancy pudge. Her eyes were wearied and hardlined and her skin was scaled and parched. When I took her in my arms she smelled of sweat. She was soft and insubstantial and her mouth was dry and sour-tasting and she tried to push me away but I kissed her again and again until she relaxed and offered one back.

Where's the baby at? I whispered.

I dropped her off at Mom's.

Her?

Jewel Hope Price. She rummaged in her purse and brought forth a picture. Shiny pale gray eyes and a juberous little nose. A little you-aint-nowhere-near-as-sharp-as-I-am smile. Fine blonde hair peeking out from a pink knitted cap and two tiny fingers from a sleeve.

Jewel, I said. Hope. Price. I devoured my daughter.

She's perfect. Perfect in every way. Linda pulled the picture around so she could look too like she hadnt yet got enough.

I looked from Jewel to Linda and from Linda to Jewel. She looks like you. And you look like a million bucks.

I look like hell.

No you dont. I hugged and kissed her again.

Where's the Subaru at? I said when the hogwild dogs knocked us apart.

It's toasted I think. It heated up on the mountain above Shoehorn. I should have let it cool but I didnt and I think I ruined it. Some guy offered a ride, dogs and all, so I came on.

It aint nothing to worry about. I counted dogs. You got one missing.

Snoot, she said. He got run over a while back.

Aw. It would of had to be the boy dog.

Yeah, she said into my chest. Theyre careless and not as smart.

She was tentative and shied off under me like she'd never done this before. Or like it had been a bad time if she had. Thin lips and tight-shut eyes and her hair stringy and wet. The used bedframe shrieked. She gripped my sides and tightened her legs on me like a pulley on a v-belt.

Roll over, I whispered. The muscles of her back and neck were flabby tumors that took a long time to break up under my thumbs and formed up again behind them. When they finally rested soft and liquid under her skin my wrists throbbed. I kissed every inch of her back like I was painting with my tongue and savored the tastes of soap and of iron water. When I'd covered all the skin I could reach she rolled toward me and let me follow along her neck and shoulders. Then she became the artist and directed my brush over her canvas with fingers that sometimes combed my hair and sometimes tried to haul it loose. When I rose over her again she came to meet me and dragged me down with nails and heels. I got desperate and thought on hoeing corn and stapling insulation and soldering pipefittings and as the rasp of her breath became an endless moan I thought of not one blessed thing. Our voices went up like tree dogs as our lonely times tore away in sheet after sheet that fluttered till there was nothing more to tear.

Beneath the open bedroom window first one dog and then another and then the whole pack joined in. Linda twitched and then humped as her laughter climbed up into a different kind of howl. I was too shot through to join her.

But it was funny.

And she can already pull herself up on my fingers. If I help a little.

I dont want to talk about her no more. I want to go fetch her home. Alison Reddy wont care for me to use her pickup.

The skin around her eyes was stretched too tight over her cheekbones. Not just yet.

No more dadblamed talk. I placed my finger across her lips. I want to lay my hands on my little girl.

She sat up and pulled the blanket around her shoulders. Remember how much good it did you to talk when we went to my home for Christmas?

Yeah. Look at what it got me.

She moved to the window and made the silhouette of a robed angel.

All right. If you want to talk there's one thing I want to know. Who give you that black eye when you run off to the shelter? That's one thing that's always chapped my butt.

You dont want to know.

I'm gonna know.

Dave did it.

Dave Sinko? Dave Sinko gave you a black eye?

Her hair bobbed as she nodded. When you didnt come home that day I knew you were drinking and I thought I'd see if Sharon was home and maybe I could stay there till you settled down. I didnt have anywhere else to go. But Dave was home and Sharon wasnt and he put a move on me and I fought back and ended up with a black eye. And then I *couldnt* come home.

Why not? What's that got to do with coming home?

You'd have had to call Dave on it and he'd have killed you. You know how he was.

My heart was going like a woodpecker that had drunk coffee. We'll see who kills who. That sonofabitch.

Dave's dead. Or I still wouldnt tell you.

Dave's dead? Dave Sinko?

He was in a wreck a couple months back. Killed Kathie Paugh and her little girl too. They were in the other car.

Getting the world rearranged the way it was instead of the way I'd thought it was took a sizeable chunk of time. Look, I said when I'd got it done. You aint got to explain nothing more to me. Sometimes the less a feller knows the happier he is.

Will you tell me something?

I dont know. It depends on what it is.

When did you figure out what happened?

I aint just sure. I've *remembered* being in the backseat for a long time, I think. But I wouldnt let myself *know* it. Cause of what it meant.

All my talk back then about just accepting what came along . . . that was all bullcrap, she said. Something to hide behind if I came up short of what I really wanted. My dreams were as big as the moon. If she'd practiced what she was going to say she'd managed not to lose the feeling behind it.

What did you want to be?

Then you and Matt came along and I got caught up in your slipstream and everything *I* wanted was straight down the toilet.

Tell me about what you dreamed about being.

She sat on the bed and hid her face with the blanket's corners. If I'd had time to think I'd have realized how stupid and cruel it was to blame you. But when you said you couldnt remember, the opportunity was there and I jumped on it. And then it was too late.

I hooked her with my feet and pulled her up over me and rearranged the blanket to cover us. Her heart was beating fast. It's all done with, I whispered. I can guarantee you I'll *never* tell. And the car is cleaner than a West Virginia checkbook. Nobody is ever going to know.

She stiffened like she had a cramp and I moved so she could address it but she hove up out of the bed and shot me a look that would kill quackgrass and disappeared down the hall toward the bathroom.

I rewound the conversation and stretched in front of the window and tried not to appear as stupid and clueless as I felt and then felt naked in the sunshine and pulled on my shorts and pants. I waited for the toilet to flush. Waited. You all right? I hollered down the hallway. I smelled my shirt and tossed it in the corner and put on my clean one and then made up the bed and listened at the bathroom door.

She was crying.

Hey. I pecked on the locked door. What's amatter?

You leave me alone.

You sick or something? I beat on the door with my fist. Come on. Open the door. I've had about enough of this.

Go. Away.

If I have it coming go ahead and shovel it on. But not like that. You open the damn door or I'll break it down.

The lock clicked and the door opened and she stood there with crazy eyes and tangled hair and a mouth that looked like a wound. How could you?

After a time I ran out of new ways to look at it and I said, Professor Plum with a lead pipe in the ballroom? It's just a guess because I aint got clue one.

You think I'm a *murderer*? I dont know who killed Matt. Some trucker like they said. I hit a deer. The only terrible thing I did was tell you that *you* hit Matt.

The door closed and the lock's click echoed in the empty house.

Scoot over.

Lilo's mouth flashed soft green and he shrugged and slid to the passenger side. Dont all that lay a heavy frost on the ole cucumbers.

I turned the ignition switch and the defroster fan whined and a squall of mouse nest blew from the vents and settled like ashes on the dashboard. A low whine commenced somewhere between my ears and the old tube radio came to life with a song as ancient as the car. Like it had been trapped there for all those years. I turned it off.

Fire her up and let's unass this place.

The choke knob pulled easy enough. I fingered the starter button beside the steering column and gripped the big wheel with a sweaty palm.

Lilo laughed.

Roll down your window, I said.

He shrugged and held out his hands. I started to reach over him but then got out and walked around the car and opened his door. That window always skreeked. I gritted my teeth.

At least an hour passed before Linda stepped out onto the back porch and dogs streamed around the corner and milled around her feet. She hooded her eyes and looked our way and Lilo waved out the window. She petted each dog and disappeared into the house.

She aint as purty as she was, Lilo said. Foalin's been rough on her.

You shut your rotten flap. The dogs heard and the whole pack loped our way and jumped and slobbered at the door but when we ignored them they raced back to the house.

She flat out ruined our lives, I said.

Lilo grinned.

But she mucked up her own, too. That's the part I cant get a grip on.

Be hard to come clean after your ole man croaked over the whole deal. That throwed a knot in the floss.

A chipmunk popped up onto the hood and stared at me until I blinked and then it chattered away.

Just a while back you had done forgive her for murder. Now you got your bowels in a uproar over a little ole lie. Hee hee. And she's pissed at you. Like you done all the wrong.

Where would be the best place to hit him? I aint faultless. I done my share.

Uh-oh. Now you're figgering on making nice. There aint nothing going to change. Not ever. Not in you, not in her. Not in nothing. That aint even your kid. Tell me them aint Sinko eyes.

It is now. I figure it's mine anyhow. But I'll make it mine even if it aint.

You think things is going to get better but they aint. Nothing ever changes one iota. He tapped his finger against the curled cover of *Moby Dick*, still on the dashboard where I'd tossed it. *The path to my fixed purpose is laid with iron rails, whereon my soul is grooved to run.* His voice exactly that one I'd imagined as Ahab's.

I almost threw the book out the open window.

Fool! I am the Fates' lieutenant; I act under orders. All men live enveloped in whale-lines. All are born with halters around their necks.

You try this here halter on for size. For one brief second my fingers fought the resistance of Lilo's neck and the green of his gaping mouth surged into the black holes of his eyes. Then he was gone. My palms clapped together with fingers tangled like I was praying in anger.

When I'd quit shaking enough to grip the door handle I retrieved the book. Matt was leaning against the car when I turned. Go on without me, I said. I'll be along dreckly.

You wont forget? His gray eyes sparkled with orneriness.

I shook my head, and he trotted away. At the end of the driveway that other figure I hadnt been able to identify joined him and together they walked out of sight.

Grover walked down the path to the house without looking my way. He carried a foil-covered plate held high away from the jumping dogs. He backed a step away when Linda opened the door and his free arm waved as he talked. He looked my way and then went inside.

At least an hour passed before he reappeared. Where the path came closest he stopped and waved. I booped the horn, and he went on.

Through the grass, her flashlight probed here and there where threats might be waiting but then centered on me when she got closer. The butter-yellow glow of the dome light turned her blue dress green. Fresh green, not the green of decay. Smells of perfume and talcum powder and cranberries drifted over me when she closed the door.

Mr. Dulaney brought some cookies.

My hand found foil and then her hand. A long shadow drifted across a sky bright with stars. Geese maybe. The dogs churned by making enough noise for a dozen.

Her hand didnt clutch mine but neither did it retreat. I traced a crease in her palm. I rolled the window up against air that had gone damp and chill and felt and heard her doing the same and the car was smaller. Intimate.

The day Matt died was the only time in my life I ever drank.

Me too, I said.

Yeah right. Her fingernail worried at my palm. I'm not blaming my bad judgment on that, though.

I do.

My thought was that I'd scare you for a while. Show you what could happen if you kept up your drinking. I couldnt see any risk because I was telling the truth to everyone but you.

But we were *there* where Matt died. I remember that.

We came along after he'd been hit. He was crumpled up there on the shoulder and I didnt even know it was him for a little bit. Not with blood and dirt all over him and he looked so little. I thought it was some kid. I was feeling for a pulse when I realized it was Matt. And then it sunk in that we'd both been drinking and that you'd been fighting with him and here we were with a dented-up fender. And I heard a car coming and I knew there was nothing we could do for Matt and I panicked and took off before we got blamed for it.

That part of it I could forgive myself for, she said. A tear luminous in the starlight fell onto her lap. But then the next morning I did it again. When you didnt remember what had happened that same lying manipulative nature jumped up and I thought I'd scare you into straightening out for good. Just for a day or two. But then your Dad died. And I thought I'd wait till that settled down. And then you disappeared.

I went walkabout.

I knew how you were. You spilled your guts about everything when you were drinking. And I pictured you sitting in a bar telling everyone how you'd killed your best friend. And I knew I had to find you before that happened.

It wouldnt of mattered. There wasnt any evidence. Because it didnt happen.

Here's the sad part. Her fingernail left my hand and I could hear it working against her own palm. I wasnt worried about you. I just didnt want
anyone to know I was the kind of person who would do a thing like that.
Tell such a rotten lie.

I rolled my window back down a couple of inches. But hows come you
let it go on all those years?

The windshield had started to fog and turn the hard points of lights into
soft candles. Her finger traced something against the glow and she wiped
it away. I'd intended to tell you when I found you but just as I started Slick
kicked in the door and till I got a chance again I had started to like that hold
I had over you. It was all I had and I couldnt stand to be rid of it. Her voice
was as soft and small as the stars.

Rivulets of water trickled down the glass and tangled into streams. Even
when I thought you killed Matt, I didnt care, I said.

I know. That scares me to death.

Why?

Because it means that I dont really know you.

It means I love you.

I hope that's what it means.

It means that after you've got used to being a murderer yourself it aint
that hard to put up with it in someone else.

Ouch.

I found the ignition switch and the wiper knob. The blades dragged
upward and then slapped down again like a mousetrap without touching
the condensation on the inside. We both leaned forward and wiped at the
glass and the sky bristled with light again. Linda's hand rustled against the
torn cover of my book.

Is this *Moby Dick*?

Yeah. What's left of it.

I read it over and over. You didnt know that, did you?

Why?

To know you. To know why it's so important to you.

It's just a book. I guess I kept it because it was one of my last ties to Dad.
But I do like the way it's wrote. Written.

She laughed, throaty and low. What's your favorite passage?

Water from the windshield had soaked the edges of the book and the
pages ruffled unevenly where they'd stuck together. I divided the book in
half and ran my fingers over the open page like I was reading Braille. *And*

here, thought I, with my own hand I ply my own shuttle and weave my own des-
tiny into these inalterable threads. The passage caught me by surprise. Like
someone else had picked it.

Neither of us spoke as a pickup with loud mufflers passed our driveway.
Chance sure took a whack at us, she said. It always gets the last featuring
blow.

Not unless we let it.

We already have.

We dont have to keep on with it.

Her silence seemed to stretch to the stars. I caught a whiff of something
like wet dog and suddenly the car felt dank and exposed. Like sleeping in a
tent while something snuffled just on the other side of the canvas. I rolled
my window tight shut.

In the bedroom today . . . She waited for my yeah before she went on.
When I realized that you still hadnt figured out the truth I got this jolt of
something. Like electricity.

Yeah?

I've felt it before. It's the kind of feeling I imagine you get when you
drink.

Mostly I just get sick.

Well, this one made me sick, too. Because by the time you were ready
to break down the bathroom door, I'd almost figured out how to use your
misunderstanding all over again. To control you. She paused but it didnt
feel like she wanted me to say anything so I didnt. If you'd have wandered
off that's what I'd have done. Started the lie all over again.

The night was so clear that a vapor trail was visible behind a jet so far
away that its navigation lights couldnt reach us. The line moved across the
sky as if written on glass from behind. But I didnt. The hard mark gradually
smudged into streamers and bits of cloud and then faded into the void. And
you didnt either.

No. It worked out.

What did you and Grover talk about?

Preacher stuff. Repentance. Forgiveness.

Can you forgive me?

Can you forgive *me*? Can you forgive yourself?

Her arm was cold and goosefleshed and thin in my hand. You aint a
problem. But I'm starting to think I aint ever going to be perfect.

We can work on that.

I laughed. Second verse same as the first.

She slid across the seat and snuggled against me and shivered.

What if I was to do something that awful again? she said. I'm scared there's a devil in me.

Are you telling me the truth now? Or has the truth got like a big old buck deer that growed so many points you cant get a good count on them?

She leaned her head on my shoulder and held onto my arm like she was in danger of falling. Gospel truth.

Then I reckon I'd hunker down and put up with it. Me and devils get along all right.

That's an awful thing to say.

What if I was to take off on another drinking tear?

Then I'd leave you. Especially now that we have a baby. As if the same jet had lapped the earth another white line started across the sky. Linda's breath was a warm breeze against my neck.

What do you think? I said.

I think it's cold. I think we ought to go to bed.

I mean about us. And Jewel. The name tingled on my tongue. Jewel Hope Price.

Tomorrow. Tomorrow we'll get her and the car.

I let her lead me from the car but just a few steps away I stopped and looked back. I know it's bad luck to be superstitious but I got to try something. I climbed back in and shut the door so the dome light wouldnt blind me and groped for the switch and the fan came to life and my thumb rested on the hard silver button beside the steering column.

Linda rapped on the window. Come on. You can fool with the car tomorrow if you still want to.

Under my thumb waited pistons that wanted to rise and fall again. Spark plugs yearning to breathe fire into cold steel once more. A rumble of exhaust. The initial cloud of smoke as the dormant engine rattled into new life. No cops would be out this late on a weekday. It could be just like old times. Linda snuggled against my arm. The car weaving just a bit as I nursed the loose steering. We'd go get our baby right now. Light off into a fresh time that didnt need sense made of it yet. I adjusted the cracked and foggy rearview mirror and saw only the black of night. No nosy neighbors to put up with. No sick neighbors to visit. No family to track down. No lawns to mow and dogs to feed and woodwork to paint and taxes to pay.

Just for a sign then. For a token of the start of our new life.

My thumb tightened against the button and Linda rapped on the window and said, Come on, doggone it. Cant it wait till tomorrow?

I turned off the switch and the fan whirred to a halt. I bumped the big wheel with my fist the way you'd bump an old buddy on the shoulder and slid out and was pleased with the way the door clicked shut behind me. After all those years. Yeah. It can wait.